Little
White
Lies

JENNIFER LYNN BARNES

FREEFORM BOOKS
Los Angeles New York

For information address Freeform, 125 West End Avenue,
New York, New York 10023.

First Edition, November 2018
10 9 8 7 6 5 4 3 2 1
FAC-020093-18264
Printed in the United States of America

Text is set in Apple Chancery, Aristocrat Std, Fairfield LT Std Light,
Trade Gothic LT Pro Condensed/Monotype
Designed by Marci Senders

Library of Congress Cataloging-in-Publication Data
Names: Barnes, Jennifer (Jennifer Lynn), author.
Title: Little white lies / Jennifer Lynn Barnes.
Description: First edition. • Los Angeles : Freeform, 2019. • Summary:
Eighteen-year-old Sawyer accepts her estranged grandmother's bribe
to live with her for a year, participate in the debutante season and
ball, and possibly meet the father she has never known.
Identifiers: LCCN 2017043894 • ISBN 9781368014137 (hardcover)
Subjects: • CYAC: Debutantes—Fiction. • Grandmothers—
Fiction. • Mothers and daughters—Fiction. • Family life—Southern
States—Fiction. • Southern States—Fiction.
Classification: LCC PZ7.B26225 Lit 2019 • DDC [Fic]—dc23
LC record available at https://lccn.loc.gov/2017043894

Reinforced binding

Visit www.freeform.com/books

THIS LABEL APPLIES TO TEXT STOCK

For my mom, who saved the invitations from every Deb event.
Who's the best mama? You are.

Little
White
Lies

APRIL 15, 4:59 P.M.

"This one's all you, Rodriguez."

"No way. I took the drunk tank after the Bison Day parade."

"Bison Day? Try Oktoberfest at the senior citizen center."

"And who got stuck with the biter the next day?"

Officer Macalister Dodd—Mackie to his friends—had the general sense that it would not be prudent to interrupt the back-and-forth between the two more senior Magnolia County police officers arguing in the bull pen. Rodriguez and O'Connell had both clocked five years on the force.

This was Mackie's second week.

"I've got three letters and one word for you, Rodriguez: *PTA brawl.*"

Mackie shifted his weight slightly from his right leg to his left. Big mistake. In unison, Rodriguez and O'Connell turned to look at him.

"Rookie!"

Never had two police officers been so delighted to see a third. Mackie set his mouth into a grim line and squared his shoulders.

"What have we got?" he said gruffly. "Drunk and disorderly? Domestic disturbance?"

In answer, O'Connell clapped him on the shoulder and steered him toward the holding cell. "Godspeed, rookie."

As they rounded the corner, Mackie expected to see a perp: belligerent, possibly on the burly side. Instead, he saw four teenage girls wearing elbow-length gloves and what appeared to be ball gowns.

White ball gowns.

"What the hell is this?" Mackie asked.

Rodriguez lowered his voice. "This is what we call a BYH."

"BYH?" Mackie glanced back at the girls. One of them was standing primly, her gloved hands folded in front of her body. The girl next to her was crying daintily and wheezing something that sounded suspiciously like the Lord's Prayer. The third stared straight at Mackie, the edges of her pink-glossed lips quirking slowly upward as she raked her gaze over his body.

And the fourth girl?

She was picking the lock.

The other officers turned to leave.

"Rodriguez?" Mackie called after them. "O'Connell?"

No response.

"What's a BYH?"

The girl who'd been assessing him took a step forward. She batted her eyelashes at Mackie and offered him a sweet-tea smile.

"Why, Officer," she said. "Bless your heart."

NINE MONTHS EARLIER

CHAPTER 1

Catcalling me was a mistake that most of the customers and mechanics at Big Jim's Garage only made once. Unfortunately, the owner of this particular Dodge Ram was the type of person who put his paycheck into souping up a *Dodge Ram*. That—and the urinating stick figure on his back window—was pretty much the only forewarning I needed about the way this was about to go down.

People were fundamentally predictable. If you stopped expecting them to surprise you, they couldn't disappoint.

And speaking of disappointment . . . I turned my attention from the Ram's engine to the Ram's owner, who apparently considered whistling at a girl to be a compliment and commenting on the shape of her ass to be the absolute height of courtship.

"It's times like this," I told him, "that you have to ask yourself: Is it wise to sexually harass someone who has both wire cutters and access to your brake lines?"

The man blinked. Once. Twice. Three times. And then he leaned forward. "Honey, you can access my brake lines anytime you want."

If you know what I mean, I added silently. *In three . . . two . . .*

"If you know what I mean."

"It's times like this," I said meditatively, "that you have to ask yourself: Is it wise to offer to bare your man-parts for someone who is both patently uninterested and holding wire cutters?"

"Sawyer!" Big Jim intervened before I could so much as give a snip of the wire cutters in a southward direction. "I've got this one."

I'd started badgering Big Jim to let me get my hands greasy when I was twelve. He almost certainly knew that I'd *already* fixed the Ram, and that if he left me to my own devices, this wouldn't end well.

For the customer.

"Aw hell, Big Jim," the man complained. "We were just having fun."

I'd spent most of my childhood going from one obsessive interest to another. Car engines had been one of them. Before that, it had been telenovelas, and afterward, I'd spent a year reading everything I could find about medieval weapons.

"You don't mind a little fun, do you, sweetheart?" Mr. Souped-Up Dodge Ram clapped a hand onto my shoulder and compounded his sins by squeezing my neck.

Big Jim groaned as I turned my full attention to the real charmer beside me.

"Allow me to quote for you," I said in an absolute deadpan, "from *Sayforth's Encyclopedia of Archaic Torture.*"

One of the finer points of chivalry in my particular corner of the South was that men like Big Jim Thompson didn't fire girls like me no matter how explicitly we described alligator shears to customers in want of castration.

Fairly certain I'd ensured the Ram's owner wouldn't make the same mistake a *third* time, I stopped by The Holler on the way home to pick up my mom's tips from the night before.

"How's trouble?" My mom's boss was named Trick. He had five children, eighteen grandchildren, and three visible scars from breaking up bar fights—possibly more under his ratty white T-shirt. He'd greeted me the exact same way every time he'd seen me since I was four.

"I'm fine, thanks for asking," I said.

"Here for your mom's tips?" That question came from Trick's oldest grandson, who was restocking the liquor behind the bar. This was a family business in a family town. The entire population was just over eight thousand. You couldn't throw a rock without it bouncing off three people who were related to each other.

And then there was my mom—and me.

"Here for tips," I confirmed. My mom wasn't exactly known for her financial acumen or the steadfastness with which she made it home after a late shift. I'd been balancing our household budget since I was nine—around the same time that I'd developed sequential interests in lock picking, the Westminster Dog Show, and fixing the perfect martini.

"Here you go, sweetheart." Trick handed me an envelope that was thicker than I'd expected. "Don't blow it all in one place."

I snorted. The money would go to rent and food. I wasn't exactly the type to party. I might, in fact, have had a bit of a reputation for being antisocial.

See also: my willingness to threaten castration.

Before Trick could issue an invitation for me to join the whole family at his daughter-in-law's house for dinner, I made my excuses and ducked out of the bar. Home sweet home was only two blocks over and one block up. Technically, our house was a one-bedroom, but we'd walled off two-thirds of the living room with dollar-store shower curtains when I was nine.

"Mom?" I called out as I stepped over the threshold. There was an element of ritual to calling her name, even when she wasn't home. Even if she was on a bender—or if she'd fallen for a new man, experienced another religious conversion, or developed a deep-seated need to commune with her better angels under the watchful eyes of a roadside psychic.

I'd come by my habit of hopping from one interest to the next honestly, even if her restlessness was less focused and a little more self-destructive than my own.

Almost on cue, my cell phone rang. I answered.

"Baby, you will not believe what happened last night." My mom never bothered with salutations.

"Are you still in the continental United States, are you in need of bail money, and do I have a new daddy?"

My mom laughed. "You're my everything. You know that, right?"

"I know that we're almost out of milk," I replied, removing the carton from the fridge and taking a swig. "And I know that someone was an *excellent* tipper last night."

There was a long pause on the other end of the line. I'd guessed correctly this time. It was a guy, and she'd met him at The Holler the night before.

"You'll be okay, won't you?" she asked softly. "Just for a few days?"

I was a big believer in absolute honesty: Say what you mean, mean what you say, and don't ask a question if you don't want to know the answer.

But it was different with my mom.

"I reserve the right to assess the symmetry of his features and the cheesiness of his pickup lines when you get back."

"Sawyer." My mom was serious—or at least as serious as she got.

"I'll be fine," I said. "I always am."

She was quiet for several seconds. Ellie Taft was many things, but above all, she was someone who'd tried as hard as she could for as long as she could—for me.

"Sawyer," she said quietly. "I love you."

I knew my line, had known it since my brief obsession with the most quotable movie lines of all time when I was five. "I know."

I hung up the phone before she could. I was halfway to finishing off the milk when the front door—in desperate need of both WD-40 and a new lock—creaked open. I turned toward the sound, running the algorithm to determine who might be dropping by unannounced.

Doris from next door lost her cat an average of 1.2 times per week.

Big Jim and Trick had matching habits of checking up on me, like they couldn't remember I was eighteen, not eight.

The guy with the Dodge Ram. He could have followed me. That wasn't a thought so much as instinct. My hand hovered over the knife drawer as a figure stepped into the house.

"I do hope your mother buys Wüsthof," the intruder commented, observing the position of my hand. "Wüsthof knives are just *so* much sharper than generic."

I blinked, but when my eyes opened again, the woman was still standing there, coiffed within an inch of her life and besuited in a blue silk jacket and matching skirt that made me wonder if she'd mistaken our decades-old house for a charitable luncheon. The stranger said nothing to indicate why she'd let herself in or how she could justify sounding more dismayed at the idea of my mom having purchased off-brand knives than the prospect that I might be preparing to draw one.

"You favor your mother," she commented.

I wasn't sure how she expected me to reply to that statement, so I went with my gut. "You look like a bichon frise."

"Pardon me?"

It's a breed of dog that looks like a very small, very sturdy powder puff. Since absolute honesty didn't require that I say *every* thought that crossed my mind, I opted for a modified truth. "You look like your haircut cost more than my car."

The woman—I put her age in her early sixties—tilted her head slightly to one side. "Is that a compliment or an insult?"

She had a Southern accent—less twang and more drawl than my own. *Com-pluh-mehnt or an* in-*suhlt?*

"That depends on your perspective more than mine."

She smiled slightly, like I'd said something *just darling,* but not actually amusing. "Your name is Sawyer." After informing me of that fact, she paused. "You don't know who I am, do you?" Clearly, that was a rhetorical question, because she didn't wait for a reply. "Why don't I spare us the dramatics?"

Her smile broadened, warm in the way that a shower is warm, right before someone flushes the toilet.

"My name," she continued in a tone to match the smile, "is Lillian Taft. I'm your maternal grandmother."

My grandmother, I thought, trying to process the situation, *looks like a bichon frise.*

"Your mother and I had a bit of a falling-out before you were born." Lillian was apparently the kind of person who would have referred to a Category 5 hurricane as *a bit of a drizzle.* "I think it's high time to put that bit of history to rest, don't you?"

I was one rhetorical question away from going for the knife drawer again, so I attempted to cut to the chase. "You didn't come here looking for my mother."

"You don't miss much, Miss Sawyer." Lillian's voice was soft and feminine. I got the feeling she didn't miss much, either. "I'd like to make you an offer."

An offer? I was suddenly reminded of who I was dealing with here. Lillian Taft wasn't a powder puff. She was the merciless, dictatorial matriarch who'd kicked my pregnant mother out of her house at the ripe old age of seventeen.

I stalked to the front door and retrieved the Post-it I'd placed next to the doorbell when our house had been hit with door-to-door evangelists two weeks in a row. I turned and offered the handwritten notice to the woman who'd raised my mother. Her perfectly manicured fingertips plucked the Post-it from my grasp.

"'No soliciting,'" my grandmother read.

"Except for Girl Scout cookies," I added helpfully. I'd gotten kicked out of the local Scout troop during my morbid true-crime and facts-about-autopsies phase, but I still had a weakness for Thin Mints.

Lillian pursed her lips and amended her previous statement. "'No soliciting except for Girl Scout cookies.'"

I saw the precise moment that she registered what I was saying: I wasn't interested in her *offer.* Whatever she was selling, I wasn't buying.

An instant later, it was like I'd said nothing at all. "I'll be frank, Sawyer," she said, showing a kind of candy-coated steel I'd never seen in my mom. "Your mother chose this path. You didn't." She pressed her lips together, just for a moment. "I happen to think you deserve more."

"More than off-brand knives and drinking straight from the carton?" I shot back. Two could play the rhetorical-question game.

Unfortunately, the great Lillian Taft had apparently never met a rhetorical question she was not fully capable of answering. "More than a GED, a career path with no hope of advancement, and a mother who's less responsible now than she was at seventeen."

Were she not an aging Southern belle with a reputation to uphold, my grandmother might have followed that statement by throwing her hands into touchdown position and declaring, *"Burn!"*

Instead, she laid a hand over her heart. "You deserve opportunities you'll never have here."

The people in this town were good people. This was a good place. But it wasn't *my* place. Even in the best of times, part of me had always felt like I was just passing through.

A muscle in my throat tightened. "You don't know me."

That got a pause out of her—and not a calculated one. "I could," she replied finally. "I could know you. And *you* could find yourself in the position to attend any college of your choosing and graduate debt-free."

Secrets on My Skin

www.secretsonmyskin.com/community

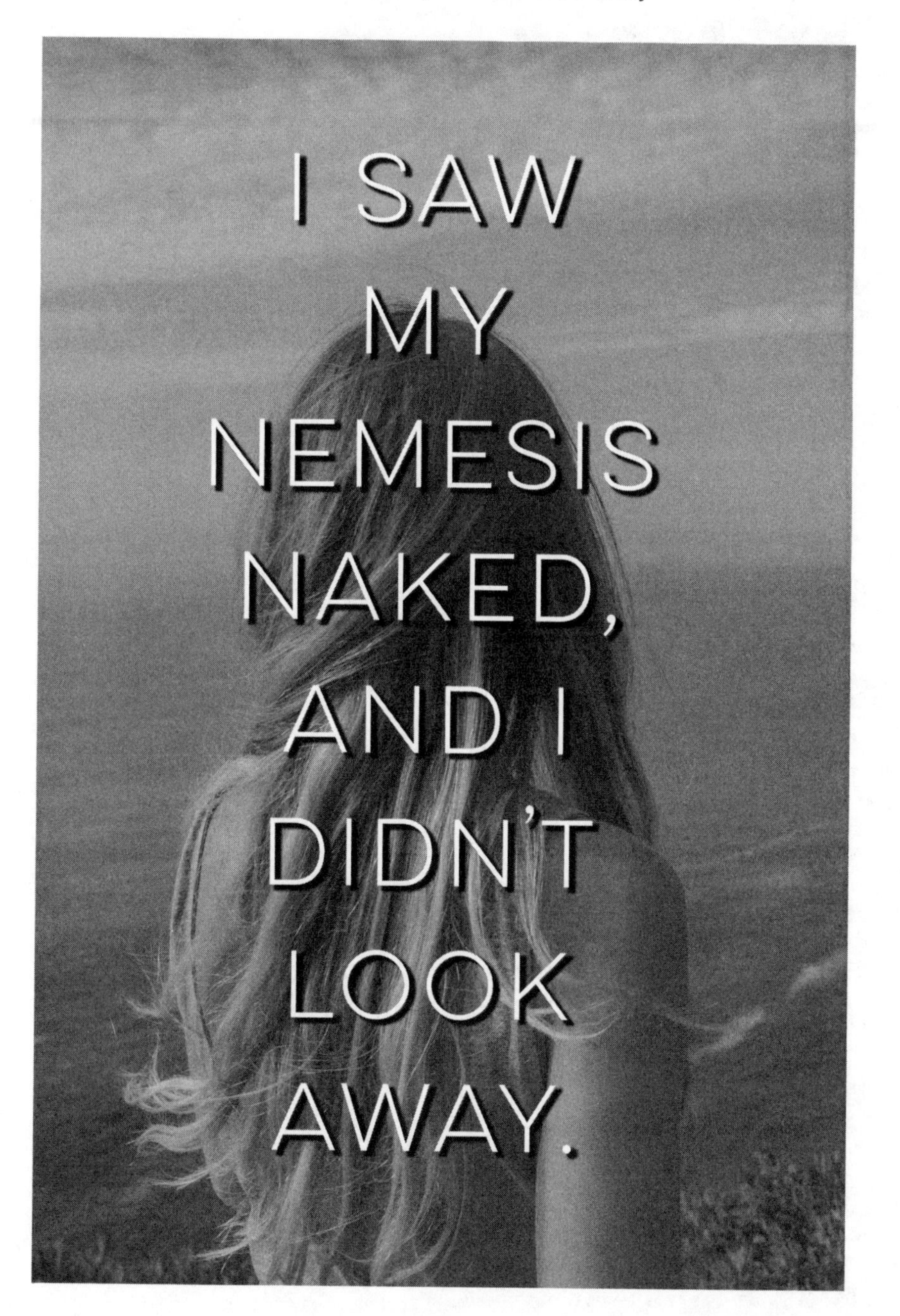

CHAPTER 2

There was a contract. An honest-to-God, written-in-legalese, sign-on-the-dotted-line *contract*.

"Seriously?"

Lillian waved away the question. "Let's not get bogged down in the details."

"Of course not," I said, thumbing through the nine-page appendix. "Why would I go to the trouble of reading the terms before I sell you my soul?"

"The contract is for your protection," my grandmother insisted. "Otherwise, what's to keep me from reneging on my end of the deal once yours is complete?"

"A sense of honor and any desire whatsoever for an ongoing relationship?" I suggested.

Lillian arched an eyebrow. "Are you willing to bet your college education on my honor?"

I knew plenty of people who'd gone to college. I also knew a lot of people who hadn't.

I read the contract. I wasn't even sure why. I was not going to move in with her. I was not going to walk away from my home, my life, my mother for—

"Five hundred thousand dollars?" I may have punctuated that amount with an expletive or two.

"Have you been listening to rap music?" my grandmother demanded.

"You said you'd pay for *college*." I tore my gaze from the contract. Even reading it made me feel like I'd just let the guy with the Dodge Ram tuck a couple of ones into my bikini. "You didn't say anything about handing me a check for half a million dollars."

"It won't be a check," my grandmother said, as if that was the real issue here. "It will be a trust. College, graduate school, living expenses, study abroad, transportation, tutors—these things add up."

These things.

"Say it," I told her, unable to believe that anyone could shrug off that amount of money. "Say that you're offering me five hundred thousand dollars to live with you for nine months."

"Money isn't something we talk about, Sawyer. It's something we have."

I stared at her, waiting for the punch line.

There was no punch line.

"You came here expecting me to say yes." I didn't phrase that sentence as a question, because it wasn't one.

"I suppose that I did," Lillian allowed.

"Why?"

I wanted her to actually say that she'd assumed that I could be bought. I wanted to hear her admit that she thought so little of me—and so little of my mom—that there had been no doubt in her mind that I'd jump at the chance to take her devil of a deal.

"I suppose," Lillian said finally, "that you remind me a bit of myself. And were I in your position, sweet girl . . ." She laid a hand on my cheek. "I would surely jump at the chance to identify and locate my biological father."

CHAPTER 3

My mom—in between alternating bouts of pretending that I'd been immaculately conceived, cursing the male of the species, and getting tipsy and nostalgic about her first time—had told me exactly three things about my mystery father.

She'd only slept with him once.

He hated fish.

He wasn't looking for a scandal.

And that was it. When I was eleven, I'd found a picture she'd hidden away, a portrait of twenty-four teenage boys in long-tailed tuxedos standing beneath a marble arch.

Symphony Squires.

The caption had been embossed onto the picture in silver script. The year—and several of the faces—had been scratched out.

Money isn't something we talk about, I thought hours after Lillian had left. I mentally mimicked her tone as I continued. *And the fact that the man who knocked your mother up is almost certainly a scion of high society isn't something I'll come right out and* say, *but . . .*

I picked the contract up again. This time, I read it from start to finish. Lillian had conveniently forgotten to mention some of the terms.

Like the fact that she would choose my wardrobe.

Like the mandatory manicure I'd have once a week.

Like the way she expected me to attend private school alongside my cousins.

I hadn't even realized I *had* cousins. Trick's grandkids had cousins. Half of the members of my elementary school Girl Scout troop had cousins *in that troop*. But me?

I had an encyclopedia of medieval torture techniques.

Pushing myself to finish the contract, I arrived at the icing on the cake. *I agree to participate in the annual Symphony Ball and all Symphony Deb events leading up to my presentation to society next spring.*

Deb. As in *debutante*.

Half a million dollars wasn't enough.

And yet, the thought of those hypothetical cousins lingered in my mind. One of my less random childhood obsessions had been genetics. Cousins shared roughly one-eighth of their DNA.

Half-siblings share a fourth. I found myself going to my mother's bedroom, opening the bottom drawer of her dresser, and feeling for the photograph she'd taped to the back.

Twenty-four teenage boys.

Twenty-four possible producers of the sperm that had impregnated my mother.

Twenty-four Symphony Squires.

When my phone buzzed, I forced myself to shut the drawer and looked down at the text my mom had just sent me.

A photo of an airplane.

It may be more than a few days. I read the message that had accompanied the photograph silently and then a second time out loud. My mother loved me. I knew that. I'd *always* known that.

Someday, I'd stop expecting her to surprise me.

It was another hour before I went back to the contract. I picked up a red pen. I made some adjustments.

And then I signed.

APRIL 15, 5:13 P.M.

Mackie kneaded his forehead. "Are you sure none of you wants to call your parents?"

"No, thank you."

"Do you know who my father is?"

"My stepmother's faking a pregnancy, and she needs her rest."

Mackie wasn't touching that with a ten-foot pole. He turned to the last girl, the one who'd successfully picked the lock mere seconds after he'd arrived.

"What about you?" he said hopefully.

"My biological father literally threatened to kill me if I become inconvenient," the girl said, leaning back against the wall of the jail cell like she *wasn't* wearing a designer gown. "And if anyone finds out we were arrested, I'm out five hundred thousand dollars."

EIGHT AND A HALF MONTHS EARLIER

CHAPTER 4

I arrived at my grandmother's residence—a mere forty-five minutes from the town where I'd grown up and roughly three and a half worlds away—on the contractually specified date at the contractually specified time. Based on what I knew of the Taft family and the suburban wonderland they inhabited, I'd expected my grandmother's house to be a mix of Tara and the Taj Mahal. But 2525 Camellia Court wasn't ostentatious, and it wasn't historic. It was a nine-thousand-square-foot house masquerading as average, the architectural equivalent of a woman who spent two hours making herself up for the purpose of looking like she wasn't wearing makeup. *This old thing?* I could almost hear the two-acre lot saying. *I've had it for years.*

Objectively, the house was enormous, but the cul-de-sac was lined with other houses just as big, with lawns just as sprawling. It was like someone had taken a normal neighborhood and scaled everything up an order of magnitude—including the driveways, the SUVs, and the dogs.

The single largest canine I'd ever seen greeted me at the front door, butting my hand with its massive head.

"William Faulkner," the woman who'd answered the door chided. "Mind your manners."

She was the spitting image of Lillian Taft. I was still processing the fact that the dog was (a) the size of a small pony and (b) named *William Faulkner,* when the woman I assumed was my aunt spoke again.

"John David Easterling," she called, raising her voice so it carried. "Who's the best shot in this family?"

There was no reply. William Faulkner butted his head against my thigh and huffed. I bent slightly—*very* slightly—to pet him and noticed the red dot that had appeared on my tank top.

"I will skin you alive if you pull that trigger," my aunt called, her voice disturbingly cheerful.

What trigger? I thought. The red dot on my torso wavered slightly.

"Now, young man, I believe I asked you a question. Who's the best shot in this family?"

There was an audible sigh, and then a boy of ten or so pushed up to a sitting position on the roof. "You are, Mama."

"And am *I* using your cousin for target practice?"

"No, ma'am."

"No, sir, I am not," my aunt confirmed. "Sit, William Faulkner."

The dog obeyed, and the boy disappeared from the roof.

"Please tell me that was a Nerf gun," I said.

It took my aunt a moment to process the question and then she let out a peal of laughter—practiced and perfect. "He's not allowed to use the real thing without supervision," she assured me.

I stared at her. "That's not as comforting as you think it is."

The smile never left her face. "You *do* look like your mother, don't you? That hair. And those cheekbones! When I was your age, I would have killed for those cheekbones."

Given that she was the best shot in this family, I wasn't entirely certain she was exaggerating.

"I'm Sawyer," I said, trying to wrap my mind around the greeting I'd gotten from a woman my mom had always referred to as an ice queen.

"Of course you are," came the immediate reply, warm as whiskey. "I'm your aunt Olivia, and that's William Faulkner. She's a purebred Bernese mountain dog."

I'd recognized the breed. What I hadn't recognized, however, was that William Faulkner was female.

"Where's Lillian?" I asked, feeling like I'd well and truly fallen down the rabbit hole.

Aunt Olivia hooked the fingers on her right hand through William Faulkner's collar and reflexively straightened her pearls with the left. "Let's get you inside, Sawyer. Are you hungry? You *must* be hungry."

"I just ate," I replied. "Where's Lillian?"

My aunt ignored the question. She was already retreating back into the house. "Come on, William Faulkner. Good girl."

My grandmother's kitchen was the size of our entire house. I half expected my aunt to ring for the cook, but it quickly became apparent that she considered the feeding of other people to be both a pastime and a spiritual calling. Nothing I said or did could dissuade her from making me a sandwich.

Refusing the brownie might have been taken as a declaration of war.

I was a big believer in personal boundaries, but I was also a believer in chocolate, so I ignored the sandwich, took a bite of the brownie, and then asked where my grandmother was.

Again.

"She's out back with the party planner. Can I get you something to drink?"

I put the brownie back down on my plate. "Party planner?"

Before my aunt could answer, the boy who'd had me in his sights earlier appeared in the kitchen. "Lily says it's bad manners to threaten fratricide," he announced. "So she didn't threaten fratricide."

He helped himself to the seat next to mine and eyed my sandwich. Without a word, I slid it toward him, and he began devouring it with all the verve of a little Tasmanian devil wearing a blue polo shirt.

"Mama," he said after swallowing. "What's fratricide?"

"I imagine it's what one's sister very pointedly does *not* threaten when one attempts to shoot her with a Nerf gun." Aunt Olivia turned back to the counter. It took me about three seconds to realize that she was making *another sandwich*. "Introduce yourself, John David."

"I'm John David. It's a pleasure to meet you, madam." For a trigger-happy kid, he was surprisingly gallant when it came to introductions. "Are you here for the party?"

I narrowed my eyes slightly. "What party?"

"Incoming!" A man swept into the room. He had presidential hair and a face made for golf courses and boardrooms. I would have pegged him as Aunt Olivia's husband even if he hadn't bent to kiss her cheek. "Fair warning: I saw Greer Richards making her way down the street on my way in."

"Greer *Waters* now," my aunt reminded him.

"Ten-to-one odds Greer *Waters* is here to check up on the preparations for tonight." He helped himself to the sandwich that Aunt Olivia had been making for me.

I knew it was futile, but I couldn't help myself. "What's happening tonight?"

Aunt Olivia began making a third sandwich. "Sawyer, this rapscallion is your uncle J.D. Honey, this is *Sawyer*."

My aunt said my name in a way that made it clear they'd discussed me, probably on multiple occasions, possibly as a problem that required a gentle hand to solve.

"Is this the part where you tell me I look like my mother?" I asked, my voice dry as a desert. My uncle was looking at me the same way his wife had, the way my grandmother had.

"This," he told me solemnly, "is where I welcome you to the family and ask you, quite seriously, if I just stole your sandwich."

The doorbell rang. John David was off like a rocket. All it took was a single arch of my aunt's eyebrow before her husband was on their son's heels.

"Greer Waters is chairing the Symphony Ball," Aunt Olivia murmured, clearing away John David's plate and depositing sandwich number three in front of me. "Between you and me, I think she's bitten off a bit more than she can chew. She just recently married the father of one of the Debs. There's trying and then there's trying too hard."

This from a woman who had made me three sandwiches since I'd walked in the front door.

"In *any* case," Aunt Olivia continued, lowering her voice, "I am just certain she'll have capital-O Opinions about the way your grandmother has arranged things."

Arranged things for what? This time, I didn't bother saying a word out loud.

"I know you must have questions," my aunt said, brushing a strand of hair out of my face, seemingly oblivious to the fact that I had been asking them. "About your mama. About this family."

I hadn't expected this kind of welcome. I hadn't expected affection or warmth or baked goods from a woman who'd spent the past eighteen years ignoring my mother—and my existence—altogether. A woman that my mom had never even once mentioned by name.

"Questions," I repeated, my voice catching in my throat. "About my mom and this family and the circumstances surrounding my highly inconvenient and scandalous conception?"

Aunt Olivia's lips tightened over a pearly smile, but before she could reply, Lillian Taft entered the room wearing a gardening hat and gloves and trailed by a pale, thin woman with brown hair knotted severely at her neck.

"Always grow your own roses," my grandmother advised me without preamble. "Some things should not be delegated."

It's nice to see you, too, Lillian.

"Some things shouldn't be delegated," I repeated. "Like party planning?" I asked facetiously, eyeing the woman who'd followed her in. "Or like greeting the prodigal granddaughter when she arrives at your home?"

Lillian met my eyes. Her own didn't narrow or blink. "Hello, Sawyer." She said my name like it was one that people should know. After an elongated moment, she turned to the party planner. "Could you give us a moment, Isla?"

Isla, as it turned out, could.

"You look thin," Lillian informed me once the party planner had exited. She turned to my aunt. "Did you offer her a sandwich, Olivia?"

Sandwich number three was literally still sitting on the plate in front of me. "Let's stipulate that I have been sufficiently sandwiched."

Lillian was not deterred. "Would you like something to drink? Lemonade? Tea?"

"Greer Waters is here," my aunt interjected, keeping her voice low.

"Horrid woman," Lillian told me pl
ever . . ." She removed her gloves. "I'm mu

That, more than the advice about rose
la Lillian Taft.

"Now," Lillian continued as the soun
against the wood floor announced the
apparently infamous Greer Waters, "Saw
upstairs and meet your cousin? Lily's stayi
can help you get ready for tonight."

"Tonight?" I asked.

Aunt Olivia took it upon herself to s
"Blue Room," she echoed cheerfully. "Sec

CHAPTER 5

I counted the steps as I made my way up the grand staircase and got to *eleven* before I paused to take in the artwork lining the wall. A blond-haired little girl blew a dandelion in one portrait and sat astride a horse in the next. I watched her grow, mahogany-framed picture by mahogany-framed picture, until a baby boy joined her in the yearly portrait, their outfits color-coordinated, her smile sweet and practiced and his served with increasingly large sides of trouble.

When I made it to the top of the stairs, I came face-to-face with a family portrait: Aunt Olivia and Uncle J.D., the blond girl, now a teenager, sitting beside John David, and the elegant Lillian Taft standing with one hand on her daughter's shoulder and one hand on her grandson's. To the right of the family portrait, there was one of Aunt Olivia in a white dress. At first, I thought it was a wedding dress, but then I realized that my aunt wasn't much older in this picture than I was now. The teenage Olivia wore elbow-length white gloves.

My eyes flitted to the left of the family portrait. There was a small, almost invisible hole in the wall. Had another portrait hung there once?

Say, for instance, one of my mom?

"I am on the verge of using some very unladylike language." The voice that issued that statement was sweet as pie.

"Lily . . ."

"Unladylike and *creative*."

As I made my way toward the second door on the left, the person who'd said my cousin's name spoke up again, tentatively this time. "On a scale of one to bad, is this really so awful?"

The reply was delicate and demure. "I suppose that depends on how one feels about felonies."

I cleared my throat, and the occupants of the room turned to look at me. I recognized my cousin Lily from the portraits: light hair, dark eyes, small waist, big bones. Every hair was in place. Her summer blouse was freshly pressed. The girl next to her was stunningly beautiful and also, based on her expression, on the verge of projectile vomiting.

Then again, I probably would have been nauseous, too, if I were lying on my stomach with my back arched and the tips of my toes touching the back of my head.

"Hello." Cousin Lily did an admirable impression of someone who had decidedly *not* been discussing felonies a moment before. For a girl who looked like she'd just stepped out of a magazine spread entitled "Tasteful Floral Prints for Virginal Ivy League Hopefuls," she had balls.

This girl and I share one-eighth of our DNA.

"You must be Sawyer." Lily had her mother's way of saying the word *must*: two parts emphasis, one part command.

The contortionist on the floor unfolded herself. "Sawyer," she repeated, her eyes wide. "The cousin."

She sounded just horrified enough to make me wonder if she considered *cousin* synonymous with *ax murderer*.

"Our grandmother sent me up," I told Lily as her friend attempted to stand very still, like I was some kind of bear and any motion might be taken as reason to attack.

"I'm supposed to help you get ready for tonight," Lily said. She caught the gaze of the doe-eyed girl next to her, who was noticeably wringing her hands. "I'm supposed to *help her* get *ready* for *tonight*," Lily repeated. Clearly, she was trying to get some kind of message across.

"I can *go* if you *two* are in *the middle* of *something*." I echoed Lily's emphasis.

My cousin turned her dark brown eyes back to me. She had a way of looking at a person like she was considering dissecting you or giving you a makeover or possibly both.

I did not like my chances.

"Don't be silly, Sawyer." Lily took a step toward me. "You aren't interrupting a thing. Sadie-Grace and I were just having a little chat. Did I introduce you to Sadie-Grace? Sadie-Grace Waters, meet Sawyer Taft." Lily had clearly inherited our grandmother's penchant for rendering her own questions rhetorical. "It *is* Taft, isn't it?" She plowed on before I could reply. "I apologize for not being there to greet you downstairs. You must think I was absolutely raised in a barn."

I'd spent six months at age thirteen learning everything there was to know about gambling and games of chance. I was willing to lay good odds right now that my oh-so-felicitous cousin hadn't been particularly enthused about the idea of a blood relation from the wrong side of the tracks being suddenly foisted upon her. Not that she'd admit to a lack of enthusiasm.

That, I thought, *would be almost as ill-mannered as threatening fratricide.*

"I was pretty much raised in a bar," I replied when I realized Lily had finally paused for a breath. "As long as you can refrain from breaking a chair over someone's back, we're good."

Emily Post had apparently not prepared either Lily or Sadie-Grace for offhanded discussions of bar brawls. As they searched for an appropriate response, I drifted toward a nearby window. It overlooked the backyard, and down below, I could see shimmery black tablecloths being spread over round-top tables. There were easily a half dozen workers and three times that many tables.

There was also a catwalk.

"Were you really raised in a bar?" Sadie-Grace came to stand beside me. She was tall and willowy thin and bore a striking resemblance to a certain classic beauty best known for marrying into the royal family. Her delicate fingers worried at the tips of ridiculously thick and shiny brown hair.

Wide-eyed. Anxious. Prone to yoga. I cataloged what I knew about her, then answered the question. "My mom and I lived above The Holler until I was thirteen. I wasn't technically allowed in the bar, but I have a slight tendency to take technicalities as a challenge."

Sadie-Grace nibbled on her bottom lip, looking down at me through impossibly long lashes. "If you grew up like that, you must know things," she said very seriously. "You must know people. People who know things."

A quick glance at Lily told me that she didn't like the direction this conversation was going.

I turned back to Sadie-Grace. "Are you by any chance fixing to ask me what my stance is on felonies?"

"We need to get you a dress for tonight, Sawyer!" Lily smiled brightly and shot laser eyes at Sadie-Grace, lest the latter even *think* about answering my question. "We'll hit the shops. And goodness knows we could stand to do something about those eyebrows."

I took that to mean that Lily had come down on the side of

makeover over *dissection*, but I got the feeling that it had probably been a pretty close call.

Beside me, Sadie-Grace assiduously avoided eye contact, her bottom lip still caught between her teeth.

I don't want to know, I decided. *Whatever my cousin's gotten herself into, whatever I overheard, I really and truly do not want to know.*

APRIL 15, 5:16 P.M.

"I'm not saying this is Sawyer's fault," the prim and proper one said delicately. "But."

Mackie waited for her to say more. The young lady, however, seemed to consider that a full sentence.

"It was an accident! You can't arrest someone for an accident!" That, from the one who literally looked like a Disney princess come to life.

"Clearly, Sadie-Grace, they can."

"But it was only maybe ten percent on purpose!"

"Girls," Mackie said in what he hoped passed for a stern voice. "One at a time. And start from the beginning."

"The beginning." The coquette of the group—the one who'd blessed his heart—sashayed forward. "I, for one, couldn't begin to say where this began. Could *you*, Lily?"

The calm, well-mannered one weathered that blow predictably calmly and with predictably good manners. The lock picker, however, seemed to take umbrage. Her eyes narrowed at Miss I-Couldn't-Begin-To-Say.

"Now that I think about it," the coy instigator continued, "I do seem to remember *something*. . . ."

The lock picker stepped forward. Her white-gloved hands started to curl themselves into white-gloved fists.

Oh no, Mackie thought. *This could get ugly.*

EIGHT AND A HALF MONTHS EARLIER

CHAPTER 6

"How would you describe your style?" The saleswoman—excuse me, *personal shopper*—had the poise of a beauty pageant contestant and the power-hungry gaze of a politician.

This did not bode well.

After ascertaining that my dear cousin Lily was blocking my exit—*smart girl*—I resigned myself to answering the question. "Do you consider 'grease stains' a style?"

Sadie-Grace's mouth dropped open in a perfect O. There was a single awkward beat of silence.

"She's looking for something classic," Lily put in smoothly. "Less than semi-formal, more than business casual, and I believe my grandmother said something about a certain shade of blue?"

"Yes." The personal shopper stretched a blink out long enough that I wondered if she was meditating on the color blue. "Cerulean. Or possibly sapphire. Less formal than semi-formal. Cocktail?"

"Yes, please," I muttered.

"Cocktail *attire*," Lily emphasized, shooting a warning look at me, "could work, if you keep in mind that the event is outdoors."

"Something summery," the personal shopper offered immediately. "A-line, in a fabric that breathes."

I'd never been much of a shopper. "Grease stains" really was the closest thing I had to a personal style. And I definitely hadn't spent any time in Miss Coulter's, the only department store in three counties, Lily had informed me, to carry *certain* brands.

Maybe, if I back away very slowly . . .

Lily sidestepped to block the exit. The personal shopper didn't notice a thing. "If you girls would like to take a look around," she told Lily, "I'll just pull a few things for your friend to try on."

"Cousin." Lily seemed to regret the correction the moment she made it, but that didn't stop her from raising her chin and repeating, "She's my cousin."

I could see the exact moment the woman in front of us accessed her mental store of family trees and realized who, exactly, that made me.

This was a city, not a small town, but from what my mother had told me about her life growing up here, I knew that the circles the illustrious Taft family ran in were very small. My mom tended to talk about the country club set the way a claustrophobic might have reminisced about time spent trapped in a storm cellar.

"Your cousin!" the personal shopper chirped. "How lovely. Now that you mention it, I *can* see a family resemblance."

I was on the small side of petite. Lily was taller, broader, and in undoubtedly better shape. Her face was heart-shaped, her skin pale, and her eyelashes nearly as light as her silk-straight hair. In contrast, I was perpetually suntanned, could have made a fortune if freckles were a monetizable commodity, and had mud-brown hair that was even less well-behaved than I was.

"Maybe," Sadie-Grace said thoughtfully after the woman had departed, "the resemblance is in your auras."

Three hours, one platinum credit card, and only two minor breakdowns—courtesy of our personal shopper and our personal shopper's replacement—later, I had a dress. And shoes. A tasteful evening bag. And murder in my heart.

"Almost done!" Lily told me cheerfully.

I would have been cheerful, too, if I'd somehow worn down my opponent until said opponent would have agreed to going to tonight's shindig *naked* if it meant getting out of this department store alive. Lily Taft Easterling was a force of nature. A delicate, demure, seemingly soft-spoken force of nature who took fashion almost as seriously as she took proper etiquette in the face of adversity.

I was the face of adversity.

I'd vetoed dress after dress. I'd flat-out refused to try on any more. I distinctly remembered refusing to even tell her my shoe size.

And yet . . .

"I'll just pop over to the cosmetics counter," Lily continued blithely, "while you and Sadie-Grace get to know each other."

I would have staged a walkout then and there were it not for the halfway-hopeful smile on Sadie-Grace's face. I'd never met someone so close to the societal ideal of beauty and so utterly unsure of herself. If I'd had to pick two adjectives to describe her, I would have gone with *vulnerable* and *cheerful*, with a close third on *naive*.

Damn you, Lily, I thought. Growing up, I'd been the kind of kindergartner who punched fourth graders for making second graders cry. It hadn't exactly endeared me to the second graders, but I couldn't do *nothing* any more than I could turn my back on the girl beside me now.

"So," I said flatly, earning a beaming grin from Sadie-Grace. "Is there anything to do besides shopping hereabouts?"

Sadie-Grace thought long and hard, then opened her mouth to reply, but instead of words, she let out a sound somewhere in the key of *eep*. Lily, deep in discussion with someone at the cosmetics counter, didn't notice Sadie-Grace's attempt to duck behind a display of designer evening bags.

"Sadie-Grace?"

She shushed me, then peeked out from behind the purses. Almost of its own accord, her left foot began tracing out graceful little half circles on the floor.

"Are you . . . dancing?" I asked.

With great effort, Sadie-Grace stilled the rogue foot. "I *rond de jambe* when I'm antsy," she whispered. "It's involuntary, like the hiccups, but with ballet."

That statement was ten kinds of odd, but I didn't have a chance to explain that to her before Sadie-Grace *eep*ed again and ducked behind me. I followed her line of sight through the cosmetics department, past the designer scarves, and straight to a couple looking at cuff links. They were in their forties, closer to Aunt Olivia's age than my mother's. There was something vaguely familiar about the man.

"Senator Sterling Ames," Sadie-Grace whispered behind me. "And his wife, Charlotte."

The senator looked up from the cuff links. He scanned the room with casual precision, and his gaze came to rest on Lily.

"Your cousin used to date the senator's son, Walker," Sadie-Grace whispered. "He's nice. But the senator's daughter . . ."

Sadie-Grace almost started rond de jambe–ing again, but she caught herself.

"His daughter?" I prompted as the senator and his wife began making their way toward Lily.

Sadie-Grace crossed herself, even though I was fairly certain she wasn't Catholic. "The senator's daughter is the devil incarnate."

Secrets on My Skin

www.secretsonmyskin.com/community

I'M THE ONE WHO STOLE
YOUR BATHING SUIT.
BITCH.

CHAPTER 7

I'd spent the majority of fourth grade learning to draw faces. I'd sold portraits for two bucks a pop on the playground, but I'd never managed to draw my own. It was like there was something missing, some facial calculus I could never quite capture because I couldn't trace the details that separated my face from my mother's back to their source.

Maybe that was why I found myself assessing the senator's features, even though he was almost certainly too old to have been a Squire the year my mother was a Deb.

"Campbell Ames is Lucifer," Sadie-Grace reiterated beside me in a dramatic whisper. "Beelzebub. Mephistopheles. Old Scratch. *The devil.*" She sighed. "Let's get this over with."

"Get what over with?" I asked.

Sadie-Grace was perplexed. She looked from me to the cosmetics counter, where the senator's wife was kissing Lily's cheek, then back at me. "What do you mean *what*? We have to go over there and say hello."

"Point of fact: we don't."

"But . . ." Sadie-Grace was at a loss for words. She listed toward

Senator and Mrs. Ames like they were a black hole, sucking her in. Apparently, it didn't matter that she'd tried to bodily hide herself from view or that she'd just referred to the senator's daughter by no fewer than five different names for Satan. In Sadie-Grace's world, when an adult you knew came within an eight-foot radius, the choices were *chitchat* and *combust*.

I followed her into the fray and ignored the grateful look she shot me in return. I had my own reasons for playing nice—and they had nothing whatsoever to do with decorum.

"We miss seeing you at our house, Lily." The senator's wife had a voice that carried: high and clear and cavity-sweet. "I just know that Walker is going to come to his senses one of these days."

Salt, meet wound, I thought as I came to stand beside Lily. I knew nothing about my cousin's relationship with her ex, but I was beginning to understand this much about Lily: The more it hurt, the harder she smiled.

And this hurt a lot.

Maybe that shouldn't have mattered to me, but I'd never excelled at standing by and watching other people bleed. It must have mattered to Sadie-Grace, too, because she overcame her jitters enough to draw the senator's attention—and more importantly, his wife's—away from Lily. "Have y'all met Sawyer?"

That did the trick. One second I was standing there minding my own business, and the next, Charlotte Ames had my hands held firmly in hers.

If you say one word about my cheekbones, I thought, *I cannot be held responsible for my actions.*

"We were just helping Sawyer pick out a little something for tonight." Lily's power smile was still firmly in place.

"Your first Deb event!" The senator's wife squeezed my hands.

"How exciting! You've missed a fitting or two, of course, but I'm sure that Miss Lillian will have you caught up in no time. That woman can move mountains."

The vat of perky subtext was clear. *You were a last-minute and probably unwanted addition! Your grandmother strong-armed someone into letting you in!*

Luckily, the experiences that had inspired me to get a GED instead of finishing out high school had left me well and truly subtext-immune.

"I take it we'll see the two of you there tonight?" Lily asked the senator and his wife politely. I wasn't sure if she'd redirected the conversation for my benefit or for theirs. "And Campbell?"

Beside us, Sadie-Grace made a small, wheezing sound.

"Sterling." Charlotte Ames laid a hand on her husband's arm. "We really should see about getting you a new pair of cuff links."

"We'll be there," the senator told Lily. He hesitated—*no,* I thought, *that's not the right word.* Men like Senator Sterling Ames didn't hesitate. They took pause.

They assessed.

"I can't say I knew your mother well," the senator told me. He had blue eyes, black hair, and a face you could trust but absolutely shouldn't. "However, the Taft women I *do* know are a force to be reckoned with." He offered Lily a small, controlled smile, then turned the full weight of his gaze back to me. "If you've inherited anything from that side of your family tree, I suspect you'll handle the Symphony Ball—and tonight's auction—just fine."

And what about the other *side of my family tree?* I thought as I watched them walk away.

"Sawyer?" Lily lightly touched my shoulder, more incisive than I'd given her credit for. "Are you okay?"

It had been a long time since I'd expected—or allowed—anyone else to take care of me. *If you don't expect people to surprise you, they can't disappoint.*

"Auction." I recovered my voice and stepped back from Lily's touch. "What auction?"

Secrets on My Skin

www.secretsonmyskin.com/community

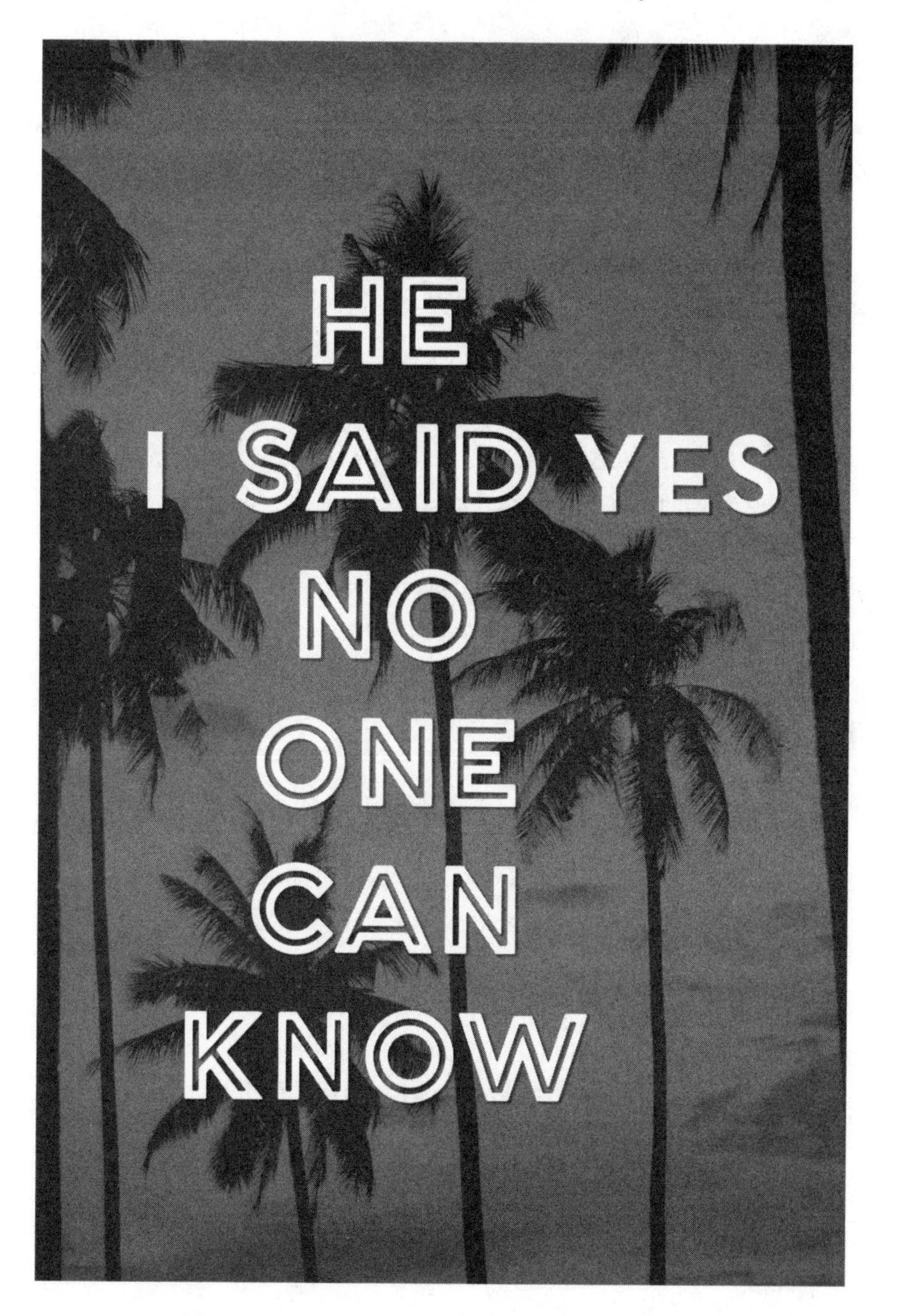

CHAPTER 8

The Pearls of Wisdom Charity Auction was apparently a Symphony Ball tradition. An hour later, I was still unclear on who or what was being auctioned.

I was fairly certain I didn't want to know.

"Sit still, Sawyer." Lily's tone was pleasant, but the look in her eyes was befitting of a stone-cold assassin.

A stone-cold assassin with tweezers.

I batted her hand away from my face. "I would rather be trapped inside a Sicilian bull than let you continue to tweeze the bejeezus out of my eyebrows."

"Did you just take the Lord's name in vain?"

"Really?" I said, raising my now-shapely eyebrows to incredible heights. "That's what you're going with? Not *What's a Sicilian bull?*"

"I would assume," my cousin said primly, "that it is a bull conceived on the largest island in the Mediterranean."

I resisted the urge to tell her that the Sicilian bull was a medieval torture device used to slowly roast the victim alive.

"You really do have excellent bone structure," Sadie-Grace said tentatively. "If you would just let us—"

I stood up. "I think I can take it from here."

Lily could not have looked more skeptical if I'd announced that I was the second coming of Cleopatra.

"There's a Lily-approved dress on the bed," I pointed out. "Shoes next to the dress. I am ninety percent sure that I can put them on myself without ushering in the apocalypse."

"Our grandmother coerced—or possibly blackmailed—the Symphony Ball Committee into letting you be a Deb. The apocalypse *is already here*." Lily took a deep and cleansing breath, but before she could continue to impress upon me the severity of the situation, a flying orange projectile bulleted past my head and hit her square between the eyes.

She blinked.

I turned toward the door, expecting to see John David. Instead, I saw Lily's younger brother *and* her father. John David was holding a Nerf crossbow. J.D. was crouched behind his son, steadying the boy's aim.

"Truce!" the smaller of the guilty parties bellowed preemptively.

Uncle J.D. made a show of looking at Lily—and the expression on her face. He took the crossbow from his son's hand and lowered his voice to a stage whisper. "Run."

John David didn't have to be told twice. Once he'd cleared out, Lily bent to pick up the dart and returned it to her father. "You shouldn't encourage him."

"But I'm the encouraging parent." J.D. pressed a kiss to the top of Lily's head. "It's what I do, and speaking of which, your mother is a bit stressed about tonight, so I just wanted to go on the record in advance by saying that you are absolutely and utterly perfect, just the way you are." Uncle J.D. turned to offer me a grin nearly identical to the one he'd given his daughter. "You settling in, Sawyer?"

"That's one way to describe it."

Lily narrowed her eyes. "Do you mind?" she asked her father, plucking the toy crossbow from his hands before turning and aiming it squarely at me. "Put on the dress," she ordered.

I snorted.

Behind her, Uncle J.D. began backing up slowly. "And with that, I take my leave. Sorry, Niece. I learned a long time ago never to involve myself in a fight between two or more Taft women."

Just like that, he was gone.

"Your mom get 'stressed' a lot?" I asked Lily. So far, none of my relatives had been what I was expecting. Aunt Olivia hadn't seemed cold or heartless or any of my mother's other favorite descriptors for her older sister.

"Mama just likes things to be perfect," Lily said diplomatically. She lowered the crossbow. "For the record, I am not trying to be difficult here, Sawyer. I am trying to help you, because for better or worse, we are in this together."

From the tone in her voice, you would have thought we were in a life raft in the middle of piranha-filled waters. Then again, I was about to make my debut in high society.

Maybe we were.

Oddly touched at the way she'd thrown her lot in with mine, I decided to go easy on Lily. She hadn't asked for this any more than I had—and *she* didn't stand to gain half a million dollars in the process.

As far as I knew.

"Relax, Lily," I said, wondering if our grandmother *had* bribed her to play happy hostess. "What's the worst that could happen?"

APRIL 15, 5:19 P.M.

"I think we can all agree this started at the auction."

"Campbell!"

"I told you. She's *Lucifer*!"

"Auction." Mackie had to raise his voice to be heard. "What auction?"

All four girls turned to look at him in unison. They looked so . . . innocent. Sweet. As pure as the driven snow.

"Officer," Lucifer said demurely, "far be it from little old me to tell you how to do your job, but if I were you, I would circle back to that." She offered him a subtle, conspiratorial smile. "If you want the good stuff, you should cut straight to asking about our accomplices."

EIGHT AND A HALF MONTHS EARLIER

CHAPTER 9

Getting dressed was more complicated than I had anticipated. The A-line number Lily had chosen was knee-length and made of a royal blue silk that had very little give. The color wasn't a problem.

The lack of straps was.

August in Magnolia County had three and only three temperatures: hot, awful hot, and damn hot. And today?

It was *damn hot* outside. I'd been in my grandmother's massive backyard all of three minutes when I started sweating. And the moment I started sweating, the dress started slipping.

And the moment it started slipping, I was surrounded.

"You must be the scandalous Sawyer Taft."

I leveled a stare at the black-haired, blue-eyed good old boy who'd issued that statement. He was my age, or maybe a year or two older. The boy beside him was similarly aged, but appeared to be about 90 percent limbs and a good 10 percent hipster glasses.

Hipster Glasses cleared his throat. "What my cousin means to say is that tales of your beauty precede you." He paused and frowned. "Or proceed you." He glanced at the other boy. "Precede? Proceed?"

"Precede," I said. "Tales of my beauty *precede* me."

That got a small, crooked grin out of the boy who'd spoken first, more genuine and far deadlier than the smile he'd worn a moment before. For a moment, Mr. Tall-Dark-and-Handsome looked almost human.

"They will find you, you know," he drawled, taking a sip of iced tea that I deeply suspected he'd enlivened with contraband. "No matter how far you run or where you hide, the debutantes of Magnolia County *will* find you."

I clamped my arms to my side, trapping my dress in my armpits and halting its rapid descent. "Yeah, well, I'm not hiding."

Neither of the boys seemed convinced. The fact that I was standing as far from the throe of things as I could manage probably didn't help my case. There were easily a hundred people in my grandmother's backyard. Slipping away from Lily's watchful eye hadn't been easy, but I needed to spend five seconds without anyone telling me how *delightful* it was to meet me. I needed to be able to hike my dress up without causing An Incident.

Most importantly, I needed to be able to watch the adults at this soiree—particularly males in the running for *mystery father*—without them realizing they were being watched.

"I have good news for you, Sawyer Taft." The blue-eyed boy drew my attention back from the crowd.

You know which one of these fine gentlemen knocked up my mom?

"In about five minutes, your fellow Debs are going to realize that my darling sister is conspicuously absent from these proceedings." The boy angled his head toward the far side of the yard. "Shortly thereafter, their mothers are going to realize the same thing."

I followed his gaze to Aunt Olivia. She was in conversation with the senator's tiny blond wife and three slightly less tiny, slightly less blond women who seemed to travel in her wake.

"My father's going to try to play it off like my sister's feeling a little under the weather." There was an edge in the boy's voice as he continued. "My mother will say something along the lines of *You know how girls this age can be* and then maniacally one-up every single bid my aunt has made in the silent auction. Meanwhile, Campbell's friends will text her. She won't reply, the same way she hasn't replied to any of *my* texts in the past twenty-four hours."

"Campbell," I repeated, remembering the look on Sadie-Grace's face when she'd told me that the senator's daughter was the devil incarnate. "Your sister is . . ."

"AWOL," the boy replied.

So this was Walker Ames. I could see his resemblance to the senator, now that I knew to look for it. The dark hair, the light eyes, the breadth of his shoulders.

"It's not like little sis to miss a chance to play Empress Supreme with her minions," he commented. "But sticking it to my father *is* like her, and if I know Cam, there's probably a guy involved." He leaned toward me and lowered his voice. "So you see, Sawyer Taft, very soon you'll be old news, no matter how scandalous you may be."

"Walker."

In unison, the senator's son and I turned to look at the person who'd spoken his name.

"Lily," he returned.

Something about the way my cousin was holding her head reminded me of the way she'd said that her mother liked things to be perfect. I was going to go out on a limb and guess that, in their days as a couple, Lily and Walker had been *perfect.*

Right up until the point where they weren't.

"I see you've met my newly acquired cousin," Lily commented.

"We were just discussing the intrigue surrounding that very

acquisition." The edge I'd heard in Walker's voice sharpened, but there was also something like longing buried deep in his tone.

"Are you drunk?" Lily asked him flatly.

He met her gaze. "Would it make you feel better if I was?"

I knew when my presence in a conversation was no longer required. I made it all of two feet away before I was joined by Walker's hipster-glasses-wearing cousin.

"The Ballad of Lily Easterling and Walker Ames," he said solemnly. "A tale for the ages, to be sure." He lifted his right hand and offered me a little salute. "I'm Boone, Walker's less explicitly handsome yet nonetheless debonair first cousin."

I gave him a look.

He was undeterred. "Mine is a subtle charm."

Despite my best efforts to the contrary, I could feel the edge of my lips twitching upward. "Are they always like this?" I asked, glancing back at Walker and Lily.

"They didn't use to be."

Before I could read much into that statement, Boone's phone buzzed. From the angle where I was standing, I could see that he'd received some kind of image.

Of lingerie. An image of lingerie—and not on the hanger.

Boone's eyes went comically wide. He looked at me, then at his phone, then back at me. "I can see how, to the untrained eye, this might seem difficult to explain."

I shrugged. "Seems pretty straightforward to me—and firmly none of my business."

"It's not like that," Boone replied quickly. "I'm in it for the artistry."

The artistry of a close-up on a black lace bra?

"Fine, you got me," Boone admitted. "I'm in it for the gossip."

"The gossip," I repeated.

"I mean, yes, technically the site lets fans submit their own PG-rated art for each secret, and technically I could get my gossip there, but I'll have you know that the fans call themselves Secrettes, which I frankly find exclusionary, and—"

"Boone," I said. "What are you talking about? What is . . . *that*?"

He turned his phone around, allowing the picture to fill the screen. "It's a photo blog," he said. "And it *is* artistic." I could make out the details of the photo now—specifically, the words that had been carefully scripted onto the girl's skin.

I said yes. He said no one can know.

"Who said yes to what?" Boone intoned. "And who told whom not to tell what precisely?" He paused. "Did I use the word *whom* correctly?"

"Secrets on My Skin." I ignored his question and focused on the emblem at the bottom of the picture.

"You've never heard of it?" Boone spoke about 70 percent faster when there were boobs involved. "It's been all the rage here for months. People anonymously submit their secrets, and this girl writes them on her body. No one knows who she is. The Secrettes think it's some girl who goes to Brighton, but I'm almost partially certain it's someone at Ridgeway Hall." He seemed to realize that flashing the picture around might not be prudent and quickly stuffed the phone back into his pocket.

"Sawyer will be joining us at Ridgeway this year." Lily slid effortlessly into the conversation, like whatever had just happened between her and Walker—who was nowhere to be seen—had been of no particular import.

"Actually, I won't be going to your school," I countered as Boone turned the world's biggest puppy-dog eyes on my cousin. "Or any school."

That was one requirement that I'd struck through with my little red pen.

"Sawyer is taking a gap year between high school and college." As if summoned by the mere thought of our contract, my grandmother inserted herself into the conversation just as easily as Lily had. "It's really quite common in Europe."

I noticed that she didn't mention my GED.

"Perhaps you could talk to my parents about gap years and their benefits for young people such as myself?" Boone offered my grandmother what I'm sure he thought was very charming smile.

"Boone Mason," my grandmother replied, like saying his first and last names was some kind of incantation to make him stand up straighter and tack the word *ma'am* onto the end of every sentence. "I believe the Squire coordinator is looking for you."

"Yes, ma'am." Boone scurried off—standing straighter all the while.

"I take it Lily has told you about tonight's auction?" In true Lillian Taft style, my grandmother—who, I realized then, was probably Lily's namesake—didn't pause for even a hair's breadth before continuing. "It's a tradition, you know, going back upward of fifty years." She held up a flat, square box, six inches wide. "Pearls of Wisdom: each Deb wears a string of pearls, while each Squire carries a first edition. At the end of the night, the necklaces and antique books are auctioned off one by one. Half of the proceeds go to the symphony and the other half to a charity of the Debs' choosing."

I glanced at Lily for some confirmation that I was not the only one who took issue with the girls being relegated to *pearls* over *wisdom*, but her eyes were locked on the box.

Our grandmother opened it, and I heard Lily's breath catch in her throat.

"Mim," she said reverently. "Your pearls."

It took me a moment to realize that "Mim" must have been what my cousins called our grandmother, and another few seconds after that for me to actually look at the necklace that had caught Lily's attention so completely. I knew very little about jewelry, but even I could tell this piece was a thing to behold. Three strands of pearls were collected together with an emerald clasp edged in finely carved silver. All of the pearls were flawless—as were the trio of diamonds that hung down from the bottommost strand, each one preceded by a black pearl that reflected a dark rainbow of colors in the light.

"Your grandfather bought this necklace for me many years ago, on a night just like this one." The wave of nostalgia in my grandmother's tone caught me off guard, and my thoughts went briefly to the grandfather I'd never known.

"Mim." Lily couldn't tear her eyes away from the box. "You can't auction off your *pearls*."

"Mim" smiled wryly. "Don't look so horrified, Lily. This will be the third time I've auctioned off this necklace, and it's never left the family yet. Your mothers each wore this necklace for their own Pearls of Wisdom. Your grandfather placed the winning bid both times." She offered Lily a knowing look. "I suspect your father has his eye on them tonight. In the meantime . . ." She removed the necklace from the box. She unclasped it.

And she turned to me.

"Sawyer, would you do the honors?"

Lily didn't flinch. She smiled—harder, wider.

I took a step back. "That's not—"

"A request?" My grandmother completed my sentence to her liking. "No, dear, it's not." My cousin watched, unblinking, as our grandmother fastened her pearls around my neck.

"What am . . ." Lily cleared her throat. "What am I wearing, Mim?"

"The Deb coordinator has something for you," our grandmother replied, straightening Lily's hair, which 100 percent did *not* need to be straightened. "And whatever it is, I am sure you will do it credit."

Lily nodded. After a fraction of a second of silence, she excused herself, running her own hand over her hair as she went.

Once she was out of earshot, I turned back to our grandmother. "Now that was just mean."

"I haven't the faintest idea what you're talking about, Sawyer."

"Lily could have worn your pearls," I insisted. "I wouldn't have cared."

"You should care, Sawyer Ann. There isn't a person here tonight who won't want a closer look at that particular piece of our family history." She let that sink in. "Whatever you think of me, I'm not cruel—not needlessly, not to my own blood. As I told Lily, your uncle J.D. will undoubtedly bid on and win this piece. Until then . . ." She attempted to straighten my hair and found it significantly less pliable than Lily's. "You and I have just ensured that every person here tonight has a very aboveboard excuse to approach you. Including people who remember your mother wearing that very necklace, *particularly* men who might not otherwise have much to say to a teenage girl."

My grandmother had just fixed it so that anyone and everyone could get a closer look at me under the guise of getting a closer look at her pearls.

Including my biological father.

"Just curious," I said, more impressed by her machinations than I wanted to be. "Am I the bait or the hook?"

CHAPTER 10

"You've been a popular one tonight." Aunt Olivia gave me a knowing look.

I was fairly certain she *didn't* know why I'd engaged with every single person who had approached. Why I'd memorized their names.

Why I'd taken a mental picture of every man's face.

"You're practically the belle of the ball," my aunt continued, and even though there was nothing pointed in her tone, I got the sense that in her *perfect* world, that honorific would have gone to Lily.

"We're lucky I haven't flashed anyone." I tugged at the top of my dress, and Aunt Olivia shooed my hands down.

"They are beautiful," she sighed.

"My boobs?"

She treated the question with absolute seriousness. "The *pearls*. I remember wearing them, of course. And then, at Ellie's Pearls of Wisdom . . ." She trailed off.

If there was one thing I'd learned growing up bar-adjacent, it was that sometimes, the best way to keep someone talking was to say nothing at all.

Sure enough, only a few seconds passed before my aunt picked up the conversational slack. "Your mama was beautiful in that necklace, Sawyer. Quiet, of course, a bit awkward, and Lord knows she was angry at the world. But beautiful."

"Angry?" I asked. My mom was many things, but *quiet*, *angry*, and *awkward* wouldn't have made my list.

"I swear, sometimes it seemed like Ellie *liked* being angry." As if she'd caught herself saying a curse word, Aunt Olivia immediately amended her statement. "Not that she didn't have her reasons, poor thing. Our father died shortly after he purchased that necklace at my Pearls of Wisdom. I felt just awful that he wasn't there to bid on it for Ellie."

My grandmother had said, very clearly, that her husband had purchased the pearls both times. I said as much out loud, and Aunt Olivia shook her head.

"Oh, no," she reiterated. "Your uncle J.D.—we'd just gotten married that summer—he bought them on Ellie's auction night, just like he'll buy them for Lily tonight. You don't mind, do you, Sawyer? Some days it seems like your cousin has been in love with those pearls since the day she was born. I always thought . . ."

You always thought Lily would be the one wearing them tonight.

This time, I didn't use silence as a means of making her put that into words. Instead, I decided to get her chatting on a different—and more useful—topic. "Is there anyone here who was a Deb with my mom?"

"Ellie and I were six years apart." Aunt Olivia fanned her face with her right hand. "I'm ashamed to say I wasn't exactly tuned in to the particulars of her social situation. Maybe if I had been . . ." Almost immediately, she redirected herself. "Water under the bridge! Now, let me think, who here was Ellie's age? Charlotte Ames—used to be Bancroft—had a little sister in that year. I believe she's a Farrow now." My aunt snapped her fingers. "And

Greer!" she said triumphantly. "Greer Richards. I'm not one to talk badly about anyone, but she was a real piece of work, and your mother was just glued to her side."

Greer Richards, I thought, rifling through my memory banks. *Recently married, chairing the Symphony Ball, and her new last name is . . .*

"Waters," my aunt corrected herself.

"Yes?"

The two of us turned to see an inordinately handsome man looking vaguely confused, as if he'd just woken from a deep and consuming sleep.

"Charles," my aunt said. "How *are* you? Have you met my niece, Sawyer? She and your Sadie have just hit it off already."

The man momentarily focused when he heard my aunt say *Sadie*. As in, Sadie-Grace—his daughter.

"Yes. Well." He smiled at me, affable, if a bit distant. "Pleasure to meet you."

Aunt Olivia melted into the crowd, and I found myself trying to gauge how old Charles Waters was.

Too old. He's too old to have been a Squire with my mother.

His gaze caught on the necklace. "Beautiful specimen," he mumbled. "Just beautiful."

I was about to reply with my thanks—as I had dozens of times already this evening—when he lifted a finger to my shoulder. I was on the verge of introducing him to the "top ten reasons you don't touch Sawyer's bare skin without permission" list when I realized that he hadn't been reaching for me.

He'd been reaching for the ladybug on my shoulder.

"Beautiful," he said again, as it crawled onto his fingertip. "*Coccinella septempunctata*," he told me. "The seven-spotted lady beetle." Almost belatedly, he seemed to realize that this was a formal affair and not an entomology conference. The ladybug took flight and he sighed. "I suppose that was horribly rude of me," he said sadly.

"Just between us," I replied, "I'm rather partial to the horribly rude. I could belch the alphabet if it would make you feel better."

He scrutinized me for a long moment and then smiled. It was pretty damn easy to see where Sadie-Grace had gotten her looks.

"Charles!" A woman appeared beside him, hooking her arm through his. She wore her dark red hair long and straight, and I could tell just by the way she held herself that the unusual color was her natural hue. "You haven't been talking our newest Deb's ear off, have you, sweetheart?"

I would have put a thousand dollars on this being the infamous Greer Waters. Sadie-Grace's stepmother was dressed similarly to Aunt Olivia, but her dress was just a smidgen shorter. Her heels were just a smidgen taller.

I would have gone double or nothing that neither of those things was an accident.

"We're ready for you backstage," Greer told me. "And look at that necklace! Gorgeous."

I let myself be shepherded to the curtained area behind the catwalk.

"I'm guessing you've seen the necklace before," I said. "My aunt mentioned that you and my mother were friends."

Greer Waters didn't hesitate. She didn't pause. But I saw something shift behind her green eyes.

"Your mother was a dear. An *absolute* dear, but I'm afraid we didn't have much in common."

Silence proved only slightly less effective on her than on Aunt Olivia.

"I was . . ." She laughed. "I suppose you could say I was horrible back then. Always in the middle of things. Just plagued with attention and admirers and secretly loving it—you know the kind of girl."

She didn't quite seem to have the hang of self-deprecation.

"Ellie Taft was a sweet little thing. But she was a bit more . . . alternative, I guess you would say? She had the world at her fingertips, and I would have sworn she didn't even want it. We were just very different people." She bared her teeth at me in a pageant-perfect smile. "Now, let's get you into position."

She clamped a manicured hand onto my shoulder and physically guided me into a line that had formed backstage, right behind Lily and Sadie-Grace.

"Stand up straight, sweetheart," she told the latter. "And remember: there is absolutely *nothing* to be nervous about."

Sadie-Grace seemed to find that statement nerve-racking in the extreme.

I stepped out of line and in front of Greer as she attempted to pass. "Greer," I said, then corrected myself. "Mrs. Waters." That bought me a few bonus points. With every intention of cashing them in, I continued. "You at least knew my mother. Do you remember who her friends were? Who she spent time with?"

Greer studied me for several seconds with an intensity I suspected she typically reserved for floral arrangements and choosing the perfect shade of pink polish. "I suppose she was close to Lucas."

"Lucas?" I repeated, my heart thudding in my chest.

"Lucas Ames."

Secrets on My Skin

www.secretsonmyskin.com/community

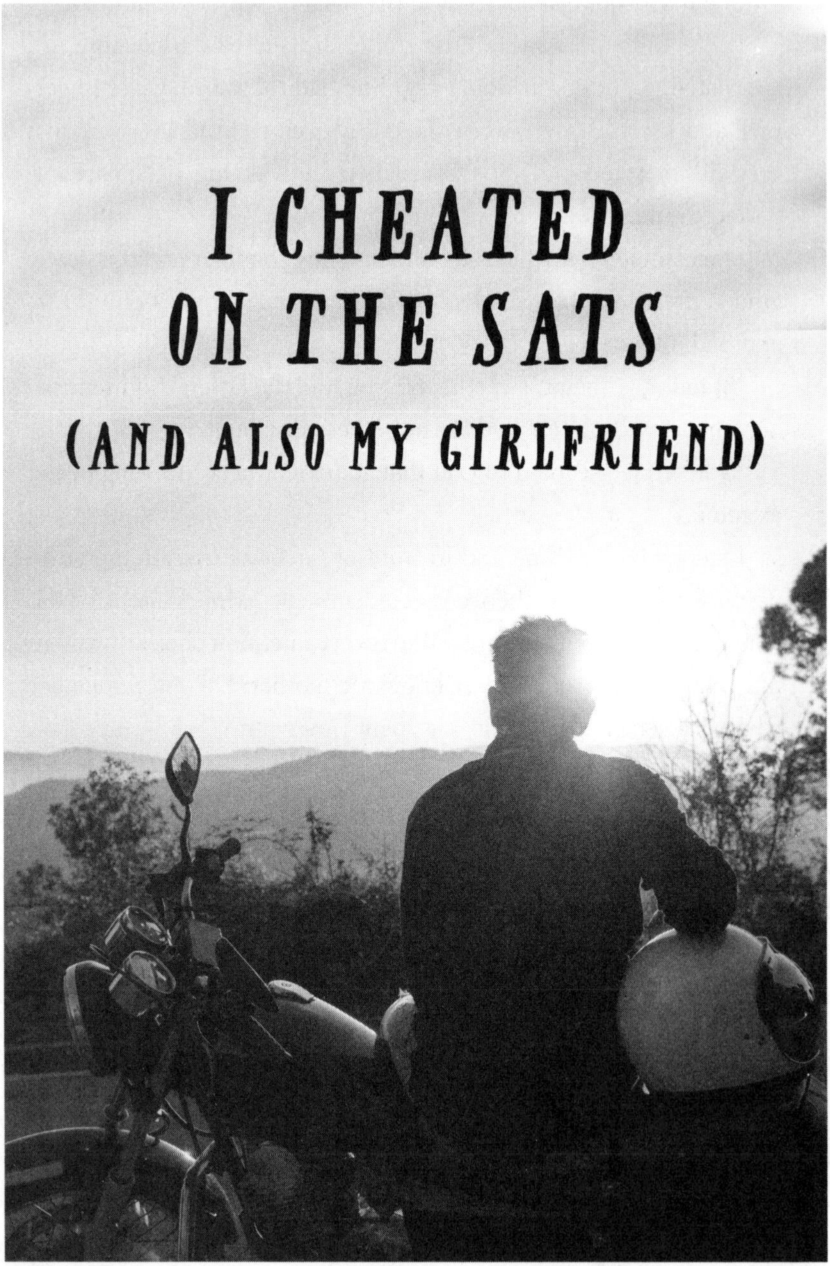

I CHEATED ON THE SATS

(AND ALSO MY GIRLFRIEND)

CHAPTER 11

As the Squires lined up in front of the Debs—*wisdom* before *pearls*—I found myself scanning the line for Walker Ames, my brain in overdrive. *Lucas Ames. Walker's uncle? A cousin?*

"He's not here," Lily murmured beside me. "Walker, I mean. That's who you're looking for, isn't it? He has that way about him. Mama always called it his helping and a half of charm."

"Lily," Sadie-Grace cut in softly.

"I'm just saying that Walker isn't here," Lily replied, her dark eyes boring into mine. "He was a Squire last year. He graduated in the spring, top of his class. He's supposed to be at college on a football scholarship. *But. Well.*"

That was meant as a conversation ender. *Walker didn't go to college,* I filled in. *And he broke up with you.*

There was probably a diplomatic way of responding, but I wasn't exactly known for my light touch. "I have no interest in your ex, Lily, except insofar as he might—or might not—be related to the unidentified dude who impregnated my mother."

"Could you lower your voice?" Lily lowered her own. "What happened with your mother isn't exactly . . ."

"Cocktail-appropriate?" I suggested.

Lily allowed herself a split second of vexation, then gathered her composure, turned back toward the front of the line, and didn't say another word to me as the auction began.

First the Squires and then the Debs were ushered down the catwalk, one by one, until there were only a handful of us left.

"They're saving you for last," Sadie-Grace whispered. "On account of your grandmother's pearls. And don't mind Lily. She's just . . ."

"A normal human being who experiences the full range of human emotions and sometimes acts upon them?" I suggested. "Don't worry, Sadie-Grace. I don't have any tender feelings for Lily to hurt."

If you don't expect people to surprise you . . .

Soon, I was the only one left backstage.

"Fancy meeting you here." Walker Ames appeared seemingly out of nowhere. He trod a straight line toward me, but I'd spent enough time at The Holler to recognize the glazed look in his eyes. If he hadn't been drunk earlier, he was well on his way now.

"Save your breath," I told him.

"Excuse me?" He had the kind of Southern manners that even alcohol couldn't dull.

"I have a rule." I paused. "Three rules, actually, but one of them is that no one interested in flirting with a teenage girl is even remotely worth flirting with, including and especially teenage boys."

I'd seen my mother go through too many breakups. I'd kissed too many boys who hadn't the faintest idea how to *really* kiss a girl back. I knew what came of putting your faith in the opposite sex, and I had no intention of letting some smooth talker leave me high and dry—now or ever.

"You're something else, Sawyer Taft." Walker's blue eyes were more focused than they'd been a moment before. His voice was softer.

"I'm a person," I corrected. "But to you?" A few feet away, Greer signaled that it was my turn to ascend the stage. "To you, I'm just another bad idea."

Hiking my dress up, I decided to hell with it and kicked off the heels Lily had purchased for me. I took the stairs barefoot and two at a time.

Let people stare. Let them judge me.

"Item forty-eight," the auctioneer announced. "Worn by Miss Sawyer Taft." He offered me an elbow to escort me down the catwalk. If I'd still been wearing the heels, I might have taken it. Instead, I made the walk myself, the exact same way I would have walked from one car at Big Jim's Garage to another.

The spotlight was painfully bright—so much so that I couldn't make out the details of the audience as the auctioneer spoke. I could, however, hear the murmurs.

"The bidding will open at ten thousand dollars."

I choked audibly on my own spit.

"Do I hear ten thousand dollars?"

My eyes adjusted in time to see my uncle raise his numbered paddle. Several other bidders got in on the action, but their conspiratorial smiles told me that my grandmother wasn't the only one who'd gone into this assuming her necklace would stay in the family.

This is all for show, I realized, wishing someone would just put me out of my misery.

Then a new bidder entered the fray. "Twenty thousand dollars."

A momentary hush fell over the crowd. People turned to look at the bidder, but his attention was focused 100 percent on me.

"Do I hear twenty-one?" the auctioneer asked Uncle J.D.

Out of the corner of my eyes, I saw Senator Ames begin to make his way through the crowd toward the bidder: a man in his mid-thirties who looked a bit like Walker.

Lucas? I wondered, and when the man promptly one-upped my uncle's bid a second time, I was suddenly sure of it. I tried to picture this man with my mother.

"Twenty-five." I could hear the tension in Uncle J.D.'s voice as he raised the stakes again.

The senator whispered emphatically in Lucas's ear. Lucas gave every impression of thinking his brother's disapproval was an absolute lark. "Thirty thous—"

Before he could finish the bid, a man around my grandmother's age stepped forward. He had an understated manner and a booming voice. "Fifty thousand dollars, final bid."

The auctioneer's gaze flicked briefly to Uncle J.D., whose whole body had gone rigid. Aunt Olivia whispered—or possibly *hissed*—something into his ear, but J.D. was frozen.

"Final bid," the old man reiterated.

The auctioneer didn't need to be told a third time. "Sold!"

APRIL 15, 5:23 P.M.

Mackie's white-gloved teenaged perps were incapable of speaking one at a time, and it was making him dizzy.

Bless your heart, he thought grimly. *I'll bless* your *heart, Rodriguez. I'll bless it real good.*

"Girls!" He hadn't meant to shout, but his head was pounding, and they wouldn't stop talking, and, damn it, he was an officer of the law!

All four of them shut their mouths and stared at him, owl-eyed.

Quick, he thought. *Say something . . . official.*

"Now, what's this about accomplices? And fifty-thousand-dollar pearls?"

There was a moment of utter silence, and then:

"They're not worth fifty thousand dollars."

"*You're* not worth fifty thousand dollars!"

"I hardly think you're in a position to—"

"Enough!" Mackie tried his luck a second time. He could do this. He could take control of the situation.

Unfortunately, that was the exact moment that the lock picker seemed to come to the same conclusion. "Tell me, Officer," she said shrewdly, "do you even know what we were arrested *for*?"

EIGHT AND A HALF MONTHS EARLIER

CHAPTER 12

If hell hath no fury like a woman scorned, then a whole legion of scorned women had no more impressive rage than a Southern lady robbed of her pearls. My grandmother was fit to be tied as she escorted me between two tables to the man who'd outbidden my uncle *and* Lucas Ames.

"Davis." She fixed him with a stare. "This was unexpected, even from you."

"Even from me?" the gentleman repeated. "If I recall, you once took great pleasure in telling me exactly how predictable I am." He turned to me and extended a hand. "Since Lillian seems to have forgotten her manners, I suppose it's up to the two of us to introduce ourselves. I'm Davis Ames. And you are, young lady?"

If my grandmother could have incinerated him with the power of her mind, I think she would have.

"Right now," I replied, "I'm someone who is very concerned for your longevity."

He chuckled, and it utterly changed his face. "Got a bit of you in her, does she, Lill?"

My grandmother's expression *almost* faltered. She was still furious, but there was a layer to that emotion that hadn't been present a moment before.

"We go way back, your grandmother and I," Davis Ames told me. "In fact . . ." His gaze went to the pearls around my neck. "I was there the day your grandfather first purchased that necklace for her." His gaze flickered back to Lillian. "If I remember correctly, I was waiting tables."

"And look at you now." My grandmother recovered her voice. The words sounded like a compliment, but I was pretty darn sure she meant for him to hear them otherwise.

"Look at us both," he replied.

Appropriately enough, that was what just about everyone at this little shindig was doing. They didn't stare, of course. *Staring* would have been rude, but every cluster of partygoers scattered around the lawn angled ever-so-subtly toward us.

I somehow doubted they were that interested in my lack of footwear.

"The pearls are beautiful," Davis Ames said decisively, "but I find I'm more interested in the young lady. You're Eleanor's girl."

I was so used to hearing my mother referred to as Ellie that the words caught me off guard—as did the sudden realization that if Lucas Ames *was* my father, this man was probably . . .

My grandfather?

"Davis, I am sure that Sawyer has better things to do than to natter away the evening with us old folks." Lillian motioned for me to turn around. She unclasped the necklace. As bitter a pill as handing them over was, Lillian Taft was not one to show weakness.

"I've heard rumors about your son-in-law's latest business venture," Davis Ames told her quietly. "Given that J.D. didn't close the door on bidding the second my idiot son opened his mouth, you might consider looking into those rumors."

Lillian held the pearls out, arching an eyebrow. There was a moment of elongated silence between the two of them.

Gingerly, he took the pearls. "Lill—"

"If you so much as *try* to give me those pearls, Davis Ames," my grandmother murmured, sugar and spice and steel, as she slapped the pearls' box into his hand, "I will end you."

I was absorbed enough in watching the interplay between them that I didn't hear a third party approaching until he stepped into my peripheral vision and spoke. "There's a bit of a rivalry between your family and mine."

I turned to see the man who had first bid against Uncle J.D.—Davis Ames's "idiot son."

"Lucas?" I inferred.

His father and my grandmother were caught up enough in their back-and-forth that they didn't notice as I took a step away from them, willing the man beside me to do the same.

He obliged. "I see my reputation precedes me."

I shrugged. "Probably proceeds you, too."

Lucas Ames snorted. "I take it you've met my nephew Boone?"

I'd spent years wondering who my father was. I'd wondered if he had a family. But there was a difference between wondering, in the abstract, if I had aunts and uncles and cousins, and trying to wrap my mind around the fact that I might well have met those people tonight.

"You knew my mother." My mouth was dry, but I managed the words.

"Way back when, I was Ellie's best friend. On my better days, she was mine. How is she? Your mother?"

"Enamored of some guy she met in a bar."

With anyone else, that probably would have been a conversation stopper, but Lucas Ames didn't bat an eye. "Good for her. As a committed bachelor myself, I'm glad to know that she hasn't joined the ranks."

"The ranks?" I asked.

"Of the domesticated. The tied down. The settled."

I almost pointed out that my mother had spent the past eighteen years raising a child, but the truth was that some days, I'd felt like I was raising her.

"Sawyer." Lillian had apparently divorced herself from the conversation with Davis Ames enough to realize that I'd strayed, because she closed the space between us and placed a hand on my shoulder. "Why don't you go see if you can find Lily?"

My grandmother was the one who'd brought up the idea of me looking for my biological father. She was the one who'd laid the pearls out as bait tonight. But now that someone had actually taken that bait, she was shooing me away.

"Not to put too fine a point on this, but I think *I* found Lily." Lucas nodded toward a table near the front of the stage. "And Walker."

Walker had his cell phone gripped tightly in his hand. Lily appeared to be trying to calm him down. Walker shook her off and started stumbling toward his father. Like a switch had been thrown, Lucas Ames went from carefree bachelor to family man mode in a heartbeat. He crossed to Walker, putting a casual arm around him, though I suspected his grip was iron tight.

"You don't look like you're feeling well, kid," he commented. "Let's get you home."

"This is one of her games," Walker said, the words surprisingly crisp. "Campbell. It's just one of her little tests. It has to be."

"What has to be?" I found myself asking.

Based on the look my grandmother shot me, you would have thought verbalizing the question that everyone was thinking was a faux pas on par with running through this whole gala buck naked.

Walker, however, didn't seem to object. He shoved his cell phone into my hands. I looked down at the screen.

"'Debs and Squires like to play,'" I read out loud.

"Sawyer," my grandmother hissed.

I ignored her and continued reading the text that Campbell Ames had sent her brother. "'If I'm missing . . . suspect foul play.'"

Secrets on My Skin

www.secretsonmyskin.com/community

CHAPTER 13

From what I picked up during the remainder of the evening, Campbell Ames had a reputation for pulling "stunts like this." It wasn't entirely clear what constituted a *stunt*, though I did gather that borrowing cars that didn't belong to her and wearing white after Labor Day were both in Campbell's repertoire. Given that Walker wasn't the only one to receive a copy of that text, his prediction that I wouldn't be the scandal du jour for long had proved right on the money.

Debs and Squires like to play. If I'm missing . . . suspect foul play.

Hours later, I rolled my eyes as I scrubbed every trace of makeup from my face. This was what happened when people had too much money and too little sense. Thanks to Campbell Ames and her little *stunt*, my mother's good buddy Lucas had left before I'd gotten a chance to ask him whether, by any chance, he and my mom had engaged in coitus roughly nineteen years ago.

Taking a perch on top of the antique desk in "my" room, I played back the day's events. I scrutinized everything: the exact words Senator Ames had said to me at the department store, the expression on Lucas's face when he'd placed that first bid, the fact that Davis Ames had ultimately purchased the pearls. At home, I would have gone for a late-night walk as I turned the details over in my mind, but here, I had nowhere to go and nothing to distract me.

If Lucas is my father, his family would want to keep that on the down low. It was a big *if.* I was assuming facts not in evidence. Just because Lucas Ames had been my mother's friend, just because he'd tried to outbid my uncle tonight didn't mean—

"Watch your foot! That's my *head.*"

I glanced toward the window, which I had cracked open after getting out of the shower.

"Watch your head," came the reply. "That's my foot!"

There was an instant of silence, followed by a muffled shriek.

I don't want to know, I thought. *It's none of my business.* And yet . . .

I slid off the desk, walked over to the window, opened it, and looked down.

Sadie-Grace and Lily, dressed in all black, were climbing down an honest-to-God trellis. Who even *had* a trellis?

It's not my business if they fall and break their necks, I thought. *It's not my business where they're going at*—I looked at the clock—*a quarter to one.*

And yet . . . I had nowhere else to go and nothing else to distract me. I stood there watching them until they had their feet firmly planted on the lawn. And then, as they attempted to sneak down the street in what I'm sure they thought was a very stealthy manner, I shook my head. I rolled up the sleeves of my nightshirt and threw on a pair of running shorts.

And then I climbed down the trellis.

I trailed my cousin and Sadie-Grace for three blocks. They ended their nighttime journey on another cul-de-sac, with homes only a little bit smaller than my grandmother's. Lily approached the front porch of one of the houses, then slipped something out of her pocket.

A key, I realized as she fit it into the lock. A moment later, she and Sadie-Grace were gone.

Is this really so awful? I heard Sadie-Grace asking in my memory.

I suppose, Lily had replied, *that depends on how one feels about felonies.*

My curiosity piqued, I headed for the front door myself. They'd locked it behind them, but I made quick work of the lock.

My stance on felonies had always been rather fluid.

The inside of the house was under construction. Tarps blocked off entire rooms. I listened for Lily and Sadie-Grace, but heard nothing. Making my way silently down the hall, I used my phone as a flashlight, and soon, one mystery was solved.

There was a portrait on the wall: Aunt Olivia and Uncle J.D., on their wedding day.

"Okay," I murmured. "So technically, Lily wasn't breaking and entering."

Technically, I was.

The fact that Aunt Olivia's house was being renovated explained why Lily's family appeared to be staying at my grandmother's, but it didn't explain why my very proper cousin had taken off in the middle of the night like a couture-clad bandit.

I made it to the living room without seeing any signs of Lily or Sadie-Grace. Unlike the rest of the house, this room seemed to be fairly untouched by the remodel. The only sign that the house wasn't lived in was the trio of boxes stacked carefully next to the coffee table. Each one had been neatly labeled.

The one labeled *Symphony Ball* was too good to pass up.

Dried flowers. White gloves. A videotape. A pillow with my aunt's initials stitched onto it in gold. A program from the ball itself. Going through the box was an exercise in masochism. Part of me wanted to know what I was in for with this whole debutante thing, but a bigger part needed to get a sense of my aunt.

My mom wasn't always the most reliable narrator. My aunt may or may not have been "heartless, image-obsessed, and a pod person," but it was incontestable that Aunt Olivia had been in her twenties, married, and fairly independent when my mother had been kicked out of the house.

She could have stepped in.

She could have *helped*.

"But you didn't." I flipped open the album only to be greeted with a familiar, fancy script. *Symphony Ball,* it declared with gracefully looping letters. Keeping an eye on the door—and an eye out for Lily—I thumbed through the album and stopped when I came to a portrait of twenty-four teenage girls in identical white dresses, standing under a familiar marble arch. I found Aunt Olivia, and my mind went to the Squire photograph I'd stolen from my mother's drawer. I didn't need to do a side-by-side comparison to know that the composition was almost identical.

"Another tradition," I muttered. I ran my fingers over the embossing: *Symphony Debutantes*. Then I flipped the page. "And Symphony Squires." Twenty-four boys in long-tailed tuxedos stared back at me. I scanned the photo for Uncle J.D., then froze. My eyes darted to the year embossed onto the photo.

"Sawyer?"

I jumped to my feet. "Lily."

"What are you—"

"I followed you." I cut her off, my heart slamming into my rib cage with the force of a sledgehammer, my brain going a thousand miles an hour. On some level, I heard Lily tell me that I should go home. On some level, I realized that Sadie-Grace had joined her.

But on another level, I was twelve years old again. I'd just found the picture in my mother's drawer. It hadn't been taped to the back, not then—not until after my mother had discovered me looking at it.

I forced my mind back to the present.

"Maybe we should tell her," Sadie-Grace was saying. "She might be able to help."

"Tell me what?" My voice was calm. The album was dead weight in my hand, but it only took a moment of misdirection and some elementary sleight of hand before I had the picture out.

Twenty-four teenage boys in long-tailed tuxedos, standing under a marble arch.

"It's late," Lily said, sticking out her chin. "You should go."

She was backlit by a light in the hallway. It wasn't until she turned her head away from me that I saw the tear tracks on her face. For a split second, she looked like my mom.

How many times, when I was a kid, had I come across her with that look on her face exactly?

"I *could* go," I told Lily, unable to tear my mind completely away from the picture in my hands. "I will, if you ask me to again. But . . ." I let the word hang in the air. "I could also stay."

I could stay, and she could tell me what was going on.

I could stay, because we were family.

I could stay and come up with an excuse to go through everything in my aunt's keepsake box with a fine-tooth comb, because this picture I'd just pilfered—the picture of twenty-four squires my aunt's age, her husband included?

It was identical to the photograph I'd stolen from my mom.

The only difference was that the year on my mom's picture had been scratched out. Four of the faces had been scratched out. I'd assumed that my mystery father had done Symphony Ball with my mother. I'd assumed that was why she had the photograph in the first place.

I'd assumed wrong.

"I think we should tell Sawyer," Sadie-Grace said decisively. "She grew up in a *bar*."

Lily hesitated, then finally managed to form a single question. "Can you keep a secret?" she asked me.

I thought of the picture I'd just stolen—not to mention the implication that my mystery father would have been an adult when my mother was just seventeen. "Like you wouldn't believe."

Wordlessly, Lily led me through the house, out the back door, and to what appeared to be a pool house in the backyard.

"Before you say anything," she told me primly, "you should know that we can explain."

"Explain what?" I said.

In reply, Lily opened the door to the pool house. There, inside, was a teenage girl, bound, gagged, and duct-taped to a chair.

"Sawyer," Sadie-Grace said ruefully. "Meet Campbell Ames."

Secrets on My Skin

www.secretsonmyskin.com/community

CHAPTER 14

As it turned out, if there was one thing capable of distracting me from the major clue I'd just found to my father's identity, it was the kidnapping and unlawful detainment of a senator's daughter.

"What the hell, Lily?"

"It's not as bad as it looks," Sadie-Grace assured me. "We've been feeding her."

I could feel a migraine coming on.

"Well, not feeding her *exactly*," Sadie-Grace rambled on, "because she's in the middle of a juice cleanse, but—"

The phrase *juice cleanse* was the last straw. "If someone doesn't tell me what's going on here, I'm walking out that door"—I jerked my thumb toward the exit—"and calling the police. Or worse: our grandmother."

Lily responded as if I had slapped her—or possibly farted deliberately in her direction. "You will do no such thing, Sawyer Taft." She lifted her chin and met my eyes. "This is just a little misunderstanding."

From behind her duct-tape gag, Campbell Ames objected vehemently to that characterization of the situation.

"We didn't mean to." Sadie-Grace was nothing if not earnest. "It just . . . sort of . . . happened."

"How do you accidentally kidnap someone?" I meant it as a rhetorical question, but Sadie-Grace seemed to miss the incredulous tone in my voice.

"It starts," she said very seriously, "with accidentally knocking them out."

"Also known as felony assault," I clarified.

"Believe it or not," Lily said, delicately clearing her throat, "we aren't the bad guys here."

Tangled auburn hair fell in Campbell's face as she did her best to lunge at my cousin, but whatever they'd bound her to the chair with—it held.

"Honestly, Sawyer," Lily continued pertly, "if you can't be bothered to keep an open mind, I hardly see the point of telling you anything at all."

"An open mind?" I stared at Lily, waiting for some hint that she recognized how ridiculous it was to accuse someone of being closed-minded about *kidnapping*.

Nada.

Deciding there was one and only one way to speed up the process of figuring out what was going on here—and how likely I was to be arrested as an accessory after the fact—I crossed the room before Lily could stop me and peeled off Campbell's gag.

"I am going to sue you, have you arrested, and utterly *decimate* you socially." Campbell glared daggers at my cousin. "Not necessarily in that order."

"Campbell Ames," Lily replied, in an unfettered tone that would have been more appropriate if the two of them had just sat down to tea, "I'd like to introduce you to my cousin, Sawyer. She clearly did not think this through."

Considering I had neither kidnapped someone nor threatened my kidnappers in a way that incentivized them *not* to let me go, I was pretty sure I was currently winning the foresight prize in this room.

"We said we were sorry!" Sadie-Grace edged back from Campbell, until her back literally hit the wall.

Campbell made a show of raking her eyes over Sadie-Grace, top to bottom, bottom to top, then turned to me. "Have you ever wondered," she said, her voice dripping honey, "what total insecurity and a complete lack of social awareness would look like personified?"

Sadie-Grace made a muffled sound. I didn't need to look down at her feet to guess that she had gone into ballet mode.

"Well, don't just stand there," Campbell commanded imperiously. "Untie me!"

Clearly, I'd been mistaken for the help. Unfortunately for Campbell, there were two kinds of people in this world: those who *weren't* condescending and needlessly cruel and those I was pretty content to leave duct-taped to a chair.

"*Now* are you ready to listen?" Lily asked me quietly.

"Are you ready to talk?" I shot back.

Lily pressed her lips together, no smile. "Campbell is . . ." she managed after a moment. "She's . . ."

Campbell smiled sweetly. "I'm what, Lillian?"

Somehow, I doubted the use of Lily's full name—our grandmother's name—was accidental.

Personally, I wasn't a big believer in subtle threats. Or subtle insults. So I swung my attention back to the least subtle person in the room. "Secrets are like bandages," I told Sadie-Grace. "Just rip it off."

Sadie-Grace took a deep breath and then opened her mouth. Campbell grunted, bucked against the chair like a wild pony, and began screaming at the pitch of breaking glass.

"Make her stop!" Sadie-Grace sounded frantic.

"Why?" I replied, raising my voice just loud enough to be heard over Campbell's ongoing shrieking. "There's enough space between houses that no one can hear her. If she wants to turn her head around three hundred and sixty degrees and puke green slime, it's no skin off my back."

Sadie-Grace took a moment to digest that. "We *have* been feeding her kale juice."

Campbell abruptly stopped with the banshee impression. She gave me a once-over, then slid her gaze back to Lily. "Cousin, you said? Now, would that be on your daddy's side or your mama's, Lily?"

"The scandalous one," I replied, planting myself firmly in front of Campbell's chair. "And speaking of scandals, I've only been here twelve hours, and I've already gathered that they're a particular specialty of yours. You like attention, and you like to break the rules. I can't help but assume that if you tried to tell anyone about this, and it was your word against Lily's . . ."

I trailed off, waiting for the implication to sink in.

Campbell let out a light peal of laughter. "Aren't you just precious?" she asked. Giving every appearance of being utterly delighted, she leaned forward, as much as she could given the restraints. "Would you like for me to tell you how Miss Propriety over there spends her spare time? When she's not volunteering for charity, studying for the SATs, standing up straight, and practicing her most virginal smiles, of course." Campbell was getting way too much pleasure out of this.

"How I spend my time is none of your business," Lily said, her voice low—and desperate.

Campbell snorted. "Keep telling yourself that, porn star."

The sudden silence following that insult was deafening.

Abruptly, Sadie-Grace jackrabbited forward. She slapped the

duct-tape gag back over Campbell's mouth, scurried backward, and crossed herself.

Twice.

Then she turned on her toes and eyed me beseechingly. "What do we do?"

Lily didn't say anything out loud, but a slight shift in her shell-shocked expression echoed the question.

"You two do know that growing up on the wrong side of the metaphorical tracks doesn't actually give a person any kind of criminal expertise, right?" I said.

Sadie-Grace frowned. "I thought they were literal tracks."

Campbell caught my gaze, and despite the strip of duct tape over her mouth, there was a triumphant glint in her eyes, one that said that we were *lesser* and she was *more*, and things would always work out to her advantage in the end.

I was a strange kid whose even stranger hobbies had gotten her kicked out of Girl Scouts. I'd been born to an unwed teenage mother. I'd been called worse than *porn star*, and there were boys I'd never so much as kissed who'd claimed we'd done a whole lot more.

I'd been looked at that way that Campbell Ames was looking at me now more times than I could count.

"Start from the beginning," I told Lily, making my way out of the pool house and nodding for my cousin to do the same. "I'm ready to listen."

Secrets on My Skin

www.secretsonmyskin.com/community

I thought she was you.

CHAPTER 15

The full story involved blackmail. Campbell was the blackmailer. Lily was the blackmailee. Unfortunately for Lily, she didn't have anything Campbell wanted, other than complete social submission, indefinitely, forever. From what I gathered, when Lily had balked, Campbell had gone to make good on her threat, and Sadie-Grace had, and I quote, "reacted on instinct" and "aggressively hugged" the senator's daughter as a means of restraint.

Campbell had fought back.

Both girls had toppled over.

And Campbell had ended up unconscious.

I didn't ask the dynamic duo why they hadn't gone for medical help, or how exactly they'd transported Beelzebub from the scene of the crime—a local country club—to the Easterling pool house. I didn't make Lily specify what, precisely, Campbell had been blackmailing her about.

I did, however, ask her to clarify one thing. "Whatever Campbell's holding over your head, whatever you did—isn't felony kidnapping just a little bit worse?"

Lily looked down at her feet. "One would think so," she said. "But I doubt my mama would agree."

I'd yet to see Lily and Aunt Olivia interact directly, but I couldn't help thinking about the way Uncle J.D. had preemptively told my cousin that she was perfect just the way she was, the way Aunt Olivia would have preferred that the Belle of the Ball title go to Lily.

There's trying, I could hear my aunt saying. *And then there's trying too hard.*

I didn't know all that much about Lily, but I thought it was a pretty safe bet that she *tried.*

"Go ahead," Lily told me. "Say that this is not your problem. Say that I have made my Egyptian-cotton-sheeted bed, and I can lie in—"

It, my brain finished as Lily went flying. There was a second of processing delay before my brain *also* registered the fact that Lily had just been ferociously tackled by a red-haired, juice-cleansed ball of fury.

Sadie-Grace gasped in horror.

"Did you *gnaw* through your bindings?" I asked the tackler, impressed despite myself.

"Get off me!" Lily grappled with Campbell's weight on top of her. Unfortunately, my cousin fought like a sorority girl at the beginning of a night of drinking, and Campbell Ames fought like one at the end.

Sadie-Grace pranced toward the fray. "Don't make me hug you!"

Campbell hooked an arm around her ankle, and a second later, all three of them were rolling on the grass like a pack of high-society hyenas.

Say that this is not your problem. Lily's words echoed in my head. Sage advice, probably. Technically, this had nothing to do with me. Technically, my cousin and I were barely more than strangers.

Then again, I'd always had a habit of taking technicalities as a challenge.

Enter the garden hose. I probably enjoyed wielding it on the catfight in front of me more than I should have.

"*Wha—*"

"Eeeee!"

"How *dare* you!" That last response came from Campbell as she climbed to her feet and stared me down through sopping-wet hair.

I spritzed her once more in the face for good measure.

Even wet as a dog and thoroughly tousled, Lily kept her composure. "Sawyer, you don't have to . . ."

"Sign your own social death warrant?" Campbell suggested. "No, she doesn't. She can turn around and walk away."

I'd never backed down from a tone like that in my life.

"So could you," I pointed out. "You could forget this ever happened, forget whatever idiotic game you're playing with my cousin, and just walk away."

Campbell tossed wet hair over her shoulder. "I'm an Ames. We never forget." She smiled. "And once I'm done with your very *naughty* cousin—neither will anyone else."

I had no idea what Campbell was blackmailing Lily about, but her tone left very little ambiguity about the fact that when she said *naughty*, she meant *slut*.

A muscle in my jaw tightening, I tossed the garden hose to the ground.

"You could say I'm something of an expert at knot tying," I commented evenly, before turning my gaze from Campbell to the other two. "I'm going to need some rope."

After I'd introduced Campbell to my superior rope-tying skills, I confiscated the cell phone I found on her person. I had literally no idea how she'd managed to send a text from it while bound and gagged, but between that and the Houdini-like escape she'd just pulled off, I wasn't taking any chances. I removed the phone's battery and smashed the rest of it beneath my heel. I may not have been a criminal mastermind, but I *had* spent a lot of time watching police procedurals.

And telenovelas.

"The way I see it, we have two options," I told Lily and Sadie-Grace, pulling them back outside—and out of Campbell's hearing. "First option: let her go."

"Pardon me?" Lily's pale eyebrows skyrocketed.

"Let her stew a little bit longer, and then call her bluff," I clarified. "Campbell's father is a senator. I'm guessing he's not a fan of the type of teen drama that makes national press. She won't sue us. She won't have us arrested. He won't let her."

Lily did not seem to find that convincing.

"She had a phone," I pointed out. "Lord knows how she managed to use it, but instead of contacting the police, she sent that text. She'd rather get people talking than deal with the cops."

"Great," Lily replied weakly. "That just leaves the threat of utter social annihilation."

"Been there, done that," I said. "The secret is not to care."

I might as well have been telling the wind not to blow. Lily was the kind of person who *tried*. She *cared*.

"It might help," I told her, "if I knew what Campbell was blackmailing you about."

Silence. Then my cousin's phone buzzed. Lily looked down at it. When she saw the message, her pursed lips paled. After an elongated moment, she lifted her brown eyes to mine and held out the phone, like the very act of doing so was the equivalent of baring her soul.

I studied her gaze for a moment before looking down at the screen. *Secrets on My Skin* had posted a new entry—a particularly salacious one, etched in gold ink along the arc of a girl's porcelain-white inner thigh. I was surprised that my prim and proper cousin had subscribed to the blog.

Right up to the point when I wasn't.

Keep telling yourself that, porn star. That was what Campbell had said before Sadie-Grace had muzzled her. Back at the auction, Boone had said that he was "almost partially sure" that the anonymous model in the pictures went to Ridgeway Hall.

Would you like for me to tell you how Miss Propriety over there spends her spare time?

Lily closed her eyes and bowed her head, saying nothing. I hit the link to go to the *Secrets* website and scrolled back through the entries. The photographs weren't identifiable, but the build and coloring fit my cousin's. None of the pictures were nudes—but the model was awfully fond of strategically draped sheets.

An entry had just been posted, but it wouldn't have been difficult to set it to post on a delay.

"You want to know what Campbell has on me?" Lily said, forcing her eyelids open. *"This."*

Lily Taft Easterling was a Southern lady. A lover of twinsets. A connoisseur of the proper utensils to use at a formal dinner.

She also, apparently, had a borderline-explicit photo blog.

"What kind of proof does Campbell have that it's you?" I asked quietly.

Lily shook her head, unwilling to answer. I didn't press her. I knew from experience that when it came to girl-parts and what girls chose to do with them, the damage was not, in any way, proportional to the "proof."

"The first option is to let Campbell go and hope she's bluffing."

Lily managed to paraphrase my own words back at me. "What's option two?"

I wasn't used to having cousins. It was still a little alien for me to think of the word *family* meaning anything other than just my mom. But I couldn't have stood by and watched a total stranger being blackmailed about something like this by someone like Campbell.

And Lily wasn't a stranger.

"Option two *also* involves letting Lucifer go." I squared my shoulders, like a general on the edge of leading her troops into battle. "But first, we dig up enough dirt on the devil to blackmail her back."

APRIL 15, 5:24 P.M.

"Blackmail is such an ugly word."

Mackie knew that the eyelash-batting rabble-rouser was baiting him. He knew it, and he didn't care, because the lock picker was right.

He had *no* idea why the girls had been arrested.

"You blackmailed someone." He tried to make it a statement, rather than a question.

"Campbell," the prim and proper one said, "*shut up*."

EIGHT AND A HALF MONTHS EARLIER

CHAPTER 16

Waking up in a canopied bed might have felt dream-like and surreal, were it not for the hundred-pound Bernese mountain dog sitting on my head.

"Don't mind her," a pleasant voice said from somewhere above me. "She just wants a little sugar."

Still half-asleep, I shoved at William Faulkner, who obligingly rolled over and presented me with her belly.

"You're not allergic, are you?" Aunt Olivia asked from the direction of the closet. "Imagine not even knowing if my own niece is allergic to dogs."

Imagine not knowing that your own daughter's pastime of choice involves artistically inscribing the secrets of the upper crust on her bikini line.

Imagine having no idea that the person who knocked up your teenage sister was a member of your *social circle.*

Imagine not even knowing there's a Debutante bound and gagged in your pool house.

The events of the previous day came flooding back, and I sat up in bed. William Faulkner, tired of waiting for a belly scratch, decided to give me some sugar of her own.

"Well?" Aunt Olivia said. "Are you?"

I swiped slobber off my cheek with the back of my hand and gave the Bernese mountain dog a scratch behind the ears before she could launch another affection attack. "Am I what?"

"Allergic," Aunt Olivia reiterated. "I swear, you girls have the attention span of gnats. I caught Lily coming out of the bathroom wearing mismatched pajamas this morning."

If the idea of clashing pj's was enough to engender a tongue cluck, I did not want to imagine how my aunt would react if she knew more about Lily's extracurricular activities.

"Not allergic," I said. I pried myself from the bed and became acutely aware of the sound of hangers skimming over a metal rod. "What are you doing?"

"Hmmmm?" For someone who'd just accused me of having no attention span, my aunt was awfully easily distracted. Before I could repeat the question, she popped out of the closet and held up a white lace sundress for my inspection. "What about this one?"

"What about it?"

"You *do* sound like your mama sometimes, don't you? But never mind that, miss—what do you think about this dress for brunch?"

"Brunch," I repeated.

Aunt Olivia faltered, in the way of someone who fears she has just committed a great faux pas. "Do they *have* brunch where you grew up?"

You would have thought she was asking me if we'd had running water.

"We have brunch," I said. I was tempted to add *And it's finger-lickin' good*, just to see the horrified expression on her face, but restrained myself. "I just hadn't planned on going to brunch today."

"We always do Sunday brunch at the club," Aunt Olivia said, like *Thou Shalt Brunch on Sunday* was the Eleventh Commandment.

"Depending on where you fall on the scale of heathen to devout, you're also welcome to join us for church this morning. No pressure, mind you."

"No pressure about church," I clarified. "But brunch . . ."

"Brunch is a family affair," a voice said.

Aunt Olivia and I turned toward the doorway. My grandmother was standing there in black pants and a white linen jacket. She wore a rope chain necklace, casual the same way the houses in this neighborhood were modest.

After eyeing my bed-head and the gargantuan dog now tangled in the sheets beside me, Lillian turned her attention to her daughter. "Perhaps not white," she said, giving the dress in Aunt Olivia's hand the once-over. "Do we have something in a peach?"

Aunt Olivia went back to the closet and came out again holding the exact same dress in a different color.

"When a style and cut are flattering," my grandmother lectured genteelly, "you buy in more than one color. One can never have too many basics." Without pausing a beat, she plucked the dress in question from Aunt Olivia's hands. "I'll take it from here, dear."

I looked for a hint of tension between them, some clue that my aunt didn't care for being dismissed, but if Olivia resented being ousted from my room, she gave no sign of it. If anything, she seemed comfortable doing what she was told.

Comfortable being the good *daughter,* I could practically hear my mom saying as Aunt Olivia called for William Faulkner to follow her out the door.

Once we were alone, Lillian laid the dress she'd chosen for me on the foot of the bed. "I could ask you what exactly you and your cousin were doing last night that necessitated sneaking back in at three in the morning, but I would be lying if I implied that I was anything less than pleased to see you and Lily taking to each other so quickly." She ran a hand over the dress to smooth out the hem. "Girls can be . . . complicated. Family, more so. If your mother and Olivia had been closer . . ." Lillian pressed her lips together, then shook her head. "You'll fare better with Lily on your side than you would alone."

"Right." I brushed Lillian's statement off. I might have come down on Lily's side the night before, but the idea that she might be on mine was still a little hard to wrap my mind around. I was good at being relied on.

Relying on others was more of a gray area.

"Brunch," my grandmother declared, ignoring my response to her last statement, "is not optional."

I could not swear that there was not a brunch clause in my contract, so I didn't argue.

I negotiated.

"I'll go," I said climbing out of bed. "I'll even wear the dress." I opened the drawer to my nightstand. "I just need you to do something for me first."

Late last night, when I'd finally crawled back through my window and detoxed from the debutante drama, I'd taken the photograph I'd stolen out of my pocket. With a thick black marker, I'd drawn four circles—one around each Squire whose face my mother had scratched out in her copy of the photo.

I handed the picture to Lillian. "I'd like the names of those four."

I could probably have made some other attempt to identify the boys in the photo, but they were men now, and I didn't believe in taking the scenic route when a blunt question could get you there directly.

Lillian was quiet for a long while as she took in the faces in the photograph. I saw a flurry of indecipherable emotions pass over her face. *Anger? Bewilderment? Surprise? Regret?*

It went on for long enough that I was starting to think that no answer was forthcoming, but the family matriarch surprised me. "I assume you recognized your uncle." She pointed to the first of the four. "He's got that boyish look about him even now."

He was the only one I *had* recognized. I hadn't thought much about what that might mean.

I hadn't wanted to.

"The one who's not quite looking at the camera is Charles Waters. I believe you two met last night." Lillian didn't so much as pause to give me a moment to process. "The tall, smug-looking one in the back row is the oldest Ames boy. The senator."

Ames. As in Walker Ames and Lucas Ames and the blackmailer bound and gagged in the pool house.

"The one on the edge," my grandmother continued, her manner and tone suggesting none of this was of much import, "is the senator's brother-in-law. He wasn't much back then, but the Ames family paid his Squire fees. Eventually, he ended up marrying their daughter, Julia."

"Does this man who married Julia Ames have a name?" I asked.

Without a word, my grandmother replaced the photo in my nightstand drawer. She pressed it shut before answering my question. "His last name is Mason. I believe you met his son, Boone, last night."

And the small world just keeps getting smaller. . . .

"First name?" I asked, as much to show her that none of this information had gotten to me as anything else.

Lillian smiled. I wasn't sure if that was a reflex—or a warning. "Thomas," she said. "Thomas Mason."

Suddenly, I felt like I'd been gargling cotton balls. My name was Sawyer Ann. My mom had told me once that even if I'd been a boy, she still would have named me Sawyer.

But in that case, it would have been Sawyer Thomas.

Secrets on My Skin

www.secretsonmyskin.com/community

CHAPTER 17

The family SUV was a Mercedes. It was also a *tank*. As Uncle J.D. pulled past the guard gate and began the ascent up the long and curving road to Northern Ridge Country Club, I was aware of two and only two things: John David's ongoing monologue on the defensibility of our position in the event of the zombie apocalypse and the name Thomas Mason.

I'd always assumed that *Sawyer Thomas* was a play on words—*Tom Sawyer,* reversed. It had never occurred to me that if I'd been born a boy, my mom might have named me after someone.

Say, for instance, my biological father.

There's jumping to conclusions, I told myself, *and then there's the Olympic long jump. Stop it.*

"John David, if you rumple that blazer, I will string you up by your toenails." In the front seat, Aunt Olivia checked her lipstick in a compact mirror. "And what's the rule about zombies at brunch?"

Lily's phone vibrated on the seat between us. I looked down. My cousin's manicured hand quickly obscured my view of her phone screen—but not quickly enough.

Secrets on My Skin. I shot Lily an incredulous look. Seriously?

My cousin refused to meet my gaze. Her father pulled onto a

circle drive and came to a stop under a cream-colored portico. I noticed the valet stand, but didn't think to look for the valet. My frustration with Lily—and the fact that she was *still* updating the blog over which she was being blackmailed—may have caused me to throw my door open slightly harder than necessary.

And *then* I saw the valet.

In my defense, I wasn't used to people opening my car door for me, and he only made a small wheezing sound when it nailed him in the stomach.

I stood and reached out to steady him by the arm. "You okay?"

The valet's hazel eyes rested on mine. "I'll live."

His accent was closer to mine than any I'd heard since entering Deb World. Though he was wearing a white polo shirt emblazoned with the club's initials, something about the way he stood told me he wasn't a polo-shirt kind of person, any more than I was a peach-sundress one.

"Nick." An older man wearing an identical shirt came up behind him and clapped a hand on the boy's shoulder. "We could use a runner. G-16."

"This way, dear." Aunt Olivia nudged me toward the building. Soon, I found myself in a foyer with forty-foot ceilings that let off into a hallway just as long.

I fell in beside Lily to avoid being herded further.

In what I could only assume was an effort to preempt any comments I might make about what I'd seen on her phone, she spoke first. "Incapacitate any valets lately?" she murmured as we made our way down the hall.

I murmured back, "Post any borderline-explicit photos?"

To Lily's credit, she didn't blanch. "I know," she said quietly. "*I know.* There's a queue. I need to disable it." She paused for a moment as a maître d' came out from behind a podium to greet her parents, then continued, her voice still hushed. "Don't forget: when eating brunch, you start with the outermost fork and work your way in."

Brunch was a four-course affair. We waited for Lillian to arrive before we were seated. Once we'd taken up position at a table overlooking a large, impossibly sparkling swimming pool, John David took it upon himself to give me the grand tour. The salad buffet was in the Breakfast Room, the breakfast station was in the Oak Room, lunch and the carving stations could be found in the Ash Hall, and dessert was in the Great Room.

I was tempted to go straight for dessert, in part because I believed in prioritization and in part because Boone Mason was currently in the process of stacking a glass plate high with a combination of cookies, miniature cakes, mousse, and crème brûleé.

If Boone's here, what are the chances that his father is, too?

"Salad first," John David told me solemnly. "And we can only talk about zombies if the zombies mind their manners."

When I glanced back toward the Great Room, Boone—and his towering plate of dessert—was gone. It took me two courses to find a pretext to go looking for him. I demurely excused myself to the ladies' room and made a stop by the dessert bar on the way. Since Boone hadn't crossed by me on his way out earlier, I tried my luck with the archway on the opposite side of the room. Another seating area, smaller than the ballroom in which my grandmother was currently holding court, was tucked away behind the arch.

At a table overlooking the golf course, Boone sat with four adults and two empty chairs. I recognized the senator and his wife. It didn't take a rocket scientist to guess that the other matched pair were Boone's parents. His mother had deep brown hair, with just enough auburn highlights to remind me that she and Campbell shared DNA.

Great, I thought. *Half of the people on my Who's-Your-Daddy shortlist are related to the girl I'm helping hold captive.* That might have merited a bit more reflection, were it not for the presence of Boone's father. Thomas Mason looked very little like he had in the Squire photograph. He'd aged well, grown into features that hadn't fit together on his teenage face. He had sandy hair, a shade or two lighter than my own, and the kind of tan that I suspected had less to do with solar exposure than genetics.

"The ladies' room is this way."

I barely heard Lily when she appeared beside me. I knew I was staring, but I couldn't stop. There were four men on my list, and two of them were sitting at that table. They'd probably been sitting at that table every Sunday for years, their kids growing older together, eating photo-perfect desserts.

"Sawyer." Lily gripped my elbow, and the next thing I knew, she'd steered me back through the Great Room, down a long hall, and into a ladies' room that had about 200 percent more furniture than any restroom I'd ever encountered.

I flopped down on what I could only assume was a fainting couch.

"Are you even familiar with the word *subtle*?" Lily asked me. "Why don't you just hang out a neon sign saying 'Thoroughly Up to No Good'?"

I'd been looking for something back there—a resemblance, maybe, or a feeling buried deep in my gut. But from Lily's perspective, I'd just been openly staring at the family of the girl she'd kidnapped.

The girl *I* had very expertly tied to a chair.

"Subtle is overrated." I climbed to my feet and surveilled the restroom. Beyond the sitting area, there was a mirror and a line of sparkling granite sinks, and past that, there were a half dozen toilet stalls.

Every one of them was empty.

"If you want to dig up the dirt on Campbell," I said, turning back to Lily, now that I knew we could speak freely, "you're going to need to be a little less . . ."

"Less polite?" Lily suggested calmly. "Less proper? Less law-abiding?"

I valiantly refrained from mentioning that law-abiding had gone out the window a while back. "Think," I said instead. "If you were blackmail material on Campbell Ames, where would you be?"

Lily closed her eyes. I had the feeling that she was silently counting to ten and also possibly considering throttling me. But when she opened her eyes again, there was a glint in them. "If I were . . . *that* . . . I might be in Campbell's locker."

We had to wait another two courses to make good on the plan. The locker Lily had referenced was in the women's locker room—completely separate from the ladies' restroom we'd already visited. Apparently, Campbell was a golfer.

Didn't see that one coming, I thought.

"She won the Junior Club Championship every year when we were kids," Lily told me, tapping her manicured nails rapidly against the lockers as she looked for the right number. "I almost won once, but Campbell cheated."

"How do you cheat at golf?"

Lily stopped in front of one of the lockers. "You lie about your score." She closed her fingertips around the metal lock on the locker. "Let's hope Cam's still using the same combination she used in middle school."

Lily tried the combination three times. After the third unsuccessful attempt, I thought she might actually resort to cursing.

"Move," I told her. As much as I hated to provide any support whatsoever for Lily's assumption that growing up outside the lap of luxury made a person a criminal by default, I had known how to defeat a basic combination lock since I was nine.

"For the record," I told my cousin, "any lock-picking ability I may or may not have acquired growing up has less to do with where I lived and more to do with the fact that I was a very weird, very obsessive little kid."

The lock popped open.

"Impressive." For once, Lily's smile looked almost devious.

With a muted grin, I began going through the contents of Campbell's locker. *Golf shoes, deodorant, a makeup bag filled with makeup, a makeup bag filled with tampons, two sports bras, one thong, and . . .*

"OxyContin." I glanced at Lily, then turned my attention back to the bottle of pills. "They're legal—prescribed to her." Behind the OxyContin, there were two other containers. "Ativan," I read off the second one. "And a multivitamin." Like the Oxy, the Ativan was prescribed to Campbell.

"Ativan is an anxiety medication," Lily told me, turning her phone so that I could see the description she'd just looked up. "Campbell has never struck me as a particularly anxious person."

"How would you know?" I felt a stab of guilt, stronger than any I'd experienced as I'd tied Campbell to the chair. When someone played dirty, I played dirtier. That was the law of the jungle. But even power-hungry gossip queens deserved *some* privacy.

I wasn't about to blackmail someone—*anyone*—about their mental health.

To distract Lily, I moved on to the vitamins. They were over-the-counter and—not surprisingly—brand name. I unscrewed the top and looked inside to verify that rich-people vitamins were virtually indistinguishable from CVS brand. They were, but that wasn't my biggest discovery in that moment.

I tilted the open bottle toward Lily so that she could see what I was seeing. The pills were white, but when I rattled the container, there was a flash of silver.

"What is that?" Lily asked.

"Only one way to find out." I fished the metal object out. It was somewhere between the size of a nickel and a quarter and shaped like a heart.

"A charm?" Lily guessed. "Lovely. I can blackmail Campbell by threatening to out her as the only person over the age of ten who still has a weakness for charm bracelets. This will surely ruin her."

I dangled the heart closer to Lily's face. "Not a charm. A tag." I had a neighbor who lost her cat 1.5 times a week. I knew that of which I spoke. "I'm betting it came off a collar." I tapped the writing etched into the tag. "Name. Phone number."

"'Sophie,'" Lily read. "Is that the owner's name, or the pet's?"

"The real question," I replied, "is why Campbell's hiding a pet tag in a bottle of vitamins in her golf locker."

Over a few rows and to our left, I heard the door to the locker room open. Moving quickly, I grabbed the last thing in the locker—a plain white envelope—and shut the door, clamping the lock back on just as a woman rounded the corner.

"Lily." Greer Waters greeted my cousin first, her smile a little too broad. "I didn't know you were playing this morning. Will your mother be joining you?"

Greer was holding a tennis racket. It felt, somehow, like she was holding a weapon.

"I was just showing Sawyer the locker room," Lily lied smoothly. "She's never played tennis before. Or golf."

I had, in fact, played tennis—much like I had, in fact, eaten brunch—but decided to roll with Lily's assertion, which Greer found suitably horrifying.

"Oh, you poor dear," she said immediately. "I'm sure your grandmother could get you private lessons."

"I'm really more interested in fencing." I couldn't help myself and picked an obscure sport at random. "Or horseback riding. Possibly badminton . . ."

Lily nudged me, and I pushed down the urge to mention yachting. We'd managed to distract Sadie-Grace's stepmother from the fact that we weren't actually standing in front of *Lily's* locker. The envelope was still in my left hand, the tag in my right.

Now would be a good time to make our exit.

"We should be getting back," Lily told Greer. "I promised my grandmother we'd be quick."

The mere mention of Lillian Taft did something to Greer. It was like she was a dog who'd just smelled a steak. *An Irish setter,* I thought, eyeing her hair. *Best of Breed and desperate for Best of Show.*

"Do tell your grandmother hello for me—and thank her for all of her help last night."

Somehow, I doubted Lillian considered herself to be the one who had "helped" with the auction.

"Will do," I said, pushing past Greer to the door. I held it open for Lily and was almost out myself when Sadie-Grace's stepmother closed the distance between us. One second she was by the lockers, and the next, she was laying a hand on my shoulder.

"Sawyer," Greer said, her voice low and serious. "It occurred to me when I got home last night that I might have been a bit short with you when you asked me about your mother. I want you to know that you can ask me anything."

People were fundamentally predictable. They didn't do complete 180s without a reason.

"In fact," Greer was saying, "if you have questions, I'd caution you against asking anyone else. When your mother took her leave, she left quite a few social fires in her wake. I'm sure you understand. There are things you simply do not talk about in polite company."

I managed a smile every bit as fake as hers. "Of course."

CHAPTER 18

After brunch, I called the phone number on the tag. The line was disconnected. As far as blackmail material went, that didn't give us a lot to go on, but I'd spent a good chunk of my life obsessed with watching professional poker, and Lily had spent the entirety of her childhood in a world ruled by etiquette and unspoken rules.

We both knew how to bluff.

It took several hours before the two of us were able to "go for a walk and catch some fresh air"—also known as visiting our hostage. Sadie-Grace was already there when we arrived. She was holding a blender.

"Campbell says no more kale."

Personally, I thought that Campbell wasn't in much of a position to be issuing orders, but I had a feeling that Sadie-Grace was the kind of person who got ordered around a lot.

"Let's see what else Campbell has to say," I suggested.

I opened the door to the pool house and dragged a chair opposite Campbell's.

Turning the chair around backward, I sat down, my legs spread to either side.

"I have some things that belong to you." I held the tag up first. There was a brief flicker of *something* on her face, gone too fast for me to tell what it was. "You have to admit," I said, taking my time with the words, "it's a weird thing to be keeping inside a vitamin bottle."

"You broke into my locker at the club?" Campbell meditated on that for a moment, then smirked. "However will I deal with the life-altering information you've surely acquired?"

When it came to sarcasm, Campbell's delivery was several paces beyond Lily's.

"I mean, you know what kind of tampons I use . . ." Campbell simpered. "For shame."

There were many ways to bluff and many kinds of tells. Based on this performance, I was guessing that Campbell's go-to maneuver was deflection.

"I called the number on the tag," I said.

There. The flicker was back, for longer this time. I had no idea what this tag meant to Campbell, but I'd gotten confirmation that it meant something, and I was betting that *she* didn't know the number was out of service.

Taking advantage of the moment, I removed the envelope from my pocket. I'd already seen what was inside, but let her think I was opening it for the first time. "Not a letter," I observed, emptying the contents of the envelope into my hand. "Not even paper." I brandished the object. "A key."

Campbell tossed her hair back over one shoulder. "Did Dame Dance-A-Lot over there tell you that I am totally and utterly over kale? Forget my juice cleanse." Campbell brandished her teeth. "If you don't want me to starve in here, you'll bring me a burger."

"You don't like hamburgers," Lily burst out.

"And," Campbell shot back, "I don't like you. But I *will* like outing you as the downright indecent little flesh kitten you are. Really, Lily, in your position, I'd be less concerned with what *our* circle will think than what the elder generations will say. Your mother. Your *grandmother.* How will they ever hold their heads up in public again?"

"We were friends once." Lily stared at Campbell. "Do you even remember that?"

"Oh, sweetheart." Campbell had mastered the art of sounding sympathetic. "I don't have friends. I have people who've proven themselves useful and those who've outlived their usefulness."

One guess which one you are, I could practically hear her saying.

I took my time standing up. Campbell wanted us to think she'd won this round, but I'd scored some points. We might not have had blackmail material yet, but this interaction had convinced me that Campbell *did* have a secret.

Maybe more than one.

When Lily extracted herself from the pool house, she retreated back inside the house. I followed her, and Sadie-Grace followed me. Lily didn't say a word as she pushed through a thick plastic sheet over one of the doorways and began ascending a wooden staircase.

The second story wasn't under construction. The decorating scheme was clearly Aunt Olivia's doing—nearly identical to the one in the house where she'd grown up.

Lily paused in the doorway of a bedroom—hers, I assumed. After a long and painful moment, she walked over to the queen-sized bed and reached under the mattress to remove a tablet.

"I never used my computer for the posts," she said softly. "It seemed safer to use something I could hide."

I wondered what else Lily had used for *Secrets.* A camera? A tripod? A few packages of Egyptian cotton sheets?

"You have to disable the queue," I told Lily. "Quit posting."

Lily's head was bowed. I couldn't see her face, and I wasn't sure that I wanted to. Her hands were gripping the tablet so hard that they shook—or maybe she was holding on to it for dear life because she was shaking.

"Are you okay?" Sadie-Grace asked hesitantly.

"I'm fine." Lily sounded hollow. She hit a few buttons on the tablet. "The blog is disabled. No more posts." She paused, then drew in an uneven breath. "I should probably delete it, get rid of as much evidence as I can."

You should, I thought. *But can you?*

I hadn't really questioned what had possessed my cousin to start this project. It hadn't occurred to me that it was anything other than a titillating little pastime, a chance she was taking because taking chances felt good. But right now? This didn't look like someone who'd had to put a hobby on hold. She didn't look like a girl who regretted doing something stupid.

She looked like she was grieving.

"Enough." Lily snapped the cover to the tablet closed. "It's done. It's over." She walked to the trash can and let the tablet fall from her hands. It landed with a clank. "Let's get Campbell her freaking hamburger and go home."

CHAPTER 19

It never even occurred to Lily or Sadie-Grace to get Campbell's lunch from McDonald's. No, our temporary hostage could only be served an organic beef burger of the finest provenance. In fact, my fellow kidnappers bought *two* twelve-dollar gourmet burgers, because neither my cousin nor her best friend could recall with any degree of certainty whether Campbell Ames was in favor of avocado as a burger topping, or against.

"You guys do realize that she's not going to be writing a review of this experience, right?" That earned me two blank stares. "Five stars," I deadpanned. "Would definitely be kidnapped again."

"Believe me," Lily replied crisply. "We realize."

Sadie-Grace nodded seriously. "Campbell never gives *anything* five stars."

It took everything I had not to start massaging my temples. "I'm just saying that if you guys are feeling guilty, maybe it's time to reconsider option one."

Let Campbell go. Gamble that she wouldn't have us arrested and weather the scandal that would result from Lily's outing as the *Secrets* blogger. Eventually, a bigger scandal would come along.

"Sawyer." Lily pressed her lips together, then forced herself to continue speaking in a pleasant tone. "It's not just what people would say. It's that they'd *enjoy* saying it. I'm Olivia Taft Easterling's daughter. I am proper and respectful and polite. I say the right thing. I do the right thing." She took a breath, but there was a long pause before she let it out. "Sadie-Grace is probably the only friend I have who wouldn't be glad to see me fall."

"That's not true," Sadie-Grace argued immediately.

"It was when Walker broke up with me."

Before Sadie-Grace could reply, Lily's phone rang, and my cousin glanced at me. "It's Mama. Whenever I even *look* at this many calories . . ." She held up the brown bag containing Campbell's burgers. ". . . she knows."

I plucked the phone from Lily's hand and declined the call. Based on the reaction from the peanut gallery, you would have thought I'd done actual witchcraft.

"Your mom will live," I said.

"She just likes to know what I'm doing," Lily replied automatically. "Where I am."

"What you're eating?" I suggested.

Lily responded to my pointed question with one of her own. "Doesn't your mama care about nutrition?"

When I was a child, we'd named our dog Pop-Tart. My mom's idea of a balanced breakfast probably didn't match up with Aunt Olivia's.

"Let's put it this way," I told my cousin. "If I was the one running the *Secrets* blog and *my* mom found out? She'd try to turn it into a mother-daughter activity and ask if she could submit some photos of her own."

Lily was either awed . . . or aghast. "They never talk about her, you know." She slowed her pace as we neared her parents' house.

"Your mama. I was in the fourth grade before I even knew she existed."

I took that to mean that Lily hadn't known that *I* existed, either.

"That's the scary thing." Sadie-Grace was wide-eyed. "With some scandals, people talk. But with others . . ."

Lily looked down. "They *stop* talking about you. Forever."

She couldn't possibly believe that the reaction to *Secrets* would, in any way, equal the one to my mom's teenage pregnancy, but I doubted she'd find *They won't exile you forever* to be comforting.

For better or worse, we definitely were not going back to option one.

"You requested a burger," Lily declared as she opened the door to the pool house. "We got you a . . ." She stopped talking.

I looked past her and saw why. Campbell was gone.

Incredulous, I stalked over to the empty chair and picked up the ropes that lay there. "How the hell did she . . ."

"I told you," Sadie-Grace whispered. "She's in congress with the Beast."

"She's flexible, she's driven by vengeance, and she has sharp fingernails," Lily corrected tersely, holding on to her composure by a thread.

Sadie-Grace was dismayed. "I knew I shouldn't have agreed to file her nails to points during that hot stone manicure!"

I couldn't help myself. "You kidnapped her and *gave her a manicure*?"

"Enough with the Monday-morning quarterbacking," Lily told me tartly. "Campbell's gone, and that's that." She plucked a handwritten note from the arm of the chair.

I moved close enough to read it. Campbell's message was all of two words long.

GAME ON.

Beside me, Lily bolted. At first, I thought she was going outside to puke her brunch up, but she kept running.

To the main house.

Up the stairs.

To her room.

I managed to keep up with her, but only just.

"It's gone." Lily sank to the floor next to her trash can, and in an uncharacteristic burst of temper, she knocked it over. "The tablet I used for *Secrets*," she whispered hoarsely. "I threw it away, and now it's gone."

CHAPTER 20

Lily and I spent the rest of the day waiting for the ax to fall, but Campbell's social media accounts remained silent, and a few discreet texts on Lily's part suggested that even Campbell's highest-ranked minions still hadn't heard from her.

The police did not show up at our grandmother's house.

By the next morning, my cousin seemed intent on pretending that absolutely nothing had happened—and disturbingly adept at doing just that.

"It's Monday," Lily declared, entering my bedroom after a purely perfunctory knock. "Typically, that would mean the club is closed, and Symphony Ball events are usually spaced at least a month apart, but—"

"Lily," I interrupted.

"*But*," Lily continued emphatically, "this particular Monday is the exception to both rules. Northern Ridge is well aware that classes at Ridgeway and Brighton start next week, and the mamas on the Symphony Ball Committee realize that Pearls of Wisdom is more for the parents than for the Squires and Debs." She finally took a breath, but it was a short one. "Today is for us."

"Today?" I repeated.

Lily stalked toward my closet. "You're going to need a bikini."

Three hours later, I'd accepted that Lily was not going to discuss Campbell Ames, her missing tablet, or any form of impending social doom. I'd also developed a new life motto: *You can make me wear a skimpy bathing suit, but you can't make me take off the board shorts and cutoff T-shirt I'm going to wear over it.*

Lily had attempted to coerce me into a designer "cover-up"—total misnomer—but I won that fight. It didn't take long after we'd arrived at the pool party for me to realize that, in this social circle, the more questionable your fashion choices, the more compliments you received. No one would come right out and say that I looked like I'd taken a pair of scissors to a Walmart T-shirt myself (I had). Instead, I was told that my outfit was *just darling.*

I was so *original.*

And wasn't it nice that I didn't get all bothered by the way I looked?

"An insult doesn't count as an insult if you phrase it as a question."

I'd retreated from the pool area and taken refuge inside the Northern Ridge Country Club Boathouse, which did not, in fact, house boats, but instead served as the upscale version of a snack shack. Apparently, I wasn't the only one who'd decided to hide out among the onion rings and shrimp cocktail.

"Coincidentally," Boone Mason continued, "an insult also doesn't count as an insult if you pretend it's a compliment, call the person you're insulting *sugar,* or self-deprecatingly and completely insincerely criticize yourself at the same time. Shrimp?"

He offered me a plate, which he'd already piled high with hors d'oeuvres.

"No, thanks," I told him, flashing back to the moment when I'd seen him at the dessert buffet the day before. My brain went into hyperdrive, searching his face for any similarity, no matter how subtle, to my own.

This was Thomas Mason's son.

"I live life by relatively few rules," Boone said, perfectly content to carry on a mostly one-sided conversation. "But one of those rules is to never turn down a free crustacean."

Physically, Boone looked nothing like me, but it was all too easy imagining him as a child, adopting an endless series of truly odd obsessions.

"I have rules, too," I found myself saying. "Anyone interested in flirting with a teenage girl isn't remotely worth flirting back with. Don't expect people to surprise you, and they can't disappoint. Say what you mean, and mean what you say."

There was a beat of silence.

"How refreshing," Boone said, in a surprisingly good imitation of the last Debutante to not-insult me. "You *are* an interesting one, aren't you?"

He offered me a crooked smile.

"I might also be your half-sister." It was one thing for me to *say* that I didn't believe in letting social niceties get in the way of the truth. It was another to walk the walk, but I hadn't come here—to Lillian's house, to high society, to today's pool party—to be demure and observe.

I'd come here for answers.

"You might be *what*?" Boone sputtered.

"Don't get your panties in a twist," I said. "Your dad is just *one* of the men who might have knocked up my mom. You might be my half-brother, but it's also entirely possible that we're cousins."

Brow furrowed, Boone ate another shrimp. It took three more

delicious crustaceans before he'd recovered enough to question me further.

"First cousins?" he asked. "Or distant cousins, destined to a star-crossed love?"

I gave him a look.

"You will eventually find me endearing," Boone promised. "And I will eventually stop flirting with you."

Without warning, a third party entered our conversation. "And why would you ever do a thing like that?"

I turned.

Walker Ames was not wearing a bathing suit. He looked like he'd just stepped off the golf course.

"We meet again, Sawyer Taft," he said. "Are you going to spend all of the Symphony Ball events hiding on the fringes?"

"She's not hiding," Boone said quickly. "She's . . ." I waited for him to say something about the bombshell that I'd just dropped on him. Instead, he shoved his plate into my hands. "She's monopolizing the shrimp, is what she's doing."

"Actually . . ." I started to say, but Boone elbowed me. *Do not say to Walker about his father what you just said to me about mine.* The warning was as clear as if he had spoken out loud.

Deciding—for once—that discretion was the better part of valor, I opted for a topic that was *slightly* less sensitive. "Heard from your sister yet, Walker?"

"Not a word." Walker glanced out the bay window toward the pool. "But I'm banking on the likelihood that someone here has."

I followed his gaze. Dozens of Debutantes and Squires lounged poolside. There was a game of volleyball going on in the water, and closer to the pool's edge, a coed chicken fight was quickly devolving into a mess of intertwined limbs and sexual tension.

I searched for Lily and found her sitting on the side of the pool with Sadie-Grace. Beside me, Walker's attention had landed in the exact same place. He'd already graduated high school. He wasn't a Squire, and that meant that my cousin wasn't expecting her ex to be here today.

"It's nice to see you sober," I told Walker dryly, deflecting his attention from Lily. "It's a good look for you. Less poor little rich boy, more borderline-functional member of society."

Walker had an automatic, default smile—that *helping and a half of charm* that Lily had mentioned. For just a moment, his go-to expression went lopsided: less handsome, more real.

"Like I said," Walker told Boone before turning to take his leave. "Why would you ever want to stop flirting with the indelible Sawyer Taft?"

Without waiting for a reply, he exited the Boathouse, but hung a left at the pool, leaving me to wonder who, exactly, Walker expected to have heard from his sister.

"He's protective of Campbell," Boone said beside me. "Always has been."

"That doesn't explain why you didn't want me to say anything to him about his father," I said.

Boone ate two more shrimp, then dodged the question. "That thing you said about my dad and his implied sperm and your mom's implied ovaries? I can't really picture it. My uncle Sterling—or, as I like to call him, Senator Bossypants—likes to say that I'm all Mason. He means that I'm not smooth, because neither is my dad."

"Nice uncle you got there," I commented.

Boone shrugged. "It's his way of getting under my mother's skin, because *she's* all Ames. Like Walker. And Campbell."

I'd grown up without siblings—or cousins. But I still recognized sibling or pseudo-sibling rivalry when I saw it. Boone was used to being in his cousins' shadows.

"My dad . . ." Boone searched for the right words. "He grew up middle class. I have no idea how he and Uncle Sterling became friends, but they did. So my dad got a taste of what this life was like, and he decided he wanted it, too." Boone paused. "He made something of himself, and he married an Ames. Some days, I think he regrets it, but back then? I can't imagine him risking all of it for some woman."

Not a woman, I thought. *A girl.*

"My mother is what one might charitably call vindictive," Boone said, almost fondly. "She would have *buried* him if he'd cheated."

Maybe Boone had the right read on his parents, but my mother had scratched Thomas Mason's face out of the picture for a reason.

And if I'd been a boy, she would have named me Sawyer Thomas.

"What about your uncle?" I asked Boone, returning to the point he'd skirted. "The senator. Any idea what he was up to, approximately eighteen years plus nine months ago?"

"None whatsoever," Boone said cheerfully. "But might I suggest *not* asking any other member of my extended family that question? We are, on the whole, a merciless lot, especially Uncle Sterling."

And that's why you didn't want me saying anything to Walker.

"I can take care of myself," I said.

Boone did not seem to like that response. "I'll see what I can find out," he promised. "About my uncle, my dad, your mom—just . . . hang tight, little buddy."

"Little buddy?" I repeated incredulously.

"Hey," Boone said, "you deal with your possibly incest-y feelings for me in your way, and I'll deal in mine."

CHAPTER 21

I made it through another hour of the pool party before I abandoned ship. A quick survey of the surrounding area told me that my only options for fresh air were an expanse of vibrantly green grass, where people were honest-to-God playing lawn games, and a back alleyway that led to the dumpsters.

I chose the dumpsters. Imagine my surprise when I found Dumpsterville occupied.

"Sorry." The boy leaning back against the building immediately straightened. His phone went into his pocket, and his eyes went to a point over my right shoulder.

"What are you apologizing for?" I asked.

The question surprised him into meeting my gaze. It took me a moment to realize that I recognized those eyes.

The valet. He was wearing different clothes today—navy-blue swim trunks and a formfitting shirt emblazoned with the club's crest.

"Lifeguard?" I asked.

"Filling in for a friend," he replied. "Don't worry, I'm certified."

"Really not my number one concern at the moment."

He managed a small smile. "New around here?"

"What gave me away?"

"Besides your accent, your clothes, and the fact that you're comfortable *not* smiling?" He leaned back against the wall, keeping his shoulders squared toward mine this time. "Absolutely nothing."

That might have actually gotten a grin out of me, but the sound of the door to the alleyway opening and closing interrupted the moment. The valet glanced toward the door. I took note of the motion. Growing up above The Holler had given me a sixth sense for bar brawlers. In a polo shirt or lifeguard uniform, it didn't matter. This was a guy used to keeping his back to the wall and his eyes peeled.

He wasn't built for walking away from a fight.

What fight? I wondered. I turned to look at the person who'd joined us and found myself facing Walker Ames.

"I should go," the valet said. He walked past me, then attempted to pass Walker.

Walker sidestepped. "Nick," he said. "It is Nick, right? Got a minute?" Walker didn't wait for an answer. That was what happened to people who grew up in a world where the answer was always yes. "We need to talk."

"I need to get back to work." Nick's blank expression never wavered. He was like stone.

Walker just kept chipping away. "This will just take a second."

Nick glanced back at me. Clearly, he wanted me to get lost, but the two of them were blocking the only exit.

"Is she with you?" Walker demanded.

"Who?" Nick said. He gestured toward me. "Her? We just met."

Walker's eyes flicked to mine. Clearly, he hadn't taken note of my presence until that exact moment. "Could you give us a second, Sawyer?"

Now it was my turn to lean casually back against the wall. "Take all the time you need."

I saw the barest hint of amusement on Nick's face.

Walker's next word banished it. "Campbell," he said, turning back to the other boy. "Is she lying low at your place?"

Nick stared Walker down. "I think you must be confused."

"And I think that you're my sister's type," Walker countered. "Look, who or what my sister does is none of my business. I just want to know if she's okay."

She's fine, I thought, *and given that she didn't go home after she busted out last night, I'd give it eighty-twenty odds that she's up to something.*

"I have no idea where your sister is," Nick said clearly.

Walker took a step toward him.

This will not end well, I thought. Walker was taller than Nick, broader through the shoulders. Nick was almost certainly a better fighter. Even though his veneer of calm hadn't cracked yet, the part of me that had grown up bar-adjacent said that it could.

"Leave him alone," I told Walker. To my surprise, someone else said the exact same words at the exact same time.

"Miss me?" Campbell stepped into the alleyway and placed a kiss on her brother's cheek. She didn't look like she'd spent the past two days duct-taped to a chair.

She looked like she'd been to some kind of spa.

"Campbell." Walker turned his irritation on his sister, Nick instantly forgotten. "Still in one piece, I take it?"

"Aren't I always?" Campbell returned lightly. "You can go, Nick." She didn't even look at him as she issued the dismissal.

Nick didn't seem to mind. An instant later, he was gone.

Campbell is here. Campbell is smiling. This cannot possibly be good.

"Sawyer, this is my sister." Manners dictated Walker introduce us. "Campbell, this is . . ."

"Sawyer Taft," Campbell finished with a smile every bit as charming as her brother's. "I know. Lily introduced us this weekend."

"You were with Lily?" Walker asked his sister. "She didn't say anything." He turned to me. "*You* didn't say anything." He shifted narrowed eyes back toward his sister. "Since when do you and Lily hang out?"

Since she KIDNAPPED me. . . . I waited for Campbell to pull the trigger.

Except she didn't. She also didn't say anything—not a word—about *Secrets on My Skin.*

Instead, Campbell gave Walker what I could only describe as puppy-dog eyes. "Look, big brother, I'm sorry about the past couple of days. Would you believe it if I said I'd had my heart broken?"

That was all it took to throw Walker back into protective mode. "Did someone—"

Campbell didn't give him a chance to finish the question. "It doesn't matter what someone did or did not do. As previously discussed, my physical and/or romantic relationships are none of your business." She softened her tone. "I needed some space, Walk. I needed Mom not to be breathing down my neck. And . . ." Campbell looked toward me, and I saw something downright chilling masquerading as fondness in her sparkling green eyes. "I needed some girl time."

"Girl time?" Walker repeated.

"Lily let me crash in her pool house for a few days," Campbell said, twirling her auburn hair around her index finger, watching my reaction as much as her brother's. "I would have told you, but Ms. Perfect is a bit of a sore spot for you these days."

"Don't call her that," Walker said immediately.

Campbell arched an eyebrow at him. "See?"

"You and Lily aren't friends anymore," Walker responded. "You haven't been friends since middle school. You don't have girl time."

"Don't we?" Campbell asked innocently. "Go ahead, Sawyer." She turned the full force of that innocent expression on me. "Tell my brother where I've been the past few days."

Or do you want me *to?* Campbell was as adroit at silent threats as her cousin Boone was at warnings.

"She's really been at Lily's?" Walker asked me. "For the past two days? You knew she was there, and you knew I was worried, and you said nothing?"

I could have denied it. I could have played dumb, but Campbell was holding all of the cards here. The plan had been to let her go *after* we'd finished digging up dirt.

"Campbell was with us," I told Walker, deeply suspecting that I would regret playing this game. "She asked me not to say anything."

All smiles, Campbell walked over to me and hooked an arm through mine. "Sawyer and I are becoming fast friends," she declared.

Walker clearly didn't believe that, but just as clearly, he was done talking—to both of us. As he retreated inside, I stepped away from Campbell's hold.

"I thought you didn't have friends," I said lowly.

"I don't," Campbell replied, pleased as punch. "I have alibis."

APRIL 15, 5:31 P.M.

"I'm the victim here, Officer." The auburn-haired coquette laid a gloved hand on her chest, halfway between pledging allegiance and a swoon. "Truly."

Mackie was skeptical, but he managed a question. A reasonable, logical, by-the-books question that he was only half-sure he wanted the answer to.

"The victim of *what*?"

EIGHT MONTHS EARLIER

CHAPTER 22

Two weeks post-pool-party, I hadn't heard a peep out of my good *friend* Campbell. School had started for Lily, but from what she'd told me, not one word had been uttered about *Secrets on My Skin*, the stolen tablet, or the weekend that Campbell had spent bound and gagged in the pool house.

We still had no clue whatsoever what Campbell needed an alibi *for.*

For the sake of my own sanity, I had to concentrate on something other than the ticking time bomb that the senator's daughter represented.

"What can you tell me about Charles Waters?" I asked my grandmother, lifting my hand to my face to block the sun. I was still waiting on Boone to make good on his promise to figure out what his father and uncle had been up to around the time I'd been conceived. In the meantime, all I could do was move on to the next name on the list.

Sadie-Grace's father.

"Lillian?" I prompted when she didn't respond to my query.

"You really should wear a hat in this sun, Sawyer." My

grandmother looked up from the rosebush she was inspecting. "The elements can be so harsh, and you only get one face."

I almost responded by telling her that You Only Get One Face would make an excellent band name, but experience had taught me that smarting off wouldn't get me any closer to answers. Instead, I slapped on a nearby sun hat and a pair of gardening gloves that Lillian had taken to leaving around when she tended her roses, in case I "decided" to join her.

My grandmother was big into allowing the rest of the family to make our "own" decisions, with nudges, hints, and guilt trips along the way. In the past two weeks, she'd learned that none of the above worked on me.

I had learned that if I wanted information, I had to give her something in exchange.

"When I was seven," I offered, eyeing the flowers, "I had a brief obsession with poisonous and carnivorous plants."

If Lillian had been around when I was growing up, she probably would have nudged me toward more *appropriate* pastimes, but as it was, whenever I mentioned anything about my childhood, she seemed to drink it up. The predictable flicker of interest in her eyes was enough to make a person wonder why, if she was so curious about what she'd missed, she hadn't bothered, even once, to take a forty-five-minute drive and be a part of my life until now.

"I actually tried to join the International Carnivorous Plant Society," I continued. "I wanted a membership card I could flash around school."

"Of course you did," Lillian said. She *almost* smiled.

I took that as an opening. "What can you tell me about Charles Waters?" I asked again. Quid pro quo. I'd given her something. Now it was her turn.

"Nature can be bloodthirsty, can't it?" Lillian let her fingertips hover over a rose thorn. "I suppose there are those who would argue that people aren't much better. Your mama, for one."

That wasn't what I'd asked, but she knew I wouldn't sidestep a conversation about what my mom had been like as a teenager.

"Ellie Taft maniacally and devotedly believes the best of people," I corrected. "Even when they don't deserve it." *Especially* when they didn't deserve it. *Especially* if they were male.

"Some people, maybe," Lillian replied. "But her family, our friends? After we lost her daddy, Ellie was . . . *Cynical* isn't the right word. At the time, I might have said *sullen*. She always took things so personally."

That was a loaded statement if I'd ever heard one.

"I remember when Charles Waters got married." Up until Lillian said that sentence, I'd been convinced she was going to ignore my question altogether. "The whole ordeal caused quite the hubbub, and you would have thought any word uttered about the new Mrs. Waters was an insult directed straight at my daughter."

"Were my mom and Sadie-Grace's father close?" I asked, trying to imagine why a teenage girl would be so defensive of the marriage of a man six years her senior.

"Not in the least." Lillian waved away the question. "It was a matter of *principle* for Ellie." My grandmother managed not to roll her eyes, but only just. "Charles's bride wasn't from around here. She was a ballet dancer from *New York*, of all places. Of course people were going to talk. Charles was . . . well, I hate to put this fine a point on it, but he's always been a bit . . . erudite."

Awkward, I translated.

"His mother was a Kelley," Lillian continued. "Oil family. Charles was the only heir, and you've seen the man. He's no stranger to *handsome*. He could have had any girl he wanted, but the poor boy seemed genuinely unaware that the gentler sex even existed until he came back from a business trip to New York married. Of course that was going to raise a few eyebrows."

Of course.

"So what you're saying is that people were nice to his wife's face and talked about her behind her back, and my mom—*heaven knows why*—seemed to find that offensive?"

Lillian must have heard the heavy wallop of sarcasm in my tone, because she was quiet for a moment. "You don't care much what people think, do you, Sawyer?" She didn't wait for an answer. "Your mama did. I wish I'd seen that then. She'd get all riled up and talk about how she hated it here, but my Eleanor wanted people to like her. She wanted to be noticed."

That hit me hard, because my mom had been *wanting*—and *longing* and *searching*—for as long as I could remember.

"What happened to the first Mrs. Waters?" I asked abruptly. I hadn't come outside to talk about the hole in my mom's life that she'd spent the entirety of mine trying to fill.

"Sadie-Grace's mama passed away when she was little," Lillian said. "Poor thing."

"How—" I started to ask, but before I could get the rest of the question out of my mouth, the door to the backyard opened.

Lily stepped out onto the patio, still wearing her school uniform. Her hair was neatly parted down the middle, her lips recently glossed. Her already perfect posture straightened the moment she saw our grandmother.

"How are your roses, Mim?"

"Bloodthirsty," Lillian replied lightly. She glanced at me. "And beautiful."

"How was school?" I asked my cousin, willing our grandmother to look at her, not me. Two weeks had been more than enough time for me to realize just how badly Lily wanted to please the great Lillian Taft.

"School was lovely," my cousin said. "Thank you for asking. Mim?" Lily swung her eyes back to our grandmother's. "Do you think I could borrow Sawyer for a moment?"

"You girls go right ahead," Lillian declared, removing her gloves. "I'll make some lemonade."

Lily waited for the screen door to close behind our grandmother before she crossed the lawn. "We need to talk."

I waited for her to elaborate.

"It's Campbell."

And there it was, after two weeks of waiting for the other shoe to drop.

"She says she has security footage of the pool house." Lily swallowed, hard enough that I could practically taste the bile rising in the back of her throat. "And she's gone through all of the files on my tablet." Lily closed her eyes. "There are pictures. Uncropped copies of the ones on *Secret*—before I edited out my face."

As far as proof went, that was ironclad—and almost certainly an order of magnitude worse than whatever Campbell had on Lily before.

"What does she want?" I asked flatly.

"For now?" Lily opened her eyes and tried not to look like she was in dire need of a fainting couch. "Campbell's demanding your presence—and mine—at a party she's throwing tonight."

CHAPTER 23

Campbell's party wasn't what I'd come to expect of the Debutante set. There were no hors d'oeuvres. The music was not instrumental. The alcohol—and there was plenty—was served in kegs.

"Let me guess," I said over the sound of three dozen teenagers in various stages of inebriation and the bass line emanating from a very expensive sound system, "Campbell's parents aren't home."

"This isn't Campbell's house." Lily somehow managed to make herself heard without yelling as we pushed our way through the foyer. "It's Katharine Riley's."

"Let me guess," I said, modifying my previous statement, "Katharine Riley's parents aren't home."

Lily herded me toward a breakfast nook off the kitchen, Sadie-Grace following in our wake.

"Katharine's parents are out of town," Lily confirmed, the acoustics providing a break from the bass line. "So is Katharine."

I wasn't sure I'd heard her correctly. "What?"

"Katharine and her family left yesterday for an out-of-town wedding. Today, Campbell just started asking people if they were coming to Katharine's party." Lily shook her head. "Within an hour or two, everyone else was doing the same thing. Half the people here probably don't even realize that Katharine's not."

I glanced back toward the kegs. "Campbell's version of throwing a party involves breaking and entering?"

"Oh, you make it all sound so sordid." Campbell Ames strolled over to stand in the midst of our group. "So glad that you three could make it."

Lily allowed her chin to jut forward. "I don't recall being given a choice."

"Relax, Lilypad, I'm doing you a favor. What exactly has a life of propriety and rule-following gotten you? A reputation for being boring and self-righteous, a boyfriend who got bored and self-righteously dumped you, and so much pent-up sexual frustration that you spontaneously decided to self-destruct." Campbell laid a hand lightly on my cousin's cheek and then gave it a solid pat. "Live a little."

Her tone left very little question that it was an order.

"In fact," Campbell continued, "live a lot. I, personally, would love to see you making friends and influencing people. Have a beverage or two. Dance on the table."

"I will do no such—"

"You will," Campbell said sweetly. "And you'll like it. And you . . ." She turned to Sadie-Grace. "You'll stay busy picking up after my guests. We can't have the Rileys coming home to a mess, now can we?"

Sadie-Grace flushed. Like everything else, it was a good look for her. I deeply suspected her vulnerability wouldn't have been quite so enticing to Campbell if she'd been less of a knockout.

"Put that down," I told Sadie-Grace when she tentatively picked up a Solo cup someone had abandoned on the ground.

"Sawyer," Lily said, her voice low.

"You," Campbell barked back at her, "dancing on the table." She narrowed her eyes at Sadie-Grace. "You, trash. Unless you two *want* me to publish a new entry to *Secrets*? One that includes our lovely model's face."

Lily paled. Sadie-Grace picked up another cup. Satisfied that the two of them had no choice but to jump at her command, Campbell allowed her full attention to land on me.

"Let's you and I take a little walk," she said. "Shall we?"

Our walk took us to the second story of the Rileys' home. A marble balcony overlooked the open floor plan below. Campbell leaned her elbows lightly against the wrought-iron railing.

"I suppose that Lily mentioned the darling memento I have of our girls' weekend?" She angled the cell phone in her hands toward me. "I especially like this shot of you tying my hands behind my back."

The photo had obviously been captured from a video. I'd held out some hope that Campbell had been lying about the security footage, but clearly, she hadn't been.

"If you were going to do something with that footage, you would have already," I said.

I'd been willing to bet against Campbell going to the police two weeks ago. The fact that she'd waited this long to make a move had done little to change my mind.

I leaned against the railing next to her. "I'm guessing at least one of your parents would find a way to blame the whole *sordid* ordeal on you."

That was a stab in the dark, but my metaphorical blade drew blood.

"You don't know anything about my parents," Campbell snapped.

"I know that Walker bought the story that you took off for an entire weekend because you needed breathing room from your mother." I let that sink in. "I know your father's a politican."

I know that your family is, in Boone's words, a merciless lot.

"Daddy would never want me to go public with this nonsense," Campbell admitted, then turned wide, innocent eyes on me, the edges of her lips flicking upward like a serpent's tongue. "But if the security footage leaked to the media, through no fault of my own . . ." She gave a helpless little shrug. "The senator would want to get out in front of the scandal, control the narrative. I'm sure the police would understand why I was reluctant to report my *friends*. Fragile young flowers such as myself are just so vulnerable to bullying from their peers."

Campbell was about as fragile as a cement truck. She was also, I suspected, fully capable of leaking the footage herself and pretending to be horrified that it had come out.

"You'd get the lion's share of the blame, you know," Campbell said casually. "Not perfect Lily. No matter what she says, everyone—your family included—will think that the cousin with the *unfortunate* background was the ringleader of the whole kidnapping fiasco."

If the police did get involved, if the blame fell on me—per the terms of Lillian's contract, I could kiss my college fund good-bye.

"Let them think what they want," I retorted. "I can handle it." I hoped that Campbell could hear the promise in my tone: *I can handle you.*

Undeterred, she turned her attention to the party below. Lily was standing near the edge of a mahogany table, a drink held in a death grip in her right hand.

"She's going to do it," Campbell told me. "If I say dance, she'll dance. She might need a little more liquid courage first, but she won't risk that security footage coming out, and she definitely won't risk me getting bored enough to upload a few uncropped photos to *Secrets*."

I gritted my teeth. "Why are you doing this?"

"Petty revenge?" Campbell suggested pertly. "You do remember the whole *kidnapping* thing, right?"

"The blackmail predated the kidnapping." I gave her a hard look. "Seriously—what did Lily ever do to you?"

"Who says she *did* anything?" Campbell pushed her ponytail back over her shoulder. "Maybe I'm just evil incarnate."

I stared at her for a moment. "Maybe you feel helpless more often than you'd like to admit."

I might not have known her, but I knew that people didn't play games like this one because they *already* felt powerful.

Campbell stared down at Lily below, her expression impossible to decipher. "I love my brother," she said. "Everyone does. They always have."

Given the way Campbell had reacted earlier when I'd mentioned her parents, I was betting *everyone* started with the senator and his wife.

"But once upon a time . . ." Campbell's gaze flicked back toward mine. "Lily was *my* friend."

I took that to mean that Campbell hadn't been a fan of the romance between my cousin and her brother. *She was supposed to choose you.*

Down below, Lily sipped at the drink in her hand. Again. And again. And again.

"I wonder how Walker would react if I released those pictures," Campbell mused, signaling that this little heart-to-heart was over.

"If you even *think* about posting a picture with her face in it . . ." I said lowly.

"You'll what?" Campbell returned. "Precious, proper little Lily made her own bed the moment she launched that site. I'll let you in on a little secret, Sawyer: What girls like us do behind closed doors? As long as the person we do it with keeps his mouth shut, that's our business. But you don't flaunt it. You don't do a striptease in the middle of a country club, you don't lose it under the high school bleachers, and you do not give the gossiping mamas anything to talk about."

The mention of *bleachers* hit me harder than it should have.

"People talk about you all the time," I countered. Walker had told me that much.

"They talk because I want them to." Campbell gave a graceful little shrug of her shoulders. "And I don't give them anything quite so . . . *intimate* . . . to talk about."

"It's not like *Secrets* is pornographic," I shot back. "The important bits are covered."

"Barely," Campbell said cheerfully.

"It's PG-13," I insisted. "Not R. Even if you do release the photos, people will find something else to gossip about soon enough."

"You think so?"

Down on the first floor, Lily had finally finished her drink. She glanced up and caught the two of us looking down at her. Campbell lifted a hand to wave, one finger at a time.

"Dance," she mouthed.

Lily bowed her head for a moment, and then she carefully hauled herself up onto the table. Slowly, the people around her caught on to the fact that something was happening and turned to look.

Lily moved her hips from one side to the other. Her hands raised themselves robotically over her head.

Campbell watched with no small amount of self-satisfaction. "There are two kinds of scandals, Sawyer." Down below, Lily had fallen into the rhythm of the music, and the crowd around her had grown substantially. "Those that ruin you, and those that don't. And if you think the difference between the two is in what someone does and not who does it, you're even more naive than I thought."

Even from a distance, I could see the flush on Lily's cheeks when a boy hopped up on the table to dance beside her. She stepped back, and Campbell started clapping.

Loudly.

"What do you want, Campbell?" I bit out as other partygoers joined in on the applause and someone yelled for Lily to *take it off*.

"Right now?" Campbell turned her back on the scene below and walked toward me. "I want to enjoy the party, knowing that you and Sadie-Grace and your darling cousin will be handling the cleanup. I also want you to bring me the key you stole from my locker at the club."

She brushed past me, but turned back to speak over her shoulder. "After that?" she said. "I'll let you know."

APRIL 15, 5:48 P.M.

Mackie had spent the past ten minutes searching for a record of the girls' arrest. Anything was better than trying to *talk* to the gown-clad foursome. He wasn't at all sure what the quartet had done, but he was starting to think that the only thing they *weren't* capable of was giving him a straight answer.

Blackmail. Theft. At one point, something had been strongly implied about indecent exposure. . . .

"Excuse me."

Mackie was grateful to even hear a male voice. It took him a moment to realize it belonged to a boy not much older than his white-gloved perps. "Can I help you?" Mackie straightened his spine as he asked the question. *I am in charge here,* he thought. *I am an officer of the law!*

"That depends," the boy replied, leaning his elbows on the counter. "Do you know where I can find Sawyer Taft?"

SEVEN MONTHS EARLIER

CHAPTER 24

"If you'd been abducted by aliens, you'd tell me, right?"

My mom's greeting almost made me smile—*almost*, because I had deep and abiding suspicions that unlike the smattering of communication I'd had with her since she'd taken off, this conversation was going to involve the kind of questions I couldn't dodge.

"It would probably depend on the circumstances surrounding my abduction," I replied, pulling my car—a beater I'd refuse to let Lillian replace—into a parking spot in front of a large white building. "How likely I thought I was to be believed," I elaborated. "Whether or not the aliens in question had a taste for human flesh . . ."

I'd clearly spent way too much time around John David in the past month.

"Sawyer." My mom's voice was uncharacteristically serious. "Where are you?"

I turned the question back around on her. "Where are *you*?"

"I'm at home," my mom replied. "Our home—and all of your stuff is gone."

"If I'd been abducted by aliens, it's highly unlikely that they would have allowed me to pack first."

I could practically *see* my mom rolling her eyes. "I would like to remind you that I have a Mom Voice, missy. I don't use it often, but I can and I will."

I'd missed her. Why was it that I never let myself register that fact until she came back?

"I went by the garage," my mom continued. "Big Jim said you don't work there anymore."

"I haven't worked there for two months." If *she* hadn't just spent two months who-knows-where with a guy she'd met at a bar, she would have known that. "I got a better offer."

The term *better* was a stretch. It had been a little over six weeks since I'd come to live with my grandmother. Six weeks of playing debutante. A full month since Campbell had stopped lying low and started lording her power over us at every turn.

"What kind of offer?" my mom asked suspiciously.

I'd known from the moment I'd signed Lillian's contract that I'd have to come clean eventually. As absentminded as my mom could be—as *absent* as she'd sometimes been since I turned eighteen—there was no way I could hide my location for nine months.

I eased into the truth as best I could. "I found a way to pay for college." That, at least, would make my mom happy. "A nine-month contract. After this, I'm set."

"Please tell me what you're doing is legal."

I let out a long breath. "Lillian's lawyers assure me it is."

One second of silence. Two seconds. Three . . .

"Sawyer, please tell me that your pimp's name is Lillian."

"Mom!"

"You're working for my mother?" Ellie Taft was known for going with the flow. She'd never sounded as much like Lillian as she did right now.

"Not working, exactly," I said. "More like . . . debutante-ing."

"You're a Deb." My mom paused. "Your grandmother is paying you to . . ."

She trailed off in horror.

"Pretty much," I said.

The rest of the conversation went about like I'd imagined. My mother could not fathom why I would have taken Lillian up on her deal, and also, did I not realize that my mother's mother was manipulation personified and wrapped in a St. John suit?

"It really hasn't been that bad," I said. *Aside from the blackmail, obligatory brunches, and lack of progress on identifying my father.*

"You're not doing this for the money, Sawyer. Don't try to tell me that you are."

The door to the large white building opened, and a familiar figure stepped out.

"I have to go," I told my mother. "And *you* have to make your way back to The Holler and beg for your job back. The apartment's paid through next month. Nonperishable groceries are in the cabinet."

"As your mom, it's my sworn duty to tell you that this is a bad idea."

On the bright side, I replied silently, *it's not the* worst *idea I've had lately.*

After I hung up, I slipped out of the car and approached the man who was waiting for me.

"Senator." I offered my hand.

He took it. "Miss Taft," he said. "Welcome to the campaign."

Given that Senator Ames was only halfway through his term, it wasn't much of a campaign yet, but six weeks without answers—and four weeks under Campbell's thumb—was my limit. I wasn't wired to sit around and do nothing. When I'd floated the idea of getting a job by Lillian, she'd offered me two options: Uncle J.D.'s investment firm and volunteering.

It wasn't my fault that when my grandmother uttered the word *volunteering*, she thought *Junior League*, and when I heard it, I thought . . . *access*.

The day after the party at Katharine Riley's house, I'd surrendered the key we'd stolen from Campbell's locker to her possession. I'd also made a copy. The fact that she'd wanted it back was proof enough that there was leverage to be had, and the sooner we found it, the better.

Meanwhile, Boone had proven to be a pretty sorry detective. All he'd been able to tell me about his uncle, the senator, was that nineteen years ago, Sterling Ames had been a law student and already married to Walker and Campbell's mother. In fact, based on the intel I'd gathered in the past few weeks, all four of the men on my list had been married at the time of my conception.

In other words: No matter how this shook out, my sire was a cheating cheater who cheated.

"Walker will show you the ropes." The senator, who'd been giving me a tour of his office space, got my attention the moment he said his son's name. My master plan in coming here wasn't what one would call *defined*. I wanted to get a bead on Sterling Ames. I wanted to figure out what kind of man he was, and if I found something that let me counteract Campbell's increasingly ridiculous demands—that we hand-wash her car twice a week, that Lily decline a nomination for student council president, that Sadie-Grace stop using conditioner of any kind in her hair—all the better.

Campbell's brother was an unexpected complication.

"Welcome to the trenches, Sawyer Taft." There was an edge of humor—or something like it—in Walker's tone. "I had no idea you were politically inclined."

Allow me to translate, I thought. *You weren't expecting to see me here, and you don't particularly want to be here yourself.* I was willing to bet big money that when Walker had dropped out of college, the senator hadn't given him much choice about "volunteering."

"How are you at fetching coffee?" Walker asked me. "Personally, I consider it my calling in life."

"Walker," his father scolded fondly. I thought back to what Campbell had said about *everyone* loving her brother, but didn't get the chance to ruminate on the relationship between father and son, because Walker was standing directly in front of his dad's office, and inside that office, nearly obscured from my line of sight, was a safe.

The kind you opened with a key.

CHAPTER 25

"Sawyer, I could hug you." Standing on Lillian's back porch, where I'd pulled my cousin to talk the moment she and Sadie-Grace had arrived after school, Lily seemed on the verge of losing her characteristic composure.

"Let's not get carried away here," I replied. "We don't know that the key from Campbell's locker fits her father's safe. *Ooof*." I had to fight to keep my balance. Unlike Lily, Sadie-Grace didn't threaten hugs. She hugged with a vengeance.

"You have no idea what school's been like," Sadie-Grace whispered fiercely. "Campbell makes me wear *plaid*."

"She makes me wear ponytails," Lily added gravely.

"I feel for you both," I replied dryly. Right now, I really didn't think that Campbell playing fashion dictator was anyone's biggest problem. The fact that she could still out Lily as the person behind the now-defunct *Secrets on My Skin* and leak the footage of the kidnapping?

That was a much bigger issue—for all three of us.

"With a little luck," I commented, "Campbell will be off all of our backs soon."

"Will I?" a voice asked behind me. Campbell loved to make an entrance, and for someone who preferred heels—the taller, the better—she walked with surprisingly light steps as she sauntered out the back door.

In all likelihood, Aunt Olivia had let her in and sent her back.

I turned to face the enemy head-on and found, to my surprise, that Campbell wasn't wearing heels. She was wearing tennis shoes, patterned leggings, and a long-sleeved, slightly oversized T-shirt. In her hands, she held a large cardboard box.

"Help yourselves, ladies." Campbell dropped the box on the porch. Sadie-Grace peered inside. Based on the expression on her face, I deduced that she was likely expecting a box of snakes.

"Shirts," Sadie-Grace said, frowning and perplexed. "Like yours."

"Presents," Campbell declared. "For my favorite fellow Debs." Campbell gave a little spin so we could take in the 360 view. Her name was written on the back of the shirt in block letters, with the number 07 underneath. On the front, written in script, were the words *Symphony Ball.*

"There are ball caps beneath the shirts," Campbell continued blithely. "I hope y'all don't mind that I took lucky number seven."

She was acting like we were actually friends, like she hadn't spent the past month blackmailing the whole lot of us.

"You made us shirts," I said slowly. In the grand scheme of Campbell's modus operandi, making us personalized clothing seemed remarkably undastardly.

"It is possible," Campbell allowed, "that I am a wee bit competitive. I like to win, and I like to be color-coordinated when I do it. Try on the leggings. I swear, they're like butter on your legs."

There was waiting for the guillotine to fall, and then there was hearing the *eek, eek, eek* of the blade creaking downward. Campbell being *nice* was downright terrifying.

We tried the leggings on. They were made of the softest fabric I'd ever touched.

"I told you," Campbell practically purred. "Heavenly."

I felt like I'd fallen into the Twilight Zone. "Far be it from me to ask questions," I said, "but what, exactly, are we meant to be winning?"

"Far be it from me to provide answers," a male voice intoned, "but I know this one!"

We seriously needed to put a bell on the door—and Aunt Olivia seriously needed to stop letting people into Lillian's house and sending them back.

"Boone," I greeted.

"Skeptical one," he returned, bowing his head slightly. He shot Lily a brief smile and then tripped over his own two feet when he attempted to do the same with Sadie-Grace.

It had not been difficult, over the past few weeks, to ascertain that Boone had a crush. Sadie-Grace was the only one he *didn't* try to flirt with, and she was the only one who didn't realize how head over heels for her he was.

"Tonight is the Symphony Ball scavenger hunt." Boone tried to recover his cool, a task which would have been monumentally easier if he'd ever had it. "Teams of five, must be coed." He gestured to the four of us. "Co." Then to himself. "Ed."

Campbell reached down into the box and pulled out a T-shirt with her cousin's name on it. "I decided you didn't need leggings," she told him.

"Always the bridesmaid," Boone sighed. "Never the bride."

"All of this is for a scavenger hunt?" I said, waiting for the catch.

Campbell met my gaze and batted her eyelashes. "What else would it be for?"

CHAPTER 26

Scavenger hunt, my ass. Three hours later, I was ensconced in a limousine with Lily on one side and Boone on the other. Campbell was sitting with her back to the privacy window, which she'd very pointedly raised. Lily held a list of items in her left hand and a handheld high-definition camera in her right.

Apparently, the annual Symphony Ball Scavenger Hunt was a *video* scavenger hunt. Limos had been provided for our convenience. The plan was for us to spend the next five hours—between now and midnight—racing around town, videotaping ourselves doing a range of mama-approved challenges in front of famous local landmarks. But to decode exactly *which* landmarks, we had to answer a series of riddles.

The list in Lily's hand contained the first clue, which would lead us to our first location, and, in turn, to a clue that would point us to the next. At the bottom of the card, scrawled in scripted lettering, was the first challenge: *One Deb and one Squire must do the chicken dance to a Top 40 song of your choice (no profanity, please).*

"I am beginning to sense that I may have made an error in judgment in agreeing to be the only boy on this team," Boone stated.

Campbell rolled her eyes. "You were born for this," she told her cousin. "And besides, I know you'll keep your mouth shut."

And there it was: the catch I'd been waiting for.

"Might I ask what Boone will be keeping his mouth shut about?" Lily inquired, her tone taking weaponized politeness to a new level.

"Simple," Campbell replied. "My dear cousin Boone and I will do the chicken dance. It will be the best and most hilarious chicken dance any of you has ever seen. And then I'm going to take advantage of the fact that our driver could not be less interested in these proceedings to duck out for a bit."

"Duck out where?" Sadie-Grace asked.

She was the only person in the limo who expected that question to be answered.

Immediately after Campbell and Boone had finished their chicken dance and the camera had been turned off, Campbell began to strip. She tossed her shirt at Sadie-Grace.

"Tuck your hair up under your cap," she said. "We're about the same size. As long as they only shoot you from the back, no one will know the difference."

Suddenly, the fact that Campbell had gone out of her way to make sure the four of us were dressed in matching outfits *with our names on them* made total sense.

Six weeks ago, when our former hostage had confronted me at the pool party, she'd told me that the three of us were her alibis. I'd assumed—erroneously, apparently—that she meant her alibis for *that* weekend.

What were the chances that the past four weeks of misery had just been Campbell's way of testing her power over us and making sure we'd do what we were told tonight?

The manipulator in question tossed her cell phone to Lily. "I recorded some voice memos for when 'I' am offscreen. Make sure you catch Sadie-Grace as herself on camera while I'm talking, and I'll see you girls in a couple of hours."

I glanced at Boone. The three of us were being blackmailed. What was his excuse?

"Don't look at me," Boone said solemnly. "She knows where I sleep."

Great. While we were parading around town, recording ourselves in front of this statue and that plaque, Campbell would be off doing who knows what. Every bone in my body said this was a bad idea.

And yet . . .

Campbell sidled up beside me. "I'm sensing some reluctance. And I'm sympathetic." Campbell gave my arm a little squeeze. "Would it make you feel better if I promised you, girl to girl and on my family's honor, that my intentions are pure?"

No. The answer was obvious enough that I didn't bother with it out loud. Campbell didn't expect me to.

"Would it make you feel better," she said instead, "if, after tonight, I promise to give you this?"

She slipped something out of her purse. *The tablet.*

"The security footage is on there, too," Campbell said. "I haven't made backups." There was almost no inflection in her tone. No sugary sweetness, no innuendo, no threat. "I swear that I haven't, Sawyer, and I promise you that if you three do this for me tonight, I will give you everything I have on Lily—on all three of you."

She's telling the truth. I knew that the way Lily knew exactly which shade of lipstick to pair with a modest pastel—instinctively.

"I also promise," Campbell continued, "that if you *don't* do this for me tonight, I'll leak the footage of my kidnapping and upload every naughty, uncropped picture of Lily I have."

Also true.

"One way or another," Campbell said, "this ends at midnight."

Whatever the senator's daughter was planning to do, whatever she needed an alibi for—it mattered to her more than continuing to torture the three of us.

She's a spoiled Southern belle who likes to play mind games, I thought. *How bad can what she has planned possibly be?*

"Do we have a deal?" Campbell asked.

I glanced back at Lily. I was only in this mess because of her, but day by day and week by week, she'd grown on me. Being blackmailed was something of a bonding experience.

I turned back to Campbell and lowered my voice. "Deal."

APRIL 15, 5:49 P.M.

"Sawyer Taft," Mackie repeated. He'd definitely *heard* the name Sawyer in the girls' various natterings, but the last name?

Taft?

That was new.

"About yea high," the boy said, gesturing lazily. "Smart mouth. Packs a hell of a punch."

Oh, God, Mackie thought. *The lock picker is violent.*

Out loud, he opted for: "Taft?" Mackie cleared his throat. "As in . . . er . . . the Rolling Hills Tafts?"

SEVEN MONTHS EARLIER

CHAPTER 27

It took an hour for us to film the first three clues—and about that long for Sadie-Grace to get the hang of pretending to be Campbell. It took two hours for me to realize how much this whole exercise was weighing on Lily. Six weeks of living in the bedroom across from hers had taught me that my cousin straightening her hair and tucking it behind her right ear was a bad sign.

The worse Lily felt, the more she needed things to appear perfect.

"*Oh, Lordy. I can't watch. . . .*" Offscreen, Boone played one of Campbell's voice memos. She was cracking up laughing. Sadie-Grace was currently on-screen, in her own shirt, attempting to make up a rap about good citizenship while standing in front of an enormous statue of praying hands.

It was going only slightly better than Boone's attempt to impersonate a camel at the entrance to the local zoo.

Lily held the camera in her left hand, as her right secured her hair in place once more.

"That's enough." I put Sadie-Grace out of her misery. Mid-rap, she'd gone from rond de jambe–ing to a battement, which was never a good sign.

"Oh, good," Sadie-Grace said, her entire body sagging with relief. "I was having a really hard time thinking of a rhyme for *hospitality.*" She turned to retrieve the next clue from the base of the praying hands.

Next to me, Lily let her left hand—and the camera—fall gently to her side. I waited for her right hand to make its move.

Another hair tuck. "It's going to be either Maynard Park or the fountains," she murmured. "Or, if they're feeling daring, the bluffs."

I hadn't been aware that our region of the country *had* bluffs. But prior to this evening, I had also never been to the botanical gardens or the historical society. Tonight was a night of firsts.

"Ladies," Boone called out. "Our destination is Maynard Park. To the Bat-limo!"

"See?" Lily said. The resignation in her tone sounded so raw that on the way back to the limo, I broke my cousin's cardinal rule and asked about her feelings, which, to Lily, was pretty much the equivalent of inquiring about her underwear.

"You okay?"

"I'm fine." Lily's reply was immediate, but she followed it with a shake of her head, negating that sentence.

"Care to elaborate?" I prompted gently.

"It's just . . ." She trailed off, then surprised me by forcing herself to continue. "Whoever put this list together might as well have simply asked Walker for a list of places he used to take me when he wanted the night to be memorable."

My cousin's relationship with Walker Ames was right up there with *Secrets* on the list of topics that Lily Taft Easterling *did not* discuss.

"He gave me a promise ring, you know." Her voice was quiet. Not bitter, not sweet. "Last spring. He was getting ready to graduate. We were at the botanical gardens. And then two weeks later . . ."

The Ballad of Lily Easterling and Walker Ames, I thought, remembering Boone's words at the auction. *A tale for the ages to be sure.*

And now, courtesy of the Symphony Ball Committee, Lily was being forced to relive their greatest hits.

She can't take another three hours of this, I thought. What I said, as the four of us piled back into the limo was: "This is ridiculous." Lest Lily think I was talking about *her,* I continued. "I am not . . ." I looked down at our next challenge. "Attempting to recite Robert Frost while stuffing my mouth full of marshmallows."

"I volunteer as tribute!"

"And neither are you," I told Boone. We still had three hours to burn. Based on the deal I'd made with Campbell, we *had* to continue to document her presence with us.

But who said that we had to continue to do so *here,* with a parent-approved list?

If we're stuck being Campbell's alibi, we may as well enjoy ourselves. Sick of playing by the rules, I crawled toward the front of the limo and lowered the privacy window. I gave the driver our next location—*not* Maynard Park.

"That's a forty-five-minute trip," the driver said.

"So it is," I replied. I reiterated the address and rolled up the window.

"Where are we going?" Sadie-Grace asked, her brow furrowed as the limo pulled away from the curb.

I leaned back in my seat. "I believe people around here refer to it as *the boonies.*"

As far as I could tell, Lily, Sadie-Grace, and Boone had all been to Europe, but not one of them had ever driven more than twenty minutes outside the city limits.

Why would they?

"Are we allowed to make the driver come all the way out here?" Sadie-Grace asked when it became clear just how far off the beaten path I was taking them. "Isn't that, like, grand theft auto?"

"Grand theft limo," Boone corrected sagely.

"Hey," I cut in. "Bonnie, Clyde, if you two are done complaining, we're almost there."

When the limo came to a stop, my three companions followed me warily out onto the street, like they half expected to step out into the Dust Bowl.

Either that, or they'd noticed the town's lone strip club across the street.

Home sweet home. I hadn't been tempted, even once, in the past six weeks to make the drive, but now, knowing my mom was back in town . . .

"It's . . . a vacant lot." Lily aimed for diplomacy as she followed my gaze to the address I'd given the driver.

"No," I corrected. "It's *the* lot."

The town I'd grown up in may not have had botanical gardens, but we did have landmarks of our own. The lot had been empty for as long as I had been alive. The grass was uneven and slightly overgrown—but only slightly. That was one of the oddest things about the lot. I'd never seen anyone cutting it. Given the contents of the field, I wasn't sure anyone *could* cut it, but the grass never seemed to grow long enough to completely mask the objects people left there.

It had started, so the local rumors went, with bottles. Glass bottles. It wasn't hard to imagine people tossing an empty into a vacant lot, but somewhere along the way, someone must have noticed the way the sunlight—or moonlight—caught on colored glass, because slowly, the lot's purpose had evolved. People left mirrors, metal, anything that might catch the light. At some point, the bottles weren't tossed anymore—they were placed.

Some people left notes in them.

A thousand notes in a thousand bottles in an empty lot that would have run the length of a city block, if we'd still been in the city. But we weren't.

By my calculations, we were roughly three and a half worlds away.

Beside me, Lily clutched her purse tighter. Clearly, she'd spotted the strip club. Instead of telling her that her wallet was safer here than it was in the city, I looked up. The night sky wasn't quite clear, a waning moon disappearing behind smoky clouds. I walked back to the limo and made one last request of the driver. Obligingly, he angled the car toward the field and flashed the brights.

Light caught on glass. A thousand bottles, a thousand notes, and between them, mementos—scrap-metal sculptures, patches of glittery fabric, the occasional hand-fashioned cross.

"Wow," Sadie-Grace said. "This is . . ."

"Trash?" I suggested, because I half expected one of them to say it.

"No." That response came from unlikely quarters. Lily's grip on her purse relaxed. Her lips curved slowly upward. "This is a place that Walker Ames has never *ever* been." She lifted the camera up and turned back to Sadie-Grace, her eyes alight. "Get out there, 'Campbell.'"

I took them to Late Nite Donuts. We visited the Methodist graveyard and the secondhand shop behind Big Jim's that always had the mannequins in the window decked to the nines and posed like they were in crime scenes.

That was Boone's favorite. Lily's was the library. There was an actual library, one town over, but I'd always preferred this one myself.

"Someone made this?" Lily asked, standing at the base of the tree and looking up.

"Not the tree itself," I said. "Obviously. But the rest of it? Someone carved the shelves when I was a kid."

I was pretty sure we were on private property, but the fence was easy enough to jump that the owners couldn't have wanted to keep people out too badly.

I suspected they were at least partially responsible for keeping the library's shelves stocked.

Recesses had been carved into the trunk of the old oak, three feet wide, a little over a foot tall, one on top of another on top of another, a makeshift bookshelf filled with tattered copies of books that even the used-book store wouldn't accept.

This was where I'd gotten my first tome on medieval torture.

"Maybe we should get back," Sadie-Grace said suddenly—and with no small amount of reluctance. "What if Campbell—"

"Campbell wants an alibi," I cut in. "I have no idea where she is or what she's doing, but I'd lay good money that we're farther away from the eye of the storm now than we would be if we'd stuck to the rules."

"The farther away we are," Boone summarized, "the better Campbell's alibi."

I told Lily to turn on the camera and issued a challenge of my own. The library wasn't the library until you climbed it.

"What's next?" Sadie-Grace had dirt on her face, grass in her hair, and a scratch on her elbow. She *still* looked like she'd come straight from a royal engagement—or stepped out of a fairy tale.

I checked my watch: forty minutes until the limo driver was supposed to circle back to the lot to pick us up. "I figured we'd swing by the gas station," I said. "Then we'll end at The Holler."

I didn't know what it said about me or the first eighteen years of my life that this was all I had to show them. Probably the same thing it said that I hadn't made the drive back here until now.

"What's the gas station?" Lily asked. Unlike Sadie-Grace, she had survived the tree climb completely unscathed. She literally could have sat down to brunch at the club without adjusting so much as a hair.

"The gas station," I said dramatically, "is . . . a gas station."

They all stared at me blankly.

"The Holler is a bar," I offered.

"*Your* bar?" Sadie-Grace asked.

I smiled.

CHAPTER 28

Trick did a double take when I walked through the door, but it didn't take him long to recover. "How's trouble?"

I could see him taking in the motley crew I'd brought with me. The overly manicured, slightly dirt-smeared motley crew.

"What's the rule about bringing the underaged into my bar?"

I knew the answer by heart. "No one serves them, if they cause problems, you'll take it out on my hide, and we slip out the back if there's a fight."

"That's my girl." Trick observed me for a moment. "Though I have to say, there's something different about you, Trouble."

The hair. The nails. The clothes. The company.

"Don't make me explain in excruciating detail how a Judas chair works," I warned. The last thing I wanted was *anyone* to start waxing eloquently on my whole-body—and whole-life—makeover.

As Lily, Sadie-Grace, and Boone finally made their way past the entrance, I worked up the courage to ask Trick, "Has my mom been in?"

"Since she left me high and dry two months back?"

I wouldn't have blamed him if he didn't give her the job back. How could I?

"She's been in, and you can stop worrying, Trouble—she still has a job." The old man put me out of my misery. "In fact, I believe she's on her break out back."

That hit me straight in the gut. As much as I'd told myself this detour had been for Lily's benefit, I wasn't fool enough to believe that it was coincidence that my mom had arrived home today, and here I was.

"Thanks for letting her come back," I told Trick.

He wiped his brow with the back of his hand. "I wouldn't have been able to hold the job for her, but your . . ." He stopped midsentence.

"My what?"

Still no answer, and I thought of all the times that this man should have fired my mother, but didn't—all the times he'd looked after me.

"I hope you're enjoying it up there," he said abruptly. "With your grandmother."

I hadn't told him where I'd been. My mom never mentioned her family, so I doubted that she'd told him, either. And that meant that the most likely source from which he'd come by my current location *was* my grandmother.

"Did she pay you?" I asked. Rose garden heart-to-hearts aside, I still knew relatively little about Lillian Taft, but I did know that money wasn't something she talked about. It was something she had—and something she *used*.

"Not a word about any of this to Ellie, Sawyer." That was all the reply I got from Trick, and all the confirmation I needed.

"Is this the first time my grandmother's paid you to hold my mother's job?"

No answer.

"The second?"

Still no answer. My mom had been underage when this man had let her rent the apartment overhead. He'd advanced her the first two months' rent. He'd hired her to clean the place before she was legally old enough to tend bar.

He'd saved her—saved *us*. I'd always believed he'd done so of his own volition. That he'd been fond of my mom and fonder of me.

I looked away before I'd realized how badly I needed to. Unfortunately, this was a family business in a family town, and instead of having a moment to catch my breath, I caught sight of a whole slew of Trick's grandsons behind the bar. Even the youngest was working tonight. Thad Anderson was only three years my senior.

"You okay?" Lily appeared beside me.

I nodded and turned away from the counter—and Thad.

"You ever hustle someone at pool?" I asked Lily, but when I attempted to walk by her, she caught me by the elbow.

"That boy behind the bar," she said. "Who is he?"

"His grandfather owns this place," I said. I would have left it at that, but Lily had uttered a full five sentences about her relationship with Walker Ames earlier. I figured I owed her something in return. "His mom used to watch me after school, when my mom was working."

"You were . . . friends?" Lily asked cautiously.

I shrugged. "I was more like an annoying little sister, until I got old enough to stay home alone."

And then I'd gotten older.

"Also," I added under my breath, "my freshman year, he had sex with some girl under the bleachers, and he let the entire school think it was me."

Lily's eyes widened comically, then her face went blank. Dangerously, lethally blank. She turned back to the bar, probably to give him what I could only assume was a very sternly worded piece of her mind.

This time, I caught *her* elbow. On the other side of the room, Boone appeared to be challenging a duo of drunk good old boys to a game of darts. Sadie-Grace stood to his side, blissfully unaware of the way that pretty much every male in the room was ogling her.

"We should go," I said.

Lily stared at a point over my shoulder. She opened her mouth to reply, then closed it again. Finally, she managed to clear her throat. "Sawyer?"

"Yes?"

She nodded past me. "You really do have your mama's cheekbones."

CHAPTER 29

Lily hung back and let me approach on my own. My mom's hair was shorter than it had been when she'd left, her eyes brighter. The moment she saw me, she lit up the room.

"Baby, you will not believe the couple months I've had."

No greeting, no surprise that I was here—just a smile wide enough to nearly break her face.

"Right back at you," I said, thinking about the couple months that *I'd* had.

"Of that, we will not speak." My mom paused, then rendered that statement null and void. "Tell me everything. Did you manage to have *any* fun? I hope you at least staged a protest in the middle of one of Lillian's formal dinners. Burned a few bras?"

"The 1960s called, Mom. They want their signature feminist protest back."

"Smart-ass." My mom threw her arms around me. "I didn't think you'd come back," she whispered, breathing in the smell of my hair.

For once in my life, I had no words. I wasn't back. Not for good. "I'm . . ."

"Too good for them," my mom finished, finally letting loose of me. "You—"

I knew the exact moment she spotted Lily, because she stopped midsentence.

"I didn't come alone." I recovered my voice and glanced back at Lily. My cousin took that as her cue to come closer.

"Olivia." The name escaped my mom's lips.

"Mom," I stated, well aware that there was more or less an entire herd of elephants in the room now. "This is Lily."

It only took my mom a second or two to recover. "Named after Lillian, I assume?"

"Yes, ma'am. It's nice to meet you." Lily was nothing if not polite.

My mom didn't do polite. "Your mama know you're slumming?"

Lily Taft Easterling had probably never even *heard* the word *slumming*, but to her credit, she didn't bat an eye. "What my mama doesn't know won't hurt her."

My mom stared a second longer, then broke into a wide, unbridled smile. "It's nice to meet you, Lily."

"Sawyer's been showing us the town." Lily couldn't have refrained from making chitchat if she'd tried. "It's lovely."

"It's something," my mom countered. "But it's ours. Between you and me, it's a good place to live a little." She eyed Lily for a moment and then leaned forward and expertly mussed her hair. "Or a lot."

Lily clearly didn't know how to respond to that, and all I could think was that this shouldn't have been her first visit. I'd grown up less than an hour away from my mother's family. It would have been so easy for them to come see us.

A crash on the other side of the room snapped me out of that line of thinking. *Boone.* He was standing with his mouth open, two darts in his left hand, and his right hand frozen in a position that suggested he'd just thrown a third.

A few feet away, a man in a ball cap was staring at a broken beer bottle on the table in front of him, sopping wet.

"It is possible," Boone said gamely, "that my aim leaves something to be desired."

The man in the ball cap put his hands flat on the table.

"I should take care of this," I told my mom. I managed to extract Boone from the situation at approximately the same time that Thad Anderson brought the man's table another round of beers on the house.

Crisis averted. Then, from behind me, I heard: "I don't think that's legal." Sadie-Grace sounded disturbingly contemplative. "But I *am* very flexible."

"Time to go," I told Lily.

She pulled Sadie-Grace away from the men she'd been talking to. I grabbed Boone by the back of the neck, and once I'd deposited all three of them safely outside, I ducked back into The Holler.

"Friends of yours?" my mom asked dryly.

"More or less." My reply surprised both of us. I wasn't exactly known for my habit of making bosom buddies everywhere I went.

"These friends of yours have names?" my mom asked.

"Boone," I said. "And Sadie-Grace."

"They have last names?"

My gut said that question was significantly less casual than it sounded. "Boone Mason. Sadie-Grace Waters."

My mom recognized the names. I'd known she would. If she hadn't already noticed that the picture she kept taped to the back of her dresser drawer was gone, she'd almost certainly be checking when she got home.

"Sawyer, what are you doing?"

I didn't answer, because I didn't have to.

"You're not back, are you?" my mom said quietly. "You're not planning on staying. Here. With me." She paused, then searched my hazel eyes for the answer she desperately wanted to hear. "If I told you to let this go, would you?"

No. Even now, she wasn't answering the questions I'd had my whole life. She wasn't going to—ever.

"I've never been very good at letting things go," I said.

"Sawyer?" Lily stuck her head back into the bar. My mom and I both turned to look at her, and Lily cleared her throat. "The limo's here."

My mom took the words like a slap. "It's just as well," she said, her mouth tightening. "My break's over."

I could see how this was going to pan out. I wasn't here to stay. I couldn't let this go, and she couldn't—or wouldn't—understand that.

"Mom," I said as she started to make her way to the bar.

She pressed a fleeting kiss to the top of my head. "When you come to your senses, I'll be here. Until then . . ." Her voice hardened. "Your limo and Lillian await."

CHAPTER 30

The driver dropped Boone off first. He said good night to me and Lily, and then stammered unintelligibly in the general direction of Sadie-Grace. After the car door closed behind him, I raised an eyebrow at Sadie-Grace, trying to focus on the here and now—and not my mom's parting shot.

"What?" Sadie-Grace frowned. "Do I have something on my face?"

I decided that subtle really wasn't the way to go here. "Boone likes you."

Sadie-Grace wrapped the fingers on her right hand around her left. "Boys always like me. Or at least, they *think* they like me, until I'm . . . me." She cleared her throat. "I have an unfortunate habit of breaking them."

"Breaking them?" I repeated.

"As in . . ." Sadie-Grace ducked her head. "Physically. We try to do things, and then I break them."

I turned to Lily for a translation.

"She is kind of . . . accident-prone," my cousin said delicately.

I made the executive decision that I did *not* want to ask any further questions. It was just as well, because an instant before the limo pulled away from the curb, the door opened again.

Campbell slid in. Her face was pale, and she stared straight ahead, like the rest of us weren't even there.

"Commit any major crimes lately?" I asked.

That jarred Campbell out of her uneasy reverie. She picked her team shirt up off of the limo floor, and a moment later, she was wearing it.

Like she'd been here the whole time.

Like whatever she'd been doing for the past five hours was nothing.

"I take it we had fun tonight?" she chirped.

Lily caught my eyes for the briefest moment. "You could say that." She paused. "You seemed to particularly enjoy taking the evening into our own hands, frolicking through an abandoned lot in the sticks, and belly dancing at a dilapidated rural gas station."

Campbell turned her head forty degrees to the left, poised and ready to strike. "Did I?"

I shrugged. "We may have gone off script."

Her green eyes caught the interior lights. "That wasn't the deal."

"If you don't want the footage that establishes you were a good forty-five minutes outside of town most of the evening . . ."

"No." Campbell forced a smile. "I'm sure what you have will be fine."

Lily hesitated for a second or two, then placed the camera in Campbell's open palm. The flicker of relief I saw cross the senator's daughter's face was more concerning than any threat she'd issued in the past six weeks.

"What are you going to do with it?" I asked. *All of that precious footage, Campbell's alibi for who knows what.*

"Exactly what our instructions say to do with it." Campbell

shimmied across the seat and lowered the privacy glass. "Excuse me, sir," she said, molasses-sweet. "But I think we're supposed to leave this with you."

Watching the glass go back up felt like watching a curtain fall—or a sword.

"He'll turn it in," Campbell said. "The committee will review our video, and at our event next month, the winners of the scavenger hunt will be announced."

"Aren't you forgetting something?" I prompted. *Lily's tablet. The security footage.*

"After the next event," Campbell promised. "As soon as the winners are announced, I'll give you everything I have. You won't hear a word from me about *Secrets* or anything else in the meantime."

That wasn't the deal.

Campbell's gaze was intense. "I mean it, Sawyer. I won't be a problem—for any of you—and at the masquerade next month, every trace of evidence I have is yours. You have my word."

"I, for one, find that extremely comforting," Lily murmured, soft and sarcastic at once.

Sadie-Grace's reply was somewhat less elegant. "Uhhhh . . . guys?"

I was still giving Campbell a hard look when Sadie-Grace repeated herself.

"Guys," Sadie-Grace repeated, her voice going up an octave. *"Look."*

I looked. The limo had just turned onto Camellia Court. Sadie-Grace's house was on one side of the cul-de-sac; my grandmother's was on the other, and down at the end, on the largest of the oversized lots, was the only house on the block set back from the street by a wrought-iron gate.

Tonight, that gate was open. There were police cars in the

driveway—three of them. Flashing blue and red lights drilled themselves into my brain with the strength of an ice pick—again and again and again.

Lily whipped around to look at Campbell. "That's your grandfather's house."

I searched for any hint of weakness on Campbell's face, any of the unsteadiness I'd seen when she'd climbed back into the car.

All I saw was steel.

"Oh, dear," Campbell said, the very picture of concern. "Grandfather's house. Whatever could have happened there?"

CHAPTER 31

I spent the night lying in bed, wondering what in the hell we had been a party to. Three police cars wasn't misdemeanor territory. Exactly what kind of felony—or *felonies*—had we aided and abetted Campbell in committing?

When I finally heard Lillian stirring downstairs the next morning, I took that as my cue to throw in the towel on sleep. If my grandmother had heard anything about what had happened at the Ames place, I wanted to know.

I joined her on the front porch for morning coffee. We were the only two people in this family who took ours black.

"Something happened last night." I took a long drink from my mug. "When we got home from the scavenger hunt, there were police cars at the Ames estate."

Lillian Taft was nothing if not unflappable. "I don't suppose there was an ambulance," she said.

My heart stopped. It hadn't occurred to me—not until just now—that Campbell might have hurt someone.

She didn't. She wouldn't. Would she?

"No ambulance," I said out loud.

"Pity," my grandmother commented. "A heart attack or two might improve Davis's disposition."

I choked on my coffee. "Lillian!"

"Oh, pish, Sawyer. Don't look at me like that. Before my morning coffee takes hold, I am allowed to make heart attack jokes about Davis Ames, so long as no one with manners is around to hear them."

Apparently, I didn't qualify as a person with manners. I took that as a compliment.

"What do you think happened?" I pressed my grandmother. "Three police cars. That seems like a lot."

I'd witnessed all-out bar brawls that had only merited one.

"We don't see much crime in this neighborhood." Lillian lifted her mug to her face and inhaled. "Davis would expect an immediate and impressive response. The senile old coot probably misplaced his car keys and reported them stolen."

I should have found her dismissal of the situation comforting, but I was taken off guard, because for the first time in six weeks, I felt like I was talking to Lillian Taft, Actual Person, not the family matriarch—or even my mother's mother.

"My mom called yesterday." This was not what I'd planned on saying. "She wanted to know where I was." I paused. "I went to see her."

"I can't imagine that she's happy you're here." Lillian set her coffee down. "I'm sure that in her telling of things, I'm an absolute villain who never reached out, never asked to meet you even once."

You didn't, I thought.

"Quite frankly," Lillian continued, perfectly content to carry on a one-sided conversation, "I'm appalled it's taken this long for my daughter to inquire about your whereabouts and well-being."

"Of course you are," I said. I'd chosen to come back here. That didn't mean I had to take her side against my mom's.

Lillian cut me a look. "Have I done something to upset you, Sawyer? Something other than providing you food and shelter and opportunities most young women would die for?"

I would never, in a thousand years, master that tone: the one that managed to sound mildly curious and gingerly self-deprecating and not at all critical, no matter how much criticism was being given.

"I took Lily to The Holler last night." When in doubt, go with blunt and unexpected.

"Pardon me?"

"The bar where my mom works. I took Lily there last night, and it appears as though someone is paying the owner to keep my mother employed."

Lillian resumed sipping her coffee. "Isn't that odd?"

"Lillian," I said. No response. "*Mim.*"

It was the first time I'd used Lily's name for her. My perfectly poised, perfectly formidable grandmother blinked, her eyes watering. She raised a napkin to her lips and gave herself the amount of time it took to blot to gather her composure, as effectively and mercilessly as a commanding officer gathering her troops.

"What would you like me to say, dear? That I committed the cardinal sin of watching out for my own flesh and blood? That I would have bought the entire establishment if I thought I could get away with it, just to make sure the two of you always had a home?"

You're the one who kicked her out, pregnant and scared and alone. You're the reason we were there.

"Now . . ." Lillian folded her hands in her lap. "Why don't we talk about something a little more pleasant?" Not a question, not a request. "What do *you* think brought the police to our street?"

CHAPTER 32

I decided it was in my best interest to get out of the house. I told myself I was leaving to avoid further questions, but the truth was that my conversation with Lillian—and seeing my mom the night before—had shaken me. I needed something to dig my teeth into, to puzzle over, to obsess about.

Say, for instance, whether or not the key we'd stolen from Campbell's locker fit in the senator's safe.

If Campbell kept her promise to hand over the tablet, we wouldn't need the leverage, but I wasn't feeling particularly trusting, and hanging out in the vicinity of people with the last name Ames also seemed like as good a way as any to figure out what had brought the police out the night before.

What we'd helped Campbell *do*.

There were only two people at the senator's office when I arrived—Walker and his father's assistant, a woman not much older than the two of us. *Leah*. My memory supplied the name, which turned out to be a waste, because Leah-in-the-red-heels headed out practically the moment I stepped in the door.

"Working on the weekend?" I asked Walker, resisting the urge to grill him about the police cars at his grandfather's house the night before.

"You know what they say about idle hands, Sawyer Taft. Devil's playground, et cetera, et cetera." Sensing I wasn't impressed with that explanation, Walker elaborated. "I needed to get out of the house."

I let myself wonder, just for a moment, what the Ames household was like—what growing up there had been like.

"I hear you had a scandalous night last night." Walker was smooth, but the abrupt subject change did not go unnoticed. "Campbell and I talk," he told me. For a split second, I thought his sister might have told him the truth, then he continued, "Dare I hope that the monotony of a day of envelope stuffing will be broken up with tales of your debauchery on the outskirts of civilization?"

"Classy," I told him. "I can see why you're the favorite child."

"I'm not the favorite," he said, quietly enough to tell me that he didn't really believe that.

I love my brother, Campbell's voice echoed in my head. *Everyone does. They always have.*

I wondered for a split second if that was what all of this was about—some desperate cry for attention. But I didn't stay thinking about Campbell for long. Instead, I remembered why I'd gone rogue the night before in the first place.

Walker Ames had made my cousin promises, then torn out her heart.

"Why does the look on your face make me think that you're planning my immediate demise?" Walker asked pleasantly, leaning toward me.

He'd broken Lily's heart, and now he was flirting with me. "I don't know," I returned. "Maybe you're not as stupid as you look."

• • •

Walker Ames and I spent the next two hours stuffing envelopes. I bided my time until he took it upon himself to make a coffee run, then headed straight for the senator's office. I didn't anticipate any problems breaking in.

If Sterling Ames didn't want people picking the lock, he shouldn't have opted for a lever-handle lock. And if he had . . .

He should have gone with one with a clutch, I thought as the lock gave way. Unsure how much time I had, I took one glance over my shoulder, then went for the safe.

The key didn't fit.

"I got you a coffee," a voice said behind me.

I turned to face the door to the office, pocketing the key.

"Black," Walker continued. "Like my soul."

If he wasn't going to ask what I was doing in here, I wasn't going to volunteer the information. Instead, I crossed the room and plucked the coffee from his hands. The name that Walker had given the barista to scrawl on the side was *Walker-Immune*.

I almost laughed at that one.

"You don't like me." Walker seemed to find that strangely satisfying.

"I'd classify my feelings more as apathetic," I said.

"You can't be apathetic," the senator's son replied immediately. "That's my thing."

Once upon a time, Walker Ames had been his parents' golden boy, the type to take his girlfriend on romantic dates, to make promises and give rings.

"So, what is this?" I asked, for Lily's benefit as much as to prevent Walker from working his way up to asking why I was in his father's office. "Pointless rebellion? Quarter-life crisis?"

Based on the expression on his face, I inferred that people usually took Walker's fall from grace a little more seriously.

"Quarter-life crisis?" he repeated. "I'm not that old."

I cocked an eyebrow at him. "Planning to live past seventy-six?"

He let out a snort. "As much as I'd like to go for *Live fast, die young,* we Ames men do tend to be long-lived."

"Speaking of long-lived Ames men . . ." I walked past him, leading the way out of the senator's office. "Is your grandfather okay? We saw all of the police cars at his place last night."

Walker closed the door behind us. "My grandfather will outlive us all and lecture our graves about how disappointed he is in our lack of grit."

Given the one time I'd met Davis Ames, that was actually fairly easy to imagine.

"There was a break-in," Walker continued. "But the old man wasn't home at the time. Someone tripped the alarm and broke into his safe."

My breath caught in my throat, and my hand found its way to my pocket, to the key—the copy I'd made before returning the original to Campbell.

"You okay?" Walker asked me. "You haven't insulted me in at least three minutes."

Someone broke into your grandfather's safe.

"I'm sorry to hear about the break-in," I said, trying to mask the way my mind was reeling. "And also: I think you're an idiot of colossal proportions for dumping Lily, and you have a very smug face."

"Thank you," Walker replied graciously. "But I can assure you that Lily is better off without me. And you don't need to worry about my grandfather. He has insurance."

"Oh, yeah?" I said, trying to sound casual. "What was stolen?"

Walker must have heard a little too much interest in my voice, because he smirked. "Say thank you for the coffee, and I'll tell you."

If I gave in too easily, he might start questioning why I wanted to know.

"I would," I replied, "but apathy is kind of my thing."

He looked at me. "Maybe," he said, his tone as offhanded as his expression was intense, "not caring is just what ordinary people see when they can't process what it looks like when someone cares too damn much."

I thanked him for the coffee.

"You're welcome, Sawyer Taft—and since a gentleman always keeps his word, I'll let you in on a little secret: There was only one thing taken from my grandfather's safe last night. *Your* grandmother's pearls."

APRIL 15, 5:50 P.M.

Mackie had known that this situation could be sticky. The girls were *wearing gloves.* But he could handle this.

"I hate to break it to you," the boy, who sounded like he was *enjoying* breaking it to Mackie, said, "but if you have Sawyer Taft back there, and she's not alone . . ."

He gave a brief shake of his head.

Mackie did not like the look of that head shake. "State your name and your business here." He would *not* lose the upper hand.

The boy did not state his name. The boy did not state his business. Instead, he leaned forward. "There's four of them, aren't there?"

Mackie didn't answer. He refused to answer. "There might be four of them."

"In that case," the boy said, "you've locked up *both* of Lillian Taft's granddaughters. Also: a senator's daughter and the beloved only child of the wealthiest man in the state."

Mackie was going to kill O'Connell and Rodriguez.

The boy shook his head again. "Bless your heart."

SIX MONTHS EARLIER

CHAPTER 33

"She stole Mim's pearls." Lily furiously sewed a white feather boa onto the bodice of a strapless dress. "*Campbell. Ames. Stole. Mim's. Pearls.*"

That had been Lily's mantra for the last month.

She'd said it the day Aunt Olivia had heard about the theft and gone into a forty-eight-hour frenzy of pissed-off baking that culminated in a fit-to-be-tied pie she'd delivered to Davis Ames herself.

She'd said it the night after the police had come to interview Lillian about the pearls—and left with a dozen of Aunt Olivia's indignantly delicious brownies apiece.

Lily had repeated that mantra every day after school when Campbell had kept her word again and again to stop playing power games, proving, at least in my mind, that neither petty revenge nor messing with Lily had ever been her real goal.

And now Lily was issuing the complaint apropos of nothing at all.

"Technically," I told my cousin, knowing I was poking a bear, but unable to help myself, "the pearls weren't Mim's when Campbell took them."

Lily looked up from the dress in her hands. "Do you want to sew your own costume?" she demanded.

"That's *my* costume?" I asked.

"Of course it's yours," Lily replied with exaggerated patience. "I'm going in Renaissance garb."

I looked at the glittery mound of fabric in her hands. The beading was so intricate—and so dense—that a person practically needed sunglasses to stare directly at it. "And I'm going as . . . ?"

Lily finished sewing the feathers into place. "An angel." As if that fact were obvious.

"An angel," I repeated. "Have you met me?"

"You, as in the girl who threw herself into the line of fire on my behalf after having known me less than a day?" Lily asked innocently. "Or the one who spends hours discussing zombie-related military tactics with my younger brother?" She paused. "Or maybe the one who can't even let herself be angry that her mother's a piece of work who's been refusing her calls all month?"

Ouch. Lily usually didn't go quite so clearly for the jugular.

"I don't want to talk about my mom."

Lily shook the dress out and laid it on the bed. "All I'm saying is that I'm fairly certain you've earned your wings."

Yeah, I thought, *setting aside the various crimes I've been an accessory to in recent months, I'm a regular Mother Teresa.* Knowing that argument wouldn't persuade Lily, I fell back on a different line of reasoning.

"I went barefoot at Pearls of Wisdom," I reminded her. *The horror.* "And I dared John David to lick that ice sculpture last week at brunch."

Lily gasped. "That was you?"

I shrugged. "Still think I'm halo-ready?"

Lily Taft Easterling was not the type to admit defeat. "I think," she said pointedly, "that Mama's going to want to sign off on both of our costumes, and there is no way she will let you walk out of this house wearing one that consists only of a clever pun written on a piece of cardboard that you wear around your neck."

That was accurate, both with respect to the level of planning I generally put into my Halloween costume and in terms of Aunt Olivia's likely response. Since our unauthorized trip to my old stomping grounds, Lily's mother had been keeping a closer eye on us, like she thought that next time, I might drag her daughter off to perdition itself.

I suspected that had less to do with where we'd gone than the person Lily had met there.

"Fine," I capitulated, knowing that any attempt at resistance would be about as effective as spitting into the wind. "I'm going to the Symphony Ball Masquerade as an angel. I'm sure it will be *lovely*."

"It will be," Lily promised—or possibly commanded. She managed not to say anything else for all of four seconds, during which she produced a delicate pair of wings and a white-feathered masquerade mask.

And then she hit her limit and burst out, "I cannot believe that *witch* stole Mim's pearls."

Lily's words proved oddly prophetic. That night—the night that Campbell had promised she would surrender Lily's tablet and the security footage—the senator's daughter showed up dressed like a witch.

Her ball gown was black, made of a fabric that shimmered when she moved. The skirt was full, but the bodice was tight, and the threadwork—in a fine, hand-stitched silver—looked like a spider's artfully spun web. Her mask was plain black and covered only half of her face. The other half was made up to the nines, her eyes accented by tiny black and white jewels, affixed to her face and arranged in elaborate swirls.

"It was nice of my grandfather to offer to host tonight," Campbell commented when I cornered her. "Wasn't it?"

Living with Aunt Olivia meant that I heard far more Symphony Ball gossip than I cared to, so I had pretty much gotten a play-by-play on the *travesty* that was Northern Ridge double-booking tonight's event with a member wedding. From what Sadie-Grace had said, her stepmother had tried everything short of ritual sacrifice to come out on top of that fight, but ultimately, the wedding had prevailed, and the masquerade had been ousted.

It had the makings of a tragedy, or what passed for one in Deb World, until Davis Ames had stepped up. He'd voluntarily opened his home to this evening's event, bringing Campbell—not to mention Lily, Sadie-Grace, Boone, and me—right to the scene of the crime.

I wonder where he keeps the safe.

My gaze went to the necklace Campbell was wearing tonight: a single blood-red teardrop—doubtlessly, a ruby—that hung from her neck, a visceral reminder that Campbell Ames had no need of stolen jewels. Whatever game she was playing, I deeply suspected it had less to do with the monetary value of the pearls than Ames family dynamics.

And I deeply did not care.

"You promised," I started to say, but Campbell looped her arm through mine and cut me off.

"Tonight," she pledged, walking me toward a cupcake station that had been set up on the far side of the room. "As soon as the scavenger hunt winners are announced and I have what I need, I'll give you what I promised."

What you need? That was ominous.

"I may be Lucifer," Campbell continued, "but I keep my word. Cupcake?"

I almost turned her down, but it was chocolate. As I did my best not to stain my costume and earn the wrath of Lily, I found myself scanning the room for my cousin. She'd agreed to let me handle Campbell, but under a nearby archway, she and Sadie-Grace kept shooting nervous looks in our direction.

To my surprise, when I turned back to Campbell, I caught her shooting a similar look at the person tending bar opposite the cupcake station.

Nick.

I'd seen him in the past months, parking cars at Sunday brunch, but he hadn't said a word to me. After a moment's hesitation, Campbell tossed her red hair over her shoulder and made her way to the bar. I followed.

"I don't suppose I could talk you into trading mocktails for cocktails, if I provide the *oomph*?" Campbell asked Nick.

"No *oomph*." Nick was calm, cool, professional. "And," he said, lowering his voice, "no interest."

I expected Campbell to lash back at him, but she didn't. Instead, she plucked a toothpick off the bar and speared a cherry out of a nearby bowl. "You aren't still mad about last month, are you?"

"Of course not." Nick used the exact same tone I'd heard him implementing with Walker in the alleyway weeks earlier. "I'm just not masochistic enough to let you stand me up twice." Without another word to her, Nick turned to me. "Good or evil?" he asked.

It took me a second to realize he was referring to the drinks he'd been mixing. The crystal martini glass on the left held a white liquid; the one on the right was red.

I glanced down at my dress: blindingly white, a perfect match for the feathers on my mask, not to mention the delicate wings at my back.

"Give me the red one," I said.

Nick managed a very—*very*—small smile.

"I'm sorry," Campbell told him suddenly. If I hadn't known better, I would have thought I'd heard a note of genuine remorse in her voice.

"You're not sorry," Nick corrected. "You're bored."

"And you're, what?" Campbell retorted. "My hobby?"

Nick shrugged. Clearly, when it came to his relationship with the senator's daughter, he'd never deluded himself into thinking he was more than a slightly forbidden, well-muscled distraction.

"I *am* sorry," Campbell said quietly, "that this is the way it had to be." Without waiting for a reply, she grabbed a white drink for herself and turned to wave someone over. "Boone!"

As Campbell's cousin scurried over, I took in the outfit he'd chosen for this evening: a bright purple tuxedo. With matching bow tie.

"What are you supposed to be?" I asked him.

"This is my offended face," Boone replied, pointing to the scowl on his lips.

"You're not wearing a mask," I observed.

"And cover my offended face?"

"Boone, be a darling and keep Sawyer entertained for me, would you?" Campbell didn't wait for a response before she turned to leave. I sidestepped, blocking her path.

"Where are you going?"

"I'll be back," she said. "And then you'll get what you want. Scout's honor." She pushed her cousin toward me. "Dance with Sawyer."

"I don't dance," I said flatly at the exact second that he executed an elaborate bow and held out his hand for mine. "Milady?"

CHAPTER 34

As Boone led me to the dance floor, I lost track of Campbell in the crowd. Davis Ames's house looked more like a museum than a home. The ground floor had an open plan and the tallest ceilings I'd ever seen. The wood floors were dark, polished to the point that they were nearly reflective.

I suddenly had a very uneasy feeling about the fact that Campbell had slipped from view.

"I got you a present." Boone began to lead me in what I guessed was suposed to be a waltz.

"A present," I repeated.

He nodded, and then he lifted his right hand off of mine and reached forward. For one horrific moment, I thought he was going to gingerly touch the side of my face, but instead, he pinched a piece of my hair between his thumb and his forefinger and yanked.

"Ow!" He was lucky we were in plain view of at least five chaperones, including my grandmother, or I would have drilled my fist into his stomach. "Your definition of a *present* leaves something to be desired."

"There's a plastic baggie in my left inside pocket," he told me. "If you pull it out, we can bag the hair."

I did as he asked, careful to mask the action as best I could. The waltz carried on.

"Your present," Boone declared, "is a mail-in paternity test. I bought you a half dozen of them. The results take forever to come back, but I've already obtained a sample of my dad's hair." He tucked the baggie with my hair in it back into his tuxedo lapel. "We can send my dad's test off tonight."

Given the obviousness of Boone's suggestion, I had to question why I hadn't thought of it first. The only progress I'd made on my search for my father in the past month involved using the internet to glean everything I could about the four men on my list.

Deep down, I had to wonder how much of what had been holding me back was my mom. She didn't want me here. She didn't want me knowing the truth.

"I am," Boone confided, "upon occasion, just south of brilliant. And I wouldn't mind having a sister." Then, because the moment was a little too serious, a little too sweet, he added, "But my mom would be a real bitch of a stepmother."

Hearing any version of the phrase *bitch stepmother* had my gaze going automatically to Greer Waters. I was guessing she wouldn't welcome any inquiries into whether or not her newly acquired husband had fathered an illegitimate child way back when.

"I know what you're thinking," Boone declared. He spun me in a circle. "How are you going to get genetic material on the other Who's-Your-Daddy candidates?"

I was still volunteering at the senator's office. The renovation on Aunt Olivia and Uncle J.D.'s house showed no signs of ending, so we were still living under the same roof, and if I asked Sadie-Grace to show me her parents' bathroom, she'd beam at me without asking too many questions about why I was rifling through her father's hairbrush.

"Getting the samples is doable," I told Boone.

As our dance came to its end, I caught sight of an Audrey Hepburn out of the corner of my eye: Sadie-Grace. As my good deed for the day, I used the last chords of the waltz to steer Boone toward her. A new song began, and I passed Boone off.

Neither one of them seemed to register the fact that they were dancing with each other until they were several feet away.

"Sawyer." My grandmother pulled me discreetly to the side of the room. She wasn't dressed in costume, unless *stately and fashionable* was a costume. She spoke in an understated murmur that I had to strain to hear. "Would you like to guess what the ever-enthusiastic Greer Waters has been impressing upon me in the last few minutes?"

My mind was still on the hair in the envelope I'd left with Boone—and the other paternity tests he'd promised me.

"Apparently, your scavenger hunt tape caused *quite* the stir." My grandmother's expression was pleasant, but we were in public. If there was one inviolable societal law in Lillian Taft's circle, it was that one was *always* pleasant in public.

"Some people get stirred up too easily," I said.

"There was some talk about whether or not what you five did was dangerous."

Five, I thought. *As in the four of us,* plus *Campbell.* She had her alibi now—ironclad and, thanks to my deviation from the plan, spreading through the gossip tree like wildfire.

"When rich people say *danger,*" I told my grandmother, "they just mean *poor.*"

I'd broken two cardinal rules: I wasn't smiling, and I was talking about money.

"Sawyer, you and your mother were never *poor.*"

I had no idea what to make of that sentence or the tone with which Lillian had said it, but I also didn't have time to wonder, because a moment later, Davis Ames descended the staircase, and my grandmother's attention shifted fully to him.

He wasn't in costume. He wasn't wearing a mask. Campbell was by his side. Had she gone to fetch him? Why?

"I understand that there are prizes of some sort to be distributed," he said, in a voice that carried with no need of artificial amplification. "For tonight's costume contest *and* a rather legendary scavenger hunt."

This was what we'd been waiting for. What Campbell had been waiting for. I still wasn't clear on why *this* was the turning point for her. Was she just biding her time until word of "our" hijinks on scavenger hunt night had spread far and wide, to solidify her alibi?

Or was she up to something?

I barely paid attention to the names that were called as the prizes were announced. Ours were, obviously, not among them—not for last month's event and not for tonight. It went without saying that behavior such as ours was not to be rewarded.

Actually, it didn't, because Greer had *literally* said as much to Sadie-Grace the week before.

I didn't care about the prizes, or whatever subtle disgrace came our way. All I cared about was getting that tablet from Campbell and putting this whole thing to rest.

Once I did, Project Paternity Test could begin.

A smattering of applause marked the final prize. In the lull that followed, the doorbell rang, which seemed odd, because Mr. Ames had brought in a valet company to park the cars out front, and one of the valets had been tending the door when I'd arrived.

As I watched, Campbell's grandfather excused himself. Campbell followed, and I trailed her and snagged her by the arm.

"The tablet," I insisted.

"It's upstairs," Campbell said, her voice surprisingly thin, almost reedy. "If you take the back staircase from the kitchen, no one will see you. First bedroom on your left. I left the tablet on the desk."

This didn't feel right. Something was off, and I didn't like that I couldn't pinpoint what that something was. I pushed back through the crowd, to the kitchen, and up the stairs, waiting for the other shoe to fall.

It didn't.

The tablet was exactly where Campbell had said it would be. I turned it on. The security footage was there. I deleted it, then checked the sent mail to verify that no files had been emailed out. Finally, I pulled up the photo reel and began scrolling.

It didn't look like Campbell had deleted or modified a single picture.

As I came to the last two photos, I stopped. One contained a naked girl, curled into a ball, her arms wrapped around her knees, her chest and privates obscured. The other was a screencap of the *Secrets* blog, taken only minutes before.

What did Campbell do? My mouth went dry, and I pulled up the site. There was, indeed, a new post—the second-to-last picture from the reel. I took in the details: the lighting, the angle, the careful handwriting in which a single sentence had been scripted onto the model's naked back.

He made me hurt you.

Slowly, I processed the obvious: the picture was black and white, so the model's hair color wasn't visible, but neither the length nor the texture fit Lily's, and there was a birthmark of some kind, barely visible at the very bottom of the frame.

This isn't Lily.

“Campbell.” I couldn’t believe that she’d *given* us this. Even if Campbell had kept copies of Lily’s pictures, Lily now had the exact same thing on her.

Why would she do that? The gesture stuck with me like food between my teeth. We hadn’t asked Campbell for this. Why would she make us wait an entire month and then give us more than we’d bargained for?

Unsettled, I walked back toward the main stairs. I paused at the top of the spiral staircase, aware that I probably should have snuck down the way I’d come, but not caring overly much. There was a bay window to my right, facing out the front of the house.

Outside, I caught sight of Davis Ames, Campbell, and a police car.

As soon as the scavenger hunt winners are announced and I have what I need, Campbell had told me, *I’ll give you what I promised.*

Tearing my eyes from the police car, I made my way back toward the kitchen stairs. If I could get through the party without drawing attention, I could figure out why the police were here.

What Campbell was telling them.

What I was missing.

But when I got to the kitchen, the police were already there. There were two officers, and they had one person between them—a boy, cuffed, being read his rights.

Nick.

CHAPTER 35

Somehow, the police—and Davis Ames—managed to keep the arrest quiet. The officers took Nick out the back, and the party wore on. I tried to object, tried to ask what was going on, but neither the police nor Campbell's grandfather paid attention to the girl in the beaded ball gown.

What just happened? My mind was a mess of memories—images and phrases and moments that hadn't meant anything to me at the time.

You're not still mad about last month, are you? Campbell had asked.

Of course not, Nick had replied stiffly. *I'm just not masochistic enough to let you stand me up twice.*

Campbell had stood Nick up. *Last month.* What were the chances she'd been referring to a very specific evening? One where a set of legendary pearls had gone missing? Had Campbell promised to meet him somewhere? After ensuring her own alibi, had she made sure that he wouldn't have one?

That seemed beyond cold, beyond heartless—even for her. I was probably being paranoid, seeing connections where there were none. I had no way of knowing what Nick had been arrested for. I had no reason to think that it had anything to do with the pearls.

And yet . . .

I am sorry, Campbell had told him, *that this is the way it had to be.*

The senator's daughter had held on to her leverage over us for the past month—long enough for her alibi to become rock solid, long enough to ensure that none of us were going to the police. Why had she insisted on ending the game *tonight*?

What had she been planning?

I told myself to stop. I told myself—again—that I had no idea *what* Nick had been arrested for, or why Campbell and her grandfather had been outside talking to the police.

The authorities must have evidence. No matter what Campbell did or did not tell them, no matter what Nick was arrested for—they don't just barge into fancy parties and slap cuffs on people out of nowhere.

My thoughts flicked to the stolen key that Campbell had insisted I return. Was it the key to her grandfather's safe? And if it was, what had she done with it once she'd stolen the pearls?

Stop. I forced myself to slow down. But as I pushed my way through angels and devils, princesses and knights, all I could think of was Campbell's entry on *Secrets on My Skin.*

He made me hurt you.

That night, I stood in front of my vanity scrubbing viciously at the makeup on my face.

"Sawyer."

I'd caught Lily up on what had happened. *Nick was arrested. Campbell might have had something to do with it.*

"Sawyer," Lily said again. She caught my wrists. "You're going to take the skin right off your face."

"So?"

She nudged me toward the edge of my bathtub, pushing me to a sitting position. "Stay." She removed the cloth from my hand and went back to the sink. When she returned, there was a container of makeup remover in her hand.

My cousin didn't say anything as she swabbed a damp cotton ball gently over my eyes, my cheeks.

This is our fault. If what happened tonight has anything to do with the pearls—it's our fault.

I'd known better than to trust Campbell. I'd known that something was off.

"We'll figure out what happened," Lily said softly. My eyes were still closed. She was still removing mascara. "No matter how quietly the arrest was handled, word will get out. People will talk—at the club, at school. We'll corner Campbell. We'll figure this out, Sawyer."

The problem was that every instinct I had—every probability I'd learned growing up bar-adjacent, the sixth sense that let me keep an eye out for trouble customers at Big Jim's—said that figuring this out wouldn't solve the problem.

At most, *figuring it out* would confirm what the problem was.

"What if she framed him?" I asked. "What if Campbell Ames framed that poor guy for stealing the pearls, and we helped?"

Was it too late to go to the cops? We could tell them that we'd falsified Campbell's alibi, claim that we'd thought she wanted to sneak off for run-of-the-mill teenage hijinks, not to commit a major crime.

Then why, I could hear someone asking, *didn't you come clean when the pearls went missing?*

"I have something that might cheer you up." Lily ducked into the bedroom and came back up with a gift bag: black, with glittery orange tissue paper. "You forgot your favor from tonight's event."

If Lily thought a Symphony Ball keepsake could put a dent in my current mood, she had mistaken me for someone with no conscience and a fondness for the saccharine and overpriced.

"Just open it," Lily prodded. She was using her *I am the granddaughter of Lillian Taft* voice, genteel and bossy in equal parts.

Shooting her a dark look, I tossed the tissue paper aside a little harder than necessary. Sitting at the bottom of the bag, in a clear plastic case with the words *Symphony Ball* engraved on it, was a USB drive.

"The scavenger hunt footage," Lily told me. "I understand there was some debate about what to do with ours, but ultimately, it was decided that the best tack to take was ignoring our little side trip. A professional videographer put together a highlight video of each group—and one of the whole event. Plus, we each get a copy of our own raw footage."

Footage of us at the lot, the library, The Holler.

"Why would this cheer me up?" I asked Lily. This was Campbell's alibi. The alibi we had given her, even after we knew what she'd done with it.

"Sawyer Ann Taft." Lily pulled herself up to an impressive height. "Do you think that you're the only one whose stomach is twisted up in veritable knots of dread right now? The only reason we're in this mess is because you stuck up for *me*. Sadie-Grace did the same. I am, by all views and possible accounts, the common denominator here, but am I moping?" In that moment, she was a dead ringer for her mother. "No. No, I am not. I will cross the moping bridge when I come to it, once we know exactly what happened tonight and not before. And this?" Lily held up the USB drive. "This should interest you."

I could not, for the life of me, see a lick of sense in that declaration.

"Why?" I said.

Lily gave me a look that strongly implied that I was being either very stubborn or very dumb. "Why did you come here?" she prodded.

"Because our grandmother offered me half a million dollars."

Lily didn't so much as blink at that assertion. "What are you looking for?" she elaborated. "Or, to be more precise: *Who*?"

In the entire time I'd been living here, I hadn't said a word to Lily about the fact that I was searching for my biological father. I had a lot of free time while she was at school. I thought I'd done at least a passable job of keeping my intentions a secret.

"Oh, please, Sawyer." Lily waved a dismissive hand in my general direction. "I am perfectly capable of putting two and two together. Your mama left in disgrace in the middle of her Debutante year. You're either here to redeem her . . ."

I snorted.

"Or you're here to find out who she was . . . *close* to . . . before she left."

Lily Taft Easterling did not use phrases like *knocked up*. *Producer of sperm* and *bastard child* were also out.

"You knew?" I asked.

"Have you ever been under the impression that you were subtle?" Lily didn't wait for an answer. "You should have learned by now that Symphony Ball is all about tradition. If *we* had a video scavenger hunt, you can bet your mother's year did as well, and if *we* were given copies of our videos . . ." She trailed off meaningfully.

Operation Paternity Test was already under way. Assuming my father was indeed one of the four faces my mother had scratched out of that photograph, I would get my answer eventually.

But *eventually* wasn't *now*.

Eventually wouldn't get me to morning and answers about Nick's arrest.

"This would be an appropriate time to ask me if I know where Mim keeps your mama's old things," Lily prompted.

I looked down at the USB drive. It was late. There was nothing I could do about Campbell or Nick right now.

But *this*, I could do. "Where does Mim keep my mother's old things?"

Lily gathered the used cotton balls, dumped them in the trash, then pivoted toward the doorway. "The attic."

CHAPTER 36

I shouldn't have been surprised that Lillian Taft's attic was insulated, air-conditioned, and neat as a pin. It ran the entire length of the house, a third floor that was only accessible through a staircase tucked away behind a door that I'd assumed led to yet another linen closet.

This definitely wasn't a closet.

"Mim isn't what one would call organized," Lily said, staring over the sea of boxes laid out in a labyrinth that criss-crossed the room. "Luckily, however, my mother *is*, and she got it in her head to organize Mim's attic a few summers back. I don't know where your mama's things are, but it's a good bet that they're all together."

It took a half hour for me to find a framed portrait, quite possibly the one that had once hung downstairs: Eleanor Elisabeth Taft, in all her debutante finery. I'd never thought that my mom and I looked alike, but at seventeen, she'd been freckled and slight, with hair several shades darker than mine and eyes at least two sizes too big for her face. There was something about the set of her lips and the tilt of her chin that was utterly familiar.

As Aunt Olivia had once pointed out, we had the same cheekbones.

The portrait hit me harder than I expected. *The white gloves. The up-do. The bouquet of white roses in her lap.* This girl? She didn't look anything like my mother. She looked . . .

"Hollow," I said out loud.

Lily popped up from behind a trio of wardrobe boxes several feet away. "Did you find something?"

I held up the portrait. "One daughter, banished to the attic in disgrace."

Lily stared at the portrait for almost as long as I had. I wondered if she was thinking about *Secrets* and how close she'd come to disgrace of her own.

"Well, don't just stand there like a bump on a log," she ordered, recovering. "Get started on those boxes."

There were easily two dozen boxes behind the portrait, stacked in columns of three, all the way back to the wall. Each one had been marked in the upper right corner in thick black marker: *E.T.*

Eleanor Taft.

The contents of the boxes were meticulously organized: elementary school projects and dolls that my mother had outgrown, photograph albums of two little girls at a lake, year after year. I found an entire series of boxes dedicated to my mother's old dance costumes.

I hadn't even known she'd taken ballet.

Near the back, I finally hit pay dirt: three boxes marked *E.T.—S.B.*

As in: Symphony Ball.

I wondered briefly at the fact that Aunt Olivia had only one box at her house dedicated to Debutante keepsakes, but that my grandmother had somehow kept every party favor, every invitation, every notecard of my mother's. There was a decorative pillow hand-stitched with the words *Symphony Deb;* a program from my mother's Pearls of Wisdom listing the items in the silent auction. There were a pair of white slippers and a pair of white heels and a small ring box—empty. What looked to be a vintage purse contained only two items: the stub of a movie ticket and a small, braided bit of ribbon.

I held the ribbon in my hand for a moment. *Three strands of white, woven together.* After a moment, I returned the contents to the purse and set it aside.

The last item in the last box sucked me in like a black hole. The memory book had obviously been put together by the Symphony Ball Committee to mark the season. The cover was made of a matte black fabric, crinkled and ridged in a way that made me think of a formal dress. There was a small square cut out of the middle of the cover, and inside, there was a picture of a single red rose.

Lily slid in beside me. The two of us sat cross-legged with our knees touching as I paged through the book, sheet by sheet. I'd never been the slumber-party, confiding-in-other-girls type. Having Lily here with me should have felt invasive, but it didn't.

Unlike Aunt Olivia's album, the one between us on the floor didn't include loose pictures. Instead, the photographs had been scanned and printed, like a yearbook—if that yearbook was printed on paper thick enough that each page could have practically stood on its own.

The book was divided up by events. *Pearls of Wisdom. The pool party. The scavenger hunt. The Halloween masquerade* . . . Lily was right. Everything we'd done, my mother had done, too. I wasn't even halfway through the book when I started turning back, scanning each individual picture in detail, looking for my mom.

There she was at the masquerade, dressed, the caption informed me, as Juliet from *Romeo and Juliet*. Her mask was a deep rose pink, accented in golden thread and beads. She wasn't alone in the picture—there was a boy beside her. It took me a moment to recognize him, beneath the mask.

Lucas Ames.

I paged back further, to the scavenger hunt, and was rewarded with a whole page of pictures of each team. My mom's had consisted of two boys and three girls. I recognized Lucas again, but barely registered his presence or that of the other boy, because almost all of the photographs were of the three girls.

Three girls, with their arms thrown around each other.

Three girls, posing ridiculously for the camera.

Three girls, pressing exaggerated kisses to each other's cheeks.

They'd done their hair in matching styles: French braids, tied to one side. Woven through each of their braids, there was a white ribbon. It stood out, stark against my mother's dark hair. One of the other girls was blond, and the third—the third, I recognized.

Her hair was red.

"That's Sadie-Grace's stepmother," Lily realized. "It looks like she and your mother were—"

"Not just passing acquaintances?" I suggested. I checked the box for video footage of the hunt and came up empty, so I flipped back further in the book and found more shots of the three girls, almost always together, always a unit, always wearing a white ribbon somewhere on their bodies. There they were at the pool party, legs dangling into the water. At Pearls of Wisdom, they stood side by side behind the stage, proudly displaying their pearls and waiting to go forth.

I flipped forward, past the masquerade. I only found one more picture of the three girls, taken at Christmastime, in front of a two-story-tall tree. They were wearing white scarves and white hats.

They weren't laughing.

I looked down at the caption—*Ellie, Greer, Ana.* I flipped past Christmas, to New Year's, Casino Night, a spa day, something called a "glove luncheon," the Symphony Ball itself.

There were no more pictures of my mother.

No more pictures of Ana.

Greer was suddenly surrounded by other girls. Other *boys.* I paused near the end of the memory book on a photograph of Greer being escorted down an elevated platform. Her father—or a man I assumed was her father—was waiting for her at the end, his arm outheld. Greer had a bouquet of white roses in one arm and the other was tucked through the arm of her escort.

Greer Richards, daughter of Edmond and Sarah Richards, I read the caption, *escorted by Lucas Ames.*

"Sawyer." Lily's voice snapped me back to the present. I looked up from the photographs.

"What?" I said. It didn't take a genius to figure out why my mother had disappeared from the pictures. At some point between Christmas and New Year's, she'd told her family that she was pregnant.

She'd been on the street by New Year's Day.

"Sawyer," Lily said again. "Your phone."

It was ringing. I pushed aside the question on the surface of my mind—*What happened to the other girl? To Ana?*—and looked down at the screen. Suddenly my mom's Debutante year didn't seem quite so pressing.

The name on caller ID, programmed in during the month I'd spent at her beck and call, was *Campbell.*

APRIL 15, 5:55 P.M.

Mackie was fairly certain that it wasn't protocol to allow perps in the holding area to have visitors, but it also wasn't protocol to have no idea whatsoever why you were holding said perps or what they had been arrested for doing, nor was it protocol for Rodriguez and O'Connell to have abandoned him to their mercies.

"Girls." Mackie kept his voice low and even. Best not to show fear. "You have a visitor."

"Is it perhaps a lawyer?" the prim and proper one asked.

"We've been thinking of lawyering up," the drop-dead gorgeous one added, tugging nervously at the tips of her white gloves.

Mackie thought about the kind of lawyer that these girls would have and shuddered. He aimed his next words to the lock picker. To the granddaughter of *Lillian Taft*.

"I thought you said that if anyone found out you were arrested, you'd be out five hundred thousand dollars." That was a pretty good shot, if Mackie did say so himself.

Before Miss Taft could reply to the zinger, however, her visitor stepped around the corner.

"I told you to wait," Mackie said, shooting the boy an aggrieved look.

The boy ignored him. "Half a million?" he said, his voice dry and barbed. "Is that the going rate for selling your soul these days?"

For the first time since Mackie had met the girls, all four of them fell silent. The boy didn't seem any more inclined to speak. He just stared at them, his expression impossible for Mackie to read.

I am not sure, Mackie thought suddenly, *that he is their friend.*

The flirt—the troublemaker, the one that Mackie just *knew* had to be the senator's daughter—recovered her voice first. It came out in a whisper. "Nick."

FIVE MONTHS EARLIER

CHAPTER 37

"Stand up straight, Sawyer." Aunt Olivia wasn't even looking at me. She was looking at the sketch in her hand: a detailed drawing of the design the committee had, after much length, selected for this year's Symphony Deb gown.

As I'd been led to understand, the selection process had gotten downright near bloody. Somehow, I wasn't surprised that Aunt Olivia had come out on top. I could make out the soft, satisfied curve of her lips as she studied the design.

"Face forward." This time, the order came from the tailor, who squeezed my chin between delicate fingers and forcibly moved my skull to the correct angle. I stared at myself in the mirror. I was wearing nothing but my underwear and bra. The seamstress looped her measuring tape around my boobs. The sound she made as she wrote down the number was unmistakably a sound of judgment. "We'll build in cups," she offered delicately.

"I should think so," Aunt Olivia replied.

"You have such a tiny waist," Lily told me soothingly.

There was nothing like starting the day off with a three-way conversation about the size of my boobs where no one actually *mentioned* my chest, but it was strongly implied that one needed a microscope to see it. It could have been worse—Lily's fitting had included some murmurings about where the dress could be let out and taken in, to create the desired silhouette.

And, it was strongly implied, to camouflage Lily's butt.

This is hell, I thought. *I have died, I am in Dante's inferno, and I deserve to be here.* This time, as I caught my reflection in the mirror, I acknowledged how hard it was to recognize the girl who stood there. Months of using conditioner that cost more per ounce than most gourmet chocolates had given my hair the kind of body and softness that could only be bought. My natural highlights *weren't* natural anymore, and somehow, my skin looked like I was wearing makeup, even though I decidedly was not.

That was just the tip of the iceberg.

The Sawyer Taft I'd been four months ago wouldn't have left Nick's fate in the hands of the girl who'd gotten him arrested.

"Sawyer?" Aunt Olivia prodded.

I snapped back to the present. "Yeah?"

My aunt winced at the fact that after lo, these many months, I still couldn't manage a *yes*, let alone a *yes, ma'am*. "Perhaps," Aunt Olivia suggested diplomatically, "you could put on some clothes."

Apparently, the tailor had finished getting the measurements she needed.

Apparently, that wasn't a particularly recent development.

Apparently, I'd been standing there in my undergarments for a while.

Only about a third as embarrassed as I should have been, I ducked back into the dressing room. As I closed the door and picked up my jeans, I found myself doing something I'd done a thousand times or more in the past month: I replayed the phone conversation I'd had with Campbell the night of the masquerade.

"I need you to do something for me."

That had been all the greeting she'd given me; the Campbell Ames version of *hello.*

"What happened tonight?" I had asked.

There had been silence on the end of the phone. I could still remember meeting Lily's eyes as I'd pressed further.

"Campbell, tell me that Nick getting arrested had nothing to do with those stupid pearls."

Campbell decidedly had not told me that. *"They can only hold him for the theft for forty-eight hours without charging him,"* she'd said instead. *"And I can guarantee you that no one is going to charge Nick with anything. They needed to arrest him. That's all."*

"They needed to arrest him," I had repeated, *"or* you *needed him arrested to ensure that none of this blows back on you?"*

"Does it matter? Either way, there won't be any charges."

"They're not going to charge him," I'd confirmed through gritted teeth, *"because I'm going to the police in the morning. I'm going to tell them the truth."*

"The truth?" The tone in her voice had been maddening and arch.

"I'll tell them that you're the one who stole the pearls," I'd threatened.

"I hope you have some evidence to back that up."

"I can revoke your alibi."

"After a month? One during which no one even asked me for my alibi, because I've never been a suspect?"

"The key," I'd said abruptly. *"The one we found in your locker."*

"The one you stole, you mean? I suppose if you didn't *want to admit to a crime, you could always tell the police that you just saw me with a key at some point. But how exactly is that incriminating?"*

"You stole those pearls."

"Why?" Campbell had asked mildly. *"What's my motive? I don't need the money, and they're not* my *family's heirlooms."*

They were mine.

"Nick will be out by Monday, Sawyer. I'll make sure of it. And until then, I need you to do something for me."

"What?" I'd asked sharply.

I'd practically been able to hear Campbell smiling on the other end of the line. *"Nothing."*

Campbell Ames had asked me to sit back and do nothing, to let this play out, and for some godforsaken reason, I'd done what she'd asked. I deserved a dozen fittings like this one—*worse* than this one. I deserved to be waxed and plucked and manicured to perfection. I deserved the worst that high society had to offer.

True to Campbell's word, Nick had been released within forty-eight hours of his arrest. Charges were never pressed. I'd been told—multiple times—that I should be *happy*.

Nick had been fired from the club. He'd lost his job, but I should have been relieved. All was well that ended well.

Like hell.

A knock on the dressing room door jarred me back to the present and filled me with the awareness that I was *still* standing around in my underwear.

"Sawyer," Lily called through the door, "if you don't hurry, we'll be late to meet Campbell."

CHAPTER 38

Any activity involving Campbell Ames ranked just above *root canal* and just below *bikini wax* on my list of preferred pastimes, but the November Symphony Ball event was being organized by the mothers of the Ridgeway Hall Debs. Since Sadie-Grace's stepmother was chairing the whole ball, that left two power players to battle it out for subcommittee supremacy: Aunt Olivia and Charlotte Ames.

Not coincidentally, my aunt and the senator's wife had also been the leaders of the two opposing camps on what I'd termed *Dressgate*. When Aunt Olivia had won that battle, Campbell's mother had simply *insisted* that my aunt let her take on the brunt of the work for the November event.

Aunt Olivia, of course, had *insisted* on helping.

Lily and I had been conscripted against our will.

"Food, Coats, Comfort, and Company." Campbell greeted us at the door to Costco with a shopping cart and a sardonic expression on her face. "It doesn't quite have the ring of Pearls of Wisdom, but charity is as charity does."

This was the first time Lily and I had been alone with Campbell since Nick's arrest—and release. The senator's daughter clearly intended to pretend that none of it had ever happened. The only reason I obliged her was that the three of us weren't alone for long.

"Pack mule, reporting for duty." Walker's hair looked like it hadn't been brushed, and the gray hue of his normally suntanned skin made me think that he needed to invest in a better hangover cure.

"I didn't know you were coming," Lily said, her voice dangerously neutral. I watched for a hair tuck, and she didn't disappoint.

"Neither did I," Walker replied. He glanced at Campbell. "Mom's on the warpath. If she asks, you called me in a tizzy about the prospect of lifting moderately heavy objects on your own, and I had no choice but to vacate the house and come to the rescue."

"You know I don't do tizzies." Campbell arched an eyebrow at him. "I'm so much better at conniptions."

"Shall we divide up the list?" Lily interjected. She wouldn't come right out and say that she hadn't signed up for this, but I knew that she preferred all encounters with Walker Ames to be of the anticipated variety.

"Divide away," Campbell said with a wave of her hand. "Who wants canned food, who wants coats, and who wants comfort?"

At this point, I had to ask. "I thought Symphony Ball was hosting a canned food drive for Thanksgiving?"

Lily blinked several times. "We are."

"That's why we're here," Campbell explained with exaggerated patience. "To buy the canned food."

I considered explaining that drives like this one usually involved donating *your* extra food, but decided it wasn't worth it. "Let me guess, we're also buying the coats?"

Lily must have decided that was a rhetorical question, because she got down to business. "I'll do food."

"That will get heavy quickly," Walker commented. "I can—"

"I'm sure I'll be just fine." Lily cut him off. "Don't you worry a thing about it."

Walker looked like he was on the verge of objecting, but Campbell spoke up first. "Given Sawyer's *unique* fashion sense, I'll do coats. Walker, why don't you help Sawyer with *comfort*?"

There were worse ways to spend an afternoon than buying books, blankets, stuffed animals, lotions, bubble bath, and chocolate on another person's dime. The only guideline we'd been given wasn't a monetary one: five carts of food, five of coats, two of comfort.

Walker and I jammed as much into our two carts as we could fit.

He tried, no fewer than three times, to help Lily load up and maneuver carts of canned food, but she rebuffed his offers and recruited multiple stock boys in his stead.

"That has to hurt," I commented after he'd been shot down a third time. If there was one thing I'd picked up during months' worth of envelope stuffing, it was that Walker wasn't over Lily. I had no idea why he'd broken up with her in the first place.

"Is that your way of calling me a glutton for punishment?" Walker leaned over his cart, his elbows on the handlebars.

"I've called you worse." I glanced at the display behind him. "Do you think I could use Monopoly boxes to extend the sides of my cart and fit more in?"

He grabbed a couple and tossed them to me. "Dream big, Sawyer Taft."

I set about experimenting with the boxes. "Interesting advice from someone who dropped out of college, broke up with his girl-friend, and started hard-core training for the future-squandering Olympics."

Walker and I had an unspoken agreement. I gave him crap, and he seemed to enjoy it. Mainly, I thought he enjoyed the fact that I hadn't known the old Walker. I had no expectations whatsoever of him—and in exchange, he'd stopped trying to charm me.

"That's cold, Sawyer Taft. Really cold." Walker picked up a teddy bear and tossed it to me. I tested the structural integrity of my cart extenders and placed the bear on top of the mound of goods already in my cart.

"As much as I enjoy these heart-to-hearts," Walker continued, "if I may be so bold as to change the subject, I need a favor."

I kept stacking my cart. "I'm listening."

"Ease up on Campbell."

I turned to look at him, unable to believe that he'd meant to say those words in that order.

"I know how my sister can be," Walker said. "And I know that whatever has you, Lily, and Sadie-Grace avoiding her like the plague, she probably deserves it. But she's had a rough few weeks." He paused. "She could use some friends."

Campbell had been having a rough time?

My expression must have said that exactly, because Walker elaborated. "She used to be involved with that guy Nick. The one who got arrested?"

Your sister is the one who got him arrested.

The only way I could keep from actually saying those words out loud was to give my cart a good push around the corner—and directly into another cart.

It took two SUVs to get our haul back to the Ames house. When we arrived, it became apparent that we weren't the only ones who'd dropped off donations. The foyer and formal living room were overflowing.

"Lily." Mrs. Ames greeted my cousin with a squeeze. "You look wonderful, sweetheart. Have you lost weight?"

That question had thorns. The only saving grace was that Walker was too busy unloading the cars to hear it.

Before I could issue a suitable—and possibly profane—reply on Lily's behalf, the senator came ambling down the main staircase. "Gathering the troops?" he asked his wife, coming to stand beside her and wrapping an arm around her waist.

"I'd say that we're past that point and well on our way to mission accomplished," Campbell mused.

The senator barely spared a glance in his daughter's direction before turning his attention to Lily and me. "It's lovely to see you, ladies. Sawyer, Walker says you've settled in nicely at the campaign."

"What can I say?" I could feel Campbell bristling beside me. "I'm a patriot."

"Speaking of Walker . . ." Charlotte Ames laid a hand lightly on her husband's arm. "I am just sure he could use some help unloading the car."

"That's my cue," the senator said gamely. "If you ladies will excuse me . . ."

He strode past us toward the door. Campbell turned to follow. "I'll help, Daddy."

"Don't be silly, Campbell," Charlotte Ames cut in. "I'm sure your father and brother can handle it."

Campbell forced a smile and met her mother's gaze head-on. "I'm stronger than I look."

"Hello, hello!" Aunt Olivia slipped in the front door as the senator made his exit. She glanced around the foyer at the mounds of donations. "How wonderful!" she gushed. "Whatever you need to get this chaos under control, Charlotte, the girls and I are at your service."

While I appreciated the emphasis Aunt Olivia put on the word *chaos* and the way Charlotte Ames gritted her teeth in response, I'd been under the impression that our servitude was limited to picking up the donations.

So why was the senator's wife suddenly chatting about "assembling baskets"?

Faced with the prospect of being instructed on the finer points of tying "an appropriate bow," I followed Campbell's suit and offered to help the guys unpack the car.

Neither my offer nor Campbell's was accepted, and I spent the next few hours of my life in the circle of hell devoted to tying ribbons on baskets. Eventually, reinforcements showed up—first Sadie-Grace and her stepmother, then Boone and his dad.

Walker and the senator had disappeared about the same time I'd wanted to start drinking.

"Are we still tying bows?" Sadie-Grace sounded hopeful as she sat down beside me at the senator's dining room table. "I only have three things in life that I am truly gifted at, and one of them is tying bows."

I shoved the basket I was currently working on in her direction. "Have at it."

Sadie-Grace studied my work and got very quiet for a moment. "Sawyer," she said morosely, "what did this cellophane wrap ever do to you?"

I took that as my cue to take a water break. In the kitchen, I was faced with a choice of lemonade and tea, sweet or unsweet. I would have given my right arm for a real sandwich, but instead, someone somewhere had decided that *cucumber* was a satisfactory sandwich filling.

Dainty little sandwiches, I thought grimly. *Bow tying. I deserve this.*

"I do hope I'm not interrupting." Boone hopped up on the counter beside the cucumber sandwiches, stacked three of them on top of each other, and then bit in. "Close your eyes and open your hand."

Without waiting for me to do as I was told, he presented me with a bright pink envelope. One eye on Boone, I withdrew a card from inside.

Congratulations, fancy script said. *It's a girl!*

Boone had handwritten the word *NOT* on the front of the card in fat red marker. When I opened the card, a single piece of paper fell out.

A report, I realized.

"As you'll see . . ." Boone hopped off the counter, polishing off the sandwiches as he went. "You are decidedly not my sister!"

It had been so long since Boone had taken my hair that I'd almost given up hope on getting the results back.

"Given that you *still* haven't obtained a sample of my uncle's DNA," Boone cautioned firmly, "I would recommend that we continue to resist the obvious animal attraction between us."

"I think I can manage." I gave him a look, sure that the primary reason he was in the kitchen was that he was hiding from Sadie-Grace, who he *still* hadn't managed to ask out. "And thank you." I hesitated, just for an instant, remembering the words he'd spoken to me at the masquerade. "For the record, Boone? I wouldn't have minded a brother."

"Brother?" A voice spoke behind us. Boone jumped. I managed to play it cool, right up until Greer Waters plucked the greeting card from my hand. The paternity test was still stuck inside. "Is your mother expecting, Sawyer?"

I could practically see the gears in her mind turning.

"Nope." If I'd grown up in this world, I might have felt compelled to provide more of an answer than that, but instead, I followed up my *no* with what I believed to be the only proper response to someone snatching something out of my hands.

I took it back.

Greer clearly hadn't been expecting me to reclaim my property. "Boone," she said, pursing her lips, "may I have a word with Sawyer?"

Boone looked at me, and I nodded. I could handle Greer Waters—and I had some questions to ask her.

"As I'm sure you know," Greer said after Boone had vacated the kitchen, "tonight, the Debs and Squires will deliver the baskets we're currently assembling. Food, coats, and comfort are just a small piece of our work—*company* is only a few letters removed from *compassion*."

Dollars to donuts said that was part of a speech she'd rehearsed. What followed, however, seemed a bit more off the cuff.

"I'd like an assurance from you that we won't have a repeat of last time."

"Last time?" I repeated.

"The scavenger hunt," Greer said, putting emphasis on each of the three words.

If you knew what we were really up to that night . . . I thought, but what I said was, "We'll stick to the plan." I offered Greer what I hoped was a good imitation of Lily's most simpering smile. "Scout's honor."

"About . . . *this*." Greer nodded to the card in my hand. "Would you care to explain?"

I didn't see how this was any of her business. "Not particularly."

"I told you that you could come to me, if you had . . . questions. I'd hate to see you drag poor Boone Mason into this. He's a darling boy, but goodness knows he marches to the beat of his own drum.

Navigating social expectations is difficult enough for him as it is."

This from the woman who'd told me that my mother was a dear, but that they hadn't had much in common. *Liar.*

"I went through some of my mom's things the other day." I openly assessed the set of Greer's features. This was a lady who hid her tells—when she wanted to. "There were a lot of pictures of the two of you together."

Greer managed an elegant shrug. "I'm afraid I was the type to hop in the middle of *every* photo."

Were it not for the fact that saying the words *Hey, what are the chances that your new husband is the one who knocked up my mom?* would have made getting a sample of his DNA that much harder, I would have thrown it out there, just to see the look on her face. Instead, I opted for a different question, also guaranteed to provoke a reaction.

"Speaking of those photos: Who was Ana?"

CHAPTER 39

Remarkably, Greer realized at that exact moment that she just *had* to recount the baskets. Left alone in the kitchen, I turned my attention back to the card Boone had given me.

Thomas Mason was not my father.

How long was I going to let my mom's ongoing silent treatment keep me from getting samples from the other three candidates on my list?

As long as I'd been focused on the situation with Nick—and beating myself up about *that*—I hadn't had to think about what pulling the trigger on the paternity tests might mean.

She'll forgive me for coming here, for finding out. I wanted to believe that. My mom wasn't perfect, but she loved me. I had to do this.

Now.

Given that the alternative was tying bows, the decision to go in search of a sample of the senator's DNA was surprisingly easy.

It didn't take long for me to locate the master bedroom. Finding the senator's hairbrush was more of an ordeal. The bathroom was enormous, with an ungodly number of built-in drawers. I went through three of them before I found something definitively identifiable as makeup and concluded that I was on Campbell's mother's side of the bathroom. Quickly and silently, I moved on to the vanity on the opposite side of the double doors.

The senator's a neat freak. I came to that conclusion after opening one drawer. *What are the chances that his brush doesn't contain a single hair?*

"Do I even want to know what you're doing in here?"

I whirled to face Campbell. "Tampons," I said. *Plausible deniability, thy name is feminine hygiene.* "I need one." I paused. "Possibly two."

Campbell frowned. "Why would you need *two*?"

"Just . . . does your mom have any lying around?" I tried to look somewhat urgent.

"Come off it," Campbell told me. "We both know what you're really looking for."

A sample of your father's DNA?

"The pearls." Campbell gave me a vexed look. "You just can't leave well enough alone, can you?"

Well enough? I could feel my hands curling into fists. "You've never needed a job, have you?" I said. "Never relied on the income that you're bringing in, never had to stand on your own two feet. Did it even occur to you that Nick is unemployed now, thanks to you?"

Thanks to us.

"You don't get to talk to me about Nick," Campbell said, her voice low.

"The charges were dropped," I mimicked, letting the words bleed sarcasm. "All's well that ends well, right?"

"Nick is a survivor," Campbell told me, looking down at her three-inch heels. "He'll be fine."

"You used him." I wasn't sure why I expected that accusation to matter to her. "Were you ever even interested?"

"He used me." Campbell lifted her eyes back to mine. "I don't blame him. I let him." She paused. "I'd let him again. Believe me when I say that I did what I could for Nick."

"You could have left him alone," I retorted.

"No," Campbell said quietly. "I couldn't."

CHAPTER 40

Two hours later, when the Debs and Squires were being assigned to groups for the evening's deliveries, I still wasn't sure why Campbell's statement that she *couldn't* have left Nick alone had the ring of truth.

"Sawyer Taft."

I looked up to see Charlotte Ames standing at the front of the room holding a clipboard.

"You're in group five. You'll be making deliveries to local nursing homes." The senator's wife didn't pause before reading off the names of the rest of my group, which decidedly did not include Lily, Campbell, Sadie-Grace, or Boone. I could only assume the Symphony Ball Committee thought splitting us up might keep us out of trouble.

By the time I was ensconced in a car with the four other members of my team—two Squires, two other Debs—I was reminded that outside of our immediate circle, prodigal granddaughter Sawyer Taft was still something of a legend. A deluge of questions and comments and not-compliments ensued. When we arrived at the first nursing home to deliver some good old-fashioned comfort, I was ready to fly the coop.

By the third, I was thinking that total sensory deprivation sounded good.

Unfortunately, instead of a nice, dark tank with no questions and no physical contact, I was somehow appointed as our group's designated hugger.

"This is so sweet." An older woman squeezed the living daylights out of me. "I'm not supposed to have chocolate, you know." She picked the book up out of her basket and lowered her voice. "Do you have anything with more kissing?"

As much as I wasn't into being *the infamous Sawyer Taft,* I was enjoying the rest of this assignment. Of the three homes we'd visited, this last one was by far the most upscale—and its inhabitants needed the most physical help.

Half an hour later, I ducked into the last room on the hall, my arms wrapped wide around one final basket. I looked for the room's resident and found him on the bed. My brain fired rapidly, three overlapping realizations fighting for my attention at once.

The room's occupant was in the bed, unconscious.

The room's occupant was hooked up to a whole host of machines.

The room's occupant wasn't much older than I was.

I walked slowly to his bedside, my grip on the gift basket tightening. He was, what? Twenty-one? Twenty-two? His dark hair looked like it had been recently cut, but something about the constant *beep, beep, beep* in the background made me wonder if he'd been awake when that happened.

"Hi." I'd read once that people could hear you, even if they weren't conscious. "Don't take this the wrong way," I continued, "but you're either a really deep sleeper or comatose."

There was no answer. I probably should have just left the basket for the patient's relatives or else taken it and given it to someone else altogether, but instead, I found myself sitting beside the bed and undoing the carefully wrapped cellophane myself.

Given the elaborate bow, I was pretty sure that Sadie-Grace had packaged this one.

"If it's all the same to you," I told the dark-haired guy on the bed, "I could use a few minutes away from the grind."

No reply.

I made the executive decision to read to him from the book in the basket. It didn't take me long to realize that it was one the old woman who'd asked for more *kissing* would have appreciated.

Coma Guy and I were having a grand old time, when I heard the door open behind me. I assumed that it was either the nurse or one of the other Symphony Ballers.

I assumed wrong.

"What are you doing here?"

I turned toward the door and sucked in a breath. "Nick." Seeing him standing there, I couldn't manage more than that.

"What are you doing here?" he repeated.

"Food, Coats, Comfort, and Company." I felt like an idiot even saying the words, but managed to nod toward the basket I'd set on the side table. "It's a thing."

"Is asking you to leave also a thing?" This wasn't the collared-shirt guy I'd met at the club, or the one who'd tended bar at the masquerade. There was nothing aggressive in his voice or posture, but nothing conciliatory, either. *No polite mask.*

"I'm sorry you lost your job." I felt like I didn't have the right to say the words, but I said them anyway. "I know you didn't steal anything."

"I'd ask how you know that, but as it turns out, I don't actually care."

He wasn't smiling, and neither was I. It felt good to drop the act.

"Is there anything I can do?" I asked. "For you?"

"Wow." Nick's voice reverberated off the walls. "It really didn't take them long to convert you, did it?" He snorted. *"Is there anything I can do for you?"*

Until he repeated my words back to me, I didn't realize how much I sounded like Lillian—or Aunt Olivia or Lily. Like I could just wave a magic wand and fix whatever it was that needed fixing.

"I should have said something." I forced the words out between clenched teeth. This wasn't smart, and it wouldn't make a difference at this point, but he was here, and so was I, and he looked enough like the comatose guy on the bed that it was a safe bet they were related. "I know who set you up, and—"

"Stop." He walked toward me, step by hypercontrolled step, stopping at the foot of the bed. "Whatever you're about to say, don't." He didn't sound angry anymore. His voice was almost gentle. "Whatever you know, whoever you know it about—I don't want you to tell me." He paused. "I don't want you to tell anyone."

"What?" I literally could not process what he'd just said.

"I want you to keep your mouth closed." When it looked like I might argue, he cut me off. "So I lost my job," he said dismissively. "Have you *seen* this place?" He gestured to the private room around us. "Do you think I could have afforded this kind of care on a valet's salary? On a bartender's?"

He didn't say where he'd gotten the money to pay the fees. It occurred to me then that maybe I'd read the situation with Campbell wrong. Maybe she hadn't framed him.

Maybe she'd *helped* him.

"Did you . . ." I started to say.

"No." He didn't even wait for me to ask the question. "But if I'd known I could get my brother into a place like this by stealing a single strand of pearls, I sure as hell would have." He let that sink in. "Right after I got arrested, an anonymous donor started paying for this. As long as they keep paying for it . . ." He looked at me, then looked down at the floor. "I don't really care what it costs me."

APRIL 15, 5:56 P.M.

Nick. Mackie filed the name away for future reference.

"I have to say," the boy drawled, wrapping his hands around the bars of the cell and leaning forward toward the girls. "Bars are a good look for you, Campbell."

Campbell. The senator's daughter.

"Nick!" The beautifully anxious—or maybe anxiously beautiful?—one bounced nearly to the tips of her toes. "You can help us, Nick. You know things. You know people who know things."

Mackie had intended to stand back and observe, but that statement had him speaking. "What kind of people?" he said suspiciously.

"We helped you, Nick," the girl named Sawyer said.

The boy—*Nick*—rocked back on his heels, smiling in a way that told Mackie he was enjoying this altogether too much.

"The first time I was arrested?" he asked. "Or the second?"

FOUR MONTHS EARLIER

CHAPTER 41

It was a truth universally acknowledged that a person in want of plastic baggies need only look in the Taft family kitchen. Aunt Olivia was the queen of Ziplocs. She'd taken over Lillian's cabinets and had entire drawers dedicated to them—every size, every type, a year's supply of each at least.

Helping myself to a gallon-sized bag, I opened it, dropped my bounty inside, and zipped it shut. Senator Ames had politician hair. I'd had zero luck getting ahold of so much as a single strand in the past month. Luckily, however, I was a full 50 percent of the team devoted to fetching coffee at his regional office, so in between his frequent trips to Washington, it hadn't been difficult to smuggle out one of his used coffee cups.

"What in the world are you doing, honey?" Aunt Olivia was surprisingly stealthy when she wanted to be.

I turned to face her and looked down at the disposable coffee cup I'd just Ziploc-ed.

"Nothing."

"That doesn't look like nothing," Aunt Olivia commented. "Exactly how gullible do you girls think I am?"

"Fine," I admitted with a sigh. "It's a coffee cup in a plastic bag." When in doubt, state the obvious.

"And why might one wish to preserve a discarded coffee cup?" Aunt Olivia was either bemused or suspicious—the patented Southern Smile she'd just whipped out made it impossible to tell which.

"Was that a rhetorical question?" I asked to buy time.

Aunt Olivia gave me a look she typically reserved for John David. "No," she said. "No, it was not."

I improvised. "It's a Christmas tradition," I said, glancing down at the baggie in my hand. I'd found, in the stretch between Thanksgiving and now, that the entire extended family tiptoed around any questions about the way that my mom and I usually celebrated the holidays.

Lily wasn't the only one who'd realized that my mother still wasn't taking my calls.

"Putting a coffee cup in a plastic baggie is a Christmas tradition?" Aunt Olivia definitely sounded suspicious now, but only about a quarter as suspicious as she should have.

"It's like hanging stockings," I spitballed. "But for people on a budget. Are those cookies hot?" I changed the topic as rapidly as I could. Aunt Olivia had spent the day baking sugar cookies. The countertops were covered with them. I reached for one shaped like a candy cane, and she slapped my hand away lightly.

"I haven't even iced them yet," she chided. "Besides which, Sawyer Ann, I can guarantee that you won't want to spoil your appetite for tonight."

This evening was the annual Christmas party at Northern Ridge. It was open to all club members—and the families of all Symphony Ball Squires and Debs. John David had spent the better part of the last week attempting to describe to me the wide array of deliciousness that would be ours for the taking at the party.

The gingerbread was supposedly the food of the gods.

But I hadn't come down here to discuss gingerbread—or for a single plastic bag.

I'd come down here for two of them.

"Do you have any lipstick I can borrow?"

Aunt Olivia could not have been more surprised if I'd asked her to personally shave my head.

"The dress Lillian wants me to wear tonight is red," I said. "I'm usually more of a clear gloss or nothing person, but . . ."

Aunt Olivia's eyes came very close to watering as she pulled me into a side hug. "My makeup's in the bathroom. You help yourself, sweetheart."

I almost felt guilty about the fact that I'd just been looking for an invitation to rifle through the bathroom she shared with Uncle J.D. so that I could obtain *his* sample as well.

"I know that this must be a very difficult time of year for you, Sawyer." Aunt Olivia laid her hands lightly on my shoulders and gave them a squeeze, "I know you miss your mama, but we are very glad to have you here." She turned back toward the stove. "I'm not one to talk badly about anyone, but I could wring my sister's neck for pulling these kinds of games on you."

I could have used that as an opportunity to make my exit, but the urge to defend my mom ran deep. "She just wants me to come home."

Aunt Olivia pulled a bowl down from the cabinet and began making what I could only assume was the icing. "It's the silent treatment, is what it is. You give her what she wants, or she cuts you out. Lord knows this wouldn't be the first time, but her own *daughter* . . ." Realizing what she was saying, Aunt Olivia brought herself up short. "That's neither here nor there." She turned back to face me again. "The point is that you're welcome here, Sawyer. You always have been."

I stared at her, my brain turning that statement over. "What do you mean I always have been?"

For a moment, I didn't think Aunt Olivia would answer. "No reason to go raising the ghosts of the past."

That was such an Aunt Olivia thing to say after she'd already raised them. I'd been told my entire life that my mother's family didn't want us. She was an embarrassment, and I was worse. They'd kicked her out. They'd cut contact.

But my mom was the one not answering my phone calls now.

"Sawyer." Aunt Olivia paused, hesitating only for a moment. "The past year has been difficult for Lily. I will confess that I was not sure how your . . . *situation* . . . would play into that, but your being here and a part of this family has been a real blessing for my daughter. And for the rest of us." Another hug, and then: "Now, shouldn't you be seeing about that lipstick?"

Aunt Olivia steered me out of the kitchen and toward the stairs. As she did, I caught sight of the family Christmas tree. Blown-glass and crystal ornaments were intermingled with ones that had been made by pudgy little hands when Lily and John David were young. Three stockings hung on the mantel—one with Lily's name on it, one with John David's, and one with mine.

For the first time, it occurred to me to wonder whether or not my stocking was new.

"Go on," Aunt Olivia said, planting an affectionate swat on my bottom. "Scoot. I promised your grandmother we'd be the first ones in line for family pictures at the party tonight."

I scooted. I barely noticed the portraits on the walls these days, but the small nail hole next to the family portrait at the top of the stairs hit me harder than it usually did. My mom wasn't always the most reliable narrator, but Lillian had never denied kicking her out. My grandmother had banished all trace of her younger daughter to the attic.

But she kept it all. I forced that thought down and walked to my aunt and uncle's bathroom. Unlike the senator—and Aunt Olivia—Uncle J.D. wasn't a neatnik. His brush was chock-full of hairs, and, luckily for me, Aunt Olivia kept an emergency box of Ziplocs in her vanity.

Uncle J.D. is not my father. The fact that I even had to think those words was ridiculous. And yet . . . my mom had asked me to let this go. She didn't *want* me to know who my father was.

She doesn't get to make that decision for me. I told myself that I had already made my choice. This didn't have to be an emotional thing. I could find my answer logically and systematically, no emotions involved. That meant investigating all four of the men whose faces my mother had scratched out of that photo.

Even my uncle.

I barely remembered to grab a red lipstick out of Aunt Olivia's drawer before I made my way back to my room. Crossing over to the bed, I opened the drawer to the nightstand, intending to tuck the samples I'd collected out of sight, but instead, my gaze fell on the photograph I'd stolen from Aunt Olivia's box.

Four faces were circled. One—Thomas Mason's—I'd drawn through with an X.

I set the baggies down on top of the nightstand and pushed the photo to the side. Beneath it in the drawer was something else I'd found myself looking at just as often in the past month: a printout of a news article. It had taken some digging for me to figure out Nick's last name, let alone his brother's first, but eventually, my internet sleuthing had turned up answers.

Colt Ryan was twenty-two, an employee at Northern Ridge Country Club. Like Nick, he'd been a valet. One night after work, he'd been walking the two miles to the nearest bus station, when he'd been hit by a car.

A hit and run.

The only coverage I'd managed to find on it was a paragraph and a half long. I'd printed the article and read it a hundred times. One day, Colt Ryan had been fine, and the next . . . *coma.*

I hadn't heard from or seen Nick once in the past four and a half weeks. I'd done what he'd asked: I'd kept my mouth shut.

"Can you zip me?"

I turned to see Lily standing in the doorway. She was wearing a black velvet dress, knee-length and fitted. She spun to turn her back toward me, and as I crossed the room to zip her dress, I realized that I'd left the nightstand drawer open.

The article—and the photo—were visible.

The zipper on Lily's dress caught. She was saying something about my accessories for tonight, but I barely heard her as I worked the zipper back down and up again. Smooth skin disappeared as I finished fastening the dress into place.

"Go ahead and put yours on," Lily instructed me, "and I'll zip you."

I did as I was told—and positioned myself to block Lily's view of the drawer.

"Penny for your thoughts," she commented as she ran a hand over my dress, smoothing the fabric.

"A penny won't buy you much these days," I told Lily as she zipped me. "Thought inflation."

"Sawyer," Lily faux-chided. "Inflation isn't something we *talk* about . . ."

I snorted. It took me a second to realize that she hadn't trailed off midsentence intentionally. I contorted my upper body to look back at her and realized that she was looking over my shoulder. Before I could stop her, she'd sidestepped right by me.

Straight for the open drawer.

She stood there for a moment, then reached. "What's this?"

I looked down at her hand, hoping that she'd be holding the article about Nick's brother. *No such luck.* She was staring at the photograph—twenty-four Symphony Squires, four with thick circles drawn around their faces, one circle crossed out.

"It's not important," I said, reaching to take it from her.

She stepped back. "That's not just a fib, Sawyer Ann. That's a lie."

"Is there really a difference?"

"Sawyer." Lily emphasized my name in a way that made the muscles in my stomach twist. "Why do you have this picture?" She was quiet for a moment. "Why did you circle Daddy?"

"It doesn't matter," I said again, but Lily knew why I'd decided to come here. She was the one who'd helped me go through the boxes in the attic. It didn't take a rocket scientist to figure out why I might have a photograph of men in our parents' generation—or why I might have circled a handful.

"Don't take this the wrong way," Lily told me, sounding more Southern-proper than she had in ages, "but if you think there's *any* chance my daddy might have slept with your mama, you are playing with half a deck."

"Lily," I started to say, but she held up her index finger—the index finger of *doom*.

"A quarter of a deck," she amended fiercely. "At most."

"I'm not the one who zeroed in on those men." I should have stopped there, but I didn't. "My mom has a copy of that picture. She—"

"She doesn't have much of a deck at all." For once, Lily didn't bite her tongue. "We both know your mama was trouble, Sawyer. As far as I can tell, she still is."

Downstairs, the doorbell rang. I barely heard it. "You don't know anything about my mother," I said fiercely.

Yes, I'd chosen to come back here. Yes, my mom had taken that badly. But that wasn't all she was. She'd been there for me my entire life. Maybe not always the way I wanted, but she'd been there. She'd thrown midnight ice-cream parties and taught me to mix cocktails and let me teach her to tie ropes. She'd never pressured me to be someone else, never once made me feel like she was anything less than delighted with *exactly* who I was.

That was more than most people could say.

"Excuse me," I said sharply, turning my back on Lily. "Me and my quarter of a deck are going to make ourselves useful and answer the door."

She followed on my heels as I descended the stairs. The doorbell rang again.

"It's probably just carolers," Lily called after me.

I would have rather faced down a half dozen churchgoers yodeling "Silent Night" than continue the conversation my cousin and I had been having upstairs. I was halfway to the foyer when Uncle J.D. stepped out of the kitchen and beat me to the door. He opened it, and I skidded to a stop. Lily nearly rear-ended me.

It wasn't carolers.

I sucked in a breath and found that no matter what I did, I couldn't seem to let it out.

"Ellie." Uncle J.D. was gobsmacked, but he covered well.

Better than I did, as I gaped at the woman standing in a little black dress and modest black heels on my grandmother's front porch.

"Mom?"

CHAPTER 42

"Squeeze in a little closer." The photographer shot the lot of us a cheesy grin that he probably hoped the whole family would mimic. "Can I get the young lady with the blond hair to tilt her chin slightly? And young man—hands out of your pockets."

Lily and John David were fidgety. I couldn't blame them, even though this surreal turn of events had achieved the opposite effect on me. I stood facing the camera, frozen, unable to so much as blink. My grandmother stood to my right side, my mom to my left.

She's here. She's wearing pearls. Her hair is pulled back into a French knot. I wasn't sure what shook me more—the fact that my mom was pretending she hadn't spent the past three months ignoring me, or the degree to which her hairstyle and dress and even her posture reminded me of Lillian.

"Perfect," the photographer declared, stepping back behind his camera. "Now, if I could get some smiles . . ."

The seven of us were standing in front of a Christmas tree that was nearly two stories tall. Every ribbon, every light, every ornament was perfect—and everything about this felt wrong.

In the old days, the photographer's flash would have gone off. Instead, one moment, he was snapping digital pictures, and the next, he was done. We were ushered off to the side, and the next family filed in.

"I'm going to find the gingerbread." John David was nobody's fool. He had even less of an idea what was going on than I did, but he had no intention of sticking around to find out. He was a good three feet away when Aunt Olivia's hand shot out and grabbed him by the back of the collar.

"What are we not going to do this year?" she asked him.

John David turned around and eyed her. "We are not," he said aristocratically, "going to eat so much gingerbread that we puke."

She smoothed a hand over his lapels and then let him loose. He was off like a rocket.

I caught my mom with the strangest look on her face.

Aunt Olivia saw it, too. "What?" she said, her voice a peal of bells, her eyes shooting daggers at my mom.

"It's nothing," my mom replied, shaking her head. "I just never pictured you with a little boy, Liv."

The fact that my mom could come here pretending she hadn't been punishing me for looking for my father was strange. The way she'd just casually shortened her sister's name—the sister who, as far as I knew, she hadn't seen in eighteen years—was downright bizarre.

The silence that followed was a second too long. My grandmother, my aunt, Uncle J.D.—they'd all been doing an impressive job of pretending that my mom hadn't shown up unannounced. You never would have known, observing us, that the adults hadn't seen each other in years. But my mom's offhand comment?

That got a response.

"Yes, well, imagining me with a son would have required spending some modicum of time devoted to thinking about someone other than yourself." If smiles were deadly, Aunt Olivia's would have downed my mother where she stood.

"Sawyer." Lillian stepped in before my mother could reply. "Perhaps you could show your mama the main dining room. It's changed quite a bit since she was last here."

My mom wove her right arm through my left. She didn't spare her mother so much as a glance, but when she spoke to me, Lillian was obviously the subject of her oh-so-pleasant statement. "She's the boss."

Hello, land mines. My name is Sawyer, and I'll be skipping through a field of you this evening. I steered my mother away from the rest of the family. As we made our way through the great room, into Ash Hall, and through to the dining room, I could feel a dozen sets of eyes—or more—pulled our way, like metal shavings to a magnet.

"That dress can't be comfortable." My mom leaned close to talk in my ear, as if the two of us were sharing delightful secrets. "Are you wearing a strapless bra?"

I managed to wait until we'd made it to the dining room before replying. "Mom."

"All I'm saying is that the Sawyer that I know would rather wear electrical tape than—"

"Can we please stop talking about my bra?" I gritted out.

At some point in our walk, I'd stopped leading her, and she'd started directing me. We ended up on the far side of the dining room, standing near one of the twenty-foot-tall windows, overlooking the pool. The thick plaid curtains—a Christmas special—had been drawn back just enough that we could see the night sky. The pool was covered and not much to look at, but the stars were a sight to behold.

"They don't shine as brightly here." My mom nudged me gently in the side. "You can't have forgotten that already."

I felt like she'd hit me. "I haven't forgotten anything."

"Look at you," my mom said softly. The words didn't sound as critical as I would have expected them to, but they packed a punch all the same.

"Look at *you*," I replied. "You're not exactly dressed for tending bar."

"Smile," my mother murmured. "We have an audience."

A quick glance told me we were drawing even more stares than we had a moment before, but I didn't give a damn about our audience.

"You've been here for a few months," my mom told me. "I spent almost eighteen years here. You're like a foreign exchange student, baby. I'm a native speaker, so *smile*."

I bared my teeth. To call it a *smile* would have been a bit of a stretch.

"That's my girl." That sounded more like my mom than anything else she'd said since she arrived, and it hurt.

If you didn't expect things of people, they couldn't disappoint you. I knew that, but a part of me would never stop expecting her to . . .

To what? I asked myself.

"You should have called me," I said. "You should have answered when I called."

"I know." She looked down at the floor. "I just kept hoping you'd come to your senses. That you'd come home."

"Home is forty-five minutes away," I pointed out. "It doesn't have to be an either/or proposition. Even if I'm living with Lillian—you can still see me."

My mom gazed out at the pool. "You're the one who left, Sawyer."

"I had a right to come here." That ended up sounding more like a question than I would have liked. "They're your family—but they're my family, too, and they're not all bad."

"If they were," my mother replied after a moment, "your coming here wouldn't have been so hard to swallow. If they were all bad—if living like this was all bad—I wouldn't have to worry that you'd like it." She looked down, her lashes casting shadows on the cheekbones Aunt Olivia envied so much. "I was never happy here after Daddy died. They probably haven't told you this, but your aunt ran away, left a note and took off in the dead of night for eight months, close to nine. The police were called. Mama, of course, asked them to keep the investigation discreet. And when my sister finally deigned to return? Your grandmother never said a word about it. We just had to pretend that Liv had been on a vacation or at boarding school or that we knew where she'd been at all times." She shook her head ever so slightly. "Except she wasn't *Liv* anymore. She was *Olivia*, and she was *perfect*. It was like all that grief, all that anger, all that *everything* . . . it just evaporated, and there I was, twelve years old and awkward as all get-out and angry at her in ways that no one would let me say. And it just . . . stayed that way." Her voice was muted now. "I didn't belong here." She turned slightly toward me. "I still don't."

"You had friends here," I said, thinking back to the photographs I'd seen in the attic. "And you obviously had a . . . *connection* . . . with someone."

"Sex," my mom corrected. "The word you're looking for is *sex*."

I opened my mouth, but didn't get a word out before a voice spoke up behind us.

"Ellie?"

For an instant, my mom looked a decade younger. Her eyes

widened. Her lips parted slightly. She turned toward the person who'd approached us. "Lucas."

For someone who'd just been insisting she didn't belong here, my mom looked awfully happy to see Lucas Ames.

"As I live and breathe," he drawled. "It's the Ghost of Christmas Past."

"You grew," my mom commented.

He grinned. "You didn't."

"Sawyer." My mom seemed to remember that I was standing there. "This is . . ."

"Sawyer and I go way back," Lucas said smoothly. "I did what I could to save her from boredom at Pearls of Wisdom, but am sad to report that neither of our families much appreciated the gesture."

"Imagine that," my mother snorted.

"My father bought your mother's pearls." Lucas waited for that to register before he dropped the bomb. "And then they were stolen."

"Someone stole Lillian's pearls?" Ellie's eyebrows skyrocketed.

"Can we not talk about the pearls?" I asked. My mom and Lucas both turned to me, like they'd only just remembered I was there. I wondered if they realized nearly the entire room was watching this little reunion with interest.

How many of these people remembered that the two of them had been friends? How many suspected Lucas of being my father?

Before I could suss out the answer to that question, Davis Ames approached with Boone's mother on one side and Campbell's on the other.

"Hello, Eleanor," Davis said smoothly.

Lucas replied before my mother could. "I was just catching Ellie up on local gossip. Who's married who, who's inherited what, all grand larcenies that have been committed in the past few months . . ."

“Lucas.” The senator’s wife gave him a look. “Please.”

“You look good, Ellie.” That was from Boone’s mother. “And, of course, your daughter is charming.”

There were at least a dozen benign replies my mom could have made without blinking an eye. *Why, thank you. Of course she is. I’m so proud of her.* But instead, what my mom said was . . .

“She takes after her father.”

CHAPTER 43

Country clubs and debutante balls may have been my mom's native language, but she was also fluent in shut-that-down, in-your-face bartender. What she'd just said about my *father* definitely qualified.

Charlotte Ames suggested that I might want to run along and find the other young folks. I ignored her. If my mother was going to say something—anything—about my father, I was damn well going to be there to hear it.

With a slight smile, my mom snagged a glass of champagne off a nearby tray and lifted it to her lips.

"I think Walker and Campbell went in search of eggnog," Lucas commented, nudging me toward the edge of the group. "But you didn't hear it from me."

"Go on," my mom said lightly. "Have fun."

I wondered again why she had come tonight. Had she given up on silent treatment–ing me into coming home? Was she missing me, because it was Christmastime?

Or was she here for something—or someone—else?

"Go on, baby."

I wanted to stay. I wanted to *make* her tell me the truth. But I also knew her. I knew that while she might take great pleasure in throwing her scandal in their faces, she wouldn't say another word with me present.

So I went. I made it about a quarter of a way around the perimeter of the room before I was accosted.

"Hide me." Sadie-Grace stepped out from behind one of the oversized curtains and grabbed my wrist.

"Hide you from what?"

Sadie-Grace lowered her voice, even though the buzz of a hundred or more people chitchatting meant that I had to strain to hear her. "Greer."

I was about to ask why Sadie-Grace needed to be hidden from her stepmother, when out of the corner of my eye, I saw Greer step into the room and scan it with military-like precision.

Sadie-Grace edged back toward the curtains. "I'm on the verge of an arabesque," she whispered urgently.

I pivoted and stepped sideways to block her from view. Unfortunately, Sadie-Grace was several inches taller than I was. Greer spotted her. She'd made it halfway toward us, beaming at Sadie-Grace with near-lethal determination in her eyes, when help came from an unexpected source. My mom approached her from the side and laid a hand lightly on her elbow. Greer turned, clearly intending to "enthusiastically" greet whoever had stopped her and then slip away.

But when she saw my mother?

Even from across the room, I could see her go ashen.

"Greer has been redecorating our house," Sadie-Grace said beside me, oblivious to anything but the fact that she'd received a reprieve. "She keeps saying that she's going to get all the pictures of my mom reframed."

I thought back to what Lillian had told me about Sadie-Grace's mother.

"Let me guess," I said, watching my mom and Greer. "Your dear stepmother hasn't found a set of frames she likes yet."

"Greer says she wants them to be perfect," Sadie-Grace replied quietly. Her hand was beginning to flit gracefully back and forth by her side. I stilled it for her, and she let out a long, labored breath. "There's only one picture my dad hasn't let her touch."

Across the room, Greer appeared to be trying to extract herself from conversation with my mother, but as I watched, my mom leaned forward and whispered something directly into her ear.

Greer let out a light peal of laughter in response. I couldn't hear it from this distance, but I knew exactly what it would have sounded like, just like I knew that it was 100 percent and without doubt fake.

"What's the picture your dad won't let her take down?" I asked Sadie-Grace, forcing my eyes away from the understated melee playing out between my mom and her dear old friend.

"It's a photo of the three of us." Sadie-Grace nibbled on her bottom lip. "My mom, my dad, and me—in front of the Christmas tree."

I knew without asking that she was talking about the tree at *this* party, just like I knew that Greer was probably determined to take a family Christmas picture of her own.

There's trying, Aunt Olivia had said the first time she'd mentioned Greer, *and then there's trying too hard*.

Across the room, Sadie-Grace's father ambled into the conversation his wife was currently having with my mom. My mom's eyes met his. Greer's hand snaked out and took up a possessive perch on her husband's chest.

I wanted to stay there. I wanted to keep watching.

Instead, I turned back to Sadie-Grace, who was practically trembling. "Got any ideas about where to hide?"

We ended up in the room where the staff had set up a few dozen gingerbread houses for kids to decorate. Cloth-covered tables ran the length of the room. There were literally hundreds of dishes full of every kind of candy imaginable on the tables.

It was chaos.

"Gingerbread?" A waiter approached us from behind with a plate that smelled of nuts and cinnamon.

"Yes, please." Sadie-Grace helped herself to a piece, then turned to tell me, in exactly the same tone that John David had used, "It's the food of the gods."

Four pieces of gingerbread later, I'd almost managed to forget the way that Greer had reacted to seeing my mother. She may as well have slapped a PROPERTY OF GREER sticker on her husband's forehead. I thought back to the memory book in the attic, to all of the pictures of Greer and my mother together.

What were the chances that Greer *knew* who my father was?

"Are you okay?" Sadie-Grace asked me. The two of us had taken up position at the end of one of the long tables. There hadn't been many gingerbread houses left to claim, so we were sharing. Her half looked like something out of Candy Land. My half looked like it had been made by a four-year-old.

Probably because I kept eating my building materials.

"I'm fine," I told Sadie-Grace, popping a lemon candy into my mouth. "It's just been a while since I've seen my mom."

That was just the tip of the iceberg. My mom's reappearance had cemented in my mind the realization that if she'd wanted to come back before now, she could have. She'd always said she'd hated it here, but she didn't seem upset to see Lucas Ames—or Charles Waters.

Swallowing the sour-sweet remains of the candy, I glanced at Sadie-Grace. "If I asked you for a weird favor, would you do it?"

"Does it involve tying bows?" Sadie-Grace asked seriously.

"No."

"Duct tape?"

"No," I told her. "It involves hair."

"I can't French-braid." Sadie-Grace made that admission as if it were her greatest secret shame.

"Not my hair," I clarified. "Your father's. If I asked you to bring me a piece of it, would you?"

Sadie-Grace wrinkled her forehead, clearly perplexed. I'd told her this was a weird favor. I could see the exact moment that clarity hit her. "Are you making voodoo dolls?" she asked suspiciously.

"No," I said. "I'm running paternity tests."

Given how Lily had responded to the fact that I'd circled Uncle J.D.'s picture, I knew that this could go badly. Sadie-Grace's father had married her mother before I was conceived. If I were in her position, I would have wanted to believe that they'd been happy.

"Do you think my father might not be my father?" Sadie-Grace was horrified at the prospect.

"No." I put her out of her misery. "I think he might be mine."

Cue blowup, I thought, *in three . . . two . . .*

Sadie-Grace launched herself at me and nearly bowled me over. This wasn't a tackle—it was a *hug.*

"Far be it from me to interrupt a moment . . ." Walker Ames dropped down into the open seat beside us. "But Sadie-Grace should probably get back to the main dining room."

Sadie-Grace, eyes sparkling, whisper-babbled something

incomprehensible in my right ear. The only word I could make out was *sister.*

I extracted myself from her steely, aggressively affectionate grip. "Why is Sadie-Grace's presence needed in the dining room?" I asked.

I expected a flippant response, but Walker's expression was measured. "Because," he said gently, aiming the words more at Sadie-Grace than at me, "her stepmother just announced to the whole room that she's pregnant."

CHAPTER 44

The timing of Greer's announcement did not seem accidental. *She runs into my mom. My mom exchanges pleasantries with her husband, and suddenly, Greer Waters is making a grand and public pregnancy announcement.*

Maybe that was just me being paranoid. Either way, Sadie-Grace reacted markedly less well to Greer's news than she had to the bombshell I'd dropped a moment before. Then again, if I'd been watching my stepmother slowly replace any and all pictures of my mother, I probably would have taken a pregnancy announcement as an indication that she was trying to replace me, too.

"I can't do this." Sadie-Grace looked like she was on the verge of prettily vomiting all over a nearby floral arrangement.

I steered her toward Lily. My cousin might not have taken the revelation of my Who's-Your-Daddy list well—and I might have avoided saying a single word to her since my mom had shown up on our doorstep—but Lily was Sadie-Grace's best friend. She could handle this far better than I could.

"Breathe," Lily ordered the moment she saw Sadie-Grace's face. "You just have to make it through tonight, and then you and I will go out and buy picture frames. Tasteful, elegant, approved-by-Lillian-Taft sterling silver frames that we'll have sent to your house as a late wedding present. I'm over often enough that it would be just terrible manners not to put them to good use. You'll get your mama's pictures back."

Sadie-Grace nodded.

"Sawyer . . ." Lily dragged her attention away from her friend long enough to glance over at me. "Are you okay?"

"I'm fine," I said, clipping the words.

Lily looked down at her hands for a moment. "Maybe you are," she said. "But I'm not. Your mother is *here*." When that didn't get a response, my cousin changed tactics. "Worrying gives you wrinkles, so I have been trying my best to keep calm, but I can only conclude that I have been less than successful." She paused. "Walker took one look at me and knew that I was upset."

Upset on my behalf? Or upset about that picture and my mother's sudden reappareance?

"He talked to me, Sawyer." Lily looked over at Sadie-Grace and then continued. "Really talked to me, like he used to."

Confiding that to me was an olive branch, Lily's way of trying to go back to the moment when she'd been zipping up my dress, right after I'd zipped up hers.

But I couldn't.

I knew, objectively, that my cousin's reaction to finding out her father was on my list hadn't been entirely unreasonable. I knew that it didn't make sense to be mad at her and give my mom a free pass, but there was a reason I'd never made friends easily. Letting people in was a risk.

I'd forgotten that, right up until the point when my cousin had seen that photograph and snapped.

"Take care of her," I told Lily, nodding at Sadie-Grace. "I should go look for my mom. After all," I added pointedly, "she's trouble."

Without waiting for a response, I walked away. I was mere feet from making my escape, when Walker Ames snagged me by the hand. I glanced back toward Lily, but she was already lost in the crowd.

The next thing I knew, I was on the dance floor. The music was the kind that brought people my grandmother's age out. Frank Sinatra seemed to be the vibe they were going for, with a side of crooning Elvis and Nat King Cole.

"I'm not an expert at good Southern manners," I told Walker, "but aren't you supposed to *ask* me to dance?"

"That does seem like something we covered in cotillion." Walker settled his free hand on my lower back. "But this way, if you feel like insulting me, you can do it away from prying ears."

"Maybe I don't feel like insulting you."

Walker pretended to be shocked. "Does this have anything to do with your scandalous mother's scandalous reappearance in society?"

"Walker?"

"Yes?"

"Shut up."

He spun me out and didn't speak again until I'd spun back in and my hand was safely trapped within his own.

"Lily's worried about you," he commented.

"Since when are the two of you on speaking terms?" I shot back.

"She needed someone."

I gave him a look. "Given your history, she probably didn't need for that person to be you."

I told myself that I wasn't being protective of Lily. I was simply stating the obvious.

"You're probably right," Walker admitted. "It took a long time and a lot of effort to convince her she's better off without me." He stared at me for a moment, an expression I couldn't quite read in his eyes. "I'd hate to undo all of that in one evening."

"Then don't."

One song faded into the next, but he didn't give me the opportunity to break away.

"I had lofty ideas about comforting you," Walker informed me. "Helping you and Lily patch things up." He leaned me backward in a slight dip. "But you're right. The part of me that wants to believe that I can be *better,* that I can swoop in and say all of the right things and be everything to everyone . . . that's the dangerous part."

My right hand was enveloped in his left. His other palm rested on the small of my back; he used it to to pull me closer.

"Walker," I said lowly. "What are you doing?"

No matter what kind of fight Lily and I were having, she didn't need to see this.

"A part of me will always miss being that guy, being a *good* guy." Walker's body was nearly touching mine now. "Maybe what I need—what Lily needs—is someone to help me remember that I'm not." Walker paused. "Maybe what *you* need is a distraction."

The song ended, and as easily as he'd gotten me out to the dance floor, he guided me to the hall. The light was dimmer here, but I could very clearly make out the plant that hung overhead.

Mistletoe.

"Walker, what are you—"

"Kiss me."

He had officially lost his mind. "Pass."

"Just once," Walker insisted, his voice quiet and rough. "Just now. I could want this, if I let myself. I think you could, too. And Lily . . ."

Lily would know that you're not a nice guy.

"You are unhinged," I told him. I forced myself to take a step back. I should have torn a strip off him.

I didn't.

Eyes still on mine, he shuddered, and the next thing I knew, the two of us weren't alone.

"There you are, Walker." His mother greeted him with a hug that struck me as territorial more than a sign of affection. "Your grandfather wants to get another photograph in front of the tree—just him and the grandchildren this time. Be a dear and find your sister and Boone, would you?"

The *would you?* somehow made it crystal clear that this wasn't a request.

"I haven't seen Campbell since we got here," Walker replied.

His mother gave his arm a little squeeze. "Then I imagine you should get to looking."

There was a moment when it seemed like Walker might push back, but he didn't. Instead, he made eye contact with me one last time, then left. I made a valiant attempt at taking my own leave, but Walker's mother slid to block my exit.

"You look lovely tonight, Sawyer. Just lovely."

I wasn't sure which was more foreboding: the fact that she'd opened with a compliment, or her tone.

"You're not as put together as Lily is, I suppose, but you do have a certain charm." Charlotte touched the ends of my hair lightly, then tucked a stray strand behind my shoulder. "You're different. You're new. Most of these kids have known each other since they were in diapers. When your aunt Olivia went into labor with John David, your uncle dropped Lily off at my house. We had an impromptu slumber party—Lily and Campbell and Sadie-Grace. We did the same when Sadie-Grace's poor mama passed when the girls were tiny, and of course I had Walker and Boone and a whole passel of little boys at my house as often as not."

"Sounds nice," I said flatly, because it did—and because I knew that the subtext here wasn't *nice* at all.

"You weren't a part of that," Charlotte continued, like I needed the reminder. "Your mama left. If Lillian had raised you, things might be different, but as it is, you're a bit of an oddity. I'm not saying you're *odd*, of course—"

"Of course not," I put in dryly.

"I'm just saying that I can see how my son might find you . . . intriguing."

"As absolutely charming as this has been," I said, mimicking her style of speaking, but not her tone, "I really should be going."

I tried to walk past her, but she caught my arm—hard. Her manicured fingertips dug into my skin and the pads of her fingers pressed down into the bone with affectionate, bruising force. "Your mother has no business being here tonight."

Far be it from me to point out the obvious, I thought, *but . . .*

"I'm not my mother. Maybe you should talk to her."

Charlotte's grip on me didn't loosen. She had about half a second to change that before I loosened it myself.

"Stay away from my son." Her voice was barely audible, but in no way could it have been described as a *whisper.*

"Maybe you should tell your son to stay away from me," I suggested, tearing my arm from her grip. "He's the one with the hair-trigger self-destruct button."

"You and Walker . . ." She stepped toward me. "It's just wrong."

There is no me and Walker, I thought, but I didn't say it, because suddenly, my mouth was dry. Suddenly, I couldn't feel the ghost of her grip on my arm.

I couldn't feel anything.

"Wrong," I repeated, struggling to hear my own voice over the echoing in my ears. "Walker and I . . . would be *wrong*."

She said nothing, but the look on her face gave away the game. *You and Walker, it's just wrong.*

I knew then. I knew, but I had to be sure.

"Wrong," I repeated a second time, "because I'm trash?" My heart jumped into my throat, beating out an incessant rhythm that warned me against continuing. I did it anyway. "Or wrong because your husband is my father?"

CHAPTER 45

Charlotte Ames didn't answer my question, and that was almost answer enough. When she turned to walk away from me, I couldn't hear anything but the thudding of my own heart. The party, what Walker had just tried to pull, my fight with Lily—it all felt about a thousand miles away.

I willed my legs to propel me back toward the ballroom, but instead, I found myself running for the nearest exit.

I asked the senator's wife if he was my father, and she didn't deny it.

She didn't deny it.

She didn't deny it.

The next thing I knew, I was barefoot and staring at the valet stand a hundred yards away. I'd come out a side exit, but under the main archway, I could see people beginning to trickle out of the party.

I thought about the fact that in a different world, Nick might have been up there parking cars—if Campbell hadn't framed him.

Campbell. Even thinking her name hit me like a sucker punch. I had known that her dad was on my list. I hadn't ever thought, in any real way, about what that might make her to me.

What that might make Walker to me.

I asked the senator's wife if he was my father, and she didn't deny it.

"Baby?"

I turned to see my mom standing behind me on the lawn. She took one look at my bare feet and kicked off her own heels. "Anything you'd like to share with the class?"

That was her way of asking if I was okay. *Now* she wanted to know.

"Did Charlotte say something to you?" my mom pressed. "I swear to God, she is an even bigger bitch than I remember."

"Maybe that's because you slept with her husband." The words were out of my mouth before I'd decided to say them.

"Sawyer!" My mom stared at me. "That's not how we talk to each other."

"Is Sterling Ames my father?" I asked. Once the question was out there, I couldn't take it back. I didn't try to. "His wife warned me away from their son."

"You and the Ames boy?" My mom's eyes widened. "Oh, honey, you can't—"

"I'm not," I said emphatically. "But when I asked Charlotte Ames if the reason she was warning me away from her son was because we have the same father, she didn't deny it."

My mom stared at me, saying nothing.

"Is Sterling Ames my father?" I asked again. I needed to hear her say it. "Is he—"

"Yes."

One word. Just one. After all these years, that was the sum total of what I got. *Yes.* The senator was my father. Lily's ex-boyfriend was my brother. And Campbell—scheming, diabolical Campbell—was my sister.

Half-sister.

"That's all you have to say?" I asked my mom. "*Yes?*"

"What else do you want?" No one did flippant like my mom. "A play-by-play of our sexual encounter?"

She said that like she was joking. Like none of this mattered.

"I had a right to know," I said, hearing in those words how close my voice was to cracking.

"And now you do," my mom said. "So you can come home."

Come home? That was all she could say?

"Oh, sweetheart." My mom pulled me into a hug, and I let her.

I let her, even though I didn't know why.

"What difference would it have made if you'd known?" my mom asked, bringing my cheek to her shoulders and kissing the top of my head. "Your daddy didn't want us."

I found my voice again. "You asked him?"

She smoothed my hair back from my temple. "He knew I was pregnant. When I left town, he could have come after me. He could have chosen us, but even at seventeen, I wasn't stupid enough to think he would. It didn't matter. I didn't need him—*we* didn't."

For as long as I could remember, it had been the two of us against the world. I took care of her. She loved me.

"We had each other." My mom stepped back from the hug and took my chin gently in her hand. "It was enough, just you and me. We didn't need *anyone*."

The emphasis she put on that last word did not escape me.

"Anyone," I repeated. "Like Lillian."

Like any of our family at all.

"She's the one who kicked me out," my mom reminded me. "I don't know what she and my sister have been telling you. . . ."

They'd said remarkably little, all things considered.

"Did she?" I asked suddenly. "Kick you out?" I paused and then rephrased the question. "Did Lillian cut contact, or did you?"

My mom stared at me. "I did what I had to do."

"That's not an answer, Mom."

"She kicked me out." My mom pulled herself up to her full height and stared me down. "When I told my mother that I was pregnant, the great Lillian Taft took over. You've lived with her. You must know how she can be. Of course *Lillian Taft* had a plan."

My mom's voice was rising. I wondered how much louder she would have to get before the partygoers exiting in the distance heard every word.

"She was going to take you." My mom's body shook with pent-up emotion. "Her grand plan was for Olivia and J.D. to raise you. Like I wasn't even your mama. Like my sister would be better for you than me." She lowered her voice slightly, but the intensity in her gaze never wavered. "I said no. You were mine, baby. Not your father's, not anyone else's. I told Lillian . . ."

She closed her eyes for just a moment.

"I tried to tell her that, and she told me to get out."

I knew the rest of the story. My mom had driven until she'd run out of gas. She hadn't gotten very far.

"She tried to apologize," my mom bit out. "But there's no coming back from that."

It took me a second to process that statement. "Lillian apologized after she kicked you out?"

"Too little, too late. We didn't need her. Or Olivia. Or anyone else." My mom smiled. "What do you say?" she asked me. "Ice cream, then home?"

She made the suggestion so casually, so lightly.

"You told me your family kicked you out and never spoke to you again," I said.

"They did," my mom replied emphatically, even though she'd just gotten through telling me something different. "Why dwell on the past, Sawyer? You wanted answers. You got answers. Now you can come home."

"What about Lillian?" I found myself asking. "Aunt Olivia? Lily?"

I half expected my mom to point out what I had earlier in the evening: that it didn't have to be either/or. That even if I went back to her, they'd only be a forty-five-minute drive away.

"They aren't your family, baby." My mom gave me a sharp look. "I am."

"What about college?" I asked.

She could have told me that I didn't need Lillian's money, that I could work for another couple of years, enroll at community college, put myself through school.

"You don't need to go to college," she said instead.

"What?" I couldn't believe she'd just said that. And yet . . . I could. My mom wanted me to put all of this behind me and come home. We would be together, and that was what mattered to her—right up until the next time she took off.

"Sawyer?" My mom reached for my hand, but I pulled back. "Baby, after everything I've done for you . . ."

That was the straw that broke the camel's back. Not the fact that I'd found out who my father was here, like this, when she could have just *told* me. Not that she had unilaterally decided we were better off without family and lied to me about it my entire life. Not the way she full-on expected me to do exactly what she wanted, or the fact that she'd already made it clear that she was capable of going radio silent on me if I didn't.

After everything I've done for you . . .

I loved her. I always had. I hadn't ever expected her to be perfect. But no matter how hard I'd tried not to—I'd expected more than this.

"Mom," I said, my voice actually breaking this time. "Go home."

APRIL 15, 5:57 P.M.

Mackie came very close to asking this Nick character why *he* had been arrested. *Twice.* But it seemed bad form to admit that the only officer of the law in the room didn't know why *anyone* in the vicinity had been placed under arrest.

"Was there something in particular you wanted to say to Miss Taft?" Mackie prodded Nick. *If he could just direct this conversation a little . . .*

Nick turned to the girl in question. "Incoming."

Incoming? Mackie puzzled over that. *Incoming what?*

"Excuse me, Officer."

Mackie did not startle. He did not jump. He simply turned slowly to face the person who'd spoken behind him.

Another boy.

"I'm here for my sister," the boy said—more order than statement.

Before Mackie could respond, the one called Nick leaned back against the bars of the cell and snorted. "Which one?"

THREE AND A HALF MONTHS EARLIER

CHAPTER 46

"I loathe putting away Christmas decorations." Lillian was standing on a stepladder, removing nutcrackers from the mantel and handing them down to me. "Every year, I tell myself that I'm going to hire someone to decorate, and every year . . ."

"You realize that you can't outsource Christmas?" I said dryly.

"Oh, hush." Lillian finished with the mantel and made her way back down to solid ground. She studied me for a moment. "I appreciate the help."

I heard the *however* coming about a mile away.

"However," Lillian continued delicately, "I have to think that a girl your age has better things to do with your afternoon."

"Nope."

Lillian's expression suggested that she was in the process of trying to be diplomatic, which was never a good sign. "Sawyer, the night of the Christmas party . . ."

Nope. Nope. Nope. It had been two weeks, and I still didn't feel like discussing anything that had happened that night. It was no secret that my mom and I had fought, but Lillian had no idea what the two of us had fought about. When I'd told my mom to go home, she had. She'd left, and she hadn't looked back.

"Did something happen between you and Lily?" my grandmother asked.

Oh, I thought. *That.*

My mom had left me standing barefoot outside the clubhouse. Eventually, I'd found my shoes and returned inside. The first person I'd seen was Lily, and for a split second in time, I'd felt relieved. I might have pushed her away earlier, but when I'd *needed* someone . . .

My cousin had marched up to me and told me that I was no better than my mama.

I felt like she'd kicked me in the teeth, like everything leading up to that moment had been Lily being polite, not Lily being family—or my friend. I hadn't managed to put together what had happened until the next day, when Sadie-Grace had told me that "everyone" had been talking about my dance with Walker. The ubiquitous *everyone* had seen him pull me closer.

Everyone had seen us duck out into the hall.

I could have told Lily that nothing happened. I could have had some sympathy for the fact that she'd offered me an olive branch, and I'd turned it down. I could have concentrated on how she must have felt, having just told me that she'd had a moment with Walker and then watching the two of us duck out for a cozy, dimly lit, mistletoe-adjacent tête-à-tête.

But every ounce of my emotional capital had already been spent. I'd managed exactly two words. The first was *screw,* and the second was *you.*

"Why don't you ask Lily?" I turned my grandmother's habit of answering a question with a question back on her.

"I'm asking you, Sawyer Ann." Lillian was just as good at using silence to her advantage as I was.

"This is me, not answering," I clarified.

"You seem . . ." My grandmother chose her words carefully. ". . . on edge. Your mama—"

"I don't want to talk about my mom."

"You don't want to talk about your mama. You don't want to talk about Lily. I can only assume that you don't want to talk about whatever other bees you've gotten in your bonnet." Lillian opened a nearby box and gently settled one of the nutcrackers inside. "Unfortunately for you, I'm a nosy old woman, and I learned my lesson a long time ago about not asking."

I got the distinct sense that was a reference to my mother.

"Sawyer," my grandmother said gently. "Are you unhappy here?"

The question took me off guard. I'd come to Lillian's world to find out who my father was. I'd found out. By all rights, I should have been ready to leave.

But . . .

But there was nothing for me back home. If I returned, I'd fall right back into old habits. I might never leave, and someday, I'd find myself resenting it—resenting my mom for keeping me there.

"I said I would stay for nine months." That wasn't an answer to my grandmother's question, but it was all she was going to get. "So I'm staying."

After the Symphony Ball, I'd have options. Money. A future.

"About the contract . . ." my grandmother started to say, but before she could get further along than that, the doorbell rang. "That must be Davis," Lillian said.

"Davis," I repeated. *As in Davis Ames.*

Lillian went to answer the door, and I followed. The past two weeks had been so crammed full of holidays and traditions that I hadn't come face-to-face with a single member of the Ames family. Aunt Olivia had mentioned offhandedly that they typically spent winter break in the mountains. I'd very conveniently *not* had to think about what my paternity meant.

Until now.

"Lil." My paternal grandfather greeted my maternal grandmother with a nod the moment she opened the door.

"Davis," Lillian replied. "I'd ask you in, but the house is just a mess. You understand."

"How could I not?"

In any other circumstances, I might have been impressed that they could turn such a mundane conversation into a subtle power play, but that barely even registered as I found myself searching my grandfather's face for any resemblance, however fleeting, to my own.

"I'll get the papers for you," Lillian was saying. By the time I'd processed that statement, she was gone, leaving me alone with the Ames patriarch in the foyer.

"Papers?" I managed. That seemed like a nice, neutral thing for me to say. As a bonus, it wasn't *Your son knocked up my seventeen-year-old mother.*

"Appraisal papers," Davis clarified. "For those blasted pearls. Insurance has been kicking up a fuss about my numbers."

"So you asked Lillian for hers?" I was impressed despite myself. He'd bought a precious family heirloom out from underneath her, lost it, and didn't bat an eye at calling her up and asking her to provide proof of how much they'd been worth.

The man had balls of steel.

"You have a party tonight, don't you?" Davis asked abruptly. "One of those Symphony Ball whatsits. Campbell has been nattering on about it all week."

His word choice might not have sounded affectionate, but his tone when he talked about Campbell was. I couldn't help wondering if he knew—or even suspected—that I was his granddaughter, too.

"You're not the type to natter, are you?" Davis Ames said in response to my silence.

I said the first thing that came to mind. "Kind of a sexist way to describe someone talking."

He blinked.

"You wouldn't describe your grandsons as nattering," I elaborated.

If anything, Davis Ames seemed to find that amusing. "Walker hasn't spoken more than a word or two to me in months," he said. "Boone *natters* on about *Star Wars* all the time."

The affection wasn't as raw in his voice when he talked about the boys, but it hit me all the same. *Campbell. Walker. Boone.*

And me.

"Here you are." Lillian reappeared and held a folder out to Davis. "I made copies, but these are the originals. Do try not to misplace them."

The way he'd *misplaced* her pearls.

"Sawyer," Lillian said, clearly pleased with her dig, "why don't you run along and get ready for tonight? Your . . . *outfit* is hanging in the closet."

Davis Ames let his gaze linger on her for a moment longer, then turned back to me. "Planning to wear an eyebrow raiser tonight, are you?" he asked.

I'm your granddaughter. Your son is my father.

Out loud, I stuck to answering his question. "You could say that."

CHAPTER 47

"You cannot be serious."

I turned to face Lily. She was standing in the doorway to my room. The expression on her face could not have been more horrified if I'd declared my allegiance to a religious sect that didn't believe in wearing clothes, only snakes.

"You like?" I asked her, knowing quite well that she didn't.

"You *cannot* wear that to Casino Night."

This was the longest continuous conversation I'd had with her since the night of the Christmas party. I honestly wasn't sure if she was giving me the silent treatment or the other way around.

"Are you *trying* to make a scene?" Lily asked, still thoroughly aghast.

"It's a tuxedo, not a declaration of war," I said, knowing quite well that to my cousin, it might as well have been. "And besides, Lillian signed off on it."

"Mim would *never* . . ."

"She had it tailored for me." That shut Lily up—temporarily. Under normal circumstances, our grandmother probably would have been as horrified as Lily, but Lillian had loosened the reins in the wake of my mom's visit.

She wanted me to be happy here.

"Sadie-Grace told me that you asked for a sample of her father's hair." Lily recovered her voice, but didn't return to the topic of my outfit. Our grandmother was the ultimate trump card, and Lily knew it. "Is there anyone in our immediate social circle you *don't* intend to drag through the mud?"

I hadn't told Lily about my conversation with the senator's wife. I hadn't told her that my mom had confirmed what Charlotte Ames had implied. As far as my cousin knew, I was still looking into the men I'd circled in the photograph, ready and willing to tear their lives apart at the seams.

Just like I'm ready and willing to come between you and your one true love, right, Lil?

"Nothing happened between Walker and me." I knew that Lily would take the very mention of his name like a slap, but I'd never exactly been a "turn the other cheek" kind of person. "Whatever people say they saw, whatever you heard—nothing happened."

"We are not talking about this." Lily spoke admirably calmly for someone whose deep brown eyes were promising bloody, bloody murder.

Doubtful that she'd believe me, I tried one last time. "I have exactly no interest—*zero*—in your ex-boyfriend, Lily."

"I find that about as unlikely as the chances that you've suddenly developed a well-honed sense of decorum."

The fact that my cousin could turn a sentence about decorum into an insult was just about the most Lily thing I'd ever heard. It was also the last—very last—straw.

"Walker's my brother." I figured that would take the wind out of her sails.

She opened her mouth to shoot back, then blinked. And blinked. And used the most *unladylike* language I'd ever heard. It was downright *descriptive*—and far more creatively arranged (not to mention anatomically impossible) than I would have predicted.

"You can curse like a sailor," I said, impressed. "Who knew?"

"Sawyer Ann Taft." Lily channeled our grandmother and her mother and a full generation or two of Southern women before them. "Would you care to repeat what you just said?"

I couldn't help myself. "About your language choices?"

"Sawyer!"

I felt a tug in my stomach, like the muscles were twisting around each other, fibers being wound into rope. I'd missed her. I didn't want to admit that, even to myself.

But I had.

"I found out the night of the Christmas party." I wasn't usually a person who talked or stepped softly, but somehow, my voice refused to rise above a whisper. "The senator's wife let it slip when she caught Walker with me under the mistletoe. Nothing happened. Nothing was going to happen, but she didn't believe that."

Neither did you, I added silently, but that wasn't the point.

"I asked my mom, and she confirmed it." I swallowed, surprised at the size of the lumps in my throat. "Sterling Ames is the one who knocked her up."

"The senator is your father." Lily seemed to be having a hard time processing. She'd told herself a story about that night—about me. If *she'd* had a childhood obsession with telenovelas, that story might have taken a few more bizarre turns, but as it was, she hadn't seen this coming.

"The senator is my father," I repeated, "and since I'm not a big fan of *incest*—"

"Stop." Lily actually placed her hands over her ears. "Just . . . you can stop there."

I waited until she'd let her hands float back to her sides before responding. “I was never a threat, Lily. I was never your competition. For Walker, it’s always been you.”

“I don’t want to talk about Walker.” She tilted her chin upward.

Far be it from me to fight the chin tilt. “Are we good?” I asked.

“Good?” Lily repeated incredulously. “You can’t just tell me something like this, and . . .”

“And expect you to go on like life is normal?” So far, that was what I’d been trying to do. I’d succeeded, more or less, until I’d seen Davis Ames downstairs.

“Have you said anything to the senator?” Lily asked. “Are you going to say anything to him?”

I don’t know. I didn’t know if I was going to confront the man responsible for half of my DNA. I didn’t know if I was going to say anything to Walker or . . .

“Campbell will be there tonight.” Lily tried to catch my eyes. “You could tell her.”

Because that *would go over well.*

“Sawyer,” Lily said.

“I could tell her,” I repeated. “Or . . .” I straightened and smoothed one hand over the lapel of my tuxedo, lifting my own chin. “I could go to Casino Night, ignore Campbell Ames, and beat the pants off of everyone there at poker.”

CHAPTER 48

My tuxedo went over about as well as I had expected. At my grandmother's insistence, the shirt underneath was black silk, the square of fabric in my pocket a fiery red. I was wearing three-inch heels—another concession to Lillian—and, around my neck, a borrowed diamond choker.

"I love your outfit. It's just so *offbeat*!" The girl beside me was better at bluffing than any of the boys at our table. If she'd wanted her fake compliment to sound like a real one, it would have.

It didn't.

Relieving her of her remaining poker chips felt good. Given that this was a Symphony Ball event, the chips held no actual monetary value. The poker tables, roulette wheels, and blackjack dealers were just here to add to the ambiance. All the glamour of Monte Carlo, none of the vice.

Or at least, that was what the Symphony Ball mamas were aiming for. To my fellow Debs and Squires, however, this was a second New Year's Eve—all of the glamour, all of the vice.

I'd counted twelve flasks since I walked through the door.

"Don't look now," a voice stage-whispered beside me. "But I'm a little loopy."

I turned to find Sadie-Grace smiling adoringly at me. Her hair was pulled back to the nape of her neck, but part of it had already come loose—probably because she seemed unable to refrain from the occasional pirouette.

"Everything okay?" I asked. I'd never seen her pirouette-level anxious before.

"Lily says you're not my sister." Sadie-Grace stuck out her bottom lip. By the grace of God, she'd somehow managed a whisper that time instead of a stage whisper. "No sisters for Sadie-Grace," she continued morosely. "Only fake babies for a fake-beautiful girl . . ."

I didn't even try to follow what she was saying. I deeply suspected there had been an alcoholic beverage of some sort—or four—involved. She needed fresh air—and probably some water.

Standing up, I laid my cards down: a flush. Several groans, a half dozen dirty looks, and an impressive bounty of chips later, I escorted Sadie-Grace to the side of the room.

"Is everything okay?" I asked her again.

Sadie-Grace let out a lovely, delicate sigh. She stared out the window. After the debacle with the masquerade, the Symphony Ball committee had made the executive decision to look past the local country clubs for venues. Tonight, we had the top floor of Eton-Crane Tower, the tallest building in the city. It was shaped like an octagon, with panoramic windows overlooking the lights of downtown and everything that stretched off into the distance.

"I know something I shouldn't know," Sadie-Grace stated.

I peered at her. "Please tell me that this doesn't end with the revelation that you've got someone tied up in your guesthouse."

"We don't have a guesthouse anymore," Sadie-Grace replied automatically. "It's a mother-in-law suite now. Greer redid it for her parents so they can come from Dubai and stay when the baby is born."

"Okay," I said, waiting. I figured it wouldn't take much silence to prod her to keep going.

I was right.

Sadie-Grace pressed her cheek against the cool window, her hair even more lopsided than it had been a moment before. "There is no baby."

I waited for her to make that statement make sense.

"I found a pregnancy test Greer took—it's negative."

"She could still be . . ."

"I saw her trying on bellies." Sadie-Grace poked her own belly button through her dress.

"Who fakes a pregnancy?" I asked, but then I remembered the circumstances in which Greer had announced her delicate condition.

My mom was there—and Greer wasn't happy about it.

Charles Waters was not my father. What threat was my mother to his newly wedded bride?

"Do you think Boone's cute?" Sadie-Grace asked suddenly, lifting her cheek off the glass and smiling. "I think he's cute."

Oh, boy . . .

"Let's get you some water."

Sadie-Grace was nothing if not obliging. After I'd deposited her at Lily's side, I decided that *I* needed some fresh air. I paused at the roulette table just long enough to bet every chip I had on a long shot. I was walking away from the table when the winning color and number were called out.

A collective gasp informed me that my long shot had paid off.

"I . . . er . . . I don't have enough chips to pay you." The man behind the wheel was wearing a tuxedo that looked nearly as expensive as my own. I wondered how often he worked parties just like this one. "If we were actually playing for money, I'd cash you out, but . . . well . . ."

We weren't playing for money. There were no stakes here.

"Not a problem," I said. It was pretty much a law of nature that winning was easiest when you wanted to lose.

By the time I finally made it out a side door, I found myself cycling back to the questions Lily had brought up earlier. *Am I going to tell Walker? Or Campbell?* I'd almost succeeded at pushing the possibility out of my mind when I stepped into the stairwell and realized that I wasn't alone.

Speak—or think—of the devil, and she appears.

Campbell Ames was standing on the landing below me. I was on the forty-ninth floor. She was on the forty-eighth—and she wasn't alone.

"I shouldn't have come."

I recognized Nick's voice, even though I couldn't see his face. Campbell's auburn hair was piled high on her head. Her dress was red, tight and fitted. It came to the floor, but there was a slit up the side.

All the way up the side.

She was standing with one leg thrust forward, her hand lying on the back of Nick's neck. "I just need you to trust me a little while longer."

"Trust you?" Nick jerked back from her touch. "Even when we were having our fun, I never trusted you, Campbell."

"They're reinvestigating the theft, Nick. My father is putting pressure on the DA to make another arrest—and make it stick this time."

I counted the length of the silence between them with the beats of my own heart: *one, two . . .*

"I don't care what your father is doing," Nick said coldly.

"You don't know my father," Campbell insisted. "I don't know why he wants this case in the news again. I don't know what he's trying to redirect attention *from,* but Senator Sterling Ames always gets what he wants."

I swallowed, my throat suddenly dry. I had a theory—a good one—about why the senator might want to control the news cycle now.

His wife had confronted me. Had she confronted him? If he knew that *I* knew that he was my father, then he might have spent the past two weeks waiting to see what my next move would be.

Waiting to see if I would go public.

He hadn't even tried to approach me, but apparently had no qualms whatsoever about throwing Nick under the bus, just in case.

"Maybe they arrest me again, maybe they don't. Either way, it's none of your concern, *Miss Ames.*"

"You need to listen to me," Campbell insisted.

He was already brushing past her.

"I know why you're here," Campbell called after him.

Nick turned, annoyed. "I'm here because you sent me a note suggesting that my brother's continued care was contingent on me coming."

That was the first confirmation I'd gotten that Campbell was the anonymous donor paying for Colt Ryan's treatment. *Did you sell the pearls to pay for it? Or just natter away to your grandfather and ask him for a favor?*

Our grandfather.

"I'm not talking about why you're here *tonight,*" Campbell—my *sister*—said down below. "I know why you got a job at the club, why you pursued a relationship with me in the first place."

There was a beat of heavy silence.

"You don't know anything."

“I know that the police never found the car that hit your brother. I know there was an event at Northern Ridge that night. I know that a lot of people weren’t in any shape to drive.”

The implications of what Campbell was saying sank in slowly. *She’s implying that the person who put Nick’s brother in a coma was coming from Northern Ridge.*

“I know,” Campbell continued softly, “that your brother used to have a dog named Sophie.”

APRIL 15, 5:58 P.M.

"Which one what?" Mackie felt ridiculous even saying the words, but he persevered, squared his shoulders, and shot the boys a very hard look.

"Which sister," Nick clarified helpfully. "I understand Walker has two of them."

The newcomer presumably named Walker ignored both Nick and Mackie and turned to the holding cell. His gaze flitted briefly over three of the girls, then lingered on the fourth. The well-mannered one.

"I got your note, Lily."

"What note?" Mackie pressed in the silence that followed.

"You four sent him a note, too?" That question—from Nick—was aimed at the one he'd come to see. *Sawyer.*

"I am going to need to see these notes," Mackie insisted.

Walker turned toward Mackie, who noticed for the first time that one of the boy's eyes was black-and-blue. It looked like he'd gone to some effort to cover the bruising, but it was visible if you looked.

Mackie's instincts buzzed. *Notes. Bruises.* Hadn't one of the girls said something earlier about accomplices?

"I'm going to need to see some ID," Mackie told the visitors gruffly.

"And I," Walker replied, "am going to need to place a call to the family attorney."

TWO AND A HALF MONTHS EARLIER

CHAPTER 49

No arrests. No news. No sudden realizations. In the month since Casino Night, every morning had started exactly the same way. I checked the news for mention of Nick's name—and the names of every single member of the Ames family.

Excluding my own.

I hadn't gone back to volunteering when the senator's office had reopened in the new year. I'd barely seen Walker or Campbell. Most days, instead of thinking about them, I found myself thinking about Nick, about what the Ames family—*my* family—had done to him.

Campbell had framed him. The senator had pressured the DA to reopen the case. Was that all?

Enter my new obsession. In addition to going back over the conversation I'd overhead between Campbell and Nick a thousand times, I'd started a new volunteering gig. Three days a week, I worked at the last nursing home we'd visited during Food, Coats, Comfort, and Company.

Colt Ryan was still a patient. If his brother had been to see him, it hadn't been when I was volunteering. *Yet.*

"What did you bring me?" Estelle—she of the fondness for the *good stuff* in romance novels—was my self-appointed greeter when I walked in the front door. "Valentine's Day is coming up. Chocolate?"

I shook my head. I'd come empty-handed today. Estelle found that a matter of some concern.

"Pretty girl like you," she said, "you should have the boys knocking down your door and drowning you in chocolate. A beau or two never hurt anyone."

I tried to decide how to best and most diplomatically say *finding out exactly what kind of man my biological father is has only confirmed my belief that anyone interested in hooking up with a teenage girl is supremely not worth hooking up with. Also: the last time someone tried to kiss me, it turned out he was my half-brother.*

I settled for "I should probably put out more."

Estelle chortled gleefully, the way I'd known she would. I was fairly certain she'd played the high-society game with the best of them in her time, but she'd clearly given up proprieties a few years back.

"I'm going to hold you to that," she swore. "Starting now." For an old woman, she moved surprisingly quickly.

One second I was facing Estelle, and the next she'd turned me forty-five degrees, placed both hands on the small of my back, and shoved. I got a face full of gray T-shirt before I realized that the person wearing the T-shirt was Nick.

He reached out to catch me automatically, and my mind went immediately to the first time we'd met, when I'd nailed him with the car door and reached out to steady him.

I was wearing my own clothes today—non-Lillian-approved ones—and it took a second for recognition to hit him.

If you knew who I really was, who I'm related to, you'd toss me right out that door.

He dropped his hands to his sides, and I cleared my throat. "Can we talk?"

"*Talking.* That's what we called it back in my day, too," Estelle said knowingly. "You treat her right, young man." She waggled her finger at Nick. "And next time," she called after us, "I want chocolate!"

I assumed the two of us would end up in his brother's room, but Nick led me outside to the stone garden instead.

"What?" he said simply.

The last time I'd seen him, he'd asked me to keep my mouth shut. I had. He didn't know I'd overheard his conversation with Campbell. From his perspective, we were essentially strangers. What could I possibly have to talk to him about?

"Is silent staring what passes for polite conversation for you high-society types these days?" Nick asked.

I responded by removing from my pocket an object that I'd carried with me for the past month: a heart-shaped tag that said *Sophie.*

"Where did you get this?" Nick's voice wasn't neutral anymore. His face wasn't, either. "Did Campbell put you up to this?"

"Campbell doesn't know I'm here. She also doesn't know that I'm her illegitimate half-sister." I hadn't planned to let him in on that little secret—just like I hadn't told Walker or Campbell—but I needed him to listen. *When in doubt, take 'em off guard.* "And in answer to your question: I stole that tag from Campbell's locker at the club months ago. I had no idea what it meant."

"But you do now?"

No. I knew it had something to do with his brother. I knew that when Campbell had mentioned Sophie's name a month ago, he'd responded with shock, and once he'd gotten over the shock, he'd gotten in her face and demanded that she "tell him."

He hadn't specified *what.*

"I know that it matters," I said. I could see the muscles in his shoulders tensing.

"Why can't your family leave me the hell alone?"

I would never get used to the Ames family being referred to as *mine.*

"I'm the reason the senator wanted to open the case back up, Nick." Confession was supposedly good for the soul. "I'm the reason he's desperate to control the narrative in the press. If you've ever wondered what a scandal in human form looks like—it's me."

I wasn't just the product of an affair. I was the product of an adult man's affair with a teenage girl. After six weeks of silence on my part, the senator had to suspect that I planned on keeping my mouth shut, but he couldn't have been sure.

I still wasn't sure.

"I don't know what's going on with you and Campbell," I admitted, scanning Nick's face, "but I know it has something to do with what put your brother in that coma."

Nick took a step toward me, then hesitated. I waited, knowing that he didn't owe me anything. If anything, I owed him.

"Not *what* put my brother in the coma, Ms. Scandal," Nick said finally, his voice low. "*Who.*"

CHAPTER 50

When I got back to Lillian's house, I did something that I hadn't done once since the night of the masquerade. I pulled up the *Secrets on My Skin* website. The most recent entry—Campbell's—stared back at me.

He made me hurt you.

He as in the senator? *You* as in Nick? The story the latter had told me fresh in my mind, I scrolled back to the very first *Secrets* post and looked at the date.

"One does not wish to question your life choices," Lily said from behind me. "*However* . . ."

"However," I suggested, "this one involves you?"

In the photo I'd just pulled up, my cousin was wearing nothing but a threadbare towel. The words inscribed on her chest, just under her collarbone and above the edge of the towel, were: *I am broken inside.*

"How long after Walker broke up with you did you post this?" I asked. I had a theory about why Lily had started this blog—why she'd *needed* to.

Lily ran one finger lightly over the picture. "One week."

I reverse engineered the timeline in my mind: A week before

Lily had posted this entry, Walker Ames had broken up with her. He'd dropped out of college. He'd started going out of his way to make sure that people didn't see the golden boy when they looked at him.

Two days before *that*, an unidentified car had plowed into Colt Ryan.

The details Nick had given me were bare-bones: His brother had gotten ill and left work early. He'd had to walk from the club to the bus stop.

Almost the entire two-mile stretch was owned by Northern Ridge.

I know there was an event at Northern Ridge that night, Campbell had said. *I know that a lot of people weren't in any shape to drive.*

Nick had taken over his brother's job because he'd believed the person responsible for the accident was coming from that party. He'd wanted to find the SOB who'd left his brother, half-broken, on the side of the road.

He'd believed that the police couldn't be trusted to do it.

When Campbell had flirted with him, he'd responded with the hope of gleaning some information about the party that night.

"Two days before Walker broke up with you . . ." I forced myself to focus on the here and now, on Lily. "Did you go to an event at the club?"

"What is going on with you?" Lily frowned.

"Just think," I told her. "Two days before Walker broke up with you."

Lily didn't have to think very hard. "The wedding."

"What wedding?" I could feel my pulse start to tick upward.

"Sadie-Grace's father's," Lily said.

Greer's, my mind amended. I tried to fit this information into what I already knew—and what I didn't.

"Was Walker at the wedding?" I asked. "Was Campbell?"

The questions must have seemed random to Lily, but she answered—in the affirmative.

Lots of people were there that night, I told myself—but lots of people hadn't begun a downward spiral almost immediately thereafter. Lots of people hadn't leapt into a physical relationship with the hit-and-run victim's brother—and then framed him for theft.

Lots of people weren't paying for Colt Ryan's care.

"Tell me what you're thinking, Sawyer Ann."

I met my cousin's deep brown eyes. I told her what Nick had told me—and then I spelled out *exactly* what I was thinking.

"I'm guessing that either Campbell or Walker was driving that car."

"You're jumping to conclusions," Lily said immediately.

"Colt Ryan had a dog named Sophie," I responded. "Nick said that her collar broke that morning. Colt took it to work to fix it." I held Lily's gaze in my own. "After the hit and run, the collar was nowhere to be found, but somehow, the tag ended up in Campbell's locker."

Maybe that was a coincidence. Maybe Walker's downward spiral was nothing more than a pre-college meltdown.

"Sawyer." Lily stared down at her hands.

"What?"

Lily took long enough to reply that I wasn't sure she was going to. "When Campbell started blackmailing me," she said faintly, "I wondered how she figured out I was the one behind *Secrets*. Why she cared who was posting."

"What does that have to do—" I started to ask, but I cut off when Lily left the room.

When she returned, she was holding the tablet she'd used for *Secrets* tight with both hands. She sat down beside me, then quietly pulled up the queue—the posts she *hadn't* gotten around to publishing.

"What if the reason Campbell wanted to figure out who was behind *Secrets* was because there was a secret she didn't want to get out?" Lily pressed her lips together. "I remember all of the submissions I got. Every one." She pulled up a picture in the queue and turned the tablet toward me.

In this particular shot, she was lying prone, her back arched and her hands digging into what appeared to be sand. Her head was thrown back and chopped out of the shot. The message was vertical, starting on one arm and continuing on the other.

I was driving.

In isolation, that sentence seemed benign. But knowing what we knew . . .

"You think Campbell sent this secret in and then regretted it?" I asked Lily. "Or do you think . . ."

Do you think it was Walker?

"I don't know," Lily said quietly. She straightened, her chin jutting out. "I do know that we can't sit here all day asking questions we have no way of answering."

"Wanna bet?"

"I'm sure you haven't forgotten what this afternoon is," Lily replied, which, of course, meant that she was sure I had. "We have our second-to-last Deb event, excepting the ball."

My first instinct was to tell her where she could shove that reminder—and the event—but my next instinct was more mathematical. *Deb event = mandatory attendance. Mandatory attendance = Campbell's presence.*

Campbell's presence = answers.

"I can honestly say," I told Lily, "that I've never found myself so motivated to attend a party in my life."

"Not a party." Lily wasn't a person who smirked, but she came very, very close.

I didn't trust that expression. "What are we doing?"

She rose to her feet and turned before answering. I could only make out one word, and that word . . .

Was *spa*.

CHAPTER 51

If there was a phrase more perfectly designed to drive fear into my heart than *Spa Day*, I hadn't heard it yet. Fifteen minutes in, I wasn't sure which was more horrific: the fact that this particular event was set to last all afternoon and well into evening, or the fact that I was going to be spending a disturbing amount of that time sans clothing.

"Relax your face." The order came accompanied with pressure from the thumbs of the "specialist" under both of my eyes. "You are carrying too much stress."

I was naked, my legs were wrapped in seaweed, and the concoction this woman was about to apply to my face was bubbling. I would have been stressed without having phrases like *hit and run*, *cover-up*, and *coma* bouncing around my head.

I was driving.

"Blink!"

The exclamation mark on the end of that order seemed to suggest that I was supposed to blink with a vengeance.

"Open!"

I opened my eyes. The next thing I knew, steady hands were

working themselves like five-legged spiders down my cheekbones. Another girl might have found this experience relaxing.

"Close!"

"Have you ever heard," I asked the specialist through gritted teeth, "of a medieval torture device known as the pear of anguish?"

My oh-so-charming conversational skills did not get me out of the facial. They also did not get me my clothes back. I did, however, earn a trip to the hot rock sauna. Since this was supposed to be a bonding activity—a Debutante-only "girls' day" in advance of our "big day"—the sauna wasn't private.

I recognized the Debs sitting there when I arrived, but didn't know them well enough to even consider shedding the towel. I kept half an ear tuned to their conversation as I forced myself to sit and allowed my brain to cycle back to the information playing in my memory in a solid loop.

Somebody was driving the car that hit Colt Ryan. Somebody submitted that secret. Somebody—most likely Campbell, unless she lied to get Nick to meet with her—is paying for Colt's care. Campbell got Sophie's tag somewhere. She kept it for a reason.

Just like Campbell had stolen my grandmother's necklace for a reason. Just like she'd blackmailed Lily and framed Nick for a reason . . .

The door to the sauna opened. I half expected it to be Sister Dearest herself, but instead, Sadie-Grace stuck her head in. She smiled when she saw me, then took up a position to my left.

"Saunas make me nervous."

I glanced sideways at the other girls. I could sit here, waiting for answers to come to me—or I could look for them myself.

"How would you like to go on a mission?" I asked Sadie-Grace.

She frowned. "The kind where you convert people?"

"Not exactly."

There were six semiprivate saunas at Omega Wellness and Spa. We found Campbell in the fifth. Lily was already in there with her. I shot a brief look at my cousin, and she gave a subtle shake of her head.

She hadn't started the interrogation yet.

There were two other Debs sitting nearby. "There's room for you," I told them, "in sauna two."

"You can't just kick us out," one objected. "Campbell—"

I sat. Sadie-Grace sat. Campbell stood, let her towel drop to the ground, and turned to the other girls. "Go." Campbell waved a hand at them when they didn't move. She repeated the gesture with an aristocratic arch of her eyebrow.

After a brief deer-in-headlights moment, the other Debutantes scattered. Campbell waited until the door had closed behind them before she turned back to us.

"Feeling modest, are we?" she asked, eyeing our towels and seemingly unbothered that she was bare as the day she was born.

"I make it a general rule not to get naked around people who have a history of blackmail," I replied.

"I got a call from Nick." Campbell apparently wasn't in the mood to play. "He said that the two of you talked."

"Did he mention I gave him the dog tag from your locker?"

Campbell's gaze darted toward Lily and Sadie-Grace.

"Don't mind us," Lily said sweetly. "We'll just be over here minding our own business and listening to every blessed word you say."

"Whatever you think you know . . ." Campbell said flatly, her eyes going from Lily's back to mine. "Leave it. Nick doesn't need your help."

"Because he has you?" I asked with a heavy dollop of sarcasm.

Campbell didn't reply. The faint hiss of steam entering the room punctuated the silence.

"You know," Lily said coyly, "I've been looking back at all of the submissions I got for *Secrets*." She paused. "There was one in particular . . ."

My cousin was better at this than I'd anticipated.

"You're looking a little flushed, Lillian." Campbell stared her down. "I think your skin is a tad too delicate for the heat. And were I in your position, I wouldn't go around talking about *Secrets*."

This could go on—and on and on and on. "Sadie-Grace," I said, deciding to speed the process up, "would you like to hear a story?"

"Telling stories is actually my second-greatest talent," Sadie-Grace said seriously. "After bows."

I amended my suggestion. "How about I tell you a story, and then you can tell me how to improve it?"

Sadie-Grace seemed delighted with the prospect. As I spun my tale, I kept my eyes on hers, waiting to feel Campbell's shift to me. "Once upon a time, there was a hit and run."

Sadie-Grace gave me a look. "That is not a good way to start a story."

"So noted." I continued, keeping the embellishments to a minimum. "The police were not overly invested in finding the perpetrator, so they never found him." I paused. "Or her."

Lily kept her eyes locked on Campbell's so that I didn't have to.

"At some point after the accident, a guilt-stricken individual submitted a secret to an anonymous blog."

Sadie-Grace raised a hand tentatively. "If this is a story, who's the protagonist?"

Good question.

"We're dealing with more of an antihero." Now I was just

shooting in the dark. "Someone who didn't *mean* to hurt anyone."

"Sadie-Grace is right." Campbell had probably never said those words before in her life. "This is not a very compelling story."

"I heard you talking to Nick at Casino Night," I shot back. When that didn't get a reaction, I said the one thing I could say that would guarantee me a response.

"Would now be a good time for a plot twist?" I asked Sadie-Grace.

"It's always a good time for a plot twist!"

"Spoiler alert." I stood and pivoted to face Campbell head-on. "This one involves my mom and your dad."

Actual, undisguised emotion flitted over Campbell's even features. First confusion, then curiosity, and then . . .

"I would never just come right out and say this, Sawyer, but your mama . . . well, you can tell she's lived a hard life, can't you? At this point, she's a mechanical bull, and the senator? He's partial to thoroughbreds."

It took me a second to get past the insult and realize that she thought that I was suggesting that her father was cheating with my mother *now*.

"Twist within a twist," I said. "My mother was seventeen at the time."

Campbell opened her mouth, but whatever retort she'd been constructing died on her tongue.

"Is this the part where you ask me if your father was the only one she was sleeping with?" I asked innocently. "Because the answer to that question is yes."

Lily made a show of looking between the two of us. "I can see a resemblance."

"Lily!" Sadie-Grace was aghast. "Their auras don't look alike *at all*."

Campbell recovered her voice, but the emotion in it was impossible for me to read. "Could you excuse us?"

Us as in me and Campbell. Lily looked on the verge of refusing, but at the last second, she shot a long, knowing look at me—and then she tugged Sadie-Grace out the door.

"So," Campbell said. "You've somehow come to believe that my daddy is your father."

"*Somehow* has a name," I clarified. "Its name is Charlotte You-Absolutely-Cannot-Become-Involved-With-My-Son-Because-It-Would-Be-*Wrong* Ames."

Campbell tilted her head to the side. "You're saying that my mother told you that you're my father's bastard child?"

When you put it like that, it did sound somewhat unlikely.

"My mom confirmed it," I said. "So, *sis* . . ." I took a step toward her. "Just between the two of us, I have to know: Which one of you was driving the car that night—you or Walker?"

CHAPTER 52

"Once upon a time, there was a girl." Campbell had the cadence of a storyteller, her tone lilting and the rhythm halfway to musical. "She had a heart of glass, and inside the glass, a heart of stone, and she knew better than to care about anyone."

I was fairly certain Sadie-Grace would have approved of *this* story—just as certain as I was that Campbell could have saved both of us a lot of trouble by cutting straight to the truth.

"There was a ball one night—a wedding ball, and the girl with the heart of glass and stone-within-glass had a little too much to drink. Her brother had a little too much to drink." She shrugged. "Everyone had a little too much to drink."

She dropped the affected style of speaking so abruptly that I wondered whether it had been for my benefit—or hers.

"Let me guess," I said, "the next part involves a horse-drawn carriage and some fairy-tale drunk driving."

"I don't have to tell you any of this." Campbell grabbed for her towel. That, more than the staccato bursts of pent-up emotion in her tone, told me that she was feeling vulnerable.

"Were you driving the car?" I asked again. "Or was Walker?"

She didn't reply.

"What about your father?" I asked. *Our father,* I corrected silently. "Did you call him after the two of you hit Colt? Did he take care of the problem?"

Sterling Ames was the one pushing for an arrest in the theft of the pearls. He was the reason that Campbell had felt the need to warn a boy she had actively and intentionally framed.

What were the chances that my biological father had pressured the authorities *not* to look into the hit and run too hard?

"Daddy called someone, and that someone took care of everything." Campbell flipped her hair over her shoulder, but it was hot enough in the sauna that some strands remained plastered to her cheeks, her shoulders, her neck. "That's what he does, Sawyer. He makes calls. He doesn't talk to me—or listen. He doesn't see me, the way he sees Walker. But if I'm in trouble, *that* gets his attention. He likes taking charge and making things happen. Quite frankly, if what you say about his relationship with your mama is true, I'm surprised he hasn't taken care of you."

Well, didn't that sound ominous?

I focused on what mattered. "You said that he doesn't see you, the way he sees Walker, that he only pays attention when you're in trouble. When you're a problem." I let those words hang in the air for an instant. "Were you the one driving that night?"

"Does it matter?" Campbell asked. If she'd wanted to, she could have denied it. She could have cast the blame on her brother. If she'd had a heart of stone-within-glass, then she would have.

She would have cared only about herself. But Campbell had told me once that she loved her brother.

Everyone does.

"It was Walker, wasn't it?" I asked quietly. There was something in her expression, something vulnerable and raw beneath the sweat and the flush. "You're protecting him."

Even though he was their father's favorite. Even though he was the one their father looked at and *saw.*

"It was me." Campbell flashed her teeth at me. "Happy? Not Walker. Me."

"You're lying." I was possibly channeling television detectives a little too much. "You're protecting him—just like you had to find out who was behind *Secrets* once you realized he'd confessed."

"*Walker. Was. Not. Driving.*" Campbell's fist tightened around the towel in her hand. She turned her back to me and wrapped it taut around her body.

"If Walker wasn't driving," I pressed, "then why exactly did he hop on the merry-go-round of self-destruction two days later?"

"Because," Campbell said, her voice low and fierce and strangely hollow, "he thinks that he was."

APRIL 15, 6:01 P.M.

After Mackie had acquired the boys' driver's licenses, it occurred to him to do the same for the girls. Holding all six in one hand, he retreated to the nearest computer station and ran all of them through the system.

Sawyer Ann Taft, Lillian Taft Easterling, Campbell Caroline Ames, Sadie-Grace Waters. None of the girls' names returned any hits. A little poking around online, however, revealed that what *Nick Ryan* had said earlier was entirely correct: The quartet in the holding cell was a perfect storm of social connections. *Senator Sterling Ames. Oil magnate Charles Waters.* Mackie stopped himself right there. He didn't need a search engine to tell him that Lillian Taft was, among other things, the Magnolia County Police Department's single largest donor.

Glumly, Mackie turned his attention to the boys' IDs. Nick Ryan returned multiple hits in the system—the juvie records were sealed, but the more recent one gave Mackie *plenty* to chew on.

"Fifty-thousand-dollar pearls," he murmured. His heart ticked up a beat. *The girls mentioned pearls.* He ran the last ID.

Walker Ames.

Mackie stared at the screen. A record had popped up, but every line in it—every single one, other than the name—was blank.

TWO AND A HALF MONTHS EARLIER

CHAPTER 53

Walker wasn't driving, but he thinks he was. I stared at Campbell.

"You were driving." My mind was spinning. "But Walker doesn't know that. He thinks . . ." I was so horrified I could barely form the words. "You *let* him think that he's the one who hit Colt?"

No response from Campbell.

"How does that even work?" I took one step and then another, until I was standing in front of Campbell instead of behind her. "You were both drunk, but he was too drunk to remember? Did you put his body in the driver's seat? Or just lie to him later?"

Campbell bolted. In a flash of white towel and tan skin, she was halfway out the door. I followed on her heels. All I could think was that Walker was my half-brother. He was the type of person who pulled a girl out onto the dance floor and invited her to insult him. He missed being a *good guy*. He chased people away, because deep down, he believed that he deserved to be alone.

"How could you?" I started to say, but before I finished, Campbell stepped to the side. I was still going forward. Somehow, I ended up outside the door, and she ducked back in. Before I could react, she slammed the door to the sauna.

I hadn't been aware that it locked until I tried to get back in.

"Campbell!" I pounded on the door with my fist. "Open this door!"

Eventually resigning myself to the fact that she had no intention of doing so, I turned to make my way back toward the changing room. *Whatever my next move is, it is not going to happen while I'm wearing literally nothing but a towel.*

Unfortunately, that thought proved to be prophetic. I made it half a step away from the sauna before I realized that when Campbell had slammed the door, she'd caught my towel. The edge was stuck between the door and the frame.

I tugged, to no avail.

I looked down the hallway—to the left, to the right—but there was no one there. No Lily, no Sadie-Grace, no spa employees.

Whatever my next move is, I realized, setting my jaw, *it's not going to happen while I'm wearing nothing but a towel.*

Unless I wanted to stand here indefinitely, it was going to happen while I was wearing nothing at all.

We shall not speak of the rest of Spa Day.

Suffice to say, I eventually obtained my clothes, and I was also asked to leave the premises. That was how I ended up back at Lillian's house several hours earlier than scheduled. I fit my key into the front door and tried to prepare myself for the Southern Inquisition.

I eased the door open an inch or two, but realized an instant later that I needn't have bothered. Aunt Olivia and Uncle J.D. were arguing too loudly to hear me.

"Are you sure there's nothing you want to tell me?" Aunt Olivia phrased the jab as a question.

"You know everything, Olivia. You'd be the first one to remind me of that." Uncle J.D. was easygoing. Uncle J.D. was a goofball—90 percent John David and only 10 percent Lily. But right now, he sounded . . . not quite angry.

Bitter.

"Allow me to rephrase, dear: are there any *financial* matters that I should be aware of?"

"Stay out of it, Liv."

"Don't call me that." Aunt Olivia's tone wasn't quite angry, either. *Cold.* "I called to check on the renovation timeline. It's ridiculous that it's taken them this long. Imagine my surprise when they said the project was halted in December."

"I'm going to work this out. . . ."

"Halted for lack of *funds*."

She just mentioned money, I thought dumbly. *Aunt Olivia doesn't talk about money.*

I thought back to the auction—to the moment when Davis Ames had outbidden Uncle J.D. on the family pearls. The old man had mentioned something about rumors.

Before Uncle J.D. could reply to Aunt Olivia's accusation, before she could press him for an answer, a door slammed.

"If you get a call from the neighbors," I heard John David call out, "I want you to know that duck had been infected with the zombie virus, and he had it coming."

The argument in the kitchen evaporated in an instant.

"Come in here," Uncle J.D. called back, "and tell us about this zombie duck."

I heard John David sigh. "I might have scared him. And he might have pooped *all over* the neighbor's car."

Deciding this was as much of a distraction as I was going to get, I opened and closed the door—loudly. "I'm home," I called. Before anyone could reply, I darted for the stairs. *Thank you, John David, patron saint of girls weathering the fallout of accidental nudity.*

I made it up a third of the grand staircase before I heard the distinct sound of a throat clearing behind me. I turned to see my grandmother standing at the bottom of the stairs.

"Sawyer," she said. "A word?"

CHAPTER 54

Lillian waited until she'd poured each of us a cup of coffee before she spoke.

"I don't want you worrying about your aunt and uncle."

"Okay." I took a long drink of coffee to avoid saying more, and she led me out to the front porch. A bench swing hung there. Lillian sat and, with an arch of her eyebrow, commanded me to do the same.

"Olivia has a way of landing on her feet. I should have worried less about her growing up." Lillian took a sip of her drink. "And more about your mama."

Since Christmas, Lillian had only tried to bring up my mom once or twice.

"I don't intend to make the same mistake with you."

I realized then that this was an ambush. Or possibly an intervention. I wondered if my grandmother had been informed about "the streaking incident."

"You and Lily have obviously mended fences," Lillian commented, making me think the answer to that question was no. "I'm glad to see it—but I also see *you*. You aren't sleeping, Sawyer. You pace around this place like a cat in a cage. Something is bothering you. This would be an appropriate time for you to share what that something is."

Oh, you know. My biological father may or may not be pressuring the DA to arrest a boy who was framed by my devil of a half-sister, who also somehow convinced her brother—who tried to kiss me—that he was the one who put that other boy's brother in a coma.

"Things are fine," I said.

"Sawyer." Lillian fixed me with a look. "*Splendid* is good, *good* is okay, and *okay* and *fine* are horrendous."

Not for the first time, I got the distinct feeling that Lillian would be rather lethal at poker. And chess.

"What can you tell me about the Ames family?" I asked. I meant the question to distract her, but that didn't keep me from leaning forward to hear the answer.

"Why do you ask?" Lillian covered her lips with her coffee mug, just long enough to obscure whatever fleeting emotions my question might have provoked.

I'd always believed in absolute honesty: Say what you mean, mean what you say, and don't ask a question if you don't want to know the answer.

And then I became a Symphony Debutante.

"I've been having some trouble with Campbell Ames." I could have told her what my mother had told me six weeks earlier. I didn't—and wasn't even sure why. "And over Christmas, Walker tried his hardest to kiss me."

Lillian didn't bat an eye at either of those statements. "Never trust an Ames boy," she said. "They're too handsome for their own good and too ambitious for anyone else's."

Ambitious wasn't exactly a word I would have used to describe Walker. The senator, on the other hand?

"Are you speaking from personal experience?" I asked. I didn't expect my grandmother to answer. Lillian Taft could dodge questions as expertly as she could use them as weapons.

Just this once, however, she surprised me.

"Davis Ames and I grew up together." There was a long pause, and then she clarified. "Not here."

She didn't mean *here* as in this geographical location. She meant this world. This social stratosphere.

This twisted, sparkling place.

"Davis was always ambitious," my grandmother mused. "He would say that we had that in common." Another pause, another discreet lift of the coffee mug to her lips. "The place we came from . . . it was the kind of place I was terrified that Ellie would end up."

Lillian so rarely referred to my mother by name. It was *your mama, your mother, my daughter.*

"I didn't do enough to keep this family together." Lillian stared out at the street. I wondered if she even realized she'd changed the subject, or if in her mind, it was all connected: her past with Davis Ames, the way she'd turned my mother out, the scandal, the fact that I was here, sitting on this porch with her, now.

You did what you could. That was what I was supposed to say, but there was still enough of the old Sawyer in me that I didn't. I wouldn't lie to her.

Or, at least, I wouldn't lie to her about *this.*

"Did you kiss him?" Lillian asked suddenly. "Walker Ames?"

"I wouldn't do that to Lily." It occurred to me then that what Campbell had told me—what she'd done to Walker—would hit my cousin a thousand times harder than it had hit me. Campbell's lie had torn Lily's life apart at the seams.

"I do not recommend kissing Ames boys." Lillian's voice brought me back to the present. "If you can help it."

CHAPTER 55

When Lily got home, I meant to tell her everything. The truth was right there on the tip of my tongue, but instead, I told her what had happened *after* Campbell had locked me out of the sauna.

"Greer Waters was the one who caught me." I shuddered.

"In your birthday suit," Lily clarified. "Sadie-Grace's stepmother caught you scampering down the halls of the spa buck naked."

"That is an accurate assessment of the situation, yes."

Lily pressed her lips together. I thought she was scowling, but then her shoulders shook, and I realized that she was trying very hard not to laugh.

"What did you say?" she asked, a giggle escaping.

I didn't particularly want to rehash this, but I did want Lily to keep smiling. I wanted to figure out what to *do* about Walker before I brought the world as my cousin knew it crashing down.

"I covered my crotch with my right hand and my boobs with my left forearm." I shrugged. "And then I looked at her stomach and said, 'You're starting to show.'"

• • •

It took Lily several minutes to recover. She laughed so hard she cried, and when she asked me if I'd managed to get any information out of Campbell, I told her that I hadn't.

I didn't want to be the one to tell her what had broken Walker. I wanted to fix it.

Late that night, I saw a familiar SUV driving down the cul-de-sac. It pulled into Davis Ames's drive and waited outside the gate. From a distance, I couldn't tell who was driving or if there were any passengers, but the last time I'd seen this particular vehicle had been at the basket-wrapping marathon for Food, Coats, Comfort, and Company.

The two most likely drivers were Walker and Campbell.

As I watched, the gates to the Ames estate opened, and the SUV disappeared past them.

The decision to add *breaking and entering* to my list of recent felonies—kidnapping, accessory to grand theft, indecent exposure—was surprisingly easy. If Walker was the one visiting their grandfather—*my* grandfather—he deserved to know the truth, and if it was Campbell, I had a roll of duct tape with her name on it.

Duct-taping my conniving half-sister to a chair might not prove practically advantageous at this point, but I was positive it would feel really, really good.

Scaling the gate wasn't a problem. Proceeding past the "skulking outside the house" portion of this endeavor proved significantly harder. I was weighing the benefits of sneaking around back when I felt something—or *someone*—brush against my leg.

Or, more specifically, my thigh.

I skittered backward and whirled. In the darkness, I couldn't make anything out right away, but I could hear the sound of heavy breathing.

The closest thing I have to a weapon is duct tape. That thought formed in my mind an instant before I managed to locate my assailant.

"William Faulkner!" I scolded in a whisper.

The dog stared up at me with what, in the dark, I could only assume was an adoring expression.

"How the hell did you get past the gate?" I asked.

William Faulkner was not forthcoming with answers. Of the 199 breeds eligible to compete in the Westminster Dog Show, there were a handful that I would have classified as capable of both stealth and getting past that gate.

The hundred-plus-pound Bernese mountain dog was not one of them.

As if sensing this evening was not going my way, William Faulkner attempted to comfort me—and by that, I mean that she bumped my body with hers, nearly sending me sprawling to the ground, and then threw her head back and started barking.

I tried to convince her to stop, but it was like she'd waited her entire life for the chance to perform the lead in a doggy opera.

I barely heard the front door to the Ames house open. I made an attempt at retreating even farther into the shadows, but Davis Ames scanned his lawn with military precision and his gaze landed first on the mammoth dog and then on me.

"Sawyer?"

"You must have impressive night vision," I called back. Realizing that I should probably make at least an attempt to explain, I racked my brain.

"William Faulkner get out again?" he asked.

I latched on to that explanation like a lifesaver. "I have no idea how she got past the gate."

That gave him a moment's pause. "How did *you* get past the gate?"

"I'm going to plead the Fifth on that one."

With the scant light from the house, I couldn't see his expression, but I had the distinct feeling that response had gotten me either a smile or a smirk.

"Your grandmother always was one for climbing trees," he commented.

"Is Walker here?" I asked. Now that stealth was out the window, the direct approach seemed to be my best bet.

"You are aware that it is past midnight."

"Sure am," I replied.

I actually heard him snort this time.

"I hate to disappoint you, young lady, but Walker isn't here. The boy hasn't been by in weeks."

Davis Ames had to have noticed the dramatic transformation his grandson had gone through in the wake of the accident. Allowing myself one second to grit my teeth and another to hide the roll of duct tape behind my back, I took a few steps toward the front door.

"Walker isn't here," I repeated. "Is Campbell?"

Davis Ames jingled the change in his pocket, then nodded toward the house. "Why don't you come inside?"

I wondered, suddenly, if he knew that his son was my father. Was that why he'd stepped in when Lucas had bid on me at Pearls of Wisdom? To prevent people from assuming that I was a bastard Ames?

Lucas doesn't care about appearances, but his brother does. Their father does.

"I should stay out here," I said. "With William Faulkner."

My companion barked again. I allowed one hand to rest on her collar.

Davis Ames didn't reply—not at first. "All right, then, young lady." When he did speak, it didn't feel like he was capitulating. "I'll send Campbell out."

CHAPTER 56

Campbell was wearing pajamas. Fuzzy ones. To say that she wasn't pleased to see me would have been an understatement.

"What do you want?" Campbell turned the porch light on. She looked younger than she had earlier in the day—and more likely to bite.

"I *want*," I said, emphasizing the word, "to tell your brother the truth."

"And you think I don't?"

I stared holes in her. "If you wanted to, you could have."

"Right." Campbell offered me a biting smile. "Because it's that simple."

"*Hi, Walker*," I said, by way of suggestion, "*you're not the one responsible for that hit and run, and also, I'm a horrible person.* Seems simple enough."

Campbell stared right back at me. "You've got everything figured out."

I shrugged. "You're not exactly an enigma."

"And you're not a member of this family." The words left her mouth like the crack of a whip. "So you can stop pretending you know anything about what it's like to be an Ames."

I hadn't been expecting a family reunion. I'd come into the search for my biological father knowing that I wasn't likely to be welcomed with open arms. Campbell's statement about being an Ames shouldn't have stung.

"How could you do that to Walker?" I didn't let myself dwell on her attack. "How could you—"

"He's *my* brother." Campbell stared daggers at me, daring me to even *think* about claiming that he was mine, too. "Walker is the one person in this world who loves me, no matter what."

"So that gives you the right to screw with him like this?" I asked sharply. "Lucky him. And what about Nick?" I took a step toward her. "Did you know who he was when he started working at the club? Did you pursue him on purpose?"

Campbell's response lagged, just by a breath. "I'm a coldhearted bitch," she said flatly. "What else would I have done, right?"

For the first time, I could hear in her voice a shade of the self-loathing that sometimes colored Walker's.

"You don't get to feel sorry for yourself," I said. "You *framed* Nick—"

"Keep your voice down." Campbell lowered her own.

I refused to do the same. If someone overheard us, so be it. "You framed Nick for stealing the necklace, and you let Walker think—"

"I'm not framing *Nick*." Campbell stepped off the porch, toward me. She stopped when she hit the grass, but only for a moment.

I was about to argue that she clearly *had* framed Nick when I processed exactly what she'd said. "Framing," I repeated. "Present tense."

She hadn't denied that she'd *framed* Nick. She'd very clearly said *framing*. As in ongoing.

As in, whatever game she was playing—it wasn't over.

"Haven't you done enough?" I said incredulously.

Campbell stopped walking once she'd stepped clearly into my personal space. Her face was just inches from mine. "*Nick*," she said, enunciating the name, "is not the one I'm framing."

What was that supposed to mean?

"Go home, Sawyer."

A muscle in my jaw clenched. "You made me a part of this the night of the scavenger hunt."

Campbell closed her eyes. "Why can't anyone just *trust* me?"

I let out a single bark of laughter, which William Faulkner seemed to find fairly exciting.

"Did that question seriously just leave your mouth?" In true Taft woman fashion, I rendered my own question almost immediately rhetorical. "You let Walker tear himself up over something *you* did. And Nick—"

"I'm doing this *for* Nick," Campbell said vehemently. "For Walker."

I nodded. "Right. And you blackmailed Lily for her own good."

William Faulkner padded forward, just enough to nudge Campbell's hand with her massive head. I expected Campbell to jerk her hand back or ignore the dog, but instead, she knelt and stroked William Faulkner's head. "I just need a few more weeks," Campbell said quietly. "After that, you can do whatever you want."

Kneeling, the formidable, heartless Campbell Ames was smaller than the dog.

"A few more weeks for what?" I didn't want to be asking. For all I knew, I was playing right into her hand, but nothing about this confrontation had gone the way I thought it would.

I still hadn't broken out the duct tape.

"You want me to trust you?" I told Campbell. "Give me a reason."

She stood, but she kept her gaze focused on the dog as she said, "I wasn't the one driving the car."

I had to strain to hear her, and when I worked out the words, my first instinct was to lash back. I was tired of playing her games. Right before she'd locked me out of the sauna and left me to prance around in the altogether, she'd insisted that this was her fault—not Walker's.

"If *you* weren't driving," I said pointedly, "and Walker wasn't, who was?"

She waited so long to reply that I wasn't sure a response was coming. And then it did. "Our father."

APRIL 15, 6:02 P.M.

Mackie wasn't sure what to make of the blank record he'd pulled up for Walker Ames. The fact that there was no arrest record for the girls, however, was completely unsurprising.

Rodriguez and O'Connell must not have entered it into the system before they'd thrown him to the glove-clad wolves.

And speaking of . . . Mackie turned to head back to the holding area. By now, the girls had probably jimmied the lock open. For all Mackie knew, he'd come back to find fine, upstanding young men and women dancing a waltz.

Or enacting a conspiracy the likes of which this station had never seen.

He was halfway back to the cell, when he heard the door to the station creak open. Mackie figured there were two options: either Rodriguez and O'Connell had *finally* taken pity on him and returned . . .

Or the Ames family lawyer had arrived.

Steeling himself, Mackie turned toward the door. The figure standing there straightened his tie. Or, more specifically, his bow tie. He wasn't any older than the lot in the back—and there was a crescent-shaped cut above his eye.

"Boone Mason," the boy said. "No relation to Perry. Do not be deceived by my boyish looks."

Mackie closed his eyes and slowly counted to ten.

"I am not a teenager," the tuxedoed boy declared in the single most cheerful lie Mackie had ever heard. "I am a lawyer. Take me to my clients."

FOUR WEEKS EARLIER

CHAPTER 57

With T-minus one month to go before our official presentation to society, I caught Lily curled up on the window seat on the second-floor landing, her tablet in her lap. After Campbell had revealed the truth—the *real* truth—about who had hit Colt Ryan, I'd come clean to my cousin about the events that had sent her ex into a downward spiral.

A month and a half later, Lily was still reeling. This wasn't the first time I'd caught her staring furtively at one of her old *Secrets* entries. It was, however, the first time I'd caught her fixated on the final post—the lone photo of Campbell.

"'He made me hurt you.'" Lily looked up from the tablet, her brown eyes searching mine. "*He* as in the senator, *you* as in Walker."

"I'm not proud of what I did to my brother." The conversation I'd had with Campbell the night I'd climbed the gate at the Ames estate came back to me. It had been the first of many, and they all boiled down to a single, crystal-clear point: *"But I will take a lot of pride in bringing my father down."*

"*He* as in the senator," I echoed Lily. "*You* as in Walker. That's one interpretation."

"Maybe I was talking about Walker when I wrote those words." I could still see the subtle, serpentine smile working its way first to one side then to the other of Campbell's lips. *"But to a jury? It's going to look like I was talking about Nick."*

Campbell had said, that night on the lawn, that she wasn't framing Nick. Slowly, I'd pieced together the real plan: framing daddy dearest *for* framing Nick. Piece by piece and move by move, she was laying a trap, one that would result in the truth coming out about the hit and run in a way that not even a powerful senator could counteract.

"I'm doing this for Walker," Campbell had told me. *"I'm doing this because Daddy would never expect it of* me."

Campbell didn't know who our father had called to handle the police that night, or what the person on the other end of the line had done to take care of the "problem." She did know that if she went to the authorities now, she could easily be dismissed as a spoiled teenager making up lies—a silly little girl, desperate for Daddy's attention.

But if Campbell could make it look like the senator had stolen the pearls for the *purpose* of framing Nick, because Nick was asking questions and getting too close to the truth? If she waited until the evidence against our father was ironclad, and *then* admitted that he was the one who'd hit Nick's brother?

Suddenly, the senator's scandalous daughter might start looking more credible than her father.

"I want in." That was what I'd told Campbell. She'd replied—more than once—that she neither needed nor wanted my help.

But here we were.

"Girls!" Aunt Olivia called from downstairs.

Lily closed the cover of the tablet. "Coming!" She turned to me, and I knew what she was going to say before she said it. "I still think we should tell Walker the truth."

So did I.

So did Campbell.

"Not yet."

Campbell was in the back seat that night. The newly minted Mrs. Waters had spared no expense on her wedding—and that meant an open bar. They weren't checking IDs, so Campbell had made use of it. So had Walker.

So had almost everyone in attendance.

As Lily and I sat in the back of Aunt Olivia's car, I turned the story over in my mind, the way I had countless times, working in new details as I'd pulled them from Campbell. I wasn't sure why I felt the need to imagine it—repeatedly, visually imagine it.

Maybe because, in a different life, with one key change eighteen years earlier, it might have been me in the back of that car—or it might have been both of us.

Campbell was slumped, halfway unconscious, across the seat lengthwise. Walker was equally out of it in the passenger seat. Their father was talking—lecturing. Family honor and self-control and blah, blah, blah. The senator expected better of Walker. Any man worth his mettle knew his limits.

Only the senator didn't. Not really, because at some point in the drive, he'd allowed the car to drift into the next lane.

Oncoming traffic. Campbell saw headlights, and the next thing she knew, her father jerked the wheel to the right.

Too far to the right.

The sound the car made as it hit something wasn't a thump. It wasn't a crunch. Campbell let her eyes close again as her father opened the driver's side door. Let Mr. Hypocritical High-and-Mighty, who'd expected better of Walker, *figure this one out.*

She hadn't known, at that point, that the object they'd hit was a person.

"Are you two excited?" Aunt Olivia asked as she pulled into the parking lot. "Of course you are. After all of this time and all of those fittings—you'll actually get to try your dresses on!"

The Symphony Ball was rapidly approaching. Each and every copy of the designated gown had been ordered, altered, and hand-sewn to exact specifications. This was the last fitting—the one where we actually saw the results of all the others.

"I am so excited," I deadpanned, "that I can hardly stand it."

"Oh, hush, you." Aunt Olivia's enthusiasm remained fully intact. "And remember: if you see Charlotte Ames, tell her how much you *love* the dresses."

"It's nice to see you three on such good terms." Charlotte Ames was indeed present inside the tailor shop. Thus far, the senator's wife had called the Symphony Ball gowns "a bit full" and "classic in a refreshingly ordinary kind of way." Now she'd transitioned from subtle jabs at Aunt Olivia to focusing on Campbell, Sadie-Grace, and Lily—and blatantly ignoring me. "Just like old times," she continued blithely.

Something tells me you wouldn't be so glad to see them acting like such good buddies if you knew why.

Lily didn't keep secrets from Sadie-Grace, and that meant that Lily's best friend knew what we knew, and she was just as determined as we were to help Walker and Nick—even if that meant helping Campbell, too.

"That dress does flatter you, Sadie-Grace, sweetheart." Charlotte Ames shook her head fondly, then turned back to the other mothers. "Then again," she said for Aunt Olivia's benefit, "what dress wouldn't?"

Beside me, Campbell cut a sharp glance toward Sadie-Grace, who was looking distinctly jittery in the wake of the compliment.

"Be nice," I told Campbell.

"Aren't I always?"

Lily slid in beside us. With deft hands, she combed her fingers through Campbell's hair and swept it back into an elegant twist. Campbell relaxed slightly under her touch, then caught herself. "Don't you dare feel sorry for me, Lily Taft."

Lily had made it very clear that she was in this for Walker's sake, but there were moments like this one where the remnants of her friendship with Campbell were evident, too.

"You should wear your hair back to the ball." Lily let the other girl's red tresses drop gently back to her shoulders and moved past her to the mirror. "And don't worry. I wouldn't dream of feeling sorry for you."

"We need them," I reminded Campbell. She'd been reluctant to accept my help, let alone anyone else's—but this wasn't a two-person job.

"This isn't a fairy tale, sister dear." That was what Campbell had said to me, as she'd begrudgingly let me in on the details. *"This is a revenge story, and it's going to be epic."*

Across the room, Charlotte Ames narrowed her eyes at the two of us. Part of the reason I'd been able to convince Campbell that we needed Lily was that the senator's wife would have put up a much bigger fuss about Campbell spending all of her free time with *me*.

Turning away from me, Campbell walked toward the three-way mirror. She waited until all four of us were standing in front of it—and out of earshot of her mother, Aunt Olivia, and Greer—before she cut to the chase. "They made the arrest today." She met her reflection's gaze. "Daddy has been pressing for it. Nick is in custody as we speak."

The thought of Nick behind bars made my stomach heavy.

"This is a good thing, Sawyer." Campbell's elevated brow challenged me to argue with that statement. "You know that."

I knew that Campbell's original plan had involved Nick being let go. When the senator had intervened to have the case reopened, she'd decided to use that to her advantage. Objectively, I recognized the fact that the way the senator had been pressuring people to make this arrest would work in our favor. I knew, as well as Campbell did, how that interference, once it came to light, would look.

Senator Ames committed the theft to frame Nick, who was getting too close to the truth about his previous crimes. When that didn't work, he used his political sway to engineer the arrest.

That was the story we wanted to tell.

"How long until we can pull the trigger?" I asked, smoothing my hands over the front of my gown and trying to look like I actually cared whether or not it succeeded in giving me the appearance of boobs.

"Sawyer! Don't you dare smudge that fabric."

Aunt Olivia had eagle eyes. I let my hands fall back to my sides and waited for Campbell to answer the question.

"It could be weeks still," Campbell murmured, turning slightly to one side and then the other, inspecting the dress from each angle. "We'll only have one shot at this."

The fact that she'd said *we* was a miracle—and not a minor one. To my surprise, Campbell followed that up by combing her fingers through Sadie-Grace's hair, the way Lily had through hers, arranging it just so around the startled girl's face.

"The closer we get to a trial," I murmured, "the more rope we give the senator to hang himself." I knew that. It didn't mean I had to like it.

"I suppose we're supposed to just sit around and wait?" Lily rose up to the balls of her feet. "Heels?" she called back to her mother.

"Two inches."

Lily adjusted her stance. I tuned out Aunt Olivia and focused on Campbell. My mind went back to that night—the one she'd described to me, the one I couldn't get out of my head.

Campbell's eyes were closed. She didn't open them until she heard her father on the passenger side of the car. He dragged Walker out from his seat and over to the driver's side.

When Campbell realized what was going on, she threw her own car door open, bent to the ground, and puked.

And that was when she saw Colt's body.

"The three of you will have to take care of Nick," Campbell murmured.

"Take care of him?" Sadie-Grace asked, wide-eyed and cautious as Campbell stopped playing with her hair. "Like . . . mob-style?"

Campbell laid one hand lightly on Lily's shoulder and the other on Sadie-Grace's and leaned forward conspiratorially—like the three of them were just BFFs. "Get him a lawyer. A good one."

"How would a teenager go about hiring a lawyer?" I asked, catching sight of the four of us in the mirror: a quartet of girls in white gowns, pure as the driven snow.

Campbell stepped back from the rest of us. "You'll figure it out," she murmured. "And *I* will handle everything else."

CHAPTER 58

As it turned out, finding a lawyer to hire for Nick wasn't the hard part. Coming up with the retainer was. Lily offered to ask her parents, but given what I'd overheard weeks before about their financial situation, I wasn't sure that was the best idea.

Not that the idea I'd come up with was much better.

I cleared my throat. "Can I talk to you?"

My grandmother was sitting behind her desk in the home office. She glanced up from the papers she was perusing. "You certainly can," she confirmed, "though perhaps you should also inquire as to whether or not you may?"

It took every ounce of self-control I had to resist the urge to eye-roll. Instead, I rephrased my question. "You got a second?"

With a roll of *her* eyes, Lillian inclined her head toward the chair on the other side of the desk. There was no easy way of approaching this, so I ripped the bandage right off.

"I need an advance on my trust."

"The educational trust due to you once you have fulfilled your end of our contract?" Lillian clearly knew the answer to that question, but for once, she made me provide it anyway.

"Yes."

"Dare I ask what you need this advance for?"

To provide legal counsel to an accused criminal—but don't worry, he didn't do it.

"I'd prefer not to say."

"I see." Lillian tilted her head to one side. She looked older somehow than she had on the day I'd met her—less polished, more real.

Or maybe I just knew her a little better.

I certainly knew her well enough now to know that my request was going to cost me.

"How much of an advance are we talking about?"

She'd been in charge of the family's finances since her husband's death. From what I'd come to understand in my time here, it had grown exponentially under her guard.

"Ballpark number?" I stalled for time.

Lillian did not believe in stalling. She picked up a pen and turned back to her papers. I spat out a number.

Very slowly, Lillian laid the pen back down. "Are you in some kind of trouble, Sawyer?"

Do you consider breaking numerous federal laws in an attempt to take down one's biological father to be "trouble"?

"I'm fine," I said.

She stared at me, long and hard. After a long moment, she smiled. "I suppose an advance could be arranged."

I hadn't anticipated this being so easy.

"I'll have my lawyer draw up the papers."

I was already rising from my chair when something about the way Lillian had said those words sent a twinge down my spine.

"What papers?" I asked.

"We'll have to amend the contract, of course," Lillian told me, reaching out to pat my hand. "With the advance—and my new conditions, going forward."

APRIL 15, 6:07 P.M.

Mackie had no idea how things had gone so wrong. In retrospect, letting the boys back to the holding area was probably a mistake. Especially the third boy.

The one who'd claimed to be a lawyer.

The one who could *not* stop talking.

At first, Mackie had listened to the rambling teenager in the tuxedo, hoping to catch something that vaguely resembled human speech. Instead, all he had picked up on was the fact that the "lawyer" had also received a note.

Mackie did not trust these notes.

"I thought you called your attorney." Mackie aimed that statement at Walker Ames—he of the curiously blank, but entirely existent, police file. "Or did you just call *him*?"

Mackie nodded—sternly, he hoped—toward the boy in the tuxedo.

"Neither, Officer." That answer didn't come from Walker Ames. It didn't come from the other boys or from any of the four girls.

It came from behind Mackie.

With a sense of foreboding, Mackie turned and found himself looking at a regal, terrifying woman. Like the girls, she was wearing a floor-length gown. Unlike the girls, her dress was black. It shone and shimmered all the way to the floor. The jacket she wore over it was beaded. Expensive.

It was her eyes that concerned Mackie the most. She looked to be in her late fifties—possibly older—and her eyes were steel blue.

"Walker called me."

"And who might you be, ma'am?" Somehow, Mackie managed to form intelligible words.

"My name," the woman replied graciously, "is Lillian Taft." She fixed him with a smile. "I'm afraid the two of us are going to need to have a little chat."

TWO WEEKS EARLIER

CHAPTER 59

"The glove luncheon is one of Symphony Ball's oldest traditions. On the night of your official presentation to society, your fathers will be the ones to escort you to the end of the walkway. They will be the ones leading your first dance as adults, as elegant, strong, charitable young women."

Greer Waters had her red hair pulled back into a sedate ponytail at the nape of her neck. Her "baby bump" was just barely noticeable underneath her pale blue dress. The speech was clearly practiced.

My mind was on other things.

"But this afternoon," Greer said with a smile, "is not about your fathers. It is about the women who've come before you, the women who've raised you. Mothers and grandmothers, aunts and sisters and more. So, mamas . . ." Greer raised a glass. "Enjoy your mimosas. You deserve it! And, girls?"

Cue a sheen of unshed tears . . .

"We are so very proud of you."

Personally, I thought my own mom—who was, of course, not in attendance at this little soiree—would have been *very* proud of the way I'd posted bail for a boy I barely knew, hired him one shark of an attorney, and also learned quite a bit about natural sedatives in the past two weeks.

Every Southern lady, I thought in imitation of Greer's tone and cadence, *should know how to drug and frame a scoundrel sorely in need of drugging and framing.*

"I remember Lily trying on these gloves when she was four." Aunt Olivia looked down at the gloves lying between her plate and Lily's and smiled fondly. "Such a bitty thing with such a big attitude."

That *bitty thing* had spent the past two weeks on logistics. Lily was every inch her mama's daughter—type A in the extreme, especially when it came to *premeditated* crimes.

"I hope this isn't too presumptuous." Greer took the lone empty seat at our ten-top round table, right beside Sadie-Grace. "But I have something for you, sweetheart."

The whole point of this luncheon, such as I'd gathered, was for each Debutante to be presented with a pair of white gloves—elbow-length, elegant, and preferably with a family history.

Symphony Ball was not designed for first-generation debutantes.

"My Deb year was one I'll never forget." Greer patted Sadie-Grace's hand, and Sadie-Grace, bless her heart, was unable to keep from staring conspicuously at her stepmother's gently protruding stomach.

"I know your mama wasn't from here," Greer continued magnanimously, "so I would be honored if you would wear my gloves."

Aunt Olivia brought her napkin to her face and dabbed gently at her lips—the equivalent, essentially, of coughing the words *trying too hard* under her breath.

"I only hope someday you'll have a little sister to pass them on to." Greer let her hand rest on her stomach. "Though my mama's instinct tells me this one is a boy."

Had I not been preoccupied with my own criminal enterprises, I would have been seriously concerned that Sadie-Grace's stepmother was planning to acquire a baby on the black market.

"Sawyer." Lillian spoke softly. I thought, at first, that I'd committed some unforgivable faux pas with my salad fork, but then my grandmother withdrew a pair of gloves, carefully wrapped in plastic, from her lap. "These were meant for your mother."

My mom had never made it to her own glove luncheon.

I accepted the gift Lillian had offered and then ducked my head. "Excuse me." This seemed as good a time as any to make my escape. I stood, allowing Lillian to think that the moment—and its significance—was weighing on me. "I have to make use of the necessary."

It took Lily exactly three minutes to follow me. "The necessary?"

"Too much?" I asked.

"That depends," Lily said. "Were you going for debutante elegance or drawing room circa 1884?"

I shrugged. "I'm flexible."

I checked the stalls, while Lily kept an eye on the door. By the time I'd finished my circuit, the third and fourth members of our little party had joined us.

"How's Nick?" Campbell's first words were more revealing than she would have liked.

"Salty," I said. "And somewhat bewildered as to why we're helping him. But mostly? He's picked up on the fact that there's a game afoot here, and he wants in."

"We could tell him," Sadie-Grace suggested hesitantly. "And Walker." It was fairly obvious that she was making the suggestion so that Lily didn't have to.

"If we tell Walker, he'll confront Daddy." Campbell looked from

Sadie-Grace to Lily and narrowed her eyes. "We don't want that—not yet."

Keeping this from Walker was killing my cousin. I'd been checking in on him as often as I could, but Lily had avoided being in the same room with him since she'd found out the truth.

"Walker's stable," I said. "Or as stable as Walker gets. And Nick . . ."

"Nick doesn't understand how our world works." Campbell walked over to the nearby sink and picked up a bottle of hand lotion. "He's a wild card."

Weeks of scheming side by side hadn't given me any more insight into what—if anything—Campbell felt about the guy she'd framed. She'd used him. He'd used her. I had literally no idea if there was anything more to it than that.

"We'll tell the boys soon," Campbell said, rubbing lotion into her hands. "Walker and Nick will know what they need to know when they need to. For now? I've looked at the different scenarios that Lily's run out, and there's one that seems to have a certain . . . panache."

"The day of the ball?" I guessed.

Bingo. Campbell didn't need to issue a verbal confirmation—it was all right there in her eyes.

"That gives us two weeks." I thought out loud. "What do we still need?"

"The audio," Campbell replied immediately. "And the pearls."

"What do you mean we need the pearls?" Lily said. "You have them."

"Actually . . ."

"Campbell!" Sadie-Grace squeaked. "What happened to the necklace?"

Our plan wouldn't work without it. To set Sterling Ames up for framing Nick, he needed to be caught with the pearls. *At a certain place. At a certain time. In certain circumstances.*

"Campbell," I said lowly. "You had better be joking."

Completely unimpressed with the death glare I was aiming in her direction, my half-sister passed me the bottle of lotion. I considered using it as a projectile.

"After Nick was arrested the first time, I brought the pearls to Daddy." Campbell's explanation was dainty and neat. "I confessed. If he'd wanted to do the right thing, he could have."

"The senator has the pearls?" Lily was horrified. "Do you even know where they are?"

Campbell shrugged. "There's a limited number of possibilities."

I actually did throw the lotion at her then. She ducked.

"Is that honeysuckle scented?" Sadie-Grace asked suddenly. She scampered to retrieve it. "Honeysuckle is my favorite."

"Do you even want to do this?" I asked Campbell. She was the one who'd been playing the long game for months. This was *her* plan. But she'd led us to believe that she had the pearls in her possession, and she didn't. At the end of the day, it was *her* family's reputation on the line. Her father's job. Her mother's social status. To me, the senator was just the asshole who'd knocked up my mom and hung her out to weather the scandal alone. But to Campbell?

This was her family—and her life.

"Growing up, Walker played football." Campbell sounded almost contemplative. "I danced. He was supposed to be smart. I was supposed to be pretty. He was Daddy's pride and joy, and I was the bane of my mama's existence. His and hers. Like towels."

"Cam . . ." Lily started to say something, but Campbell cut her off.

"Unfortunately for Daddy, Walker is not the one who inherited his morals. Walker isn't the Machiavellian one. Walker is not the born politician." She watched as Sadie-Grace sniffed at the lotion, then continued. "I knew when I gave the senator the pearls that his desire to make sure that *my* involvement in the theft stayed a secret would have him encouraging the police to focus on any other suspect—especially if that suspect was Nick. I also knew that it would help to have the senator's fingerprints on those pearls. I wore gloves when I handled them. Since Daddy never intends for them to be found, he wasn't so careful. So in answer to your question, Sawyer . . ." She tossed her hair over her shoulder. "Yes, I am sure I want to do this. I owe it to Walker—and to Daddy."

I'd never been so glad that my mom had left town and raised me worlds away from Sterling Ames.

"Do you have any idea where your daddy is keeping the pearls?" Lily asked. Like me, she must have deeply suspected that Campbell had just about reached her capacity for sharing.

"Either the house or the office or a location I can have a special friend pull from Daddy's GPS." Campbell's expression dared us to ask about her "special friend."

Silently, Sadie-Grace handed the bottle of lotion to Lily.

"So what we need," Campbell concluded, "is to know for a fact that Daddy Dearest will be otherwise occupied while we search."

Lily and Campbell both turned to me.

"What?" Sadie-Grace asked them. "Why are we looking at Sawyer?"

"Because," I told her, "nothing says 'distraction' like 'bastard daughter.'"

CHAPTER 60

The most convenient thing about having a remarkably small chest was that there was always room for padding. Since I've moved into Lillian's house, my *assets* had been enhanced with everything from water bras to foam held in place with boob tape.

Actual boob tape.

Today, however, marked the first time that I'd padded my chest by wearing a recording device. Sadie-Grace had acquired it. I did not ask how or where, and in return, she had only attempted to fluff up my chest once. As I reached out and rang the bell, I admitted to myself that I could have probably just used the audio recording function on my phone.

But what fun was that?

I waited a full five seconds before I rang the doorbell a second time. Campbell had promised that her mother wouldn't be home—and that, at least for the next few minutes, her father would be.

I heard footsteps coming. I measured them—too heavy to be Charlotte's, too crisp for Walker's.

Game on.

"Sawyer." The senator did an impressive job of looking both happy and utterly unsurprised to see me. "Always a pleasure to find one of the lovely Taft ladies on my front porch. Unfortunately, I have to inform you that Campbell isn't home."

She's staking out the house, waiting to send Lily and Sadie-Grace the all clear to search your office, while she does the same thing here.

"I'm not here to see Campbell," I said politely.

The senator adopted a slightly more aggrieved expression, full of fondness nonetheless. "I'm afraid Walker is not in any condition to be receiving visitors."

I took that to mean that Walker had been self-medicating again. Even a "stable" Walker wasn't necessarily a sober one. The fact that Sterling Ames could stand there and act like he had no part in that made me want to hit something.

Hard.

Instead, I tried to sound sympathetic. "It must be difficult for you." I tried to imagine how the senator would refer to Walker's long and painful downward spiral. "This . . . *stage* of his."

The senator managed a smile. "He's sowing his wild oats." That was the story, the acceptable one. "Boys will be boys, I suppose."

And snakes will be snakes.

"I'll tell him you stopped by." The senator had the door halfway closed when I stepped forward and wedged my foot into the entryway.

"I'm actually not here to see Walker or Campbell." I allowed a hint of something that wasn't sunny or polite into my tone. "I came to see you."

I'd give the man this: He had an excellent poker face. Maybe I'd inherited mine from him.

"I'm happy to make time for any of my constituents," Sterling Ames said. "You'll need to make an appointment with Leah, of course."

Leah-in-the-red-heels. The assistant.

"I've been talking to my mom." I didn't expect a visible reaction, and I didn't get one—but the door stayed open. "About her Debutante year."

The senator was a man who understood subtext. Better yet, he knew quite well that it could be used as a threat.

"About what happened back then," I continued, decidedly not specifying that what *had happened* was that this man had impregnated my mom.

There was a slight tic in my biological father's jaw. That was it—all the acknowledgment I was going to get.

"I'm sure talking to your mother has been very therapeutic."

I needed to get him out of the house. I needed to keep him from shutting this door. Subtext wasn't working, so I answered his statement with a shrug. "Not as therapeutic as talking to the press."

There was a beat of silence. *Cue reaction in three . . . two . . .*

The senator stepped out onto the front porch, shutting the door behind him. He didn't even look at me as he spoke. "Let's take a walk."

In the silence that accompanied our brisk walk away from the house, it took everything I had not to access my mental bank of famous movie quotes and murmur a message to Campbell. *Houston, we are go.*

"Sawyer." The senator had regained whatever shred of calm he'd lost. "What are your plans for next year?"

This wasn't how I'd expected him to respond to my threat, but the whole point of this endeavor—besides the audio I was recording—was to distract the man, so I played along.

"My plans?"

"For the future," the senator clarified.

I have a very elaborate, very detailed plan. I'm in the middle of orchestrating it right now.

"College," I said aloud. "I've always enjoyed history."

"Not the most practical degree."

I shrugged. "I could make more as a plumber than I could in most white-collar professions straight out of college."

"Do you have aspirations to plumb?"

The question was pointed, but there was enough humor there, too, to make my stomach twist. Senator Sterling Ames was too easy of a man to like.

Just keep him talking. Keep him out of the house—and away from his office.

"I'm not a person who's ever had many aspirations." I decided to nudge the conversation forward—just enough so that he wouldn't forget that there was more at stake here than the pros and cons of a liberal arts degree. "I aspired to make sure the bills were paid. I aspired to make sure there was money for groceries. And I was really dedicated to the goal of not being sexually harassed more than twice a day."

I felt a stab of something like guilt, but sharper and colder. It lingered, because what I'd just said? That wasn't a fair assessment of my childhood. I'd taken care of my mom as much as the reverse, but I'd never wanted for anything.

Especially a father.

Especially one like him.

"What can I do?" the senator asked. "For you?"

This was just a distraction, part of the plan, a cog in a very complicated machine. But I couldn't ignore the fact that this was also me walking side by side with the man who was responsible for half of my DNA. There he was, inquiring into my well-being.

"Think, Sawyer," the senator said softly. "What do you want?"

I got it then. It should have been apparent from the get-go. If I'd been approaching this objectively, it would have been.

"You're paying me off."

That earned me a dose of disapproving silence in response. One did not simply *say* that one was being offered a bribe—unless, of course, one was hoping to catch one's sperm donor saying something incriminating on tape.

The more threatening, the better.

"There is one thing . . ." I let that hang in the air for a few moments. "There's a boy. His name is Nick Ryan, and you had him arrested for grand theft."

Throwing water on a grease fire wasn't smart, but occasionally, it *was* fun.

"Be smart, Sawyer. Don't get dragged down by a loser like that."

"You asked me what I wanted," I insisted. "I don't want money. I don't want advice about my future. I don't want anything from you, except for your family to drop the charges."

Or, you know, for you to run your mouth off about Nick, the pearls, and your intentions. Tomato, to-mah-to.

"I'm afraid, at this point, that's out of my hands. You would have to bring your concerns to the DA."

"You know the DA," I said. "You're the one who pressured him to press charges against Nick in the first place."

I didn't get a confirmation. I didn't get a denial. I got a heaping side of fatherly advice. "Your mother made some very poor choices when she was your age, Sawyer. I would hate to see history repeating itself."

The anger buried deep in my gut loosened. I could feel it rising up, and for the first time in months, I empathized with my mom. I felt for the stupid seventeen-year-old girl she'd been and the cold dose of reality she'd faced when she turned up pregnant by a man like this.

"I would hate," I countered, parroting the senator's phrasing back at him, "for anyone to find out that you knocked up an impressionable teenage girl when you were a full-blown adult." I probably should have stopped there, but I couldn't quite help myself. "A married adult. An adult in law school, already on your way to a promising political career."

One second the two of us were walking, and the next we'd stopped. His hand was lying on my shoulder. He didn't grip it, didn't squeeze, didn't apply bruising force—but every survival instinct I had said that he wanted me to know that he could.

This was my father.

This was the answer to the giant question mark that had dogged my life.

"It would be very inconvenient if you were to continue down this line of thought."

Inconvenient. I swallowed, weathering the blow. That was what I was to him—all that I was. I would have preferred a threat.

"I wouldn't want to inconvenience you." There was no reason for me to sound gutted. I was the one playing him here. I was the one recording this conversation. I was the one with the upper hand.

So why did I feel six years old and alone?

"Smart girl." The senator allowed his hand to fall from my shoulder. "Because if you do become inconvenient?" His tone turned almost affectionate. "I'll kill you, sweetheart."

CHAPTER 61

I managed to keep the senator out of the house for another twenty minutes. That was the plus side to walking and talking—once he'd issued his little threat, he had to walk back. As he did so, I texted Lily, Sadie-Grace, and Campbell to give them a heads-up.

I've got the music.

As far as texts sent from one teenager to another went, that was pretty run-of-the-mill. Much less suspicious than saying that I'd gotten the audio clip we needed.

It was nearly a full minute before a reply came in—from Campbell. *I've got the dresses.*

What else would we be talking about, two weeks before our Debutante ball? What a perfectly *normal* conversation.

I smiled as I made the mental translation. *She got the pearls.*

APRIL 15, 6:08 P.M.

"These four young ladies and the young man in the tuxedo are to be presented to the whole of society in just under fifty-two minutes. Whatever this unfortunate *situation* entails, Officer, I am certain that it can wait until tomorrow."

THREE DAYS EARLIER

CHAPTER 62

"How can we tell Walker?"

"Yes, Lily," Campbell replied. "*Now,* we can."

"*You* can," I corrected. Campbell had told me that she didn't want to be the one to tell Walker how thoroughly he'd been betrayed.

"I'll call him," Lily said softly.

Him as in the boy she'd once loved.

"What else do we need?" I asked an hour later.

Campbell glanced out the window. At first, I thought she was watching the conversation going on between her brother and Lily down below, but then I realized she was considering my question.

"A lot of luck." Campbell glanced down the street toward Sadie-Grace's house. "And a contortionist."

APRIL 15, 6:09 P.M.

Having a gaggle of Debutantes in a jail cell was bad. Having *Lillian Taft* demand you let those Debutantes go?

Even a rookie knew that was much, much worse.

"Don't just stand there with your mouth flapped open, young man. Unlock that cell."

Mackie snapped his mouth closed. This was serious business. He had taken an oath.

"I'm afraid I can't let them go, ma'am. Not until we've sorted this out."

TEN HOURS AND FORTY-EIGHT MINUTES EARLIER

CHAPTER 63

The day of our Debutante ball started with compulsory manicure-pedicures. Not for all of the Debs. For Lily and for me. By this point, I really should have been used to being polished, buffed, plucked, conditioned, coerced, and—

"Ouch!"

The manicurist who'd just relieved me of part of my cuticle submerged my feet in bubbling water. *Hot* water.

"Oh, hush," Lily said. "It feels good. Beauty is pain."

"Pain," I gritted out, "is also pain."

As the manicurist put down one tool of torture and picked up another, the door to the shop opened. I'd been expecting it, but the sight of Walker Ames standing there was still jarring.

There was a bruise around his right eye—most likely delivered by someone else's right hook. His eyes themselves, however, were clear. Not bloodshot. Not vacant. This wasn't the Walker who drowned himself in alcohol and flaunted his flaws for the world to see.

This was a person who had recovered some trace of faith that he was—that he *could be*—a good guy.

Ever the gentleman, he took a seat and waited for Lily's manicure to be completed. When that proved to be a lengthy process, he allowed one of the manicurists to give his own hands a look.

"Very manly of you," I commented.

Walker gave me an austere look. "I try."

"There's trying," I said, imitating Aunt Olivia, "and then there's trying too hard."

I'd gotten used to giving him crap—and besides, it seemed like the kind of thing a sister would do.

Even if he didn't know I was his sister yet.

I was going to tell him, but I wanted to wait until this was all behind us. Lily had already rocked his world once when she'd told him what had really happened the night a drunk driver put Colt Ryan in a coma. Campbell had been convinced that as soon as Walker knew the truth, he would confront their father. Based on the bruise around his eye, I had to wonder if she'd been right.

Soon, Lily excused herself to speak with him alone. I lingered in the doorway to the salon to make sure no one else overheard what they were saying. Walker wasn't here just to keep Lily company. He wasn't here for the sole purpose of letting her lay a gentle hand on his battered face.

"Let's keep this PG," I called out.

This wasn't a grand, romantic moment. It was a *criminal* one. Or at least, it was supposed to be. The anticipated criminality, however, was taking its sweet time coming around.

He pressed his lips to hers.

After averting my gaze for a full five seconds, I decided that Walker and Lily had had enough alone time. I was ready to get this party started.

Walker was here to deliver a package from Campbell. *The pearls.*

As I approached them, Walker pulled back from the kiss and handed Lily a box.

This is it. Except . . .

"That box is too small," I said flatly.

As Lily opened the box and found a pair of earrings inside, Walker turned to me. The expression on his face was almost, but not quite apologetic. "My sister said to tell you that the plan has changed."

In consolation, he handed me a box identical to the one he'd handed Lily. Another pair of earrings.

"She was supposed to send the necklace so that we can plant it in your father's car," I said, my voice low.

Walker shrugged. "You try telling Campbell what to do."

CHAPTER 64

We'd had a plan. A detailed, meticulously thought-out plan that Campbell was apparently content to unilaterally amend at the last minute.

I was going to kill her.

Completely unbothered by my ire, she'd suggested that we should meet in person—at Lily's parents' place, where we wouldn't be overheard.

"What in the name of God's green earth are you doing?" I demanded when Lily and I arrived to find Campbell lying on her stomach on a pristine white lawn chair beside the pool.

Campbell replied without so much as bothering to roll over. "It feels like the first day of summer, doesn't it?"

"It's mid-April," Lily said flatly.

"Regardless," Campbell continued, "this place is practically abandoned, and I could hardly lay out by *my* pool. If my mama knew I was risking a sunburn today of all days, she would skin me alive."

I could practically see my cousin counting backward from ten and reining in her temper. "You were supposed to send the pearls with Walker so that we could plant them in your father's car for the police to find."

"No." Campbell finally turned over and sat up to face us. "*Sadie-Grace* was supposed to plant the pearls in my father's precious sports car—along with a few other choice items—after Sawyer does her due diligence and makes some teeny tiny alterations to its engine." She shrugged. "But things change."

"I spent the morning being tortured with cuticle shears," I told her humorlessly. "And now I'm seriously considering the merits of tying you up in the pool house."

Campbell had the audacity to smile. We'd planned every aspect of this day, every minute detail, and she was sitting in a bathing suit *smiling* at my threats.

"Good times." Campbell yawned and stood, stretching her legs with the grace of a predator cat. "Relax, girls. I nixed the original plan because I have a better one. The pearls are exactly where they're supposed to be."

Now I was the one counting to ten. "And where is that?"

Campbell removed her ponytail holder and shook her tresses down her back. "Why," she said, "on the way to my father's mistress."

APRIL 15, 6:10 P.M.

"Until we've sorted this out." Lillian Taft was aggressively unimpressed as she repeated Mackie's words back to him. "And what, pray tell, might *this* be?"

NINE HOURS EARLIER

CHAPTER 65

"Your father's mistress?" I echoed what Campbell had just said. "Because this wasn't enough of a soap opera already."

Campbell shrugged. "I know my father, and that means that I am aware that no matter how well we plan this, there is a chance that he will lawyer or bribe or weasel his way out of any real consequences. If we want him to pay, we need a backup plan. We have to hit him where it hurts."

"His reputation." Lily was the one who filled in the gap.

"It's not so much *having* a mistress," Campbell said, "as it is being caught."

I thought back to what Campbell had said when she'd explained to me just how damaging *Secrets* could be to Lily. Some things weren't so much a matter of purity as discretion.

"And how are the police supposed to discover that your father's mistress has the pearls?" I asked.

Campbell reached down and picked something up off the ground beside the lawn chair. She rose again and offered it to Lily.

"A camera," my cousin stated. "With a telephoto lens."

"You have a God-given talent for taking dirty pictures." Campbell smiled sweetly at Lily. "How would you feel about putting that to good use?"

As much as I hated to admit it, I could see the logic behind Campbell's alteration to our plan. If the story we wanted to push was that the senator had framed Nick for the purpose of preventing him from looking further into the hit and run, people were going to question why Sterling Ames hadn't actually planted the pearls in Nick's possession. That the senator had been holding on to the pearls because he *could* might have been the truth. But the idea that he'd stolen the pearls and given them to his mistress?

That was salacious.

Stupid and borderline implausible? Maybe. But at the end of the day, salacious sells.

"Would it have killed you to tell us about this part of your plan earlier?" I asked Campbell.

She shrugged. "I just found out about Leah last week."

Leah. I registered the name, and my brain connected the dots. "His assistant?"

Leah-in-the-red-heels. Leah, who wasn't more than a few years older than us.

A tiger doesn't change its stripes.

"I have a massage in fifteen minutes." Lily still hadn't agreed to take compromising pictures of the senator's mistress. She looked down at the camera. "Then makeup at two and hair at two thirty."

"Then it's fortunate, isn't it," Campbell replied pleasantly, "that I texted Leah from my father's phone and asked her to meet him in their normal hotel room at noon. You didn't hear it from me, but I deeply suspect she'll be dishabille." She smirked. "Except for the pearls."

CHAPTER 66

My hair and makeup appointments were right before Lily's. After the fiasco on spa day, Aunt Olivia had decided that I should forgo the massage.

Campbell's last-minute alteration to our plan had me on edge, but I just kept telling myself that it made sense. We wanted the senator arrested. We wanted the truth about the hit and run to come out. We wanted a conviction—for the accident *or* the theft. But if that proved a bridge too far, the biggest scandal we could possibly generate would have to do.

"Sit still, sweetie." The man tying my hair back into God knows what kind of knot had issued the exact same order eight times. Each time, he dragged the endearment out a little bit longer.

I tried to turn to look at him, but he had a strong enough grip on my hair that the effort was futile. I sat still.

Right about now, Sterling Ames is arriving at the club. . . . In laying out the plan for today, a particular Symphony Ball tradition had proved most useful. Apparently, the one piece of wisdom that had been passed from one generation of Squires to the next was that when you were the parent, and it was *your* daughter's turn to play

Debutante—you did not want to stick around for the last few hours of preparations.

Although it wasn't official, a large number of the fathers were, even as I sat here, gathering in the men's grill at Northern Ridge for drinks.

"There." The smile was audible in my hairdresser's voice, but it wasn't until he spun my chair sideways, angling my body toward the mirror, that I could see why. A makeup artist had already had her way with my face. My eyes looked larger, my lashes impossibly long. My hair had been swept back from my face, smoothed, curled, and piled on top of my head. A single tendril—closer to mahogany than the color of mud—hung down on each side, framing my cheekbones.

I looked like my mom. For the first time in months, I considered ending our silent standoff and giving her a call.

Afterward, I told myself.

What I said to the stylist was: "I'm going to get some air."

Get some air, sabotage a car that cost as much as an Ivy League education—same difference. Campbell had made an alteration to our plan, but my role was largely unchanged.

Wearing jeans and a button-down shirt—a must, Lily had assured me, so that I could get dressed later without damaging my makeup or hair—might have been less conspicuous had the rest of me not been ball-ready. Whatever the makeup artist had put on my lips, I was fairly certain at this point that the color could withstand a nuclear bomb.

Sadie-Grace—who hadn't had her makeup done yet and nonetheless looked ten times better than us mere humans ever would—met me behind the portico. The two of us might not have been the ideal people to blend into the background today, but it just so happened that I had an inside source.

One who used to be a valet.

Campbell had assured me that the senator would be driving his 602-horsepower Lamborghini Huracán. Nick had assured me that whenever one of the members broke out a car like that, the valets knew better than to park it out front.

They parked it where they could all ogle it themselves.

Unfortunately for them, the sheer number of Debutante fathers descending on the men's grill in hopes of escaping ball preparation meant that there wasn't much time for ogling.

And that meant that Sadie-Grace and I—temporarily—had the car to ourselves.

It felt wrong to monkey with an engine that could have doubled as a work of art, but desperate times called for desperate measures. I was mostly through with what I needed to do when things went south. I heard the footsteps, but not in time to divest myself from the inner workings of the Lamborghini.

Someone's here. Think of a cover story. I scrambled, but before I could say a word, the person who'd approached spoke.

"Uhhhh . . . hey, guys."

I breathed an internal sigh of relief. This was bad—but it could have been much worse. "Hey, Boone," I said, trying to act like I hadn't just been caught red-handed.

"You look nice," Boone told me. "And possibly felonious. Felony-filled?"

"Felonious," Sadie-Grace said quickly. "I think. And she's not. I'm not." She paused for a breath—her first. "Hi." Sadie-Grace turned the full force of her smile on Boone.

In the past nine months, the closest Boone Mason had gotten to asking Sadie-Grace out had been on Casino Night. She'd thrown up on his shoes.

"Hi back," Boone said. There was a long pause, and then he leaned up against the car. "Need another lookout?"

Thank goodness, I thought, *for inept romance.*

Four more minutes, and I was done. Sadie-Grace and Boone were . . . otherwise occupied.

Really? I thought. *Now?* After all of the times he'd managed to flirt—badly—with every other girl in the near vicinity but couldn't manage to do so with her and all the times she'd been completely oblivious to—or possibly anxious about—his interest, they were making out *now*?

I cleared my throat. Sadie-Grace's left foot, which was tracing ecstatic little circles on the ground, caught Boone's right one just as he attempted to shift his balance. One second the two of them were standing there, and the next, he was on the ground and bleeding from the eye.

"Eep!" Sadie-Grace turned to me. "I told you! I break boys!"

More footsteps. I ducked behind the car—and pulled the eep-ing Sadie-Grace to do the same. Boone, who I could only assume was still bleeding, climbed to his feet as one of the valets approached.

"I'm glad to see you are all taking care of my uncle's car," I heard him say. "But I have a lady friend coming to see it."

I could practically *hear* him winking.

"Man-to-man, can you look the other way? I fully intend to work my magic, and I'm going to need a moment."

Boone's "moment" bought us time for me to hand him three notes—one for him, one for Walker, one for Nick.

"Don't deliver them yet," I said. "And don't open yours."

Boone eyed me carefully. "Dare I ask what kind of shenanigans are afoot?"

"I wouldn't recommend it," I said.

Sadie-Grace placed a chaste kiss on his cheek and a hand on his chest. "Neither would I."

APRIL 15, 6:11 P.M.

"I'm afraid, ma'am, that I have been unable to ascertain why the girls were arrested." Mackie congratulated himself on striking the perfect tone between respectful and deserving of respect. "I believe you will have to ask them yourself."

To Mackie's surprise, Lillian Taft responded to that statement by turning back to the four girls. "Care to enlighten me, children?"

TWO HOURS AND SEVEN MINUTES EARLIER

CHAPTER 67

The trunk of a Lamborghini Huracán was not what one would call spacious. "You're sure you'll be all right?" I asked Sadie-Grace.

She folded herself into a freakishly small ball, arching her neck at an angle that did not look, in any way, possible. "You know how I told you I was really good at tying bows and telling stories?"

I nodded.

"I am *awesome* at riding in trunks."

As the minutes ticked down, I tried to get a rough count of the number of ways this could go wrong and the number of laws we'd already broken.

"Sadie-Grace in place?" Campbell came to stand beside me. Tonight's ball was drawing close enough now that no one would question our presence at the venue—which, luckily for us, was Northern Ridge.

The only thing someone *might* question was why we weren't sequestered inside, putting on our dresses.

"If she gets hurt . . ." I said.

"As long as you've done your job right, she won't." Not bothering to spare another word for me, Campbell withdrew her cell phone from her pocket.

Showtime.

"Daddy?" Campbell let her voice wobble. "I just talked to Walker. He's so angry. I think he's been drinking. He kept raving about going to the press."

I could practically imagine the senator cursing on the other end of the line—but no. He was in the men's grill. One wouldn't want to cause a scene.

"I did what you told me to," Campbell continued. "I said that he was mistaken about what happened that night. I told him that he was the one who . . ." She trailed off.

Just a silly little girl, easily cowed.

"I think Walker is going to do something stupid. Something big. He said he's going back to where it all started." Campbell managed an impressive sniffle, even as a wicked grin spread over her face. "The site of the crash."

The senator came for his car, as planned. Campbell and I were in the ladies' sitting room, as planned.

Lily arrived with my dress, and the three of us stripped. I was fairly certain no Debutantes had ever gotten gowned and gloved up so quickly.

We made certain we were seen on our way back through the club. Greer asked us if we'd seen Sadie-Grace. Once we'd told her we hadn't, Campbell snagged a bottle of champagne. We ducked out of the building, giggling. If anyone came looking for us, the oh-so-discreet staff would mention, oh-so-discreetly, that we were simply off somewhere celebrating in advance of the ball.

Better to be seen breaking minor laws than suspected of something worse.

APRIL 15, 6:12 P.M.

Mackie turned expectantly toward the cell. Finally, he was going to get some answers.

The prim and proper one spoke up first. "Honestly, Mim," she said. "We don't know."

Mackie stared at her. "You don't *know* why you were arrested?" He tried not to sputter. "But what about the blackmail? The pearls? The indecent exposure . . ."

"Wait. Are they supposed to tell us what they're arresting us for before they arrest us?" The beautiful, tear-prone heiress managed to sound both surprised and insulted.

"Now, see here . . ." Mackie started to say, but before he could get out any more than that, the door to the station opened.

Good grief, he thought. *What now?*

But to his utter and absolute relief, it wasn't another teenager. It wasn't another society titan.

It was O'Connell and Rodriguez.

ONE HOUR AND THIRTY-TWO MINUTES EARLIER

CHAPTER 68

I looked down at my wrist, even though I was wearing white gloves and no watch. All three of us had left our phones back in the sitting room.

"She's late," Lily said. "Isn't she?"

Sadie-Grace was supposed to be here by now. Her part in the plan was fairly straightforward. Once my "adjustments" to the engine kicked in and the senator did what Campbell had assured us he would do in response, Sadie-Grace just had to let herself out of the trunk, plant a certain something—that *wasn't* the pearls—on the senator, do a little switcheroo, and . . .

"Here!" Sadie-Grace came bounding around the bend in the road. "I'm here!"

And there we were: four Debutantes on the side of the road, one mile from the action.

"You need to get dressed," Campbell said. "Hurry."

As she retrieved her dress from the spot in the woods where she'd left it, wrapped in plastic, Sadie-Grace caught us up.

The senator had driven to meet Walker.

Walker wasn't there.

The car wouldn't start up again.

“And?” Campbell prompted as she forcibly turned Sadie-Grace around and zipped her.

“And,” Sadie-Grace said giddily, “he drank the scotch in the glove box!”

It was a strong, expensive scotch—strong enough to hide the taste of . . . other things. After a single drink, he would have been out of it. Per the plan, Sadie-Grace had popped out of the trunk, switched the laced scotch for a normal bottle, helped the senator to ingest a few more shots of *that*, and then left him with a parting gift. By the time anyone found him, his blood alcohol level alone would be more than enough to explain his . . . condition.

Campbell glanced over at me. “How long will he be out for?”

“Long enough.”

“How much time do you think we have until someone spots the car?”

Until we got closer to the ball, the road would see very little traffic, and—not surprisingly, given his desire to be discreet—the senator hadn’t exactly parked in plain view.

“If we’re lucky?” I said. “An hour. Maybe two.”

APRIL 15, 6:13 P.M.

"Rodriguez! O'Connell!" Mackie felt a wave of relief go through his body. "This is *Lillian Taft*." He paused to let that sink in. Then, feeling vindictive, he crossed his arms over his chest. "She'd like to know why you arrested her granddaughters."

Why, bless your heart, Mackie thought. *Bless your precious little hearts.*

Instead of the horror Mackie had expected to see on their faces, Rodriguez and O'Connell just shrugged.

"We didn't arrest them," Rodriguez said.

O'Connell cleared his throat. "They were in there when we got back from patrol."

That announcement was met with the most terrifying silence Mackie had ever heard in his life. Lillian Taft looked from one police officer to the next to the next, her gaze finally landing on Mackie.

"If none of you arrested my granddaughters," she said, enunciating every word, "then who did?"

ONE HOUR AND EIGHTEEN MINUTES EARLIER

CHAPTER 69

My tongue caught between my teeth as I worked the pick in the lock.

"Are we *sure* this is necessary?" Lily had never been thrilled with this part of the plan.

I glanced back over my shoulder at the empty hallway. The evidence had been planted. The scene had been set. Someone would eventually call the police about the car on the side of the road—if they hadn't already.

Everything was in place.

"It's necessary," I confirmed. I felt the lock give, and the door to the cell popped open. Once the four of us were inside, I closed the door.

We heard the lock engage—and then there was silence.

"To success," Campbell said finally. "And to unholy alliances."

"To friendship," Sadie-Grace corrected. She glanced at Campbell. "Or something vaguely friendship-like."

"Sadie-Grace, we don't have *friends*." I stole Campbell's line, wondering how long it would be before we were discovered in the cell—and how long we could keep an officer occupied once we were. "We have alibis."

APRIL 15, 6:17 P.M.

"Gentlemen, as far as I can tell, there is not a single person in this entire unit who wants to own up to having arrested my granddaughters and left them in a cell for over an hour."

Mackie was dumbfounded.

"What about them?" Rodriguez asked, nodding to the three teenage males present. "What are they doing here?"

"I imagine," Lillian Taft said, "that they came here to protect the girls."

Protection, Mackie thought. *They don't need protection!* He was certain—just certain—that he was the only one who saw it, but one of the girls winked at him.

She looked right at him and winked.

"You have three seconds to unlock that cell." Lillian Taft never so much as raised her sweet, Southern voice. "I would hate for this to get ugly."

TEN MINUTES LATER

CHAPTER 70

I almost felt bad for the rookie cop who'd been stuck with us for the past hour and a half, but we were at T-minus thirty minutes until the start of the ball, and I was fairly certain that if we were even a second late, Lillian would murder us all.

"Come along, girls."

It had taken a bit longer than expected to get things sorted out, but once it had become clear that there was no record of our arrest, they had no choice but to let us go.

Free and clear.

We were halfway out the door when the cops brought someone else in. Like Boone, he was wearing a long-tailed tuxedo. His eyes were glassy, and his speech was blurred.

"Do . . . you . . . any idea . . . I am?"

My grandmother startled. "Sterling Ames!" She glanced between him and the officers holding him upright. "What is the meaning of this?"

"Found him by the side of Blue River Road," one of the officers said. "Clear case of drunk driving. Bottle of scotch was still open beside him."

Thank you, Sadie-Grace.

"He had *this* gripped in his hand." The other officer held up a plastic bag. Inside was a pet tag. "Can't make hide nor hair of it yet."

Nick froze beside us. He'd known we were up to something. We'd brought him here so that he would have an alibi. The fact that he was present to tell the cops exactly what they had in that evidence bag?

That was an unexpected bonus.

"That was my brother's," Nick said, his voice throaty and low. When no one replied, he looked up. "Hit and run," he told the cops. "Last May."

"I remember that," one of the cops said. "It was over on . . ." He stopped talking, his eyes going wide.

Nick finished the sentence for him. "Blue River Road."

Senator Ames picked that moment to attempt to focus his gaze on his daughter. "Campbell?" he said, belligerent and bewildered.

She leaned toward him and murmured her reply. "See me now, Daddy?"

APRIL 15, 6:34 P.M.

Mackie stared at the drunk man in the holding cell. This wasn't his case. After the way that last one had gone, he wasn't sure he'd be working a solo case for a while. But he lingered, because there was something very familiar about the man's face.

"I'm telling you, I'm a senator!"

That gave Mackie pause. *A senator. The same senator whose daughter I had in that cell?*

"I don't care if you're the pope," one of the other officers said. "We can't let you go until you've sobered up."

"Not to mention the charges . . ."

"Charges?" For a man who still couldn't stay on his feet, the senator did an impressive job of sounding irate. "This wasn't me. It was the girls! My daughter. Sawyer Taft . . ."

"Taft," Rodriguez repeated. "Hey, rookie. Was she one of the ones . . . ?"

Mackie cleared his throat. "Sawyer Taft has been with me for the past hour and a half."

TWENTY-THREE MINUTES LATER

CHAPTER 71

We made it backstage with exactly three minutes to spare. Greer Waters was holding a clipboard, her whole body practically vibrating with intensity. Her eyes lit on us. "There you four are," she said, in equal parts relief and accusation. "Do you have *any* idea . . ."

Belatedly realizing that Lillian was standing directly behind us, Greer gathered her composure.

"You and I," she told Sadie-Grace, pleasantly furious, "are going to be having a chat."

Before Sadie-Grace could shudder at that, I murmured into her ear, "Maybe you can *chat* about the pregnancy she's faking."

Greer couldn't possibly have heard me, but her eyes narrowed slightly nevertheless. "Well," she said brightly, "there's nothing to do now but move on. Girls, you'll be escorted by your fathers—alphabetical order, please. Remember: When you make it to the end of the walkway, your father will offer your *left hand* to your Squire escort. *Left*."

She paused for just an instant, before her borderline-manic eyes landed on me.

"Sawyer, I believe that one of your grandmother's friends has graciously volunteered to—"

A voice interrupted her from behind. "That won't be necessary."

I turned to see my mom standing behind me. The last time I'd seen her, she'd walked away—because I'd told her to. I'd been hurt and incredulous and angry that she couldn't even register the effect that anything she was saying or doing had on me.

"I'll be escorting Sawyer," my mom told Greer calmly. "If she'll have me."

The fact that she was here meant something. But after Christmas, I didn't want to read into that too much.

My mom must have seen some trace of that on my face, because she lowered her voice. "Your grandmother came to see me."

I glanced at Lillian, wondering what she'd said to bring my mom here.

"I'm sorry," Greer told my mother stiffly. "But you *cannot* . . ."

"Of course she can," Lillian said simply. "If that's what Sawyer wants."

Somehow, in the past nine months, Lillian had come to know me well enough to know that this *was* what I wanted. I wanted my mom—and my grandmother and Lily and the rest of my family, without having to choose.

"Truly," I said, in imitation of a proper miss, enjoying the flustered expression on Greer's face more than I should have, "I think that would be just lovely."

"It's settled, then," Lillian declared.

Greer looked like she'd attempted to swallow a frog and gotten the poor creature stuck in her throat. She wanted to argue, but one did not argue with Lillian Taft.

She turned her attention to another target. "Campbell. Your father seems to be running late."

With any luck, one of the officers would have, by this point, discovered the USB I'd slipped onto the counter when we'd left. On it, they would find a picture of the senator's mistress wearing the stolen pearls—and very little else.

They'd also find a few select clips of the audio recording I'd taken of the senator's conversation with me.

"You know the DA. You're the one who pressured him to press charges against Nick in the first place."

"It would be very inconvenient if you were to continue down this line of thought."

And then the kicker: *"If you do become inconvenient, I'll kill you."*

In a day or two, Campbell would come forward and give her testimony—about the hit and run *and* the way her father had forced her to help him frame Nick. That testimony would be backed up by a digital diary she'd been keeping, conveniently time-stamped, for the last nine months, where she'd painstakingly poured her heart out about how her father had *made* her tell lies about Nick, made her keep quiet about the hit and run.

"Pardon me." Davis Ames strode toward us. "My son has run into some difficulties. If Campbell doesn't mind . . ." He looked to his granddaughter, his expression inscrutable. "I'll escort her tonight."

The show must go on, and it did.

"Campbell Caroline Ames." Even from backstage, the announcer's Southern drawl was perfectly audible. "Daughter of Charlotte and Senator Sterling Ames, escorted by her grandfather Davis Ames."

I knew the second that her grandfather solemnly transferred her arm to her Squire's, because the announcer moved on to announcing his name, his family ties, and so on.

"You didn't have to come." I looked over at my mom. Our last name put us near the end of the alphabet.

"Yes, I did, baby." My mom leaned up against me, bumping my shoulder lightly with her own. It was a familiar gesture.

It meant *I'm here*.

"I should have handled this better. I know that, Sawyer. How could I not? But I spent so many years trying to prove to myself and to you that I could do this. I could be everything you needed." She looked down at the ground, her fingers playing at the edges of her sheer and sparkling sleeves. "I used to be so terrified, when you were little, that your grandmother would find a way to take you from me."

And then, right after I'd turned eighteen, I'd chosen to come here of my own free will.

"No one is taking me away," I said.

"Your grandmother said the same thing," my mom murmured. "Lillian came to me, eating crow and singing your praises—singing *my* praises for raising such a strong and independent young woman."

There was a pause as I heard the announcer begin the presentation of another Deb.

"She said that you have a good head on your shoulders, that you're kind, even though you'd prefer for people not to notice."

It was on the tip of my tongue to object, but I had the self-awareness to realize that would only prove Lillian's point.

"She asked you to come here," I said instead.

The indomitable Ellie Taft was quiet for a moment. "She shouldn't have had to."

My mom listened as they announced Lily's name: "Lillian Taft Easterling, daughter of John and Olivia Easterling, escorted by her father, John Easterling."

"It's okay," my mom told me, "to want your own life. And it's okay to need people. Family."

"You're my family." Those words were no less true than they'd been nine months earlier. She was my mom. She loved me.

And just this once: She'd surprised me.

As our turn approached, my mom let out a long breath. "Don't trip. Don't fall. Just walk."

I wasn't sure if she was talking to me—or herself.

The next thing I knew, the announcer was calling, "Sawyer Ann Taft."

We stepped out onto the stage. The lights were bright. As I slipped my arm through my mom's and we made our way down the walkway, I thought back to the auction.

My, how things have changed.

"Daughter of Eleanor Taft." The announcer paused, just for a moment, then registered the fact that there was no father's name to read. "Granddaughter," he continued smoothly, "of Lillian Taft, escorted by her mother, Eleanor Taft."

My mom squeezed my hand. I squeezed back. And then she handed me off to my Squire escort.

"Boone Davis Mason, son of Julia and Thomas Mason . . ."

CHAPTER 72

Boone and I were required to dance together. I expected him to ask me what exactly he'd been a part of this afternoon—the car, the notes, our "arrest." Instead he adopted an overly serious look.

"The cut over my eye is quite dashing, is it not?" he asked.

I rolled my eyes. "Sadie-Grace thinks she broke you."

He sighed happily. "Yeah."

I decided to let him have his moment.

"Don't look now," Boone said as our waltz was coming to an end, "but I believe you have a gentleman caller."

I glanced back over my shoulder, expecting to see some other poor sap of a Squire who'd been told he had to dance with me, but instead, all I saw was one of the massive ballroom windows, overlooking the Northern Ridge pool down below.

Standing next to the pool was Nick.

Sneaking out of one's own Debutante ball was harder than it should have been for a criminal mastermind such as myself. But eventually, I managed to make my way outside.

"Fancy meeting you here," I told Nick.

"That's all you have to say?" he asked incredulously.

From his perspective, this whole evening probably did merit an explanation.

"The DA has already dropped all charges against me. You and Campbell," he said. "You . . ."

"Make quite a team?" I suggested.

He stared at me. "How did you even—" he started to ask.

Given that I'd recently caught someone else's damning words on tape, I cut him off. "I'm going to plead the Fifth on that one," I said. "But for the record, when I was a kid, I watched a lot of police procedurals and telenovelas."

I would like to say that the dance was Nick's idea, but that would be a lie.

I'd always believed in absolute honesty. I'd believed that people were fundamentally predictable. I'd believed that no one who wanted to flirt with a teenage girl was remotely worth flirting back with.

For a long time, I'd believed in being self-sufficient and independent and, with the exception of my mother, alone. And then I'd come here.

For reasons I couldn't quite pinpoint, I found myself holding my hand out to Nick, a boy I barely knew, one I'd framed and unframed and hit in the stomach with the door of a car. "Can I have this dance?"

He could have refused. He probably should have.

He didn't.

This time, someone really did cut in. Based on the voice, I thought at first that Walker was the one who'd followed me outside, but when I turned, I found myself staring at Davis Ames instead.

Nick was gone before I could so much as say good-bye. I expected Davis to lead me back inside, but he didn't. Instead, he took my hand. "I probably shouldn't have to tell you this," he said as we started to dance, "but I'll lead."

I waited for him to get to the point. I had no idea how much he knew about what had happened tonight, or what, if anything, he knew about me. But I did know, from Lillian, that he was ambitious.

I knew that he valued family.

And I just helped put his son in jail.

"Still not much of a talker, I see." The old man offered me a small, self-satisfied smile. "Note that I've banished all forms of the word *nattering* from my vocabulary."

"Congratulations."

"Spitfire," he murmured. "Like your grandmother."

For a second, I thought that was why he'd asked me to dance. Maybe I looked the way Lillian had, when he'd first known her. Maybe this wasn't about my connection to his family—or the events of the past twenty-four hours—at all.

"I don't suppose you would happen to know anything about the series of frantic calls I've received from my son's attorney, would you?"

And there it is. "Can't say that I do," I lied cheerfully.

There was another long stretch of silence. "I've helped my son out of a jam or two before." Davis Ames sounded almost reflective. "He has indicated to me that you might be a problem for this family."

A problem. All things considered, that was rich. "Has he indicated to you that I'm your granddaughter?"

With as much time as I'd spent avoiding saying that, the words came out surprisingly smoothly. In response, the Ames family patriarch choked, then coughed.

"My dear," he said, once he had recovered, "I wish that you were."

"There's no use pretending." I stopped dancing and took a step back from his grasp. "Your daughter-in-law as good as told me. My mother confirmed it. And your son? He's awfully invested in keeping me quiet for someone who *didn't* knock up a teenager eighteen years ago."

There was another silence—this one, measuring. "I'm not denying that my son had a lapse in judgment."

"I'm thinking of legally changing my name," I quipped. "Do you think I should go by Lapse or Judgment?"

"He got a girl pregnant." The old man's voice was far gentler than I would have expected. "He was an adult. She was a teenager. I handled it."

Handled it. The words hit me, hard. *Just like you "handled" the hit and run that left Nick's brother in a coma?*

Campbell had said that her father had called someone that night. *Someone* had made his little problem go away. *Someone* had blocked the investigation. *Someone*, I thought, *had needed to be convinced that Walker was the one driving that car.*

"Campbell had a few things to tell me earlier," Davis Ames said, eerily perceptive when it came to my train of thought. "I believe that after tonight, my son will have to handle things for himself."

I doubted that Campbell had told him everything. Even if she had, I couldn't persuade my brain to focus on that. I'd finally told Davis Ames that I was his own flesh and blood, and he'd denied it.

Denied me.

"You know what," I said quietly. "Don't worry about me telling anyone that your son is my father. I have no intention of becoming a problem."

I turned and walked back to the party. I was halfway up the stairs when I realized he was following me. As I reached the door to the ballroom, he placed one hand on it to prevent me from opening it.

"Miss Taft," he said softly. "My son got a girl—a young girl—pregnant years ago."

I know. I know this. I—

"But that girl," he continued, "was not your mother."

I whirled around to face him. He couldn't really expect me to believe that, could he?

"Her name," he said, "was Ana."

CHAPTER 73

If the old man hadn't mentioned Ana by name, I wouldn't have believed him. But the fact that he had had made me consider the possibility that he was telling the truth.

The senator didn't knock up my mother. He knocked up her friend. If Davis Ames had spoken truly, then the man I'd helped set up tonight bore no relationship to me at all. *But* . . .

My mom had said that he was my father. The senator's own wife had certainly seemed to believe that he was. And when I'd confronted him, he hadn't denied it. Sterling Ames knew exactly who I was. He knew that my mother was Eleanor Taft.

If he wasn't my father, then why in God's name would my presence—my existence—have been seen as a threat?

I tried to think back to my conversation with the senator. I'd said that I'd been talking to my mother. I'd said that she'd told me what had happened. I'd told him that it would be a shame if a reporter found out that he'd knocked up a teenage girl.

I never actually specified which girl. That was a ridiculous thought. Why would the senator have assumed that I was talking about Ana, instead of my mom? Even if Ana *was* the one he'd gotten pregnant, what did that have to do with my mom or me?

Seated between Lily and Boone at dinner, I stared across the table at my mother. She was sitting to my grandmother's left. Aunt Olivia and Uncle J.D. were to her right.

The last thing I was in the mood for right now was a formal dinner. I couldn't stop thinking about the album I'd found from my mom's Deb year. Ana had disappeared from the Symphony Ball pictures around the same time as my mother.

"Smoked salmon with *fromage blanc* and watercress." A waiter appeared to my left and set an appetizer plate down in front of me. "Enjoy."

Across the table, I saw a waitress doing the same.

Ana disappeared from the pictures. Ana was pregnant. I wondered if it had been a scandal. I wondered if word had gotten around, the way it had about my mother—or if, with Davis Ames interfering, Ana had simply faded away from society, with no one the wiser.

What were the chances of two teenage girls—friends—ending up pregnant at the exact same time?

I don't even know Ana's last name.

"You had the vegetarian option, sir?" I barely heard the waitress over the sound of my own thoughts. "Parmesan crisp with cucumber and zucchini summer salsa."

I blinked and managed to focus just in time to see the waitress setting the plate down in front of Uncle J.D.

"I didn't know your dad was vegetarian," Boone told Lily, loading up his fork with a good third of his salmon.

"He's not," Lily replied. My ears were ringing so loudly, I barely heard her continue. "But he hates salmon."

Hates salmon. Hates salmon. Hates salmon. Across the table, my mom said something to her sister's husband. Uncle J.D. smiled—an easy smile, a familiar one.

My entire life, up until this year, my mother had only told me three things about my father.

She'd only slept with him once.

He hated fish.

He wasn't looking for a scandal.

When my mom excused herself to go to the ladies' room, I followed. Withholding information I expected, but it wasn't like her to lie to me.

Just like it isn't like Lillian to have turned out her own daughter. Even temporarily, even in a moment of temper.

Girls can be . . . complicated. Lillian's words echoed in my mind. *Family, more so. If your mother and Olivia had been closer . . .* She hadn't finished that thought. And months later: *Olivia has a way of landing on her feet. I should have worried less about her growing up. And more about your mama.*

My mom had let me think the senator was my father. She hadn't corrected Charlotte Ames's assumption. I could only assume the senator's wife knew that there was *a* pregnancy . . . a young girl . . . and since everyone *knew* about my mother's scandal . . .

She assumed I was the result.

I made it to the powder room door all of three seconds after it had closed behind my mom. I wasn't even sure what I was going to say to her—what I *could* say to her—but as it turned out, I didn't get to say anything at all.

My mom wasn't the only one in the room.

Greer was standing in front of a mirror, adjusting her stomach. She must not have heard my mom come in, but she heard me. She whirled, adopting a serene *Madonna with Child* expression, but it was too late.

Her belly was crooked.

"Well, this is rich," my mom said. I wasn't sure she realized that I was in the room. I wasn't certain that it would have mattered if she had.

"Ellie, I would prefer we keep things civil this evening, wouldn't you?" Greer made at attempt at steering the conversation, but my mom wasn't one to be easily steered.

"It's ironic, is all," my mom said lightly. "That you've spent this Debutante season pretending to be pregnant, and you spent ours pretending that you weren't."

What?

Greer adopted an expression of concern. "Are you feeling all right?" She turned to me, barreling on. "I do believe your mama might not be feeling well, Sawyer. Perhaps you should fetch—"

My mom turned around the moment she realized I was there. She must have seen something in my face, because when she met my gaze, the emotion in her own eyes shifted. We'd *just* made up, just cleared the air. "Sawyer . . ."

"Don't mind me," I said, feeling like I'd stumbled into some kind of twisted Debutante wonderland. "You two were just having a conversation about Greer's fake pregnancy."

"Why, I never!"

I humored Greer's outrage and offered her a response. "Pardon me. It's not Greer. It's Mrs. Waters." Before she could reply, I channeled my grandmother and continued. "There just never was a good time to tell you that Sadie-Grace knows you're not pregnant."

Greer's poised, controlled expression never faltered. It *deepened*.

"Oh, give it up, G," my mom said. "Nobody cares what kind of con you're pulling on your poor husband."

I cleared my throat. "Well, Sadie-Grace might."

Greer collected herself and attempted to push past us. "I will not lower myself to your level."

"What did my mom mean?" I asked when she was nearly to the door, "about your Debutante year?"

There was no answer—from either of them.

I turned to my mother. "Sterling Ames is not *my* father." I still expected—fully expected—my mom to tell me that I was wrong, that he was, that there was an explanation.

She didn't.

"What happened to Ana?" I said.

The name sent a virtual shock wave through the room.

"What happened to her baby?" I asked. And then I turned to Sadie-Grace's stepmother, thinking back to what I'd just overheard. "If you were pregnant, what happened to yours?"

Three Debutantes, together in nearly every picture. White ribbons tied on their wrists, woven through their hair.

Three Debutantes.

Three pregnancies . . .

"Greer lost her baby," my mom said. "Right around Christmas."

"Ellie." Greer let loose of my mom's name, like it had been ripped from her throat by force.

"It was her idea, you know," my mom said softly. She wasn't facing me, and she wasn't facing Greer. It was almost like she was talking to herself. "The pact."

"Pact?" I repeated.

Three Debutantes. Three pregnancies. The white ribbons. Senator Ames considering any truth that my mother had told me about my conception to be a threat, even though I apparently wasn't his *daughter.*

"Pact," I said again. My heart stopped beating. I wasn't sure it would ever start up again. "I was the result of a *pregnancy pact*?"

CHAPTER 74

I left the ball and didn't return to Lillian's until the next morning. I spent most of the night at a bar on the outskirts of town that reminded me a bit of The Holler. If anyone thought I looked out of place in a white ball gown, they seemed to know better than to comment on it—after the first guy.

By dawn, I still hadn't wrapped my mind around the reason that Sadie-Grace's stepmother hadn't wanted me asking anyone questions about my mom and the events leading up to my conception. The reason she'd insisted they barely knew each other.

She was pregnant, too.

From what I'd gathered in the chaos that had followed my mom's revelation, the pact had been Greer's idea—one she'd come up with after she got knocked up herself. Instead of averting her own scandal, she'd chosen to diffuse it. She'd found two other girls—girls who came from prominent families, but were a little lost, a little vulnerable.

Lonely.

Three girls. Three pregnancies. An inseparable bond. Until Christmas, when Greer had lost her baby and hung her friends out to dry.

I wasn't an accident. Despite everything I was trying to wrap my mind around, that little tidbit might have been the hardest. *My mom slept with her sister's husband, and she got pregnant on purpose.*

I'd asked my mom to tell me the truth, and this time, she had. Lily's dad was my dad.

I'd thought that I understood who my mom was, warts and all. I'd thought I understood why she'd reacted the way she had when I'd come back here—but, no.

Now that I knew the truth, she hadn't even tried to defend herself.

My mom slept with her sister's husband, and she got pregnant on purpose. No matter how many times a person thought those words, they didn't get any less twisted. I tried again as I parked my car on Camellia Court, and once more as I let myself in.

Lillian was waiting for me, wearing a robe, sitting on the porch with two cups of coffee.

I sat down next to her. In addition to her nightgown, she was wearing the infamous pearls.

She caught me looking at them and lifted the coffee mug to her lips. "Apparently, the police found them in the possession of Sterling Ames's mistress. A present, she said. I hear he even wrote her a note."

Campbell, on top of everything else, was an excellent forger.

"Davis Ames got the pearls back?" I asked.

She allowed her fingertips to linger on them for a moment. "Since his security obviously leaves something to be desired, he's given them to me. For safekeeping, you understand."

I nodded. I waited for the questions to come—about where I'd been, why I'd disappeared, how I'd managed to smudge my dress with such a *unique* shade of grime.

Instead, Lillian took another sip of her coffee. "Davis wanted me to tell you that his son has entered a plea."

We'd hoped for a trial. A scandal. *Maybe* a conviction. Probably not. But a plea?

"Davis," Lillian said softly, "is very good at getting what he wants."

Translation: he'd *made* his son take a plea deal. Hell, he'd probably dragged the DA away from his house in the middle of the night to make it happen.

"He also mentioned something," Lillian continued mildly, "about Sterling Ames not being your father."

My eyes whipped up to hers—not because I was surprised she'd gone there, or because I hadn't expected the Ames patriarch to tell her, but because I had to know for certain. "You knew."

Maybe not about the pact. But about my real *father.*

"Ellie . . ." Lillian searched for the right words. "She was so angry after your grandfather died—with the world, with me, with her sister. Grief looks different on different people. My Liv grieved intensely, but she decided to do so alone, and when she came back from *wherever* it was she went that year . . . she was fine." My grandmother paused. "She *seemed* fine, anyway. Ellie and Olivia never got along after that." She pressed her lips together. "I should have paid attention." Another slight, incriminating pause. "Your uncle did. He always had time for Ellie, treated her like a little sister, ran interference when Olivia or I would criticize her. It was obvious she had a crush, but I assumed it was harmless."

"It wasn't." I stated the obvious, and I wasn't just talking about my mom's role in this. J.D. had been an adult, and she'd been seventeen years old. Like a *little sister* to him.

"Did you know?" I asked Lillian. I needed to hear her say it.

"Did you know who my father was?" I swallowed. "Did you know my mom got pregnant on purpose?"

Silence stretched out between us.

"Not at first," Lillian said finally. "As soon as Ellie told me she was expecting, I went into crisis management mode. There would have been a scandal, of course, but nothing we couldn't have handled."

I thought back to the night of the Christmas party, when my mom had told me how Lillian had planned to handle things.

"You suggested that Olivia and J.D. raise me."

"Ellie flew off the handle." Lillian paused, but forced herself to continue. "She said that I acted like Olivia was so perfect, and then she asked me who I thought the father was. She told me she'd gotten pregnant on purpose, and she walked right up to the edge of telling me by whom."

"You told her to get out."

"I couldn't let her say it," Lillian said. "God forgive me, I couldn't let her say it."

So you kicked her out before she could.

"I should have kicked him out, of course." Lillian sounded so matter-of-fact. "But even before she'd tried to tell me who the father was, Ellie was so clear that *she'd* initiated. She wanted me to know that this was her doing. That you were *hers*."

I wondered if that was how Greer had sold the pact to my mom, to Ana. That if they got pregnant, if they had babies, they would have someone. Someone who would love them unconditionally.

Someone who would be *theirs*.

"You and Lily are only two months apart, you know." Lillian's voice broke for the first time. "Right before Ellie came to me, defiant and triumphant and daring me to even *try* to take you away from her—Olivia had come to me, too."

"She was pregnant," I said.

Two daughters, both pregnant by the same man.

"Did J.D. know?" I couldn't bring myself to call him *Uncle* now. "About me?"

"He must have," Lillian replied in a muted voice. "But he's never given even the slightest indication of it."

What kind of man does that make him?

"Why did you bring me back here?" I asked. "You practically dared me to find out the truth. If you knew, if you even suspected—why would you do that?"

Lillian sat her coffee mug down. Her posture was perfect: her spine straight, her chin held just so. In profile, she looked like she was sitting for a portrait. "You're eighteen," my grandmother said. "Your mama kept you from me for eighteen years, and maybe that was my penance. Maybe that was what I deserved for willful ignorance, for sticking my head in the sand. But *you* deserved better—and so did she."

I thought about the way that Lillian had paid Trick to hold my mom's job. The way she'd been paying him for years.

"I needed," Lillian said, "to make this right."

"What about Lily?" I shot back. "And John David and—"

"I don't know." It was terrifying to hear the formidable Lillian Taft say those words. "If you want to leave, if you feel about me the way your mama did—I wouldn't blame you, Sawyer. I got nine months. I got to watch you flourish here. I understand that's likely more than I deserve."

When I'd negotiated for an advance on my trust, Lillian had negotiated for more time. Summers, to be exact, starting with this one and extending through college. But if I walked out the door right now, I deeply suspected that my grandmother would still give me the money. Contract or no contract, amendment or no amendment, I could leave half a million dollars richer. *Free.*

Alone.

Maybe that would have been the right choice—not just for me, but also for Lily. Thinking my cousin's name—*she's not just my cousin, she was never just my cousin*—made me remember every moment we'd spent together, every secret we'd shared, every scandal we'd averted, every felony we'd co-committed. I thought about Walker and Campbell, about Sadie-Grace and Boone and the fact that as downright insane as the past nine months had been—I hadn't gone through any of it alone.

"I won't hold you to my terms, Sawyer." Lillian forced herself to spell that out. If I wanted to leave, I could leave.

But for better or worse, I had people here. *Family.* I also had questions—about Ana. She was just a girl in a picture, a ghost from the past. She was the situation that Davis Ames had *handled.* I didn't even know her last name. I didn't know if she'd had the baby. I didn't know what had happened to it if she had.

But if I stayed here, I *could.*

"Sawyer?" My grandmother must have seen a shift in my expression.

"A lady," I said, "always honors her contracts."

Lillian bowed her head. Her shoulders trembled, but when she looked up again, she'd gathered her composure. She reached across and put her hand over mine. "Bless your heart."

ACKNOWLEDGMENTS

This book owes a great debt to the incredible team of publishing professionals who brought it to life. Kieran Viola, editor extraordinaire, is the best advocate, sounding board, first reader, and provider of feedback a person could ask for. I am also extremely grateful to Emily Meehan, whose enthusiasm for this project from day one has been invaluable, and to the entire team at Freeform—especially Cassie McGinty, Dina Sherman, Holly Nagel, Maddie Hughes, Elke Villa, Frank Bumbalo, and Mary Mudd—for their support. A special thank-you goes out to Marci Senders, who designed the beautiful cover, and Jamie Alloy, who designed the interior art.

I would also like to thank my agent, Elizabeth Harding, for her unerring support and guidance, as well as the rest of my team at Curtis Brown, especially Ginger Clark, Holly Frederick, and Sarah Perillo. Thanks also go out to Madeline Tavis and Olivia Simkins for their assistance!

I am grateful to my family, especially my husband, who is everything I could ask for in a partner and whose generous and freely given support enables me to do more than I ever could on my own, as well as my adorable toddler and baby, who only tried to eat my manuscript a couple of times apiece. I am also grateful for my extended family and support system—parents, siblings, colleagues, and friends.

Finally, special thanks go out to the two people whose love for this story propelled me through even the hardest days of writing-with-an-infant-while-sleep-deprived: Rachel Vincent, who sat across from me at Panera and told me how excited she was every single time we met up to write, and my mom, Marsha Barnes, who didn't stop asking me about this book from the moment I read her the first chapter to the second she finally had an advanced copy in her hands.